Praise for

BLOOD VINES

"A pulse-pounding, page-turning, absolutely can't-put-it-down roller-coaster ride of a read! Get ready to stay up all night." —#1 *New York Times* bestselling author Lisa Gardner

"*Blood Vines* is as mysterious and delicious as a fine cabernet . . . TOP-NOTCH SUSPSENSE."
—Linda Castillo, *New York Times* bestselling author of *Sworn to Silence*

"A fast-paced, intense story that's hard to put down."
—*RT Book Reviews* (4 stars)

BREAKNECK

"SPINE-TINGLING." —*Star Magazine*

"A GRIPPING STORY that unfolds with breakneck speed, heart-quickening suspense, and characters you can't help but root for." —Bookreporter.com

"TOP PICK! Filled with well-developed, multidimensional characters, Spindler's latest boasts fast-paced action and emotional tension. . . . The intricately woven plot makes this novel a sure winner for readers who like to keep guessing all the way to the end." —*RT Book Reviews*

"A MUST-READ. In this gripping new thriller, we are introduced to a tough, new detective duo set to take the crime fiction world by storm. . . . A great read."
—*Evening Telegraph* (UK)

"BREAKNECK SUSPENSE . . . *Breakneck* is a taut thriller, which proves Erica Spindler is still a master of suspense.

With adrenaline-fused prose, you will find yourself sitting up into the wee hours, unable to put the book down until you reach the very last page." —*Ulster Tatler* (Ireland)

"A FIRST-CLASS THRILLING READ . . . *Breakneck* grabs the interest immediately and never lets go. This is a timely and enthralling piece of work, and has a message for all computer users." —*Fresh Fiction Review*

"ERICA SPINDLER NEVER DISAPPOINTS . . . *Breakneck* literally moves at breakneck speed."

—ReadertoReader.com

. . . and FOR ERICA SPINDLER'S PREVIOUS BESTSELLERS

"Creepy and compelling . . . a real page-turner."
—*Times-Picayune* (New Orleans)

"Shocking, emotional . . . engrossing." —Stella Cameron

"A smooth, fast ride to the end. Spindler is at the controls, negotiating the curves with consummate skill."
—John Lutz, author of *Single White Female*

St. Martin's Paperbacks Titles
by Erica Spindler

Watch Me Die

Blood Vines

Breakneck

Watch Me Die

Erica Spindler

St. Martin's Paperbacks

WATCH ME DIE

Copyright © 2011 by Erica Spindler.

For information address St. Martin's Press, 175 Fifth Avenue, New York, NY 10010.

Library of Congress Catalog Card Number: 2011015756

ISBN: 978-1-250-00327-0

Printed in the United States of America

St. Martin's hardcover edition / June 2011
St. Martin's Paperbacks edition / March 2012

St. Martin's Paperbacks are published by St. Martin's Press, 175 Fifth Avenue, New York, NY 10010.

10 9 8 7 6 5 4 3 2 1

Acknowledgments

The idea for *Watch Me Die* sprang from a newspaper piece about a stained-glass restoration artist and her heroic effort to save New Orleans's ruined windows after Hurricane Katrina. That artist, Cindy Courage of Attenhofer's Stained Glass, was kind enough to allow me into her studio. She shared personal accounts of past restorations, verbally and through visual documentation. She attempted to "teach" me the complex process, its history and terminology—even lending me copies of her precious out-of-print reference books. In addition, her Katrina experience inspired me to create Mira Gallier, *Watch Me Die*'s main character. Thank you, Cindy!

Everyone in the New Orleans and Gulf Coast region suffered loss in the wake of Hurricane Katrina, but the lives of some, like my Mira Gallier, were especially tragic. I wanted to honor those who had been so badly hurt by depicting the storm and its aftermath as accurately as possible. Thanks to all those willing to relive the nightmare with me, and also to those who connected me with them: Eva Gaspard, Beth Wolfarth, Linda Weissert, Andi and Patrick Cougevan and Karelis Korte.

No thriller would be complete without a glimpse inside the world of law enforcement. Thanks to the NOPD and Officer Garry Flot for answering my questions.

Huge thanks to my former assistant, Evelyn Marshall, for all the help, support and insight (and for listening to the occasional rant). You will be missed.

A final mention to all the usual suspects: my agent, Evan Marshall; my editor, Jen Weis, and the entire St. Martin's Press crew; the folks at Hoffman/Miller Advertising; my God for the blessings; and my family and friends for all the love.

Chapter One

He had been alone so long. Among the living but not *of* them.

Until now.

Mary had come back for him. They'd been together all those many years ago, separated by his father's will and the whole screwed-up, broken-down world.

But that was the past. She was again within his reach, and this time they would not be torn apart.

It had begun.

He climbed the stairs to his grandmother's bedroom, treading softly, careful not to wake her. Moonlight crept around the edges of the closed drapes, creating bright knifelike slivers on the dark stairs.

He knew these steps so well he could climb them blind. How many hundreds of times had he carried up a tray of food or drink first for his mother, struck down while still so young, now for his grandmother?

He peeked in at her sleeping form. She lay in her bed, head propped up on pillows, coverlet tucked neatly around her. He wrinkled his nose at the smell—of age and illness. She'd become so frail over the past months. So thin, not much more than skin and bones. And weak. Hardly able to lift her head.

Unable to fight him off.

He frowned. Now, why had he thought that? He loved his grandmother; he owed her his life. When his mother had passed, she'd sacrificed everything to raise him. For these past twenty-two years, she had supported and guided him. She had believed in him. In who he was and who he was meant to be.

He shook his head, clearing it. He had told her about Mary's return. They'd argued. She'd said terrible things about Mary. Ugly, hateful things. Each word had pierced his heart.

But in this, his love for Mary, he would not be swayed.

He crossed to the bed. The jagged moonlight fell across her torso and onto him. He lifted his hands into the light, spreading his fingers.

Blood staining his hands.

The blood of the lamb. Splattering on impact.

You're troubled.

He blinked at the clearly spoken words. He looked behind him at the empty room, then down at his sleeping grandmother. "Who's there?" he asked.

You know me. I am the one who's always with you.

"Father," he whispered, "is it you?"

Yes, my Son. What troubles you tonight? It has begun. You should rejoice and fear not, for through the Father the Son will be glorified!

"One of your Holy ones, Father. I had to. He came upon me so suddenly—"

A martyr. He will be remembered, sanctified for his role on this day of new beginning.

At his Father's words, certainty washed over him. Renewed purpose and peace. "Yes, Father. It is indeed the day you foretold and the one I have awaited. I'm in your hands, Father." He bowed his head. "I am your servant. Direct me."

Leave the old one now. Remember, only one can stand beside you.

"Mary."

Yes. Her moment is coming as well.

He eased one of the bed pillows from behind his grand-mother's head. He gazed down at her, drinking in her face, emotion swamping him. What would he do without her?

Tears stinging his eyes, he plumped the pillow and bent and carefully replaced it, cautious not to awaken her.

He pressed a kiss to her forehead. "Good night, Grandma. Sleep well."

Chapter Two

Homicide Detective Spencer Malone angled his vintage, cherry red Camaro into the spot between the coroner's wagon and crime scene van, stopping sharply. Coffee sloshed over the rim of his partner's coffee cup and onto his paisley shirt.

"Crap, that's hot! Drive much, Malone?" Detective Tony Sciame blotted the spot with the back of his tie. "And here I wanted to look good for my party."

Malone cut the engine and shot a grin his way. "No worries, Tony. It blends right in." He and Tony had been partners for better than six years. Their partnership worked despite the differences in their ages, investigative styles and—thank God—fashion sense.

Had worked. Today was Tony's last day on the force.

"Was that a shot?"

"Hell no, partner. Just a fact." Spencer slung open his door, then looked back at Tony. "You're still going to look real 'purty' for your party."

"Kiss my ass, Malone."

They climbed out of the Camaro, slamming their doors in unison. A couple of uniformed officers looked their way.

Located on Carrollton Avenue at Fig Street, Sisters of Mercy Catholic School and Church straddled two distinctly different areas of the city—Uptown and Mid-City. Unfortunately, as the years had passed, the affluent had begun moving farther uptown, leaving Sisters of Mercy to the middle class and the working poor.

Still, it was a beautiful campus occupying a massive amount of land for an urban location. Its buildings, with their stone construction and barrel arches, owed more to Romanesque architecture than the fanciful Creole style the city was known for.

"Always wondered what the inside of this place looked like," Tony said. "And what do you know? Last day on the job and I get to find out."

"You're livin' right, Tony. No doubt about it."

They reached the exterior perimeter. Malone recognized the log officer—he and his brother Percy used to raise some serious hell together.

That was the thing about being a Malone. With three brothers, a sister and various other extended family members on the force, he was always running into someone who had a connection with one of his nearest and dearest. Not all of that history was the kind one wanted to be reminded of.

"Yo, Strawberry," he greeted the man, nicknamed for the birthmark on his ass. "How you doin', man?"

"Not so bad." He held out the log. "Hear you're getting married. Never thought I'd see the day, dude. It's like the end of an era."

Tony guffawed. "Trust me, kid, he's only a legend in his own mind. What've we got?"

"Vic's in the sanctuary. Priest got whacked. Can you believe that shit? Who does that?"

"That's what we're here to find out." They ducked under the tape and followed the walk to the massive double doors and into the church narthex. The interior was cool and hushed. Through the open doors directly ahead, the sanctuary was bathed in colored light.

Malone stepped through. Stained-glass panels lined both
side aisles. They were beautiful, but that wasn't what had
him sucking in a sharp breath. Someone had taken a can of
spray paint to them.

"Holy Mary, Mother of God," Tony muttered.

Malone silently seconded the sentiment, then turned his
attention to the scene. Twelve glass panels, he counted. The
tall, narrow windows looked to be about twelve by five feet;
each depicted a scene from the life of Christ.

He backed up, taking in the graffiti on the first window to
the left of the entrance, then swiveled slightly to take in the
next, gaze moving from one panel to the other until he had
visually circled the room. Scrawled on each of the first eleven
panels, buried among random marks and shapes, was a single
word. On the twelfth, the perp had drawn a smiley face.

"Take a look, Tony. He left us a message: 'He will come
again to judge the living and the dead.'"

"As I live and breathe, one of the Malone boys."

Spencer turned. Detective Terry Landry stood behind
him, grinning from ear to ear. At one time Terry and his
brother Quentin had been partners.

"Landry, how the hell are you?"

He slapped him on the back. "Great, man." He grinned at
Tony. "What're you doing here? I thought you were heading
for the big R today."

"My last hurrah. Besides, couldn't let Malone here
handle it on his own. The department would actually like this
one closed."

Landry laughed and looked at Spencer. "Who drew the
short straw?"

Malone knew Landry referred to his next partner. He
also knew that word around the department was that he had.
"Bayle."

Landry's eyebrows shot up. "Karin Bayle?"

"The very one."

His expression said it all. "Didn't know she was back
from medical leave."

"Officially returning to active duty tomorrow." Landry started to say something else, but Malone cut him off. "Thanks for calling us in, man. This one has crazy written all over it."

"Not my call. Your captain's." He turned his gaze to the front of the church. "You get a look at the vic yet?"

"Heading that way now."

He nodded and they fell into step together. "Body was found a couple hours ago by one of the nuns."

The center aisle formed a T at the altar. The body was located on the right arm of the T, near the side exit. As Malone approached the victim, he worked to tune out the activity around him—everything from the snap and flash of the scene photographer's camera to the easy camaraderie between the CSI techs—and concentrate only on the victim, the scene and what they had to say to him.

Crime scenes had a story to tell. But they had to be gently coaxed. And carefully listened to. But still, some were stubborn and remained mute.

Malone wondered what this scene would bring.

The victim lay facedown. The back of his head had been bashed in. Blood had matted in the man's fringe of white hair, leaked from the wound and created a dark stain on the wine-colored carpet. His arms splayed forward, as if he had tried to break his fall.

Malone squatted beside the body. He'd been elderly. Judging by the thin, age-spotted skin on the back of his hands, maybe in his seventies. He wore pajamas and slippers. His left slipper had dislodged as he fell.

Malone shifted his gaze to the side door.

"What's with the PJs?" Tony asked.

"Bet he lived in the rectory," Malone said, standing. "My guess, he got up in the middle of the night to go to the bathroom, saw someone or something and came to investigate."

"And surprised the vandal."

Malone nodded. "He surprised him, then tried to run. See the way he's positioned, arms forward and feet back?"

"So what'd our perp use for a—"

"Excuse, me, Detectives?" called a uniformed officer from the side door. He motioned them over. "It looks like we recovered the weapon."

Chapter Three

At any given moment, the demons could descend upon Mira Gallier. Sometimes, she marshaled the strength to fight them off, denying their dark, tormenting visions. Their taunts and merciless accusations.

Other times, they overpowered her and left her scrambling for a way to silence them. To obliterate the pain.

Last night they had come. And she had found a way to escape.

Mira lay on her side on the bed, gazing blankly at the small rose window she had created in secret, a wedding gift for her husband-to-be. In the tradition of the magnificent Gothic windows, she had chosen brilliant jewel colors; her design had been complex and intricate, combining painted images within the blocks of color. For her, the window had been a symbol of her and Jeff's perfect love and new, beautiful life together.

She had never imagined how quickly, how brutally, that life would be ended.

It hurt to look at it now and Mira rolled onto her back. Her head felt heavy; the inside of her mouth as if stuffed with cotton.

Eleven months, three weeks and four days, shot to hell by one small blue, oval tablet.

What would Jeff think of her now? Even as she wondered, she knew. He would be deeply disappointed.

But he couldn't be more disappointed in her than she was in herself.

On the nightstand, her cell phone chirped. She grabbed it, answered. "Second level of hell. The tormented speaking."

"Mira? It's Deni."

Her studio assistant and friend. Sounding puzzled.

"Who'd you expect?" she asked. "My husband?"

"That's not funny."

It wasn't, she acknowledged. It was angry. And sad. Jeff was dead, and she had fallen off the wagon. Neither of which had a damn thing to do with Deni. "I'm sorry, I had a really bad night."

"You want to talk about it?"

The roar of water. A wall of it. As black and cold as death, brutal and unforgiving. Jeff's cry resounded in her head. Calling out for her to help him.

But she hadn't been there. She didn't know what that last moment had been like. She didn't even know if he'd had time to cry out, to feel fear, or if he had known it was the end.

And she never would.

He was dead because of her.

"No. But thanks." The last came out automatically, what she was supposed to say, even though gratitude was far from what she was feeling.

"You used, didn't you?"

No condemnation in Deni's voice. Just pity. Still, excuses flew to Mira's lips, so familiar she could utter them in her sleep. They made her sick. She was done with them.

"Yes."

For a long moment Deni was silent. When she finally spoke, she said, "I take it I should reschedule your interview?"

"Interview?"

"With Libby Gardner. From Channel Twelve, the local PBS affiliate. About the Magdalene window. She's here."

Mira remembered then. Her work on the Magdalene restoration was being included in a sixth anniversary of Katrina series the station was planning. "Shit. I forgot. Sorry."

"What should I tell her?"

"How about the truth? That your boss is a pill head and basket case."

"Stop it, Mira. That's not true."

"No?"

"You suffered a terrible loss. You turned to—"

"The whole city suffered that same freaking loss. Life goes on, sweetheart." She spoke the words harshly, their brutality self-directed. "The strong thrive and the weak turn to Xanax."

"That's such bullshit." Deni sounded hurt. "I'll see if she can reschedule—"

"No. Get started with her. Explain how the window ended up in our care, describe the process, show her around. By the time you've done that, I'll be there."

"Mira—"

She cut her assistant off. "I'll be in shortly. We can talk then."

Mira hurried to the kitchen. She fixed herself a cup of strong coffee, then headed to the bathroom. When she caught sight of her reflection in the vanity mirror, she froze. She looked like crap. Worse even. The circles under her hazel eyes were so dark, her pale skin looked ghostly in comparison. She was too thin—her copper red hair like the flame atop a matchstick.

She wore one of her husband's old Ts as a nightshirt: GEAUX SAINTS, the front proclaimed. Mira trailed her fingers over the faded print. Jeff hadn't lived long enough to see his beloved NFL team win the Super Bowl.

It's your fault he's dead, Mira, the voice in her head whispered. *You convinced him to stay. Remember what you said? "It'll be an adventure, Jeff. A story we can share with our children and grandchildren."*

The air conditioner kicked on. Cold air from the vent above her head raised goose bumps on her arms and the back of her neck. No, she told herself. That was bullshit. Isn't that what her shrink, Dr. Jasper, had told her? Jeff had been a fifty percent partner in the decision. If he had felt strongly they should leave, he would have said so.

His family blamed her. Her and Jeff's friends had been subtle in their accusations, but she read condemnation in their eyes.

She stared helplessly at her reflection. The problem was, she blamed herself. No matter what her shrink said or what the facts were.

She moved her gaze over the destruction of her bathroom—drawers emptied, makeup bags and carry-ons rifled through.

As if thieves had broken in and turned her home upside down in search of valuables.

But she had done this. She was the thief. And the eleven months, three weeks and four days she had robbed herself of couldn't be replaced.

Her cell phone went off. She saw it was Deni, no doubt calling to say the reporter had taken a hike. "Pissed off another one, didn't I?" she answered.

"Something really bad's happened, Mira."

She pressed the device tighter to her ear. "What?"

"It's Father Girod, he's . . . dead. He was murdered."

An image of the kindly old priest filled her head. He had approached her after Katrina about his church's stained-glass windows, destroyed by the storm. In the process of restoring the twelve panels, she and the father had become friends.

Grief choked her. "Oh, my God. Who could have . . . When did—"

"There's more." Deni's voice shook. "Whoever did it also vandalized the windows."

Chapter Four

Malone and Tony sat across from their superior officer, Captain Patti O'Shay. Always insightful and tough, in recent years she had shown her resiliency as well. She had bounced back from the murder of her husband, the chaos of Katrina and the betrayal of her oldest friend.

Malone respected both what she had accomplished as a woman on the force and the way she had done it—with integrity and her head held high. He admired her dedication and determination, both of which he saw in her expression right now.

And he could honestly say that his respect for her was in no way influenced by the fact that she was his aunt and godmother.

She hadn't called them into her office for an ordinary case drill. Something was up.

He asked her what.

"First, tell me what you've got so far."

Malone began. "Looks like the victim interrupted a vandal, or vandals, so they killed him."

Tony stepped in. "Smashed him in the back of the head with a brass candleholder from the altar. We retrieved it and two spray-paint cans from the scene. All three are being processed."

"Perp left us a message, graffitied on the stained-glass windows: 'He will come again to judge the living and the dead.' Punctuated with a smiley face. That's it. Nothing was stolen and nothing but the windows was vandalized."

"So what does it mean?" she asked. "Why break into a church just to graffiti the windows?"

Tony replied first. "Priest interrupted him before he had a chance to do anything else. Murder wasn't on the agenda; he freaks out and takes off."

"I've got a different take," Malone said. "He does it because it's really important to him."

The three fell momentarily silent. A fanatic was more dangerous than even a hardened criminal. Malone would choose hunting down a hundred criminals over a single zealot. The zealot's sense of purpose and destiny changed everything.

"Let's not get ahead of ourselves here," Captain O'Shay said. "At this point it looks like we have a case of simple vandalism and a wrong-place-wrong-time murder scenario."

She shifted her gaze to Tony. "You get a get-out-of-jail-free card for this one, Detective. I'm thinking you have a party to go to."

Tony didn't make a move. "Thank you, Captain. But if you don't mind, until Slick's new partner arrives, I'll hang with him."

She smiled affectionately. "Get the hell out of here, Detective. I think 'Slick' can bring Detective Bayle up to speed pretty quickly. Besides, there are a whole lot of people out there wanting to shake your hand."

"All right, then." Tony cleared his throat and stood. "You're on your own, hotshot."

Malone stood, crossed to his friend and hugged him. As he did, a dozen honest but gushy sentiments sprang to his lips, ones about gratitude, friendship and admiration. Instead he clapped him on the back and stepped away. "I'll see you out there, Tony. Try not to eat all the cake."

As Captain O'Shay's door snapped shut, Spencer forced a lid on his sense of loss and turned back to her. And found her gazing at him not as his tough-as-nails superior officer but as his beloved aunt Patti.

"You're going to miss him."

"Hell yes, I'm going to miss him. He always had my back."

"And you had his. Trust. It's what makes a strong partnership."

He folded his arms across his chest. "What are you getting at?"

"Are you sure you want to take Bayle under your wing? I'm giving you the out."

His arched his eyebrows in surprise. "I thought this was settled."

"I'm talking to you now as your captain *and* your aunt. I'll partner her with someone else. You have major issues on your mind right now, with Stacy still recuperating and wedding plans to navigate."

"I said I'll do it, I'm not going back on my word."

"Bayle melted down on the job. Completely lost it."

"I'm aware of that. I'm also aware of her incredible service during and after Katrina. She's a hero, Captain."

"She is. But I'm not totally convinced she's beaten her demons. And frankly, I'm not convinced you're on solid ground yet either."

"We've all suffered with PTSD to some degree since Katrina. Then the frickin' oil gusher in the Gulf comes along, followed by another insane hurricane season. She snapped."

He looked down at his hands, then back up at Captain O'Shay. "And I'm fine."

"Really? Stacy almost died."

Just hearing those words, knowing how true they were, stole his ability to breathe. He looked away, working to hide it from her. He couldn't shake the image of Stacy in the hospital bed, pale as the sheets, fighting for her life.

Patti O'Shay wasn't fooled. He should have known better than even to try. Her expression softened with sympathy.

"Speaking of heroes, the chief's awarding Stacy the Medal of Valor."

Fury took his breath. Stacy hadn't even been on the job. Her sister Jane had been in town; they'd been sightseeing in the French Quarter. Stacy had seen a stranger snatch a child and reacted. She'd tackled the man and wrestled him to the ground. He'd had a gun and shot her, the bullet penetrating her right lung.

They called it a sucking chest wound. With every inhale, the victim sucked more blood into her lungs, with every exhale released a foamy mixture of it mixed with air. And each breath put her one step closer to drowning in her own blood.

"You think I take comfort in that?"

"Maybe you don't. But Stacy does and she deserves that medal. She probably saved that girl's life. If he had managed to get her into his vehicle, well, we both know the stats on getting her back alive."

He did know. And he was proud beyond words of Stacy's quick thinking and courage. But he didn't know what he would have done if he had lost her. He cleared his throat. "I believe in Bayle. I'm standing by my offer."

"First sign she's losing it, your loyalty is to me, this department and your own safety. Is that understood?"

"Absolutely, Captain."

"Good. It's settled." She leaned forward. "Father Girod was a beloved member of the Sisters of Mercy parish and of the entire community. He was a fixture there for fifty years. The media frenzy has already begun and the pressure to close this case will be intense."

Malone agreed. He'd seen evidence of both. Before he left the Sisters of Mercy campus, reporters from every local news outlet had been on scene. They'd also been outside headquarters, and Superintendent Serpas had given a statement.

Captain O'Shay continued. "I have a personal interest in this case. I knew Father Girod." She paused. "I grew up in the Sisters of Mercy parish, attended school there through the eighth grade. Father Girod baptized me. He performed my wedding ceremony and he counseled me after Sammy's death.

"I want the son of a bitch who killed him caught," she went on. "And I want it done fast."

"We'll get him, Aunt Patti. I promise you that."

Chapter Five

Mira had called all her Sisters of Mercy and archdiocese contacts and had learned little more than what had appeared in the media: Father Girod had interrupted a vandal and been killed. She had been refused access to the windows and thus was unable to discover the extent of the damage. The church was a crime scene, she'd been told, and until the police released it, no one would be allowed in.

Mira had tried to explain that the sooner she attended to the windows, the better. But no one had seemed to care.

Father Girod would have cared. He had loved those windows—perhaps he had even died for them—and she wasn't about to sit back and do nothing.

Mira had done her best to focus on other things: the rescheduled PBS interview, a new restoration in Hammond, ordering stock for the studio.

Patience may be a virtue, but it wasn't one of hers. So here she was, NOPD headquarters.

She had been referred to Detective Spencer Malone in ISD, the Investigative Support Division.

"I have to see him," she said to the officer at the information desk. "It's about the Father Girod case."

The woman studied her a moment, then nodded. "Sign in."

She picked up a phone and dialed. "A Mira Gallier to see Detective Malone. Says it's about the Girod homicide."

A moment later, Mira was through security and heading up to the third floor. A dark-haired man met her at the elevator. He was extremely handsome, saved from pretty by a nose that looked like it had been broken one too many times.

He smiled and held out a hand. "Detective Spencer Malone."

She took it, realizing she knew him from somewhere. "Mira Gallier," she said, struggling without luck to remember where. The past six years had been such a blur.

They shook hands. He motioned to their right. "My office is this way. Can I get you a coffee or—"

"Nothing. Thanks."

His office consisted of a cubicle with a cluttered desk, a file cabinet and two chairs.

"Have a seat," he said, then took the one behind the desk. He cocked his head, studying her. "I think we've met."

"I was thinking the same thing. But I can't place it."

"You had many run-ins with the law?"

She knew he meant it as a joke. Problem was, she had. "Storm related." She folded her hands in her lap. "My husband went missing during Katrina."

"I trust you found him."

"In St. Gabriel," she said, referring to the massive temporary morgue that had been set up to process Katrina's dead.

"I'm sorry."

"Me, too."

He sent her a quizzical glance, then flipped open a notebook. "You said you have information regarding Father Girod's murder."

"Not exactly. What I told the desk officer was that I needed to talk to you about it."

He laid down his pen, obviously annoyed. "Okay. How can I help you?"

"I understand the church is a crime scene. But I need to get into it."

"May I ask why?"

"The stained-glass windows. I restored them after Katrina. I know they've been vandalized and I need to assess
the damage."

He nodded, then swiveled to a stack of folders on the
right side of his desk. He selected one, opened it and pulled
out several photos. He laid them in front of her.

She caught her breath. It was worse than she had feared.
On some of the panels, the graffiti covered at least thirty
percent of the window. The smiley face affected her like a
final kick to the gut.

Her eyes flooded with helpless tears.

She looked up to find him studying her. "You really care
about those windows."

"It's hard to explain." She sniffed and he handed her a
box of tissues. She took one and wiped her nose. "After the
storm, the destruction . . . all over the city . . . It wasn't just
buildings and windows in ruin, it was people's lives. It was
my life. In a weird way, each window I restored was like
putting a piece of me back together. My blood, sweat and
tears went into each one." She plucked another tissue from
the box and dabbed at her eyes. "For someone to do this, to
desecrate them this way, is obscene."

"Do you have any idea who could have done this?"

She blinked against tears. "No."

" 'He will come again to judge the living and the dead.'
That mean anything to you?"

"It's from the Creed," she said without hesitation. "A
statement of belief."

"Look carefully at the photos. At the graffiti. Do you
see it?"

Mira was about to ask what she was looking for, when it
emerged. "Oh, my God."

"Any idea why our guy might have left us that message?"

She shook her head. "None."

"Where were you last night, Ms. Gallier?"

"I'm sorry. Last night? Why do you ask?"

"This is a murder investigation. And frankly, I find it interesting that you're so moved by spray paint on glass, yet seemingly not at all by the loss of human life."

Angry heat flooded her cheeks. "That's not true! You don't understand at all."

He leaned casually back in his chair. "So make me understand."

"I'm devastated by Father Girod's murder. He was a beautiful person. But I can't help him." She leaned forward, fists clenched in her lap. "But I can save the windows. Which he loved. Their restoration, the restoration of his church, was important to him."

She struggled to control her emotions. "With spray paint on glass, the sooner we get to it, the better. The heat bakes it on, and if you haven't noticed, it's August."

She stood. "I was home, by the way. Alone. Absolutely no alibi."

"One last question," Malone said. "Anybody hate you enough to do this to hurt you?"

Jeff's dad, she thought. But that would be crazy, even for him. "No."

"I'm opening the scene in a few hours. You'll be able to get in then."

"Thank you, Detective." Mira turned. A woman stood in the doorway. She was tall and blond, her chin-length hair pulled away from her face. She was gazing at Mira with an expression that made her feel like an insect or science class specimen.

"Hello," the blonde said.

"Ms. Gallier, my partner, Detective Karin Bayle."

"Nice to meet you," Mira said.

"Same to you." The woman smiled.

Mira glanced back at Detective Malone. "Thank you for your help."

"Take one of my cards." He stood and came around the desk. "If anything else occurs to you, call me."

Chapter Six

Wednesday, August 10
8:00 A.M.

"Morning, partner," Spencer said, waving Bayle in. "Perfect timing."

"I would have been here earlier," she said, "but Captain O'Shay wanted to meet with me first thing. She's not convinced I'm a hundred percent."

"Are you?"

She met his gaze evenly. "Absolutely."

"Good. We've got work to do."

"Before we . . . Look, Spencer, thank you. For taking me on."

He waved off her thanks. "I'm happy to do it. Besides, I need a partner."

She lowered her gaze, expression twisting with regret. "I'm really sorry about everything that's happened."

"You don't have to talk about it."

"I want to. It's the elephant in the middle of the room. I lost it. Broke my partner's trust, checked out." She met his eyes. "I'm lucky the department took me back."

"You're back because you're a good cop," he said softly. "But you're also a human being."

"Thanks." She laughed without humor. "Tell that to all the

folks out there. I was not a welcome sight this morning. I'm sure you'll hear about it."

"I can take it."

"Good thing." She jerked her thumb toward the now empty doorway. "What was that all about?"

"Name's Mira Gallier. She came in to talk to me about the Sisters of Mercy case. About the windows, really. She'd restored them after the storm and was worried about them."

"Not about finding Father Girod's killer? Curious."

"That's what I thought. She told me I didn't understand."

"Do you think she's connected in any way?"

He pursed his lips and shook his head. "I don't think so, but I'm not ruling anything out."

"Fill me in."

She took the seat across from him and he handed her the case file. While he talked, she flipped through his and Tony's notes. When he stopped, she looked up at him. "I'm thinking this wasn't random."

"I'm thinking the same thing. We've already interviewed the primary players. I'm thinking we should widen the net."

She inclined her head in agreement. "An angry parent. Maybe a parishioner with an axe to grind. Or even a student. Sisters of Mercy goes through high school, maybe somebody didn't graduate. Kid could've been harboring a major hard-on toward the school. Planned to lay down some serious payback via spray paint on their prized windows—"

"But did not expect Father Girod to catch him in the act."

"And worse, since the priest recognizes him, he can't just run away."

"He panics and bashes the old man's head in."

"My thoughts exactly." She smiled. "This partnership just might work."

Returning her smile, he stood. "I never doubted it. We both can put up with Stacy, surely we can put up with each other?"

"Sure that's not backward?" She stood, too. "As in Stacy can put up with both of us?"

He made a face. "Then God help us both."

The squad room quieted as they passed through. Small-minded, Malone thought. As if each of them hadn't fucked up big.

"What?" He stopped, looking around. "Is there a problem?"

Not expecting an answer, he turned back around and headed out of the squad room.

"You didn't have to do that," she said.

"Wouldn't have missed it for the world."

"No wonder Stacy's so happy," she said lightly. "How is she? I stopped by your place yesterday. Your mom said she was sleeping, so we didn't get a chance to talk."

He felt himself tensing, felt the familiar knot form in his chest. "Steadily improving. If she wasn't, I wouldn't be here."

"Any idea when she'll be back on the job?"

"The doctors aren't certain. Probably the end of the month. If it's up to her, it'll be sooner than that."

Bayle smiled. "That's the Stacy I know and love."

The one he did, too. As annoying as her stubborn streak could be, he loved her for it.

"I can tell it's been tough," she murmured. "Sorry for bringing it up."

"Don't be. Scared the living shit out of me is all." He paused. "If I'd lost her, I might have gone out of my mind."

They stepped onto the empty elevator. As the doors slid shut, she met his eyes. "I get that," she said. "Totally."

Chapter Seven

They started with the church secretary. Malone had seen time and again that the person who manned the front desk was the most informed person in a company. Not with the inner corporate protocols or the financial ins and outs, but with the people, personalities, conflicts and drama.

Churches, ironically enough, were often hotbeds of the last two. Malone supposed that was because being a part of a church community was like being part of a family—and nobody pissed you off more than your brothers and sisters.

Vicky Gravier sat on Sisters of Mercy Church's front line. Everything that happened, at some point, went through her. At the moment, her office was quiet.

She looked up as they entered. Her eyes were red and puffy from crying.

"Ms. Gravier? I'm Detective Malone. And this is my partner, Detective Bayle."

She nodded. "I remember you from yesterday." Her eyes flooded with tears and she grabbed a tissue from the box on her desk. "I haven't been able to stop crying."

"We're very sorry for your loss."

"It's everyone's loss." She blew her nose loudly. "He was practically a saint. Everyone loved him."

"Ms. Gravier—"

"Vicky, please. That's what everyone calls me. Except the children. They're to call me Ms. Vicky."

"Okay, Vicky." He smiled. "As you know, we're trying to catch whoever did this and bring them to justice. We're hoping you can help us."

"I'll try." She dabbed her eyes. "What can I do?"

"Yesterday you told me you worked as the Sisters of Mercy parish secretary for six years."

"Yes. I took over when Bea retired."

"In your position, we're guessing you know pretty much everyone who worships at Sisters of Mercy."

"It's a huge parish," she said. "But yes, if they're regular worshippers, I know their name."

"And likewise, you're probably plugged in to everything that goes on."

She nodded. "Absolutely. It's part of my job. Now, that doesn't include what's going on at the school. They have their own Ms. Vicky."

"That's her name, too?"

She blushed. "No, her name's Anna Hebert. I meant someone like me."

"Gotcha." He smiled. "You probably also know when people are unhappy or grumbling. And why they are. Am I right?"

She suddenly looked uncomfortable. "I do. But I'm not nosy. I'm just the one who's always here."

"Exactly. That's why Detective Bayle and I have come to you. Here's what we're thinking. This crime wasn't random." She looked confused and he explained. "That means whoever did this specifically chose Sisters of Mercy to vandalize."

Bayle stepped in. "We feel strongly the perpetrator may be someone who feels like they have an axe to grind with the church or Father Girod. Can you think of anyone?"

"I don't know." She shook her head. "There are always

people who have issues with the way things are being done. It's the nature of the community."

"What kind of issues?"

"You know, like how money is being spent. That's a big one. Complaints about who's on the various committees, what ministries are being promoted. Even who Father is praying for or how long it took him to make a home visit. It can get pretty silly."

"Let's start with the money, then. Did anyone have a problem with the stained-glass windows being restored after the storm?"

She thought a moment. "Insurance paid the lion's share, then we had a benefactor put up the rest. Seems to me there might have been a few on the pastoral council urging Father to use the insurance money for other upgrades, but they were shot down. There were some hard feelings over it."

"How hard? Do you think they might have been angry enough to retaliate by vandalizing the windows?"

"I don't want to gossip. It's a sin, you know."

"Telling the truth isn't gossip," Malone said. "And I can't speak for God, but sharing what you know so we can catch a killer hardly seems like a sin."

She looked relieved. "There were two parishioners who were particularly vehement about it. One left the parish over it. But I can't see either of them doing anything like this."

"How long ago was this?"

"At least three years."

"Could we have their names and a way to contact them?"

"Sure. Hold on."

She accessed the information and wrote down the names and addresses. She slid it across the desk. "Paul Snyder's the gentleman who left Sisters of Mercy. That's the last address we had on him."

Malone thanked her, then went on. "Let's think generally now. Any recent blowups between the church or Father Girod and parishioners? Any misunderstandings, hurt feelings or other drama? Anything that might lead you to think it could be connected to the vandalism and murder?"

She thought a moment. "There was a situation recently. It involved a long-standing and faithful parishioner. He was furious with Father Girod, said he didn't do enough to help his son."

"What happened?" Bayle asked.

"His son died in a car wreck. He was only twenty-one." She crossed herself. "It was a terrible tragedy and we were all brokenhearted."

"Why would he blame Father Girod for an accident?"

"Tim, that was the boy's name, had struggled with alcohol and drug addiction for years. One afternoon, his dad called here, asked for Father Girod. Said it was an emergency. He was frightened. Timmy had taken some sort of drug and was swinging between wildly emotional and aggressive.

"Father Girod could always reach Tim." Her tears started again. "That's the way he was. There was this peace that flowed out of him and surrounded whoever was near."

She cleared her throat. "Father Girod didn't get there fast enough. Tim took off in his car, lost control and ran head-long into a tree. He was killed on impact."

Malone exchanged a glance with Bayle. She inclined her head ever so slightly in silent agreement. This was definitely someone they wanted to speak with, the sooner the better.

"How long ago was this?" Malone asked.

"A few months is all. Let me see . . . the funeral was the same weekend as the high school graduation. It made it all the sadder, young people starting a new life, moving on . . . And poor Tim Thibault, his life ended."

"We'll need the father's and mother's names. The names of siblings, if any. Their address."

"Earl and Joy. Tim was an only child." Her face puckered with regret. "Do I have to? They're still grieving and it seems wrong to do anything to add to their distress."

"Yes, Vicky, you have to. But we'll be gentle, I promise."

Chapter Eight

Thursday, August 11
10:10 A.M.

Before leaving the Sisters of Mercy campus, they paid a visit to Vicky's counterpart at the school. Anna Hebert was just as forthcoming as Vicky had been and handed them names of several disgruntled parents, as well as those of a half dozen of the students who seemed to stay in trouble.

Of all the leads, Earl Thibault seemed the most compelling. They agreed to pay him and his wife a visit first.

The family lived on Carrollton Avenue near City Park. In the style of the area, the home was a raised bungalow with arched windows and a wide front porch. There was nothing grand or ostentatious about the structure, but it was solid—and solidly middle class.

They slowly climbed the stairs, Malone using the moments to prepare himself. Facing a grieving parent was one of the most difficult things he had to do. He wasn't a father himself, but he could imagine how incredibly deep the pain of losing a child must be. And in this case, bitter as well.

They reached the porch and he glanced at Bayle. "You or me?"

"You," she said tersely.

He nodded and rang the bell. A woman answered. She

wore paint-splattered shorts and a T-shirt and gardening clogs.

"Mrs. Joy Thibault?"

"Yes?"

"Detectives Malone and Bayle, NOPD." He held up his shield, Bayle did the same. "We need to ask you and your husband a few questions."

She moved her gaze between the two of them. "What about?"

"The murder of Father Girod."

"Come in. It's too hot out there." She stepped aside so they could enter, then shut the door behind them.

The smell of fresh paint nearly knocked him over. Malone smiled at the woman. "Doing some updating?"

"Needing to keep busy. Both of us." She motioned them to follow her.

They did and landed in a large, light kitchen. "Have a seat. Can I get either of you a glass of iced tea or water?"

They both declined. She poured herself iced tea and faced them. "Poor Father Girod. He was a sweet, loving man. Truly a man of faith." She fell silent a moment. "Your showing up here isn't a surprise."

"And why's that, Mrs. Thibault?"

"You're looking for someone who might have been angry with the church or Father Girod. My husband surely fits that description."

"What about you, Mrs. Thibault? Don't you fit it as well?"

"No. I made peace with the direction our son had decided to take some time ago. I didn't condone or accept it, but I had to let go." Her voice thickened and she excused herself and went for a tissue. "That doesn't mean I gave up on him or stopped loving him. I didn't. I just gave it over to God."

"I'm sorry for your loss."

"Thank you." She brought the tissue to her nose. "But Earl wasn't able to do that. He never could surrender. And he still blames himself."

"Is your husband here?"

"Yes." She took a sip of her tea, the ice clinking as she

tilted the glass. "He was laid off recently. A part of me is angry about that. He worked for that company for sixteen years. And after all that service, after losing his only son, they lay him off?" She shook her head. "But God has a plan, doesn't he? And I have to trust that plan will take us somewhere good."

She laughed self-consciously. "I see by your expressions you think I'm either addled by grief or terribly naïve."

Malone shook his head. "Hardly, Mrs. Thibault. Truth is, I wish I could believe like that."

She smiled slightly. "I wish you could as well, it's a wonderful feeling. I'll pray for you, Detective."

Malone glanced at Bayle and found her looking at the woman both with longing and as if she were some strange, mythical creature. Totally foreign yet intriguing. He wondered what Bayle clung to that she desperately wished she could let go of.

"Your husband," Malone reminded her. "We need to ask him a few questions."

"Of course. I'll get him."

She returned after a couple minutes—without her husband. She waved them over. "Follow me."

Her husband sat in a computer chair in what had obviously been his son's room. All the furniture had been moved away from the walls, toward the center. Drop cloths covered the floor and some of the furniture. On the walls was a fresh coat of a buttery lemon color.

"She's painted his room," he said. "It doesn't smell like him anymore."

"Mr. Thibault. I'm Detective Malone and this is Detective Bayle, NOPD."

"I know who you are. Joy told me."

"We need to ask you a few questions."

The man didn't respond, so he went on. "Are you aware that early Tuesday morning someone vandalized the Sisters of Mercy sanctuary windows? And that person also murdered Father Girod?"

"I heard about it."

"Where were you Tuesday night, Mr. Thibault?"

"Here."

"Home?"

"No," he corrected. "Here. In Timmy's room."

"May I see your hands, Mr. Thibault?"

He held them out. They shook slightly. That amount of spray painting would have left quite a bit of residue on the fingers, under the nails and nail beds. It would have been near impossible to remove all traces, even with solvent.

Malone inspected them carefully. They were clean.

"I didn't do it. I wish I had. Maybe I'd feel better."

"You don't mean that, Earl."

He looked at his wife, expression naked with pain. "Don't tell me what I mean, you don't know."

Malone glanced at her wounded expression. She did know, he thought. And was living in her own private hell.

"We understand that you blamed Father Girod for your son's death."

Earl let out a deep, shuddering sigh. "Sometimes it helps to blame someone else."

"Why's that, Mr. Thibault?"

"Because for those moments, you stop blaming yourself." He started to cry, silently, his shoulders shaking.

Malone looked at Bayle and shook his head. There was no rage here, only grief.

"Thank you, Mr. Thibault. We're sorry to have bothered you."

He didn't respond and Joy Thibault walked them out. When they reached the door, Malone turned to her. "I hate to ask you, but could I see your hands?"

Silently, she held them out. Lemony flecks dotted her hands, wrists and forearms. Otherwise, they were clean.

"Would you and your husband agree to being finger-printed? We would be able to officially eliminate you both as suspects."

She looked surprised but nodded. "Anything that would help."

He thanked her and they headed to the car, not speaking

again until they were buckled in. Bayle shifted into Drive and pulled away from the curb.

She glanced at him. "You and Stacy plan on having kids?"

"After that, I'm leaning toward not."

"The world is so effing screwed up."

"Little Miss Sunshine."

"You disagree?"

"I prefer to remain hopeful."

"Like Mrs. Thibault back there."

He looked at Bayle, surprised by the anger in her voice. "It works for her. And frankly, if I had to choose between his attitude and hers, hers wins. Hands down."

She changed the subject. "Where to?"

"Next name on the list."

Chapter Nine

Thursday, August 11
11:50 P.M.

Mira stood gazing at the Sisters of Mercy windows. She and Deni, aided by Deni's boyfriend, Chris, had worked on them nearly nonstop for the past thirty-six hours. Now, the only evidence of the vandalism that remained was the lingering smell of the acetone they'd used to clean them.

"We did it," she said softly, looking at Deni, standing beside her. "I feel like I just fought a battle with the devil and won."

Her friend met her eyes and smiled. "It's a great feeling, isn't it?"

"It is. And if every part of my body wasn't screaming protest, I might even do a happy dance."

"Too tired for the Corner Bar?"

The cleaning process had been grueling, both a physical and mental workout. The respirators were unnatural and cumbersome to wear, her upper body ached from the repetitive motion used in the cleaning process, her back and feet hurt from balancing on a ladder for a day and a half, and her eyes burned from straining not to miss a single fleck of the spray paint.

Even so, Mira knew there was no way she'd be able to sleep. "Are you kidding? A drink at this point is a must."

"My God, they're beautiful," Chris said, coming up beside them. "Father Girod would be pleased."

Mira smiled at him. "I prefer to think that he *is* pleased."

Deni tucked her arm through Chris's. "We're thinking alcohol."

"Good by me," he said. "The Corner Bar?"

"Is there anywhere else?"

"The truck's loaded," he said. "Everything but your coveralls."

"Let's go then," Mira said.

The two exited before her. She set the alarm, then made certain the door was locked and met them at the truck. After removing and stowing their coveralls, they climbed into the vehicle, Chris driving and Deni in the middle. The Corner Bar, appropriately named because it sat on the corner of Willow and Dublin streets, was a true neighborhood joint. All the regulars lived or worked within walking distance of it. And that included Mira and her crew—the studio was located just a couple blocks over.

As they walked in, the owner called out a greeting. They returned it and ambled over to the bar.

"How's it going, Sam?"

"S'okay. Business is steady." He wiped the bar top. "What're you three doing out so late?"

"Celebrating a job well done," Chris answered, sliding onto one of the bar stools.

"We restored the windows at Sisters of Mercy," Deni added.

Sam's face puckered. "Poor Father Girod. He was a hell of a great guy."

"He was," Mira agreed, taking the stool next to Deni. "How did you know him?"

"Went to Sisters of Mercy my whole life. He baptized both my kids and presided over Maggie's funeral. May she rest in peace." He crossed himself, then turned his attention to the reason for their visit. "The usual?"

When they all agreed, he set about making cosmos for Mira and Deni and got a bottle of Abita Amber for Chris.

He set the drinks in front of them along with a bowl of pretzels. "As old as Father Girod was, after Katrina he was out in the heat, helping gut flooded homes. Can you believe that?"

They said they couldn't, and after a couple more moments, he excused himself to help another customer. Mira lifted her glass. "To you two, for working your asses off. I couldn't have done it without you."

"No, you couldn't," Deni agreed. "Slave driver."

She laughed. "I am a little intense when it comes to my windows."

"I loved it," Chris said. "It made me feel like I was really doing something important. You know, making a difference."

Deni looked at him, grinning hugely. "Isn't it cool! I knew you'd love it!"

Chris had been a great find, and it had been Deni who had found him. Chris was a carpenter and handyman for the New Orleans archdiocese, and Deni had met him while doing prep work for a window at St. Rita's. They hit it off and started dating.

"Your being with us really made a difference, Chris," Mira said. "Thank you."

"Does that mean we can sleep in tomorrow?" Deni asked hopefully.

"It does. Take the entire day off if you want."

"You know me better than that, but a few extra hours of sleep would totally rock."

Chris and Deni started talking to each other about their plans for the upcoming weekend; Mira fell silent, sipped her drink and listened to them. She remembered being that way with Jeff—totally lost in each other, in being a couple. She wondered if she would ever feel that way again.

"Are you okay, Mira?"

She looked at Chris, realizing how long she had been quiet. And how exhausted she suddenly felt.

"I hate to be the wet blanket, but suddenly I can hardly

keep my eyes open. And unlike you two, I have to be up early for an appointment with Dr. Jasper."

Her therapist, who had been with her through it all, the deepest and darkest times, the good, bad and ugly.

"You want me to drive you home?" Chris asked. "I could pick you up in the morning?"

"And interrupt your sleep? No way. Just get me to the studio; my car knows the way from there."

For a moment he looked like he might argue, but he didn't. They each called goodbye to Sam and headed out.

As they cleared the door, Mira noticed a man huddled on the sidewalk at the corner of the building. One of the city's many homeless, she thought. The picture of misery, he sat head down and knees drawn up, hugging himself, rocking back and forth.

"That poor guy," she said. "Maybe he needs help?"

Deni caught her arm. "Don't get too close. He may be dangerous."

"C'mon, Deni," she said, gently shaking off her friend's hand. "What could he do to me?"

"He may have something and be contagious."

"She's right," Chris said.

"I can't believe you two." She started toward the man. Deni hung back but Chris fell in step behind her.

The man didn't seem to notice when she stopped beside him. He had long, dark, stringy hair. With his head resting on his knees, it fell forward, hiding his face. Even though it was August, he wore an army fatigue jacket and boots. She wondered if he was a vet and felt even worse for him.

"Hello," she said. "Do you need some help?"

He lifted his head. The light was behind him so she couldn't clearly make out his face, but she had the impression of hawkish features and a dark, intense gaze.

"The Lord protects His lambs," he said. "They shall not want."

"That's true," she replied softly. "But He also wants us to help each other. Have you had anything to eat tonight?"

He simply stared at her. She reached into her purse and drew out a twenty-dollar bill. She held it out. "Promise me you'll get something to eat with this."

"The very hairs on your head are numbered. Do not be afraid; you are more valuable to God than a whole flock of sparrows."

"Mira," Chris said, touching her elbow, "come on."

She ignored him. "Please take it," she said. "You need it, so I'm not leaving until you do."

He silently studied her a moment, then reached up and took the bill. Without a word, he tucked it into his coat pocket and returned his head to his knees.

"He didn't even say thank you," Deni whispered as they fell into step together. "That's just rude."

"I didn't do it for his thanks. If I was in his position, I hope someone would do the same for me."

She had been in that position, Mira realized. Alone in her pain. Shutting out the world, refusing help.

She glanced back at the man. He had lifted his head and was watching them walk away. She sensed his longing. To belong. To be part of the world again.

A lump formed in her throat and she looked away. Was that his longing she sensed? Or was it her own?

Chapter Ten

Friday, August 12
1:30 A.M.

At Stacy's scream, Malone came fully awake. He found her sitting up beside him, trembling so violently the bed shook. He sat up and gathered her against him.

She clung to him and he pressed his cheek to the top of her head and rocked her slightly. "It's okay," he said softly. "I'm here. You're safe."

As the moments ticked past, her trembling ceased and her breathing evened. Still, he didn't loosen his grip.

He couldn't. When she relived the nightmare, so did he. His emotions ran the gamut from thankful to terrified. He closed his eyes, drawing in a quiet, steadying breath. And worried. Her nightmares seemed to be getting worse instead of better; they were coming more, not less, frequently.

Stacy slipped out of his arms and drew the sheet to her chin, turning her head away. "Don't do that," he murmured. "Don't shut me out."

"I can only imagine what you must be thinking," she said, looking at him, eyes bright with tears. "The badass you fell in love with has turned into a quivering mass of . . . of girly goo."

"Girly goo?" He laughed and pulled her back against his chest. "What the hell is that?"

"This. Me. Weepy and timid. Clingy."

"Look, Stacy"—he tipped her face up to his—"yeah, I fell in love with your swagger. But I also fell in love with the part of you that wants to save everyone and everything. The part that tears up during those chick flicks you make me watch. I fell in love with your unfailing honesty and fair-mindedness, your devotion to family and doing the right thing."

He rested his forehead against hers. "I love every part of you, Stacy Killian."

"Even the girly goo part?"

"Even that."

She rubbed her nose against his. "I am pretty great, aren't I?"

He laughed again. "Did I mention your sense of humor?"

"I wasn't being funny."

"Oh, yes, you were." He lay down, bringing her with him. He tenderly kissed the angry scar below her right clavicle.

She stiffened. "Won't I look charming in my strapless wedding gown?"

"To me, it's beautiful." He trailed his finger lightly over its ridges. "You should love it, too. Show it off on our wedding day. Immortalize it in our photographs."

"You're nuts."

He leaned up on an elbow and gazed down at her. "You probably saved that child's life. You didn't hesitate. You knew what you saw and acted on it. That child is alive and home with her parents because of you. I couldn't be prouder of you or that scar."

She searched his gaze, struggling, he saw, with her emotions. "I keep thinking about that day. Wondering if I could have done something differently."

"What do you mean, do something differently? You saved a child's life, Stacy."

"But I got shot. Almost killed. I had to take him out, right there in front of all those people . . . families with children. If I'd called for backup—"

"That monster might have gotten that little girl into his van. You know the stats. Once the kid's in a vehicle, probability of a recovery drops dramatically."

"I know. And I—" She shuddered. "Jane's so traumatized by it she's afraid of letting the kids out of her sight for a minute and wakes up half a dozen times a night to go check on them. The kids are having nightmares about their aunt Stacy bleeding all over the sidewalk. I hate that I exposed them to that."

He threaded his fingers through her hair. The blond strands against his fingers always reminded him of summer. "You didn't, sweetheart. That sick son of a bitch is the one who exposed them. You're the white knight."

She was silent a moment. When she spoke, desperation colored her tone. "Why me, Spencer? Why was it me who was there? Why, with so many people around, was I the only one who saw him snatch that little girl? Even her parents were oblivious."

"I don't know. But I do know her parents thank God you were."

Moments passed with just the thrum of her heart against his chest. He broke the silence. "Maybe you being there wasn't even about you. Have you considered that?"

"How so?"

"Maybe it was about that little girl?"

She rolled onto her side, facing him. She placed her hands on his chest. "Thank you," she whispered, voice thick.

"For what?"

"For being here. For loving me."

He pulled her closer to him, all the things he wanted to say bottling up in his chest. Things about being unable to breathe without her, about loving her with an intensity that terrified him.

Since he couldn't say them, he simply held her.

Chapter Eleven

Mira sat across from her therapist, exhausted to the bone yet strangely energized. The words tumbled one over the other as she told the doctor how, for the past two days, she, Deni and Chris had worked around the clock to save the Sisters of Mercy windows.

Dr. Jasper had heard about the vandalism and murder. Everyone in New Orleans had—it had been splashed from every news outlet. Father Girod had been very popular. The community was outraged; his funeral had taken on the quality of a rock concert. Because of the vandalism, the service had been held at St. Louis Cathedral on Jackson Square in the French Quarter. The church had been filled to overflowing, mourners spilling out onto the square.

"The detective I spoke to thought my urgency over the windows was weird," Mira said.

"Did he?"

"Yes." She rubbed her palms on her thighs, the summer-weight denim rough against them. "But Father Girod loved those windows. To him, they were sacred. He would have wanted me to react that way."

"You're certain of that?"

"Yes." She nodded for emphasis. "One hundred percent." Mira fell silent a moment, then went on. "The detective even asked where I was the night it happened and if I thought someone could have done it to get back at me."

"Do you think that might be a possibility?"

"There's only one person who hates me that much, and I hardly think he would stoop so low."

"Your ex–father-in-law."

Mira agreed. "I just can't picture the high and mighty Anton Gallier breaking into a church, spray cans in tow. Though he could have hired it done."

The last she had actually considered a possibility. But that wasn't his style either. Hands-on cruelty was what he preferred. His own peculiar brand.

"What would be the fun in that?" she said sarcastically. "He'd want to see my reaction. Know for sure how badly he hurt me."

"You stayed sober through this?"

"Yes." Mira caught herself looking guiltily away, as it all came crashing back: awaking in the middle of the night to the river of grief pouring over her, swallowing her. Her desperate search for pharmacological relief.

Mira clasped her hands in her lap, feeling the steep drop from hero to zero. Just the week before, she and Dr. Jasper had spoken of ending their weekly sessions. Mira was ready, they had both thought so.

Now she had to tell her she had fallen from grace.

Even as the familiar urge to dodge the truth tugged at her, she met the therapist's eyes directly. "I relapsed. Monday night. Before all this happened."

Dr. Jasper's expression registered neither surprise nor disappointment. The therapist knew her better than anyone since Jeff and wouldn't make excuses for her. But she wouldn't condemn her either.

"Where did you get the Xanax, Mira?"

"Not on the street, if that's what you're thinking. And I didn't steal it from a friend." She had resorted to both before——as well as doctor hopping and visits to so-called pill factories. "I tore the house apart. I found one in a piece of my carry-on luggage."

"And if you hadn't? What would you have done?"

Mira hesitated. Would she have hooked up with one of her reliable sources? Headed out in the middle of the night, alone, without a thought for her safety or anything else but her need for oblivion? She wished she could answer that she wouldn't have.

But she couldn't. And she despised herself for it.

Dr. Jasper leaned forward. "You're in recovery, Mira. It's a process. A journey."

"Screw that. I want to be pissed at myself."

"You've done incredibly well. It's been almost a year." Dr. Jasper crossed her legs, the movement of fabric against fabric making a rustling noise. The therapist was the epitome of elegance and well-heeled beauty. Although Mira knew her to be a decade older than her own thirty-three, they looked close in age. "What do you think precipitated this relapse?"

"You tell me. You're the expert."

Dr. Jasper didn't reply, but Mira hadn't expected her to. The comment had been bullshit, and they both knew it. She sighed. "I woke up and it was like . . . he was there. Or had been there, standing beside the bed, gazing down at me. It was so real." She looked down at her hands, clenched in her lap, then back up at the therapist. "I thought, for a moment, that maybe everything else had been a dream."

"Go on."

"And it all came crashing back," she said simply.

"The day you lost him?"

"Yes. And everything since."

"Then what?"

"I ran for cover."

"Shelter from the storm."

The storm of her emotions. The truth. "Why now, Dr. Jasper? After all these months?"

"The sixth anniversary is just around the corner. We tend to mark traumatic events, even if only subconsciously."

Six years since Katrina had blown her life to bits. "It makes sense, it's just . . ."

"Just what?"

She met the doctor's eyes. "That it feels like a lie. And I don't want to lie to myself anymore."

When Dr. Jasper didn't respond, Mira's cheeks grew hot. "It doesn't do any damn good, does it? It changes nothing and I'm so sick and tired of—"

Unmoved, the therapist asked, "So sick and tired of what?"

"Everything. This." She jumped to her feet. "Of missing Jeff. Of reliving every freaking moment of that day. I want my life back." She met the therapist's eyes defiantly. "It's mine, dammit! And I want it back!"

"So take it back. Only you can."

"Right. And how do you propose I do that? Jeff's gone. I can never get him or what we had back."

"No, you can't." She paused. "But you can make a new life for yourself."

"Haven't I?" she asked bitterly. "Isn't this it?"

"Living in the past and blunting the pain of the present isn't a new life." Dr. Jasper leaned forward slightly. "Let me ask you something. How difficult was the last year for you?"

"I don't follow."

"Staying clean. Until Monday night, how difficult has it been? On a scale of one being a piece of cake and ten being hell on earth?"

"Not a piece of cake, but . . ." *But not that difficult.* "A four. Some days even a three."

"Why do you think that is?"

Mira frowned, not comprehending.

Dr. Jasper went on. "I know from our sessions that in the past twelve months, you've experienced some version of that night many times."

"True."

"What was different?"

The Magdalene window. It popped into her head so quickly, it took her by surprise. Mira frowned. "Why would my work on the Magdalene restoration make any difference in my ability to stay clean?"

"Substituting one addiction for another isn't unheard of. In fact, studies indicate it's common."

She shook her head. "The window's been a cause, not my crutch."

Dr. Jasper laced her fingers in her lap. "It's consumed you for these past months. You've given the project everything, your talent and every spare minute, you've begged for donations, and in your quest, even alienated people close to you. Do you deny any of those things?"

"No."

"They're all classic signs of addiction."

"You're saying that for the last year, the Magdalene window has been my drug of choice?"

"It's possible. Maybe your relapse was precipitated by the fact the window is complete. Soon to be installed. Essentially, about to be taken away from you."

And what does she do? Run for her original drug of choice.

"Great," Mira snapped. "I finally get back to the point where I'm loving my work and feeling connected again, and *you* tell me it's some sort of unhealthy obsession?"

"I didn't tell you that's what it was. I offered it as a possibility." She cocked her head. "And I didn't use the term *obsession*. That was your choice."

Mira scowled at her. "I hate when you do that. Turn my words around on me."

"You're supposed to." Dr. Jasper's lips lifted in a small smile. "If it's not at least a little uncomfortable, I'm not doing my job effectively." She glanced at her watch. "With that, our time's up."

Chapter Twelve

Mira pulled into the gravel lot behind her studio and parked her Ford Focus. Her session with Dr. Jasper had left her on edge and vacillating between being disheartened and pissed off. Not with the therapist. Or even herself.

At the situation. At the fact she'd been able to turn something as healing as her art into a way to stay numb.

She climbed out of the car, slamming the door. A moment later, she rounded the front of the building. A converted chapel, located just off River Road, a few miles from the Uptown bend in the Mississippi River, the ninety-year-old building fit her needs perfectly. Constructed entirely of cypress boards, it consisted of three rooms, one of which was large enough to serve as her workshop, and lots of windows to provide natural light. Most important, it sat on natural high ground that hadn't flooded during the storm.

She let herself in. The smell of acetone and mud hit her first. Next, she became aware of the light, the way it spilled through the artworks, creating patches of color on the floors and walls. Through the day, as the sun moved, the colors and patterns would shift, creating a kind of life-sized kaleidoscope.

In the months immediately after Jeff's death, she'd worked only because the destruction had been so great. She hadn't felt the pull of the glass, had been unable to see its beauty. The feeling of purpose and completion her art usually provided had been replaced by something cold and mechanical.

It had been an awful, barren place to live, though she preferred it to the chemically induced euphoria she had turned to.

Mira crossed through what had originally been the church narthex but was now a storefront, and into the small kitchen. Using her single-serve Keurig pot and a pod of her favorite blend, she fixed herself a cup of coffee then headed with it to her workshop.

Pocket doors separated the work from the retail areas. She slid them open and stepped into the room, then closed the doors. Organized chaos reigned. Six large tables, some supporting restorations in progress, others cluttered with buckets of tools, stacks of journals, catalogs and the occasional abandoned water bottle, formed two rows. Every inch of wall space was covered with a seeming mishmash of sketches, posters, photos, ads and articles, much of it covered in a layer of studio grit.

That such a precise art form could be created in such a disorderly environment still astounded her.

Sipping her coffee, Mira made her way past the racks of colored glass, the bins of lead, zinc and copper came, heading for the rear of the studio—and the heart of the Magdalene window, the large center panel depicting a grieving Magdalene at the foot of the cross.

The other four panels were wrapped and racked, ready to be transported to their new home. Mira had been unable to let this one go.

Another indication that Dr. Jasper had been right.

Mira stopped in front of it now. Done in the Bavarian style of painting on glass, the artist had achieved an amazing amount of detail. Mira had tried her hand at the process, a complex layering of enamel paint and kiln firings, and found it exacting to the point of maddening. Calling her finished product sophomoric in comparison to this would be giving herself way more credit than she deserved.

This artisan had managed to portray Mary Magdalene's deep pain at the loss of her beloved. Mira understood the saint's pain; she had connected with it immediately.

She, too, had lost the love of her life.

"Good morning, Maggie," she said softly, perching on the edge of a table, gazing at the saint's anguished expression. "You're going to be disappointed with me. I fell off the wagon."

Mira paused, as if waiting for a response, then continued. "Dr. Jasper thinks it's because we're about to say goodbye. I hate thinking she's right, but I do."

Mira heard someone arriving. Deni, she thought, glancing at her watch. She had hoped for a few more minutes alone, but she wasn't surprised by her ever-prepared assistant's early arrival.

Mira turned her thoughts back to Dr. Jasper and what she'd said about substitute addiction—an addict trading one dependency for another. It happened all the time.

Is that really what she'd done? Used her obsession with saving the Magdalene window like a drug? And now that Magdalene was complete, would she fall apart?

Even as every fiber of her being rebelled against the thought, she admitted not only that it was true but also that she had already begun.

No. She curled her hands around her mug. *She couldn't go back to that desolate place. She wouldn't.*

She heard Deni moving through the retail area. "I'm in here," she called.

Behind her the pocket door slid open. Mira got slowly to her feet, fixing a welcoming smile on her face. "I thought you were supposed to sleep in," she said, turning around. "I should send you . . ."

The words and smile died on her lips. It was the homeless man from the night before, the one she had given money to. But unlike the night before, this morning she could clearly see his face. The expression in his eyes made her skin crawl. They burned with an unnatural intensity.

"I saw you last night," she said as steadily as she could. "Outside the Corner Bar. I gave you twenty dollars, remember?"

He didn't respond, just continued to stare at her. She cleared her throat. "There're no drugs here. I don't keep any cash on the premises. If you're hungry, there's a mission on Baronne Street."

He took a step toward her. "And the Lord said, in the end the wheat will be separated from the chaff. And the chaff will be plunged into the unquenchable fire."

"I don't want any trouble," she said softly, "and I'm certain you don't either. Just leave now. No harm done."

Something he held caught the light, glittering. A knife, she realized, heart leaping to her throat.

Mira glanced around. Her only chance of escape was the fire exit in the back corner of the room. She eased in that direction.

"In the end, the Shepherd will gather together his flock." His voice rose. "What awaits false prophets is far worse than eternal damnation!"

He took another step, then another, lifting his hand.

Not a knife, she saw. A long, thin shard of glass. One of hers. He must have found it while digging through her trash. Blood dripped from his hand.

He stopped within striking distance. She saw that a small cross had been crudely tattooed between his eyes.

"The flesh will be peeled from their bones, roasted and eaten by demons."

From outside came the sound of conversation, then laughter. Deni, for certain this time. And Chris.

The man heard them, too. It registered on his face. In the next instant, he lunged at her, going for her throat. She screamed. His fingers, slippery with blood, circled, then clawed at her neck. She fell backward against a worktable. A bucket of tools toppled, crashing to the floor.

She didn't have time to think, let alone fight before he

was off her, running for the fire exit. As the fire door popped open, the alarm sounded. Mira sank to the floor, legs shaking so violently they wouldn't hold her.

Deni and Chris rushed into the room. Chris reached her first, squatting down in front of her. "Are you all right?"

"Mira!" Deni cried. "You're bleeding!"

"Call 911," Chris ordered.

Mira looked down at her front, at the blood smears on her shirt. *He'd been bleeding, his hands at her throat sticky.*

"No, I'm fine." Mira struggled to stand up. "He had a piece of glass, but he didn't cut me. He grabbed my throat but—"

Then she realized. She brought her hand to her neck. Her cloisonné cross was gone. Jeff had bought it for her on their honeymoon in Portugal, and the lunatic had ripped it from her neck.

Another piece of Jeff taken from her.

"It was the man from last night. He took my cross necklace."

"What man? Not that bum you gave money to?"

She nodded and Chris frowned. "How did he find you?"

"I don't know." She brought her hand to her throat again, grief overwhelming her. "Why did he do this?"

They both looked devastated for her. They understood the cross wasn't simply a necklace but a piece of her lost past.

"Maybe the police will be able to get it back," Chris offered. "If we call them now—"

The police. The windows. "Oh, my God," she said. "Could it be?"

"Could what be?" Deni asked.

" 'He will come again to judge the living and the dead.' The message on the Sisters of Mercy windows. Just like last night, the guy quoted Scripture. But today he said almost the same thing that was written on the windows. The detective wondered if the vandalism could have had something to do with me."

Chris spoke first. "I think we should call 911."

"No. I have another number to call. I'll get it."

Chapter Thirteen

"That's why she recognized me," Malone said as Bayle eased into the Gallier Glassworks parking area. He and Stacy lived just down the block and around the corner.

"Who?" Bayle asked.

"Mira Gallier. When I interviewed her, we both thought the other looked familiar but didn't know where we might have met. Now I do. Not only are we practically neighbors, but Stacy and I have been here, to her store. We bought a piece of her work."

Bayle parked but didn't shut down the vehicle. "Now that I see the Glassworks sign, I recognize her, too. After Katrina, Gallier was in the news a lot."

"She told me her husband died in the storm."

Bayle shrugged. "Something about that, I don't remember what."

Malone nodded. There'd been so many bizarre and tragic stories in the news then, so many accusations, it was difficult to remember the facts of each.

They both alighted from the vehicle and slammed their doors in unison. Without speaking, they crossed to the front door.

Mira Gallier opened it. "Thank you for coming, Detective Malone."

Though her tone was steady, her expression was traumatized. Blood stained her white knit shirt and was smeared on her chest and throat.

"Are you all right?" he asked.

"Yes. He didn't hurt me."

"I think you met my partner, Detective Bayle."

She nodded and moved aside so they could cross the threshold. Malone shifted his gaze to the two people with her, a woman and a man. The woman was young; early twenties, he guessed. She was petite, pixieish with her short, spiky dark hair and heart-shaped face. The man looked slightly older, medium build and height with blond hair and brown eyes.

Gallier saw Malone's gaze and introduced them. "Detectives, this is my studio assistant, Deni Watts, and her boyfriend, Chris Johns."

He nodded in greeting, then shifted his attention back to her. "Tell us what happened, Ms. Gallier."

"I was the first to arrive this morning—"

"What time was that?"

"Around ten." She stopped, as if struggling to put her thoughts together. "I'd given Deni the morning off. We've been working nonstop cleaning the Sisters of Mercy windows."

"How's that going?" he asked.

"We finished. Last night."

"I'll have to stop by and take a look at them." He glanced at the spiral notebook in his hands, then back up at her. "So, you were the first to arrive at about ten this morning?"

"Yes. I made coffee and headed into the workshop."

"Where's that?"

She pointed to her left. Pocket doors stood open. Bayle crossed to them and peered through.

"Go on."

"I closed the doors behind me and—"

"Why?"

The question came from Bayle. Mira turned her way. "I'm sorry, what?"

"You were all alone. Why close the doors?"

She gazed at Bayle a moment before answering. "Habit. We keep the two areas separate because the studio materials make such a mess."

Malone took over. "What happened next?"

"I heard someone out here, moving around. Figured it was Deni and I called out."

"But you gave her the morning off."

"Deni's like that." She flashed an appreciative smile at the woman. "Dedicated."

"Go on."

"I didn't lock the door when I came in. Technically, we were open for business, though we don't get a lot of foot traffic."

"But it wasn't your assistant?"

"No. It was a homeless man I'd given twenty dollars to last night."

Malone glanced at Bayle; she was watching Gallier intently. "And where and what time did that happen?"

"The Corner Bar. Around one A.M. I felt sorry for him."

"That's only a few blocks from here," Malone said. "He's probably taken up residence in somebody's backyard or shed. Go on."

"He was holding what I thought was a knife."

"But it wasn't?"

She shook her head. "A piece of broken glass. One of ours. He was bleeding."

Bayle stepped in. "Is that his blood on your shirt?"

Mira brought a hand to her throat. "Yes. He—" She cleared her throat. "He was standing there, staring at me. Spouting all this crazy stuff about Jesus and judgment, false prophets and burning in hell. That's why I called you, Detective Malone. It just seemed so weird that somebody spray-painted that message on my windows at Sisters of Mercy, then today . . . this happens. It just—" She suddenly sounded unsure of herself.

"I wondered if they could be connected? If this guy could be the one who killed Father Girod?"

"Did he say the exact phrase from the church windows?"

"No."

"What did he say? Can you remember exactly?"

"I don't think I'll ever forget." She clasped her hands together. "He said, 'In the end, the Shepherd will gather together his flock. What awaits false prophets is far worse than eternal damnation.'"

She stopped, shuddering. "The last thing he said really freaked me out. 'The flesh will be peeled from their bones, roasted and eaten by demons.'"

"Whose bones?"

"The false prophets'," she said. "That was it. He said the worst awaited 'false prophets.'"

Chris stepped in. "He was quoting Scripture last night, too. But not all that judgment stuff. It was more like, 'God's got you in His hands and will take care of you.'"

Malone made a note. "You did the right thing calling me," he said. "Don't worry about what's connected, leave that to us." He smiled reassuringly. "That's our job. You just tell us what happened next."

She nodded. "I heard Deni and Chris. He must have, too, because he just suddenly . . . leaped at me. He grabbed at my throat, I thought—"

Her voice turned thick. Deni put an arm around her. "I thought he was going to kill me. But he just took my necklace and ran."

"Mind if I take a look around your workroom?" Bayle asked.

"Go ahead. Deni, could you show her where—"

"I've got this," Chris offered, then motioned to Bayle. "This way."

After they'd disappeared into the workroom, Malone continued. "Can you describe him?"

"Dirty, baggy clothes. Army fatigue jacket. Boots." She fell silent a moment. "He was a medium height."

"What about his age?"

She pressed her lips together a moment. "It's hard to tell with people like that, but . . . He wasn't a kid but not an old man."

"Hair? Skin?"

"He was white. Dark hair. Long." She motioned about her jawline. "But it was his eyes that—" She shuddered and rubbed her arms. "They were crazy. Bright, even though they were dark. Like they were lit from inside."

"Anything else? Some defining mark or—"

"A tattoo. Between his eyebrows. A cross."

"A cross?" he repeated. "Between his eyebrows? That sounds like Preacher. And this whole area is his favorite stomping ground."

"Who's that?" she asked.

"A street corner zealot. Been around for years. Doesn't have a history of violence, though things change. It'd help if you could come down to headquarters and look at some photos, confirm it for us."

"Can I get cleaned up first?"

"Of course." Malone checked his watch. "How much time will you need?"

"Not long. I keep some things here."

"Malone," Bayle said from the workroom doorway, "you'll want to see this."

He joined her in the other room, aware of Gallier and her assistant following him.

Bayle motioned a trail of blood from the doorway to a small puddle in the center of the room. The perp had entered the studio bleeding, crossed to the center of the room and stopped.

"And there." Bayle indicated a point six feet in front of that, to a spray of glass and tools on the floor.

"That's where I was standing," Gallier said. "When he grabbed me, I fell against the table and knocked everything off it."

Malone crossed to the spot and squatted beside the conglomeration. He indicated a long, triangular piece of glass smeared with blood. "Is this the piece of glass you saw in his hand?"

"It is."

Spencer looked up at Bayle. "From her description, it sounded like Preacher. He's been known to get in people's faces."

"Anything to get his message across," Bayle agreed. "I'll radio this in, communications can put out a BOLO."

"Bolo?" Mira asked.

"Be on the lookout."

"Should I clean this up?" Deni asked. "Or will you guys send a, you know, CSI team?"

God help them, TV had made everyone an expert. "I'm afraid you're looking at the CSI team for this one." At her crestfallen expression, he smiled. "Don't worry, Ms. Watts, every sworn officer is trained in evidence collection."

In the end, they collected the blood-smeared piece of glass and a couple drops of blood, the latter just in case this did end up connecting to the Sisters of Mercy homicide.

Gallier walked them to the door. "Do you still need me to come look at photos?"

"Give us an hour. We'll cruise around. Maybe we'll get lucky and pick him up."

"Thank you, Detectives. I'd really love to have my necklace back. It was a gift from my late husband."

"Was it valuable?" Bayle asked.

"To me it's priceless."

"Monetarily."

Mira stiffened. "Does that matter? Isn't it enough that it was stolen and I want it back?"

Bayle had the people skills of a pitt bull, Malone decided and stepped in. "Of course it's enough. But it makes a difference in our investigation. For example, if it's worth a lot of money, he might try to pawn it."

"Oh." For the first time since they arrived, she looked near tears. "Less than fifty dollars."

Moments later they were buckled into the Taurus. Bayle started the engine. "Do you think she was telling the truth?"

He glanced at her in surprise. "Yeah. Why?"

"Something just seemed a little off about her."

"Honestly, didn't pick up on that. Though I found it interesting she called the Sisters of Mercy windows 'her' windows."

She rolled her shoulders. "Think Preacher could be our guy?"

"Could be. Geographically it works. The whole God's wrath thing works. At this point he's looking better than anyone we've interviewed so far. One thing bothers me, though. He didn't hurt her."

"Come again?"

"Why would the same guy who killed Father Girod run off without harming her? The situations were similar."

"Don't know. Could Gallier be lying?" Bayle offered.

"Always a possibility. But why would she? All he took was her necklace, one she admitted wasn't worth much. Certainly not enough to make an insurance claim. Besides, her story hangs together. We even have the bloody piece of glass."

"True. But she could have planted it. Manufactured the whole tableau."

"Could have." He looked at her, curious. "But again, why?"

"People do crazy things for attention."

It was true, though in this case it seemed far-fetched. He told her so.

She laughed and pulled out of the parking area. "Keeping me grounded, Malone. I like that."

"Here to help." He pointed down Carrollton Avenue as they approached it. "Why don't we swing by the Riverbend? Preacher's been known to hang out there. On the way, I'll give Vicky over at Sisters of Mercy a call, see if Preacher has any history with them."

Chapter Fourteen

Preacher liked to hang out on street corners and share the Word. His particular fire-and-brimstone version of it, anyway. But there'd been no sign of him around the Riverbend that morning. Malone and Bayle checked with each business—all of them familiar with the street evangelist from having shooed him away from their doors many times.

A maniac shouting about frying in the eternal fat vat tended to hurt business.

Preacher was also known to hop the Carrollton Avenue streetcar and treat the captive commuters to his doomsday message. Invariably, the driver would boot him off; undeterred, he would simply catch the next one to come along.

He would make a day of it—until the NOPD arrived.

Again, nobody had seen him.

Mira Gallier was waiting for Malone when he arrived back at the station. He noted that she had cleaned up and come alone. "Sorry," he said, approaching her. "Have you been here long?"

She shook her head. "Just got here a couple minutes ago. Did you find him?"

"No luck yet. If it's Preacher, he'll show up." He motioned for her to follow him. "Looks like you're feeling better."

"I'm not shaking anymore." She held out her hands. "See? Rock solid."

"That was pretty fast. Good for you." He sat her in an interrogation room. "Can I get you a soft drink, coffee, anything?"

"No, thanks. How long do you think this will take?"

"It's all up to you. Depends on how long it takes for you to ID him."

Malone had called ahead and had a six-pack of photos prepared for her inspection. The single sheet consisted of mug shots of six similar-looking men, three of whom had tattoos on their faces.

He laid the page on the table in front of her. "Take all the time you need."

Turned out, she didn't need more than a moment. "That's him," she said, pointing to the grainy photo.

"You're certain."

"Positive. Is that Preacher?" When he nodded, she gazed at the picture for a long moment. "He's one creepy dude."

"That he is." Malone cocked his head. "Ironic that he spends twenty-four/seven warning people to repent and be saved, but he's so friggin' scary most folks would choose hell over a minute in heaven with him."

She smiled. "Wasn't quite as creepy when I gave him twenty bucks last night."

It was the first time he'd seen her smile. It lit up her face, altering her angular features, making her beautiful.

"I guess that's it, then?" she said and stood.

"Yup. We'll call you when we arrest him." He motioned the doorway. "I'll walk you to the elevator."

When they reached it, she held out her hand. "Thank you, Detective."

He took it. "You're very welcome. By the way, I know where you recognized me from. My fiancée and I live in the

Riverbend area. We were in your shop, she bought a fleur-de-lis panel for our front window."

She smiled. "The one with the sunflower behind it?"

He reached around her and pushed the call button. "The very one."

"I remember Stacy. I hope she's doing well?"

"Great, thanks."

"Tell her I said hi."

"I will."

The elevator arrived and she stepped onto it. He held the door open. "If you happen to see Preacher, or if he shows up at your studio again, call me. Anytime, don't hesitate."

She opened her mouth, then shut it, as if there was something she wanted to say but worried she shouldn't. Curiosity won out. "What's he been arrested for?"

"Disturbing the peace. Resisting arrest. Trespassing. Burglary."

She seemed to be attempting to come to grips with it all. After a moment, she said, "Do you think he meant to hurt me? I mean, I gave him money, so he followed me? I don't get it. And you said he's never been violent, so why the piece of glass? And why take my cross that way?"

"I wish I knew, Ms. Gallier. An impulse, maybe. He thought the glass was pretty, or your cross caught his eye so he grabbed it. Crazy people don't need reasons. At least not ones that make sense to the rest of us."

As the elevator doors whooshed shut, Spencer couldn't help but recall what Bayle had said earlier about people doing crazy things for attention and his immediate negative reaction to it. Far-fetched was what he'd said. He wasn't certain why, but he didn't find it as out-there as before.

He went in search of his partner. When he had tried the Sisters of Mercy secretary earlier, she had been out of the office. He hoped Bayle had heard back from her.

He found Bayle at her desk, just ending a call. She grinned at him.

"Good news, partner. Preacher used to hang around Sisters

of Mercy. He'd show up for mass some Sunday mornings, make folks a little nervous, but he was always respectful, just sort of slip in and out. But the last time he showed up for worship, he caused a ruckus."

"How so?"

"Stood up during the homily and announced the end was near. He did everything but foam at the mouth, and finally they had to drag him out. Vicky said children were crying, the whole bit."

He whistled. "Not a pretty picture."

"Before they got him out the door, he shouted that same line he'd used on Gallier, about flesh being stripped from bones and eaten by demons."

"Tasty."

"Then he promised retaliation and called Father Girod a demon."

"When did all this go down?"

"The Sunday before the murder." She smiled again. "Just got off a call with the lab. Fingerprint tech got a beautiful set of prints from the candle holder—"

"Which we can compare to prints collected from our Mr. Preacher during a previous arrest."

"Called the request in already."

"I'm thinking this investigation is taking a turn for the better."

"Me, too." She leaned back in her chair, expression as satisfied as a cat's. "Life is good."

Life, it turned out twenty minutes later, wasn't so great. The prints weren't a match. Not even close.

Chapter Fifteen

Friday, August 12
1:00 P.M.

Mira arrived back at the studio just as Deni's beginning glass class was letting out. She watched the half dozen women exit, her thoughts on what Detective Malone had said about Preacher's reasoning.

For some odd reason, it comforted her.

Mira supposed it did because that simple observation was held together with the same thread as "bad things happen to good people" and "good people sometimes do bad things."

The exiting students were chattering about their creations and already looking forward to the intermediate class. Several of them waved at her, a couple called out a greeting.

Offering classes had been Deni's idea. She'd designed the curriculum, advertised the classes and now taught them. They'd become so popular that Mira had decided to convert the storage shed out back to a teaching studio. She could hear Chris pounding on it now. Part of deciding the teaching studio made sense was knowing Chris was available to do the job.

She entered the studio. "Deni," she called. "I'm back."

"In here," her assistant answered from the workroom. "Come see."

Deni wasn't alone. She and a man were standing in front of the Magdalene window.

Mira stopped short, recognizing him from the back, not believing her eyes. Jeff's best friend, Connor Scott. "Connor? Is it really you?"

He turned. "Hi, Mira."

With a squeal of delight, she ran to him and was enfolded in his arms. She hugged him tightly. "Where have you been?" she asked, tears trickling down her cheeks. "You just disappeared. No word to either of us."

"I'm so sorry." He released her, drew back and saw her tears. "Don't cry."

"Tears of happiness." She wiped them away with the heels of her hands. "Where have you been?"

"Iraq. Then Afghanistan."

She saw it then, the shadows in his blue eyes, the new furrows around them. He looked the same but a lifetime older as well. The way she must look to him. They had both lived that lifetime in the past six years.

She shook her head. "But I don't understand. One day you were here, the next gone. Nothing. Why didn't you tell us?"

"I had some personal stuff going on and I didn't know what to do. So I ran away. It was either join a circus or the marines." His lips lifted slightly. "I thought the military might toughen me up."

It had, she saw. Not just his body, which felt like steel against hers, but his spirit as well. Gone was the spoiled young man whose idea of hardship had been missing out on front-row tickets or having to choose between lobster or steak.

"This explains the buzz cut." She stood on tiptoes and ran her hand over his flat top. "Grow out the back and you could have the makings for a world-class mullet. Sexy."

He laughed, caught her hand and kissed it. "You always could make me laugh. Both of you could."

Her smile died. "He's gone. You know that, right?"

"I know." He curled his fingers around her hand. "I should have been here for you. For both of you. I'm so, so sorry."

He was. She saw the regret in his eyes. And secrets as well. Ones he didn't want to share.

"Would you like a tour?" she asked, stepping away, slipping her hand from his.

He moved his gaze over the workroom, then brought it back to her. "I would."

"The old studio was destroyed," she said. "Everything in it."

"I figured. When I heard about the Seventeenth Street canal, I didn't think there was a chance the studio would have survived." He crossed his arms. "Yet you stayed in New Orleans. Why? You could have gone anywhere."

"I thought about leaving. But I couldn't. All my memories, my memories with Jeff, are here. And the windows needed me."

He cocked an eyebrow, clearly amused. "The windows needed you?"

"Katrina wrecked them. The city's entire history in stained glass lay in ruins. You weren't here. You didn't see it."

"We saw pictures. We—"

"That's not the same. A picture can't convey the"—she paused—"magnitude of the destruction. Its scope. Everywhere you looked, miles and miles of it."

She crossed to the Magdalene window. "The windows were just a small piece of the destruction. But they were my piece." She looked over her shoulder at him. "I had the unique skill set necessary for their recovery. How could I abandon them?"

It was a rhetorical question, and he didn't respond. Instead, he motioned around them. "You found a fitting place to work on them."

She smiled. "I think so, too. Though it was by accident. My first requirement of the property was that it hadn't been flooded during the storm. That narrowed the search considerably. Uptown and the Garden District. The French Quarter and the Riverbend area, plus a few other pockets."

She led him outside. Chris was on a ladder, nailing

plywood to a newly framed overhang. "Deni's classes have been so popular, we decided we needed a classroom. Once it's complete, we'll add some youth classes."

Chris looked their way and she waved him over. "Come meet an old friend of mine," she called.

He climbed down the ladder, grabbed a towel to wipe his face and neck, then ambled over. "Good to meet you," he said. "I'd shake your hand, but as you can see, mine are a mess."

Connor held out his. "It's okay, man. Just got back from Afghanistan. A little sweat and dirt doesn't scare me."

They clasped hands. "Connor Scott."

"Chris Johns. Good to meet you."

Mira smiled at Chris. He continued to surprise her. He seemed wiser than his twenty-something years, more self-assured. Like he totally had his shit together. No wonder Deni liked him so much—she was the same way.

"How's it going?" Mira asked.

"Right on schedule. Waiting on the electrical inspector."

"I'm sorry it's been so hot."

Chris smiled. "Last I checked, you didn't control the weather."

"Wish I did." She fanned herself. "However, I could have chosen a better time of year to do this."

"I'm happy to have the work."

"Stay hydrated," Mira called.

He turned back and saluted. "Yes, ma'am!"

"Seems like a nice guy," Connor said.

"He is. I feel really lucky to have him. Almost six years since Katrina and it's still hard to find good workers."

They finished the tour back in the workroom, in front of the Magdalene panel. Deni was working on a rose window from an Uptown mansion.

"Your assistant said this has been your pet project."

"You could say that." She jammed her hands into her front pockets, thinking of Dr. Jasper's theory. "It's pretty much consumed me for the past year."

"I want to hear all about it." He held her gaze. "And everything else."

"Seems we both have a lot to share."

His expression grew solemn. "I'll explain everything. But not now. Not here. How about tonight?"

"Perfect."

"Are you still in the house on Frenchmen Street?"

"I am."

"You supply the wine, I'll bring the food. You still addicted to the Cuban sandwiches from Fefa's?"

"They're gone. Since the storm, a lot of places are. But I'm not a picky eater anymore."

One corner of his mouth lifted in the lopsided grin she remembered from the old days. "I see that. You're about to blow away."

She laughed. "Haven't been hungry in five years."

"I'm sorry."

"Say that again and the dinner's off."

"Never again, then." They fell silent. His gaze didn't waver from hers. "God, I've missed you and—" He bit the last back, but it hung in the air between them.

Jeff.

He and Jeff had been prep school roommates, university fraternity brothers; Connor had been Jeff's best man at their wedding. After the wedding, the three of them had been the best of friends. Many a night they had sat around her and Jeff's kitchen table with a bottle of wine, talking and carrying on until the wee hours.

She cherished those memories.

"I'm really glad you're back," she said.

"Me, too." He looked away, then met her eyes once more. "See you tonight. Six?"

"Thirty."

A catch in her chest, Mira walked him to the door, then watched until he drove off.

Deni was over in a flash. "*Who* was that?" she asked. "You know what I mean."

"I told you, an old friend I haven't seen since before the storm."

"An old boyfriend?"

"No. A friend of Jeff's. That's how we met. The three of us spent a lot of time together."

Deni looked disappointed. "I was thinking he had a crush on you."

Mira laughed. "Hardly. We're like brother and sister."

"Too bad. He's cute."

"That he is. And nice, too."

"So maybe y'all could move past the brother-sister thing and try a romantic—"

Mira didn't let her finish. "He was a friend of Jeff's."

"And yours. Who better to fall in love with?"

"Drop it, Deni." It came out sharper than she'd intended and her friend looked hurt. Mira lightly touched Deni's arm. "Sorry. I'm not ready. Not nearly."

"I understand. It's just—" Deni hesitated, then pressed on. "It's been almost six years, sweetie."

"I know. But I . . ." She struggled for the right words. "The truth is, Deni, fifty years might not be enough."

Chapter Sixteen

The house on Frenchmen Street had been in Jeff's family since the mid-1900s. Located where Frenchmen met Esplanade Avenue, a stone's throw from the Mississippi River, it was as close to being a French Quarter property as possible without being one.

The Marigny neighborhood had been developed in the first decade of the nineteenth century by a Creole millionaire of the same name. The architecture reflected both its history and French lineage. Mira's home, a perfectly preserved Creole town house, consisted of three stories with a central courtyard and wrought-iron balconies.

It'd been left to Jeff by his maternal grandmother. Although the Gallier family had tried to wrest it away from Mira after Jeff's death, she had fought to keep it.

She hadn't cared about its astronomical market value, because she never planned to sell. It had been her and Jeff's home, the only one they had shared in their five years of marriage.

The place came with other history as well. Supposedly, Marie Laveau, the famous voodoo queen, had been an "adviser" to the first lady of the house and a frequent visitor. In addition, the original owner had been in on the scheme hatched by New Orleans mayor and Napoleon sympathizer Nicholas Girod to rescue the exiled emperor from Elba and install him in what was now the French Quarter's Napoleon House restaurant. Jeff used to say that the pirate Jean Lafitte, an integral part of the plot, had once slept in the back bedroom.

It had all seemed very romantic at first, now it was just . . . home.

Connor arrived at six thirty sharp. He brought po'boy sandwiches and lilies. "I remembered how much you loved them," he said, handing her the flowers.

"Thank you." Mira buried her nose in the fragrant blossoms, breathed deeply, then lifted her gaze to his. "Nobody's brought me flowers in a long time."

"I'm glad I'm the one who remedied that. May I?"

"Of course." She stepped aside so he could enter. "Please tell me that's a bag from Mother's."

"Is there anywhere else to get a debris po'boy in New Orleans?"

She smiled. "Not one that tastes like this."

"I dreamed about these in Iraq. And about being here. With you and Jeff."

Sudden tears stung her eyes. "I guess two out of three isn't bad."

He caught her hand, squeezed her fingers, then released them. "The house looks no worse for wear."

"It came through the storm unscathed. We were lucky."

She heard the edge in her voice and wondered if a time would come when she didn't.

They walked to the kitchen, with its old brick walls and floor-to-ceiling windows that looked out over the lush courtyard, and sat at the hundred-year-old butcher-block table.

"Still a fan of cabs?" she asked.

He was, and while she opened the bottle of cabernet, he unpacked their sandwiches. He remembered where the plates were stored and got two. As she eased the cork out of the bottle, he set the roll of paper towels on the table.

It was all so painfully familiar, her hands shook as she poured the wine.

He unwrapped his sandwich. "If they're not sloppy, I'm going to be pissed."

They were. Ridiculously so, with beef and gravy, "dressed" with mayo, lettuce and tomato.

"There's no way I'm eating this without a knife and fork," she said, standing. "Want some?"

"Are you kidding? Amateur."

She was, she saw as she returned to the table: he had already eaten a third of his sandwich, spilling hardly a drop of gravy. He was attacking it like a starving man.

"How long have you been back?" she asked, scooping up a forkful of gravy and beef.

"A couple days."

She cocked an eyebrow. "That explains your table manners. Civilization sinking in yet?"

He grinned. "With minimal success."

"I see that."

He took it the way she meant it and laughed. "How much can sink in? I slept for the first twenty-four hours and have been awake for the last twenty-four."

"What was it like over there?"

"Brutal."

He didn't embellish on that and she took another bite. "Why'd you join up like that, Connor? Why'd you disappear?"

"I needed a place to hide."

Mira frowned. "I don't understand."

He ignored her question, picked up his glass, swirled, sniffed, then tasted. "My God, that's good. One of the many things I missed."

"Why hide from us, Connor?" She leaned toward him. "Jeff was your best friend."

He looked as if she'd struck him. "You were both my best friends."

"When you just up and disappeared, it broke his heart. It broke mine, too."

He caught her hand, holding it tightly. Too tightly. His skin felt leathery, his palm callused against hers. She didn't pull away or complain, though his grip hurt.

"I promise I'll tell you everything, just not now. Okay? I thought I was ready, but I'm not. I need time."

As suddenly as he'd grabbed her hand, he released it. "Maybe I should go—"

"No." This time it was she who caught his hand, only softly. To comfort. "Don't leave. Tell me when you're ready. I trust you."

They fell silent. He drank his wine while she picked at her sandwich.

She broke the silence. "I haven't had one of these in ages."

He eyed her mutilated sandwich. "You still haven't."

"Would you like some of it?"

"Sure, pass it over."

He picked up the untouched half. "No flowers. No po'boys. What the hell have you been doing?"

"Surviving."

"Shit." He set the sandwich down. "That was insensitive of me."

"I was just being honest." She forced a smile. "How many times did we sit around this table doing a version of this? Eating something uniquely New Orleans and drinking wine—"

"A lot of wine."

"Talking and arguing?"

"About something stupid."

"But laughing, too."

"Yes." He met her eyes, the expression in his serious. "I'd like to get to that place again. Where we are now is—"

"Awkward," Mira filled in for him, then sighed. "I don't want to feel like this anymore, Connor. I don't want pity or sympathy, and I want to stop missing him."

She got to her feet and crossed to one of the courtyard windows. She leaned against the casing and stared out at the night. "It's my fault," she said softly, after a moment. She looked over her shoulder at him. "I should have been the one who died, not him."

"No. It's not true. Don't say that."

"How much of the story do you know?"

"Some. From my folks."

Who heard it from Jeff's. "Then I'm surprised you're talking to me."

"Do you really think I'd judge you that way? C'mon, Mira."

She held his gaze for a long moment, then looked away again. "I wanted to stay for Katrina. It was my idea."

"Which he went along with."

"Yes, and once I convinced him to stay, we were both excited about it. Truthfully, we figured the worst would be the wind and rain, then losing power. But secretly, we wanted it to be big. Jeff and Mira's big adventure. We were so naïve, so stupid."

"Like everyone else."

"No," she corrected. "Lots of people did the smart thing and evacuated." Mira unlatched the window and lifted it. Hot, sticky air greeted her. But heady as well, with the scent of night jasmine and the sound of insects and music from the Balcony Music Club up the street.

"We stocked up on everything we thought we'd need. Water, coolers of ice, batteries and lanterns. Nonperishables. A Red Cross radio."

"Sounds like you did everything right."

Except leave, she thought, breathing in the heavy air, releasing it slowly, memories unfurling. "Jeff got a gun."

"That doesn't sound like Jeff."

"And the marines doesn't sound like you."

"Maybe none of us knew each other as well as we thought we did."

She didn't want to think that and told him so.

He shrugged. "So, Jeff got a gun?"

"Yeah. I hated it and it scared the crap out of me. But it was a deal breaker for him. He was afraid we might need it if the unthinkable happened."

The unthinkable. It had happened. In more ways than they had imagined.

"We had made up a shelter in the closet under the stairs. For us and Ginger. We made it through the storm, though there were a couple times I wondered if we would." She looked back at him. "You can't imagine . . . the wind beat at us and beat at us . . . For hours. Screaming and howling. It felt as if it was tearing at the house, that it might rip it from its foundation at any moment. I remember pressing my hands over my ears and praying for it to stop.

"Occasionally it did, because of the storm's bands. We'd scramble out of the closet and run to the windows to see what was happening. Then it would begin again."

He stood and came up behind her. He laid his hands gently on her shoulders. Comforted, she reached up, covered his hands with hers and went on. "Then, finally, it was over. We were fine. The house was mostly intact. We were so"—her voice cracked—"lucky. The damage around us was much worse."

Connor didn't comment, didn't move. Waiting. Understanding that she had shared only the beginning of the story.

"I was worried about my studio. About my windows. I'd just finished a big job, a church in Violet. Installed the windows just a week before the storm." She cleared her throat. "Jeff offered to go check on whatever he could. We heard there were trees and power lines down, that travel was near impossible. He told me to stay. Thought I'd be safer—"

She tightened her fingers on Connor's. "Safer," she repeated. "Because of debris in the roads. And we thought it wise for someone to be at the house. He left the gun with me."

"So he got in the truck and left?"

"We thought everything was over. We thought it was safe for him to go." She looked up at him, pleading. "I wouldn't have let him drive off if I thought he'd never come back."

He gently massaged her shoulders. "Of course you wouldn't have."

"You believe me, don't you?"

"Why wouldn't I?"

His softly spoken question sounded like an indictment to

her and she jerked away from him. "Because I'm a rich widow now! Don't try to pretend you haven't heard the whole story from your family."

"I'm not pretending anything. But since I haven't heard the story from *you,* I haven't really heard it, have I?"

She went on, trembling. "The Seventeenth Street canal burst. A block from my studio. From where they found Jeff's truck, they speculate he was on foot when it happened. It would have been like a tidal wave rushing at him."

She started to cry, but when he made a move to hug her, she turned away. "And it would have been fast. There would have been nowhere he could go. And no time even if there had been a way to escape."

"How long before you knew what happened?"

"It was three days before the lake and floodwaters leveled, another week before they could collect bodies. It was agony not knowing. The whole time I kept telling myself he was fine. Holed up somewhere without a way to get in touch with me."

"His body was never recovered. Right?"

"No, they did recover him! It's just that"—she struggled for control—"they couldn't one hundred percent identify it *was* him. The condition of the body, from being so long in water . . ."

She choked on the last. How did one voice the horror of the pathologist's report, months later? Of a body being ravaged by both the elements and predators?

"What about dental records?"

"Gone," she whispered. "That's one of the things people just don't get. His dentist's office was totaled, all the records destroyed."

Mira retrieved her glass from the table and drained the last of the wine. "Jeff's family accused me of murdering him. Of using the opportunity the storm presented to dump the body."

"That's ridiculous. I know you didn't kill him."

"How?" She met his eyes in challenge. "You weren't here."

"Because I know you. And I know how much you loved him."

Tears swamped her. "No one else . . . no one else believed in me like that."

He drew her into his arms. Sinking into his embrace, she pressed her face against his chest and cried. He held her that way until her tears had run their course.

She eased out of his arms. "Lovely," she whispered, voice thick. "I've made a complete mess of your shirt."

"I have other shirts." He looked down at the mascara and foundation smears, then back up at her. He laughed. "Besides, my shirt is nothing compared to your face."

Mira wiped under her eyes. "That bad, huh?"

"Rabid raccoon, run amok."

She went for tissues, wiped her eyes, then blew her nose. "The police investigated. The Gallier family, as you know, is very influential. Their ties go all the way to the attorney general's office."

Connor snorted with disgust. "What the hell evidence did they think they had?"

"Before Jeff left that day, he gave me a shooting lesson. He insisted I had to at least know how to shoot, in case looters or other crazies showed up while he was gone."

Connor nodded. "It makes sense."

She sat heavily. "The gun had been fired and my prints were on it. But the DA refused to charge. No body, no murder. And even if the pathologist had gotten a hundred percent identification, there'd been no gunshot wound."

"I'm sorry they put you through that," Connor said.

"But it wasn't over yet," she said, tone bitter. "Next, they brought a wrongful death civil suit against me."

"Which failed as well."

"Yes." She laughed, the sound hollow. "So here I am, a rich widow who would give up everything for just one more day with my husband."

"I should have been here for you."

"You're here for me now," she said. "Thank you."

After that, they left their sorrow and regret behind. They

remembered good times and laughed about them, they spoke of the future and their hopes and dreams.

It wasn't until he had driven off that she realized he'd told her nothing of the past five years of his life or why he had disappeared the way he had.

Chapter Seventeen

Saturday, August 13
2:30 A.M.

"Jeff!"

Mira shot up in bed, breathing hard, her cry seeming to hang in the stillness of her bedroom. She darted her gaze over the interior. The dream had been so real. He'd been here, standing beside the bed, talking softly to her.

"My sweet star. How I've missed you." Star. He'd begun calling her that after they'd learned Mira was actually the name of a star. No one else had ever called her that.

Why had that crept into her dreams tonight? It'd been years.

Seeing Connor again. Remembering the old days.

She sat up and reached for the bedside light. Her fingers brushed against something hanging from the lamp's switch. Frowning, she wrapped her fingers around it. A fine-weight chain. Like a—

It couldn't be. Her mind must be playing tricks on her. She turned on the light. A whimper of fear slipped past her lips.

It couldn't be, but it was.

Her cloisonné cross hung from the lamp switch.

Mira stared at it, heart beating wildly. The metal shone

like it was brand-new. She reached for it, then froze, the full ramifications of the moment overcoming her. Someone had been in her house. While she slept. Not just in her house, beside her bed. Close enough to touch her.

My sweet star. How I've missed you.

Jeff's voice in her head, bringing a wave of comfort. And longing.

Not Jeff. Of course not Jeff.

Preacher.

He could still be in the house.

With a cry, she leaped out of the bed. She grabbed her capris off the floor and shimmied into them, then slipped into her flip-flops. She snatched up her cell phone, started to dial 911, then dug in her pants pocket for Detective Malone's card instead.

He answered on the second ring. "Malone."

It vaguely registered that he sounded as if he had been asleep and that she didn't have a clue what time it was, but her words spilled out in a panicked rush anyway. "Detective, it's Mira Gallier. My necklace, it's back!"

"Slow down. You say your necklace is—"

"Back." Her voice rose. "He brought it back. He was in my house! While I was sleeping!"

"He's gone now?"

"I don't know. I woke up and saw it and . . . Do you think he might still be here?"

"Where are you now?"

"In my bedroom." She suddenly realized he could be under her bed or in her closet. Quietly listening. Planning his next move.

"Mira?"

"Yes?" she whispered.

"I'm sending a cruiser over now. I'll be right behind."

"Don't hang up!"

"I've got to put you on hold for one minute. But I won't hang up. I promise."

True to that promise, he was back in moments, though those moments seemed unbearably long.

"The cruiser is on its way and so am I." On his end she heard the slam of a car door, then an engine roaring to life. "There was a unit not three blocks from you, so you should be hearing sirens about now."

As his words registered, the scream of a police siren reached her. "I hear them!"

"Good. Now wait where you are until they're at your door. They'll identify themselves. Understand?"

A minute later they arrived. She ran for the door, still clutching her cell phone to her ear. She flung the door open. The two patrolmen ordered her to wait outside, then entered the house. As she stepped onto the porch, Detective Malone skidded to a stop in a red Camaro, cherry light on top flashing crazily.

As he hurried up the walk, she suddenly felt calm.

When he reached her, he smiled and indicated her phone, still pressed to her ear. "You can hang up now," he said.

She felt like an idiot even as she said, "Okay. Bye."

Chapter Eighteen

A search of the house turned up nothing. Except the cross, hanging on the bedside light, just as she'd described. Malone thanked the patrolmen, then crossed to where Gallier stood, shivering despite the steaminess of the night.

He held out the necklace. "I don't think we'll be needing this. It's been wiped."

She fastened it around her neck. "Thank you."

"House is clear. Windows are all locked. No forced entry." He noticed that even though the necklace was fastened, she kept a hand over the cross.

"Did you lock the doors before going to bed?"

She nodded. "Yes."

"You're certain?"

"Absolutely."

"So how'd he get in?"

She shook her head, obviously surprised by the question. "I don't know."

"Just to be certain, think back. When you let the officers in the front door, was it locked?"

She dragged a hand through her short hair, which only enhanced her bed head. Some women rolled out of bed looking adorable, some trampled. Gallier fell into the latter category.

"I ran to the door." She said it as much, it seemed, to herself as to him. "I had the phone pressed to my right ear. I reached out . . . flipped the dead bolt, then pulled the door open."

She looked him in the eyes. "It was locked. Definitely."

Malone searched her expression. "So how did Preacher get in?"

"Did you check the kitchen windows? The ones that face the courtyard? I opened one tonight. The far one."

"Let's check it again."

It was locked. Malone slid his gaze over the room, noting the two wineglasses on the counter by the sink, an empty bottle beside them.

He indicated the glasses. "What time did your company leave?"

"Around ten."

"Could he have left the necklace?"

"No," she snapped. "Someone you called Preacher ripped it off my neck yesterday morning. And how do you know my company was a he?"

"Just took a shot." He moved his gaze over the room again, before settling it back on her. "Let me ask you another question, Ms. Gallier. Are you positive you were wearing the cross when you had your encounter with Preacher?"

"Yes. I don't take it off."

"Are you certain this is the same piece of jewelry?"

"Yes! My husband bought it for me while we were on our honeymoon in Portugal. I've never seen another one like it. Why don't you believe me?"

"It's not that I don't believe you, but I have to look at this from every angle."

"Including the she's-a-total-whack angle?"

"It happens."

"I'm not crazy. I always wear that cross. I even shower with it on."

"Okay. There's not much I can tell you at this point. We'll

keep looking for Preacher and bring him in when we find him. I suggest you be more vigilant than ever about safety. Set your alarm. Double-check door and window locks, here and at your studio. If Preacher has targeted you for some reason—"

"Targeted me? For what?"

"That I don't know. But if he's visited you twice, it's no longer random. You have a dog, Ms. Gallier?"

"I did. A golden retriever. I lost her in the storm."

At his hip, his cell phone vibrated. His brother Percy, he saw, looking at the display. "Excuse me."

He took the call. "Malone here."

"Hey, bro. You at a scene?"

"Just leaving."

"Good. I've got something for you."

"What's that?"

"Not what, who. We found Preacher. Unfortunately, he's dead."

"Where?"

"French Quarter. Public restrooms on Decatur."

"Just down from Café Du Monde?"

"The very ones. Later."

Malone hung up and turned to Mira. He saw the questions in her eyes but ignored them. "I've got to go." He started toward the door. "I don't think you have anything to worry about, but if something comes up, call me or 911."

Chapter Nineteen

Preacher had met his end in a men's room. Public restrooms in the French Quarter were few and far between—which could explain why so many drunks used the street as a urinal.

A few of the most dedicated of partiers were still about, mingling with the unfortunate folks heading into work. They gaped at the scene—patrol units, lights flashing, coroner's wagon and yellow crime scene tape stretched across the mouth of the alleyway like a drunken grin.

Malone greeted the first officer, then signed the scene log. "My brother around?"

"In the can with the vic. You'll want booties."

Malone nodded.

He got some from a tech, slipped them on and made his way there. Hazmat booties meant one of two things: a need to keep the scene free of contamination or to protect yourself from it. He saw right away that in this case, the booties applied to the latter. An adult human possessed five to six liters of blood. It looked to Malone like every bit of that was pooled around Preacher's body.

The coroner's photographer was just finishing up. Percy stood at the periphery, waiting.

Malone greeted him with a punch to his shoulder. "Rebound." Percy was four years younger, better looking, more athletic and much taller—just shy of six foot five. His height, years playing basketball and knack for hooking up with recently single women had earned him the nickname.

Malone was close to all of his six siblings, but his bond with Percy was special. They just "got" each other.

Percy turned and smiled. "Hey, man."

"Thanks for the heads-up on this."

"Glad to help."

Malone indicated the body crumpled in front of the far sink. "Crazy bastard. Looks like he preached to the wrong badass."

"Appears that way. Check out the love note. Far side of the body."

Malone made his way around. Scrawled in blood were the words *Jugment Day*.

Malone glanced back at his brother. "Somebody flunked spelling."

"That tells us something about our perp. Obviously not a rocket scientist or Ph.D."

"Judgment day," Malone mused. "What are we talking about here?"

"The end. The day you face your maker."

"The day Preacher here spent his life telling folks about."

"Maybe somebody finally had enough of the sermons?"

The photographer had finished, and Ray Hollister, the coroner's investigator, had taken over. Malone and Percy moved closer.

"He was stabbed in the throat," Hollister said. "Right in the carotid artery."

"That explains the blood."

Hollister fell silent again and Percy glanced at Spencer. "Looking a little haggard, my man. How's Stacy?"

"Healing physically. Still struggling in other areas."

Percy nodded. "That's to be expected, I think."

"Is it? I'm a little worried. It seems to be getting worse, not better."

"She'll pull through. Stacy's made of some tough stuff."

Spencer thought of her worry about turning into a mushy girly-girl. Ironic, considering. "You're right," he said. "She will."

His tone lacked conviction and Percy frowned. "Dude, we're talking about the woman who agreed to the whole white dress, extravaganza thing, which she dreaded, just because she knew Mom would pitch a holy fit if you eloped." He clapped him on the back. "Show some faith."

"Thanks for putting it that way. You're right. I just hate to see her hurting."

Hollister, squatting by the body, looked over his shoulder at them, clearly annoyed. "Malones one and two, you want to pay a little attention to Mr. Preacher here? The sooner I can wrap this up, the sooner I get back to bed."

"Like *that's* going to happen," Spencer said. "Besides, me and Rebound are in the middle of a family reunion."

"Every scene is a Malone family reunion. It's getting old, okay?" The man grinned. "By the way, Spencer, I expect an invitation. After putting up with your shit all these years, I'm expecting a meal and free booze. Lots of free booze."

Spencer groaned. Percy laughed and fitted on Latex gloves. "What've we got?"

Hollister studied the wound. "Looks as if our vic was standing at the sink and was attacked from behind. Deep wound. Ragged edges." Using a metal probe, he eased the wound open. "Pulling the weapon out did much damage as the initial strike."

Percy looked at him. "Blood spray over the sink, wall, mirror. His assailant wouldn't have walked away clean."

A fact made plain by bloody footprints leaving the scene. "So the middle of the French Quarter, perp walks out like that. Ballsy."

"We are talking the French Quarter." Percy frowned. "I'm thinking, it wouldn't have even been that late. Friday night, there should have been a good number of people around. Somebody should've seen something."

"Our perp could've used that to his advantage," Hollister offered. "Blended into the crowd."

"Could Preacher have done it to himself?" Malone asked. "You know, Judgment Day. Making a statement."

"So how'd he write the message in blood?"

"Cut himself somewhere before doing the deed."

They both looked at Hollister. "Problematic. A wound like this, he would have lost all voluntary function almost immediately. Plus, where's the weapon?"

"Besides, bro, we've got bloody footprints leaving the scene."

"Who discovered the body?"

"A gutter punk, about forty minutes ago. Ran out screaming. That drew the attention of a bartender on his way home from work. He called it in."

"And the gutter punk?"

"Gone."

"Could be his footprints?"

"I'm not ruling anything out yet," Percy said. "The dude was crazy, and it would take crazy to do that to yourself."

Malone looked back at Hollister. "What do you think, how long's he been dead?"

"A few hours. Rigor mortis is under way, lividity is evident. We'll get his internal temperature at the morgue."

Malone glanced at his watch. "It's after four now. Any chance he could have been on Frenchmen and Esplanade at one, one thirty?"

"Three hours ago?" Hollister shook his head. "Not impossible, but it'd be tight."

"What's up?" Percy asked.

Instead of answering, Malone asked a question of his own. "You go through his pockets yet?"

"First officer checked for an ID. But otherwise, no, we haven't done a complete search. What're you looking for?"

"A cross necklace. Lady's. Preacher snatched it yesterday morning; the victim said he returned it tonight between one and one thirty in the Marigny. I'm just looking for confirmation."

His brother nodded. "I'll give you a call when I know for sure."

Chapter Twenty

"You and I have to talk."

Malone looked up from his computer screen. Bayle stood in his cubicle doorway, a PJ's coffee cup in her hand and fire in her eyes. "What's up, partner?"

"Funny you're calling me that this morning. A laugh riot."

"I don't understand."

"Preacher's dead, and you don't call me? You go to the scene and don't notify me? What the fuck, Malone?"

"I didn't see any reason to wake you in the middle of the night."

She closed the distance to his desk and plunked down her cup. She bent so they were nose to nose. "I'm not some fragile princess who needs her beauty sleep. I'm your partner. This is *our* case, not just yours. Got that?"

She was right. But her in-his-face approach still got his back up. "Noted."

"That's it? What the hell were you thinking?"

"I wasn't, okay? My bad. Sorry."

She collected herself. For the first time, he saw that she wasn't just angry but hurt as well.

Truth was, he didn't blame her. No way he would have excluded Tony that way. His irritation evaporated. "It won't happen again."

"Thank you."

The fire seemed to go out of her. She grabbed her coffee and sank onto the chair in front of his desk. "My guess is, one of your sibs called you about Preacher. Which one?"

"Percy."

"Fill me in."

He did, beginning with the means of death and ending with Percy's promise of a call when he had a report.

"Judgment Day?"

"Without the *d* in *Judgment*."

"Theories?"

"Two. First, someone who'd had enough of Preacher's preaching followed him into the john and offed him. Second, he offed himself to make a statement. Far-fetched but intriguing."

"He have the cross on him?" she asked.

"That's the thing—Gallier got it back last night."

"Excuse me?" She waited, paper cup poised halfway to her lips, eyebrow cocked.

"Gallier called me last night in a panic. The necklace was back, hanging on her nightstand lamp. She figured Preacher had somehow gotten into her house and left it."

"Wow, and here I thought you'd only excluded me from one call. I really do owe you for my good night's sleep."

"I deserve that."

She smiled and brought the cup to her lips. "Gallier's story, you don't sound so convinced."

"She seemed genuinely freaked out. But the house was locked up tight with no sign of a forced entry."

"So how'd he get in?"

"Exactly. Plus, I'm waiting on the path report and Hollister's official TOD. But initially, Preacher at Gallier's at one thirty, then dead in a French Quarter john a couple hours later?" He shook his head. "I'm thinking she was confused, didn't even have the cross on in the first place. Preacher intended to kill her when he grabbed her throat, then ran when he heard the other two arriving. Or she's making the whole thing up."

Bayle looked thoughtful. "But why?"

"I like your original thought, a sick need for attention. Could be a form of mental illness?"

"I've got another scenario," she said. "She found Preacher and killed him. To get her cross back."

"It was a damn grisly job, Bayle. Deep wound, lots of blood."

"She cleans herself and the necklace up and calls you in a 'panic.' "

"Why the big ruse?"

"She has to have a story to back up her wearing the necklace again."

He had a hard time reconciling the wisp of a woman with big wounded eyes and the person cold-blooded enough to plunge a blade into a man's throat. But it made a certain twisted sense.

"She had a male visitor last night," he said. "I didn't get a name, only asked if she thought he could have left the necklace."

"You have it?"

"I left it with her. At that point, I saw no reason not to. It was a simple snatch and run, and she had her property back. It had also, obviously, been wiped."

Malone could see she wasn't happy about his decision, but she kept it to herself.

His phone rang. It was Percy. "Preacher had nothing on him. No cross necklace or anything else, no wallet, money or ID."

"Scenario number three, random robbery gone south?"

"Possibility, bro. Though who'd think Preacher a good mark, I don't know."

Malone didn't know either, thanked him and hung up. He turned back to Bayle. "No cross on Preacher. Or anything else."

"Not surprised."

"I say we get a name from Gallier. Something here is definitely screwed up."

Bayle nodded. "You do it. She seems to trust you. Or thinks she can manipulate you."

He smiled. "I'll go with trust, if that's okay?"

He brought up Gallier's number on his cell phone and dialed her. She answered, sounding like a totally different woman from the night before. Moments later, after a bit of schmoozing, he had the name.

"Connor Scott," he said, holstering his phone. "An old friend and a vet, just back from Afghanistan."

Chapter Twenty-one

The house was one of those pointed out on tours of the Garden District, the iron fence famous for the romantic story associated with it. The Greek revival, center hall–style home sat well back on its large corner lot.

Malone took in the magnificent garden and ancient live oak and decided it made sense that Connor Scott, longtime friend of Mira Gallier, lived in this house. New Orleans royalty hung with New Orleans royalty. Such behavior was deeply embedded in the city's culture, fostered by private schools, elite Mardi Gras krewes, exclusive country clubs and political deals made over one-hundred-year-old cognac. The gaping divide between the utterly rich and the tragically poor, protected by an army of the folks in between who kept things running.

People like him. And Bayle.

As they entered the gate and headed up the brick walk, Malone noted a security camera mounted in the oak tree along the pathway, then another at the front door.

They rang the buzzer. "NOPD here to see Connor Scott."

"Hold, please."

A moment later a man opened the door. He wore khaki

shorts, a white T-shirt and dog tags on a chain around his neck. He smiled and his face creased in all the right places, the way certain movie stars' faces did.

Malone took an instant dislike to him. And judging by Bayle's vibe, she did, too. "Connor Scott?" Malone asked.

"That's me."

Malone held up his shield. "Detectives Spencer Malone and Karin—"

"Bayle," Scott said, glancing at her.

Malone looked at his partner in surprise. "You two know each other?"

"A friend of a friend," Connor answered, "years ago. How're you doing, Karin?"

"Good. You?"

"Very well, thanks."

Buried under the polite exchange was a layer of intense emotion. What kind, Malone wasn't certain. But he intended to find out. He tucked the question away for later.

Scott turned back to him. "How can I help you this morning?"

Malone noticed that his eyes were a striking color, an odd cross between light green and gray. "We've come about one of your friends. Mira Gallier."

Alarm shot into those eyes. "Is she all right?"

"She's fine. May we come in?"

"Sure." He swung the door wider and stepped aside.

Malone quickly took in the grand foyer. Marble floors. Sparkling chandelier. Antique table at its center, set with a huge spray of fresh flowers. Reminded him of a hotel.

"Nice place," he said.

"My parents'. I'm staying here until I get settled."

"You've been away?"

"Just finished my tour of duty in Iraq and then Afghanistan. I've only been home a few days."

"What branch of the service?" Malone asked.

"Marines."

He nodded. Scott was clearly strong enough to have taken

out Preacher; as a marine, he would have been trained in how to do it.

"Thank you for your service. It is appreciated, no matter which way public opinion is blowing."

He smiled slightly. "Thank you for yours."

Bayle spoke up. "Where were you last night, Mr. Scott?"

"Considering the reason for your visit, I think you already know. I had dinner with Mira Gallier."

"Where?" Malone asked.

"Her place."

"What is your relationship?"

He stiffened. "We're friends. Old friends."

"What time did you arrive?"

"Six thirty."

"And leave?"

"Ten, ten thirty."

"Are you certain of the time?"

"Yes." He frowned. "Why is this important?"

"Just crossing our t's and dotting our i's, that's all."

The man knew it was bullshit, so Malone added, "There was a break-in at Ms. Gallier's last night. Just following up."

"A break-in?" His surprise seemed genuine. "But she's okay?"

"I spoke with her this morning and she seemed fine. What did you do after you left Ms. Gallier's?"

"Came here. Watched TV for a while, then went to bed."

"Anybody else here?"

"No." He cocked his head. "This is a lot of questions for just following up on a break-in."

"You know cops."

"Actually, no, I don't know cops."

His tone made it clear he was on to the fact there was more going on than a break-in and that he had answered his last question.

They thanked him and returned to the car. Malone looked at his partner. "When I said who we were going to interview, why didn't you tell me you knew him?"

"I didn't recognize the name." She fastened her seat belt. "Literally, we met once or twice. Hello, goodbye, that's it."

Spencer started the car. "And how did you know him?"

"He told you, a friend of a friend."

"That's bullshit, Bayle."

"Excuse me?"

"What I picked up between you two was too strong for that explanation to be anything but. Were you involved with him?"

"No. Not that it's any of your damn business."

"Who was the friend?"

"Why the interrogation?"

"Who was the friend?" he asked again.

"Someone I dated." He waited and she sighed heavily. "Okay, someone I was in love with. He didn't feel the same way about me and it ended badly."

"And Scott?"

"Was a part of it. They worked together. Okay? If I never saw him again, it would be too soon."

Which explained the weird vibes from both of them. He nodded, then slipped the car into gear.

"If you don't mind, I'd really appreciate you keeping that to yourself."

"You got it." He glanced at her, then pulled away from the curb. "You can trust me, you know."

"Trust is a door that swings both ways," she reminded him. "So back at you, Malone."

Chapter Twenty-two

Saturday, August 13
11:00 A.M.

When Mira arrived at the studio the next morning, Connor was waiting for her. He stood beside his car, in the shade of a dogwood tree. As she parked, he came to meet her.

"Morning," she said. "What brings you by?"

"Really?" He looked as tightly coiled as a snake. "You don't know?"

"No." She frowned. "Is something—" Then it dawned on her. "The detectives called you, didn't they? They said they might."

"They came to see me."

She slammed her car door, surprised. "Okay. That seems a little over the top, but whatever."

"Actually, it's a lot over the top, Mira. We need to talk."

"Sure. But inside," she said. "It's too hot out here."

He nodded and together they rounded the building, then headed into the studio. Deni heard them and called out a greeting from the workroom. "We're in here."

Mira glanced at Connor. "I need to say hello. Come with me?"

He nodded and followed her. Deni and Chris were sitting on the floor in front of the Magdalene window. They were sharing an Abita root beer and some cheese crackers. The sun was positioned just so and the light flooded through the window, setting the color on fire.

"Hey, you two," Mira said as she and Connor entered. "What's up?"

"Taking a break," Deni said, smiling back at them. "Hi, Connor. I thought that was you out there."

"Yup, it was me."

Chris looked over his shoulder. "We were just talking about you, Mira."

"Really?"

Deni elbowed him. He winced and rubbed his arm. "What?"

Mira laughed and crossed to stand beside the couple. "Okay, spill it."

"It's no big deal," Deni said. "We were just saying that you look like her."

"Like who?"

Chris motioned the window. "Maggie here. There's a resemblance."

"There's not," she replied. "You two are nuts."

"No," Connor said, "I see it, too. Something in the eyes."

"Really?" She tilted her head and studied the stained-glass image. "I don't see it, y'all. Maybe—"

"Oh, my gosh!" Deni exclaimed, cutting her off. She jumped to her feet. "Your cross, you got it back!"

"I did. Last night, but—"

Her assistant hugged her. "I'm so happy for you."

"Me, too." Chris stood and gave her an awkward hug.

"What happened?" Deni asked. "How—"

"He brought it back."

"Who?" Deni frowned. "You don't mean that Preacher guy?"

"I do. I woke up and my cross was . . . there. Hanging off my nightstand lamp." The two simply stared at her, as if trying to understand, and she added, "So it must have been Preacher, but I don't have a clue how he got in. Neither do the police."

"*Who* was in your house?" Connor asked.

Deni answered for her. "This psycho person the police called Preacher. He wandered in here the other morning when Mira was alone and attacked her."

Mira jumped in. "It was pretty scary, but he didn't hurt me."

"But we thought he had." Deni glanced at Chris as if for confirmation. "He had this long piece of glass, the police thought he probably got it out of our trash. There was blood everywhere—"

"The blood was his," Mira said quickly. "He yanked off my cross and ran."

Connor frowned. "And you're saying *he* was in your house last night?"

"Must have been," she said. "My cross was back. How else could that be?"

"You seem pretty calm about it all."

"I've been through worse."

"Well, I'm glad everything's okay," Chris said, "but maybe you should think about getting better locks or something."

"I think so, too," Deni said. "I mean, that guy was a freak. And he was in *your* house."

"Enough, okay." Mira held up her hands. "I'm taking care of it. I promise. If you need me, we'll be in the kitchen."

She shot a warning look at Connor, too, who seemed about to comment, then turned and headed for the kitchen.

She went straight for the coffee station. "Want a cup?" When he shook his head, she set about brewing one for herself. "So what did you want to talk about?"

"I can't believe you're asking me that. Two detectives paid me a visit this morning. They asked me all sorts of questions about our dinner last night and my whereabouts after."

"I don't see what's so weird about that. Detective Malone said he might call you, to double-check the time we were together."

"He checked a hell of a lot more than that. It doesn't make sense."

She brought the mug to her lips. "I don't understand."

"Tell me exactly what happened the other morning, in detail."

She did, from the moment she first heard Preacher rummaging around to the moment he ran off. "He said all this crazy stuff to me. About false prophets and eternal damnation." Mira shuddered, remembering. "There was something really freaky about his eyes. Scared the crap out of me."

"And what about last night?"

"I'd been dreaming about Jeff, that he was beside the bed. He called me his sweet star. And I woke up."

"Go on."

"I was unsettled and reached for the light. That's when I . . . there it was." She brought her hand to her throat, to the cross. "It didn't hit me at first, that he must have been in the house. When it did, I was terrified."

"That's when you called the cops."

"Yes. Detective Malone. He'd given me his card that morning. In a few minutes a cruiser showed up, then Detective Malone. But they didn't find anything, not even a clue how he got in."

Connor stood, wandered to the small window above the sink and gazed out. Mira suspected he was playing with the pieces, fitting them together in a way that made sense to him.

After a moment, he turned back to her. "Here's the deal, Mira. The questions the detective asked me don't make sense, not in the context of what you've just told me. They wanted to know what I did after I left your house and whether anyone could corroborate my story. Like maybe they thought I was guilty of something. Or you were."

"Guilty of what?"

"Don't know."

Mira thought back to the things the detective had asked, the way he had responded to her answers. "He did wonder if maybe I had been confused about my necklace. That maybe I'd had it all along and nobody had actually broken in last night. But I wasn't confused." She met Connor's eyes. "I wasn't."

"I believe you."

"But they don't, is that what you're saying?"

He opened his mouth to respond, then closed it as if he had changed his mind about something. He shrugged. "You're probably right, it's nothing. They're just doing their jobs and I'm just being paranoid. Wouldn't surprise me, we were trained not to trust anyone but our own. And even then . . . Never mind. Forget I came by this morning."

She reached out, catching his hand. She laced her fingers with his. "I'm sorry. When you're ready and want to talk about it, I'm here."

He looked down at their joined hands, then slipped his from hers. "I need to let you get to work. And I suppose I need to be productive."

"Are you working yet?"

"Dad wants me to come back on board with him."

The Scott family was in banking, among other things. Connor had gone straight from university and a finance degree to work for his father. He'd never seemed all that interested in his career.

"What do you want to do, Connor?"

"That's the problem, I don't know. Not that, though. Overseas I learned that life's too short to waste it doing something you don't love."

"How would you like to help install the Magdalene window? I could use a strong back."

"Sure. When?"

"The next few weeks. I haven't set the date yet." She smiled. "But I warn you, it's going to be intense. You'll see a side of me you've never seen before."

"I consider that a personal challenge. You're on."

Mira linked her arm through his and they exited the kitchen. As they entered the retail area, Deni stepped through the front door. She held a CD sleeve.

"What's that?" Mira asked.

"Libby Gardner was just here."

Mira smiled. "Is that our interview?"

"Not exactly. It's the segment that's playing tonight."

"You look upset. What's wrong?"

"She wanted to give us a heads-up. Before it aired."

Mira's stomach sank. "A heads-up? About what?"

"Jeff's dad."

Mira's knees went weak. Anton Gallier had promised to make her pay for his son's death, though his campaign against her had started long before Katrina. He had accused her of being a gold digger, had been vocal about the fact his only son was marrying beneath him and had threatened to disown Jeff if he went through with the marriage.

Jeff had shrugged off his father's antics. That old dog's bark, he had assured her, was much worse than his bite. After Jeff's death, however, she had learned that the elder Gallier had very sharp teeth.

But she'd thought it was over.

"Libby said Anton Gallier engineered the whole thing." Deni moved her gaze between them. "Used the anniversary and his influence with the station. She only saw it this morning."

"Let's look at the interview," Connor said. "It may not be as bad as your imagination is making it out to be."

Mira shook her head. "It'll never be over, will it? I'll never be free of him."

Deni reached a hand out, expression twisted with sympathy. "Oh, Mira . . . honey—"

"No." She took a step back, unwilling to accept the pity. "It's been six frigging years. Everything he's tried has failed. So he resorts to a . . . smear campaign."

Connor plucked the CD from Deni's hands. "We don't have any idea what he's resorted to. Do you have a computer?"

"My office."

He headed for it; Mira and Deni followed. He loaded the disc into the computer and skipped ahead until he found what they were looking for: a section called "Six Years Later: The Dead, Dying and Still Missing."

It was as bad as Mira feared. Worse. A devastated father.

Grieving the loss of his only son. Bemoaning the failure of the criminal justice system. Twisting the truth in a way that made him seem as much a victim as his son.

He never came right out and accused her. Never spoke her name. Never offered any facts.

But the editors had cleverly segued from his interview to hers. Only those who had been living on a desert island would miss the connection. And if they didn't quite get it, a Google search would take care of that, pronto.

Without a word, Mira left the office. She went to the workroom and stood in front of the Magdalene window. She gazed at the saint's face, into the eyes Connor had said resembled hers.

It hurt so bad, all she wanted to do was crawl into a Xanax-fueled euphoria and pretend it wasn't happening. For a moment, she let her mind go there: track down her connection, score—then oblivion. Pleasant and problem free. Who would care, really?

She would, she told herself, fisting her fingers.

And then the bastard would have won.

"We'll sue him," Connor said, coming up behind her. "We'll sue the station."

"It'd go nowhere. He has very deep pockets and an army of lawyers on retainer. And what do I have?"

"We can't let him get away with this."

She thought of where she had been these past six years, what she had endured, then overcome. She shook her head. "There is no *we*, Connor. This is about me. My decision. And you're right, I can't let him get away with this. And I won't."

"What are you going to do?"

"I'm going to go and have a conversation with him."

"I'll go with you," Connor said.

"I've got to do this alone."

"Let me drive you, then."

"Let him, Mira." That came from Deni, standing in the doorway, Chris beside her. "You're upset now, after you see him—"

"No." She retrieved her purse, slung it over her shoulder, then met Connor's eyes. "I appreciate the offer, but I've got this. I'm going to find that son of a bitch and let him know he can't break me."

Chapter Twenty-three

Mira found her father-in-law at his club having lunch. It hadn't been difficult; the man had been meeting his power-broker cronies at the Crescent City Club every Saturday afternoon for as long as she had known him. On a number of occasions he had coerced Jeff into joining them.

Each time Jeff had come home late, stinking drunk and reeking of cigar smoke. Not her happier memories.

That today's would not be, either, was a given. Nothing good would come from confronting Anton, but she couldn't stop herself. She was no longer going to lie down and let the man steamroll over her.

She alighted the elevator on the club's third floor. It was a private men-only club, and the interior reflected that. Lots of rich leather and gleaming mahogany, masculine yet under-stated.

Although women were allowed on the third floor and in the restaurant, most stayed away. She'd been there only once before—in search of Jeff.

A butler approached her. "Can I help you?"

"I'm looking for Anton Gallier. It's urgent that I speak to him. I'm his daughter-in-law."

The man looked her over, unmoved by the urgency in her voice. No doubt he had been in this position before. "I'll see if he's available."

She started to press her point, then let it go. She was speaking to her father-in-law, and no one was going to stop her. And certainly not this underpaid, monkey suit–wearing goon.

She gave the butler several moments' head start, then followed. By the time he realized what she had done, she had spotted Anton.

"I need to talk to you, Anton Gallier!" she called out. The dining room went silent. All heads turned her way. The butler grabbed her arm, she shook him off. "Or are you afraid? That all these people will see what a snake you are?"

A waiter joined the butler. They each took an arm and started to haul her out.

"Wait!" Anton called, patting his mouth with his napkin and standing. "Let her go. I'm quite eager to hear what she has to say."

The two released her.

"This is my daughter-in-law," he announced. "Former, since my son is dead. Look at her, isn't she lovely?"

Heat stung her cheeks. Mira knew she looked like a maniac. But he'd always been able to make her feel like crap, even when she had tried as hard as she could to achieve "lovely."

She reached his table. He smiled benignly, though it affected her like the hiss of a snake. "I just want to let you know, I'm not letting you get away with this. Not anymore."

"With what, my dear?"

"Your smear campaign. Your attempt to further discredit me."

He laughed. "You've gotten a sneak peek at tonight's segment."

"I have. You did everything but call me a murderer."

"I *have* called you a murderer. Repeatedly. Since I don't have enough proof, I'll just have to settle for making your life a living hell. The same that mine has been since you killed my son."

"I'll get a lawyer."

She realized how ridiculous that sounded. To a man like him, her threat was pitiable.

She tipped up her chin. "You won't break me, Anton Gallier."

"If that's a challenge, I accept."

Real fear shuddered through her. He had the ability to grind her into the ground. The money, the resources and the connections. The desire.

She kept it from showing. And she kept it from affecting her. She would not live in fear. Not anymore.

Defiantly, she told him so.

His mouth tightened. He leaned toward her. "You're weak," he said softly. "A pill head. Isn't that right? Can't handle life. Poor baby. Had to run and hide."

"I'm not hiding anymore, you son of a bitch. And I'm not running. You're on notice."

She turned to walk away and he started to laugh. She froze, then faced him, furious. "Don't you dare laugh at me."

"What are you going to do, little girl? Kill me?"

"Maybe I should. I doubt anyone would miss you."

He smiled again, obviously pleased. "That sounded like a threat, Mira. How about I—"

"Back off, Anton!"

Mira turned. *Connor had followed her.* He closed the distance between them, stopping at her side, and laid a reassuring hand on her arm.

"Leave her alone."

"The knight on the white steed arrives to save the damsel in distress." Anton picked up his cocktail and held it high. "To the white knight."

"Shut up, Anton. You're drunk."

Mira hadn't realized it before, but he *was* drunk. His face was flushed, his eyes dulled by the alcohol.

Connor caught her arm. "Come on, Mira, let's get out of here."

"Did you tell her, Connor?" Anton called, after them. "Did you tell her the real reason you joined up?"

Connor's steps faltered. He turned slowly around. "That has nothing to do with this. Or you."

"No?" He took an unsteady step toward them. "I think it does."

Mira felt Connor's anger—it rolled off him in waves.

"Jeff's *best* friend," he said. "That's what you were. But you're glad he's dead, aren't you?"

For a split second, Mira was certain Connor was going to let loose of his tightly leashed fury. Instead, he looked at her. "Let's get out of here. He's not worth it."

"Tell her!" Gallier shouted, coming after them. "Tell her why you joined up!"

They reached the elevator. The car was waiting and they stepped on. As they turned, she saw Anton's face as he charged toward them, twisted with bitterness and rage.

The doors slid shut and the car started its descent. It reached the first floor, and they hurried off and out onto Poydras Street. The midday sun momentarily blinded her. When her eyes adjusted, she realized Connor was walking away from her.

Mira hurried after him. "Wait!" She caught up with him and grabbed his arm. "Where're you going?"

"Away from here."

He was angry. Shaking. She searched his gaze. "What was Anton talking about? Why *did* you join up like that, Connor?"

"Not now, Mira."

"Why not now?" People streamed around them, some casting curious glances their way, but most oblivious. "What're you hiding from me?" She curled her fingers around his. "What could be so bad?"

He opened his mouth, then closed it as her cell phone sounded. She ignored the call. "What was he talking about, Connor? What haven't you told me?"

"Better get that," he said. "It might be important."

"Not as important as this. Not as important as you." She tightened her fingers. "Talk to me. What are you hiding from me?"

He gazed at her, his expression tortured. After a moment, he bent and pressed a kiss to her forehead. "Bye, Mira."

Fear shuddered through her. The words, his gesture, sounded so final. She couldn't bear to lose him again.

She started to go after him, then stopped as her phone went off again. Whoever was calling wasn't giving up. She dug the device out of her purse and answered. "What?"

"Mira, it's Deni. Where are you?"

"Just leaving the Crescent City Club. Why?"

"Those two detectives just called. They asked for you, when you might be back. They said they need to talk to you. About Preacher."

Chapter Twenty-four

Malone hung up the phone. Gallier was not at her studio but was due back this afternoon. If he and Bayle popped over there now, they could question her employees and be waiting for her when she arrived.

He was certain Bayle would want to, once she heard the bombshell news: the crime scene guys had most likely found the weapon used to kill Preacher—a piece of stained glass nearly identical to the one he had brandished at Mira Gallier.

Malone collected the just-delivered path report and headed for her cubicle. "Hey, partner, got a minute?"

She looked up, simultaneously shoving what she had been looking at into a drawer. Blinking furiously, she waved him in. "Sure."

Either she had something in her eyes or she'd been crying. "Are you okay?"

"Absolutely." She cleared her throat. "What've you got?"

"Path report," he said, dropping it in front of her.

"Vic bled out," he said as she removed the contents from the file folder. "But if our perp hadn't gotten him, his own body soon would have."

"Stage-four cancer," she said. "Poor bastard."

Spencer slouched in the chair across from her desk. "It'd spread pretty much everywhere but his brain."

"Wonder if he knew?"

"Pathologist said he would have been in big-time pain."

"Seems to me the dude's gone to a better place. He sure preached that message, anyway." Bayle glanced back down at the report. "No defensive wounds. Nails were clean. No secondary wound, either."

"Eliminates the suicide theory."

She slid the report back into the folder. "Now that I've got the facts, I'm ready for the commentary."

He smiled. He liked her style. "I spoke with Percy this morning. They may have found the murder weapon. A piece of colored glass, in the trash."

"Hello," she said, straightening. "Did you say colored glass?"

"I did. Wicked looking. Six inches long, pointed, shaped like a carrot. Tape around the bottom edge, to make a grip. Tape was filthy. Glass had been wiped."

"Sounds familiar."

"Very," he agreed. "What do we have so far on the bloody footprints?"

"Men's size nine athletic shoe."

"We know it's a man's shoe?"

"Could be a lady's extra wide, size ten."

"Big foot. Brand?"

"Nike. I should have the individual model number in the next day or two."

"I'm thinking, in light of the new evidence we might want to—"

"Yes."

"You know what I was going to say?"

"That we need to go over to Gallier Glassworks for another round of questioning."

"The assistant, carpenter and Gallier?"

"My thoughts exactly." She got to her feet, a slow smile spread across her face. "My God, are we a great team, or what?"

* * *

After stopping for a quick sandwich, they headed for the glass studio. Mira Gallier hadn't returned, but both her assistant and the carpenter were there.

They started with Deni Watts. Malone let Bayle take the lead. "The piece of glass Preacher found in your recycling bin, do you remember what it looked like?" The young woman said she did, and Bayle went on. "Is it uncommon for there to be remnants of glass that size and shape in the bin?"

"Not at all. We work with glass, Detective. We're as careful, and as frugal, with the materials as we can be, but we have accidents."

"Accidents?"

"Breakage. We reuse as much as we can, Mira's a stickler for that, but a piece like that"—she indicated the photo Bayle had handed her—"there's nothing we can do with it."

Bayle made a note, then met the girl's eyes once more. "How likely would it be that two identical pieces wind up in that bin?"

"Identical? Impossible. You can't re-create the by-product of an accident."

"Okay, then two very *similar* pieces?"

The assistant nodded. "It doesn't happen every day, thank goodness, but it does happen. Once I screwed up a break four times in a row."

"A break? What's that?"

"I'll show you." She led them into the workroom, to a table with a job in progress laid out on its top. What looked like a pattern—rectangular, maybe two by four feet—was affixed to the table; pieces of colored glass had been cut to fit the pattern. Like a puzzle.

"This isn't a restoration," she said. "It's an original design we're doing for a home uptown."

Malone cocked his head. It was simple, a repeating pattern of purple, green and gold fleur-de-lis and clear beveled glass. "Somebody likes Mardi Gras," he said, referring to both the colors and image.

"That's our bread and butter, actually. Fleur-de-lis, egrets, magnolias. That's what most of my students want to start with as well."

He heard the pride in her voice. "You're the teacher?"

"And I designed the curriculum. Mira didn't offer classes before I came on board. We've really grown since then."

"Kudos," he said.

She smiled. "Thanks." She selected a square of glass and laid it on the pattern. With a tool that looked like an X-Acto knife, she scored it, tapped the score, then snapped it. "That's a break," she said.

Bayle smiled. "You make it look so easy."

"You want to try it?"

Bayle took a step back. "No, thanks. *Klutz* is my middle name. I imagine it's easy to get hurt?"

"God, yes. Look at my hands." She held them out. They were riddled with cuts, scrapes and scars. "You want to be paying attention when you're doing this. You learn quickly to respect the medium."

"Where were you last night and early this morning?"

She looked from one of them to the other. "Are you serious?"

"As a judge," Bayle said.

"Um, let me think . . ."

"After Preacher attacked Mira and took her cross. It wasn't that long ago."

"Right." She shifted from one foot to the other. "I think I went to a movie."

"You think you did? Or you did?"

"I did."

"What did you see?"

She hesitated. "The new Tom Cruise flick. I forget the name." She laughed nervously. "I'm bad with names."

"Was it good?" Bayle asked.

"It was okay. I'm not a huge fan."

"Did you go alone?"

She clasped her hands together and shook her head. "I went with my sister. She is a big fan."

"What show?"

"The seven o'clock."

"And after?"

She looked like she might throw up. "Got a daiquiri. At Daiquiris and Creams on Vets."

"I love those," Bayle said, smiling. "The White Russians are my favorite."

"I'm a piña colada girl. That's what I had last night. We stayed for a while. Listened to some music. I dropped Cyndi off around eleven."

"We'll need her full name and a number where we can reach her."

"I don't understand. Why?"

"To confirm you were with her during those hours," Malone said.

"But why?" Her voice rose slightly. "I haven't done anything wrong!"

"I'm sure you haven't," he said, tone soothing. "We're just following procedure."

"That's what we have to do in a homicide investigation," Bayle added.

"Homicide," Deni squeaked.

"Preacher is dead. He was murdered shortly after Mira's cross was returned."

"Oh, my God. I need to sit down."

Instead of going in search of a chair, she plopped down on the floor. Spencer and Bayle exchanged glances. He squatted in front of her. "Are you all right, Ms. Watts?"

"Yes," she whispered.

"You seem pretty upset."

"It's just so . . . awful. I've never . . . met anybody who was . . . murdered before."

"I didn't think you'd met him."

"Pardon?"

"You said you heard Ms. Gallier scream and ran into the workroom, but Preacher was already gone."

"That's right."

"So you haven't actually met someone who's been murdered."

They'd flustered her. "Not met, you know, but who crossed my path."

He looked up at Bayle. "You have any more questions?"

"Nope. That'll do it."

He looked back at the young woman and smiled. "Thanks, Deni. We really appreciate it. What's your boyfriend's name again?"

"Chris."

Malone nodded as if only just remembering. "He was here yesterday, right?"

She nodded. "But he didn't see any more than I did."

"I'm sure you're right. But as long as we're waiting for Mira, we might as well chat with him, too."

Bayle stepped in. "He's outside, yes?"

She started to stand. "He is. I'll take you out."

Malone offered her a hand. "Don't worry about us, Deni. You have things to do, and we've kept you from them long enough. Besides, we know the way."

She looked as if she was going to argue, took one glance at Bayle and shut her mouth.

They exited the workroom by the back door, simultaneously going for their shades. When they were out of earshot, Malone said, "I'm impressed. How'd you get her to back down so quickly?"

"I gave her my don't-fuck-with-me look."

He chuckled. "Who would've thought I'd be the good cop in our relationship."

"I put the *b* in *bitch*, baby." Her tone grew more serious. "That was a little weird, by the way. She was either hiding something or outright lying. And the way she reacted to learning Preacher had been murdered seemed melodramatic."

"I agree. And it was pretty obvious she didn't want us to talk to her boyfriend. I wonder why."

"Don't know. Let's see if we can find out."

Chris was atop a ladder, painting. They stopped and looked up. "Hey, Chris. Can we talk to you for a minute?"

"Sure. I needed a break anyway."

He climbed down the ladder and went for the water cooler. He pulled out a gallon jug and drank directly from it.

"How many of those you go through a day?"

"Quite a few. Mira's always reminding me to stay hydrated."

"Good advice. How long have you worked for her?"

"Only about six weeks." He took another long swig from the jug, then set it back in the cooler. "Nicest person I've ever worked for. Considerate. Gentle. Cares about people."

Malone made a note. "How about Deni? How long have you two been a couple?"

He thought a moment. "We've been dating four or five months. But yeah, I guess you could call us a couple now."

"How'd you meet?"

Chris laughed. "In church. At least that's what my mother likes to say."

"But you didn't?"

"No, we did, just not in that context." He grabbed a towel from the back of his pickup truck and wiped his face. "I was doing some work for the archdiocese and she was there to evaluate a couple windows."

"You have a faith life, Chris?"

The kid looked surprised. "Wow, that was random, but yeah. You know, without faith, what do you have? Especially after something like Katrina. You know what I mean?"

Malone did. The storm had had a strong effect on people's faith. For some it had cemented their belief in God; for others, it had broken it.

Chris tossed the towel back over the truck's tailgate. "Besides, my mother dragged me to mass twice a week for my whole life. She'd kick my ass if I said I didn't believe."

Malone laughed. His mother had done the same, dragged each of them to mass and made it clear that nonbelief was the same as stabbing her in the heart.

"I'm with you on that," Malone said, glancing down at his notes, then back up at the young man. "Yesterday morning, when Ms. Gallier was attacked, you get a look at that guy?"

"That Preacher dude?" He shook his head. "Deni and I were just walking in the front door when Mira screamed."

"You ever notice a guy like him around here before?"

"Around here? Just the other night, at the Corner Bar." He paused, as if in thought. "Usually I see those types in the French Quarter and outside Saints games, but I never look hard at them. You know how it is, you can have a bucketful of faith, but you still don't want to talk to one of those guys."

Malone did indeed know. He appreciated the handyman's honesty. "By the way, Chris, where were you late last night?"

"How late?"

"Between ten thirty and five this morning."

He laughed. "Are you kidding? I was asleep. I'm usually out cold by nine thirty, sometimes earlier than that."

"Pretty early for a young guy like you," Malone said.

"You try working out in this heat all day. Completely sucks the life out of me."

"Was Deni with you?"

"Nope. She and I caught a quick bite to eat after leaving here, then went our separate ways."

"You know where she was last night?"

"You'd have to ask her that." He glanced back at the building in progress. "If you're cool with it, I need to get back to work."

Malone heard a car door slam. Gallier, he thought. He would like to get to her before Deni spilled everything. "Sure, Chris. Thanks for your help."

By the time they reached the door to the workroom, Gallier was already there. She looked completely rattled.

"I'm sorry it took me so long to get here, there was an accident on I-10."

Malone made a mental note to check that. "No problem. While we were waiting we talked to Deni and Chris."

"About Preacher. Deni told me. She said . . . he's dead? That he was murdered. Is that true?"

"Yes. Sometime late yesterday or early this morning."

She moved her gaze between them, expression uncertain. "That's when I got my cross back."

"That's right."

"Oh, my God." She brought a hand to her throat, to her cross. "But how is that possi— I mean . . . When did you say?"

"About the same time your cross was returned. Would you know anything about that?"

It took a moment for his words to register; he saw the instant they did. Her eyes widened and she went white. "Of course not. How could you think . . . why would you—"

She crossed to one of the stools set up at the closest worktable. She sat hard.

Her shock looked genuine. Of course, as he was certain Bayle would point out, that didn't mean squat. Many a guilty-as-hell perp came off as innocent as a choir boy. Or in this case, choir girl.

"What happened?" she managed after a moment, meeting his eyes. "How . . . where—" Her throat seemed to close over the words.

Bayle answered in her no-nonsense, deal-with-it manner. "How, his throat was slit. Where, a French Quarter john."

"Something interesting was found at the scene," Malone said. "A piece of glass almost exactly like the one he attacked you with."

"Even the same color," Bayle added.

"Which is why we're here."

Gallier looked at them, obviously struggling to connect with where their questions were heading. "Was it . . . are you saying . . . was it the murder weapon?"

"We're not at liberty to say."

He saw that she took that exactly the way he hoped she would, as a yes. "Do the words *Judgment Day* mean anything to you?"

"Judgment Day?" she repeated. "Other than it being the day foretold in the Bible when Christ will—" She bit the words back, a strange expression coming over her face. "When Christ will judge the living and the dead. Why are you asking me that?"

"It was scrawled in blood on the floor by Preacher's body," Bayle answered. "It could simply be the killer's way of sticking it to Preacher, for all his street-corner sermons."

"Or it could be connected to Father Girod and the Sisters of Mercy windows," she whispered.

"Yes. And, it seems, you're connected to both."

Chapter Twenty-five

Monday, August 15
7:30 P.M.

He stood in the doorway and gazed at his grandmother; she slept deeply. She had grown so weak. She barely moved. Her frame had become skeletal, yet he couldn't get her to eat. Day after day, he took away her untouched tray of food and drink.

He needed her advice. It was she whom he had always turned to. She whom he had counted and leaned on.

She couldn't die, he thought, panic tugging at him. He needed her. He needed her counsel.

He tapped on the bedroom door, then poked his head inside.

"Grandma? Are you awake?"

She didn't respond, didn't stir. He crept across to stand beside her bed, then fell to his knees.

"I'm so troubled, Grandmother. I don't know what to do. I need your help."

Still she slept. His eyes flooded with tears, even as shame washed over him. How could he bring this to her now, when she was so ill?

He was weak, he acknowledged. And small.

He hung his head but went on anyway. "There's so much

bad in the world, Grandmother. So much evil. I'm over-whelmed by it."

A consequence of the Fall.

Not his grandmother, he realized, lifting his head. "Who's there?"

You know me. You know what must be done.

"No, I don't!"

It's what you were born for, my Son. Evil must be destroyed.

"Counsel me, Father! I feel so lost. So alone."

Do you recall the devil's temptation in the desert?

He nodded.

When the devil said, "Throw yourself down from this mountain for your Father will command His angels to protect you," do you remember this?

"I recognized his deceit. For it is written: 'You should not put the Lord your God to the test.'"

And when he promised you all the world if you would bow down and worship him?

"I faced the liar with the truth: 'Worship the Lord your God and serve only Him.'"

And is it not also written that he left you then to wait for a more opportune time?

A more opportune time, he realized. Of course. That time was now. "The Evil One is the great liar; he takes many forms. He twists your Holy Word to use against us."

Yes. Beware. Your enemy the devil prowls around like a roaring lion, looking for someone to devour.

"Peter 5:8." Tears of gratitude and thanksgiving rolled down his cheeks. "I am Your dutiful son and faithful servant. In Your glorious name, I will flush out the serpent and destroy him."

Chapter Twenty-six

Mira paced, her every nerve seeming to jump and hum, as if she had drunk too much coffee or downed one too many energy drinks. Her mind raced. Connor had been right about the way the police had questioned him. The things they had asked.

They wondered if he had killed Preacher. Or if she had convinced him to do it. To get her cross back. Then, as a cover, she had concocted the whole break-in story.

It was crazy. Absolutely nuts.

"He will come again to judge the living and the dead." And scrawled on a floor in blood: *"Jugment Day."*

She dug her phone out of her back pocket and navigated to the photos she had taken of the vandalized windows. A knot settled in her stomach, and with it a vague unease.

What did it all mean?

Her thoughts rocketed to her father-in-law, his thinly veiled accusations. She brought her hands to her face. She didn't want to do this alone. She didn't want to be alone. Not with her thoughts and fears. Not when everything seemed to be falling apart. Again.

She had called Connor. Hours ago. She'd left a message. He hadn't called her back.

"Did you tell her, Connor? Did you tell her the real reason you joined up?"

What was he hiding from her? And now, was he hiding *from* her?

Who else could she turn to? Deni? Dr. Jasper?

No one else was left in her life, she realized. Her parents were gone. Her one sibling she'd never been particularly close to, and after Jeff's death she'd completely shut her out. She'd done the same thing to her old friends.

She had created this narrow, empty little world for herself. A world that consisted of very little human interaction, just her windows, her grief and her pills.

No, she thought. Not anymore. Connor was back. She was letting him in. Wasn't she? And Deni? Chris and Dr. Jasper?

Connor could have his secrets; she had hers. She didn't care; she just needed him in her life.

She snatched her phone off the coffee table and punched in Connor's number. This time he answered. "Connor, it's Mira. Where are you— No, don't answer. I just want you to know, I don't need an explanation why you left. I don't need to know your secrets. I'm just glad you're back in my life. I need you."

As the words spilled out, it was as if something heavy was being lifted off her. She felt lighter. Freer.

"Wow," she said with a laugh, "you must think I've completely lost my mind. Maybe I have, but I just know that—"

"I'm on your front porch."

It took a moment for his words to sink in. When they did, she ran for the door and threw it open. And stopped short, surprised.

Connor wasn't alone. By his side stood a wiggling mass of golden fur, with a wagging tail and, she discovered a moment later, a warm wet nose.

Mira squealed. "Oh, my gosh! Who's this?"

"Nola," he said. "Say hi, Nola."

Mira laughed and squatted in front of the dog, who proceeded to give her a big wet kiss. "I think she just did."

"Obviously a good judge of character."

Mira laughed again and scratched the animal behind the ears. "She's a sweetheart."

"I hoped you'd say that." He bent and ran a hand down the dog's back. "She's two. A golden retriever mix. I got her from the pound."

"Why would anyone have given her up?" Mira asked. "She's so sweet."

"Some people aren't dog people. They take one on, then realize they're not up to the challenge."

"Kind of the way some people have children." Mira ran a hand along the dog's silky back. "She sort of reminds me of Ginger."

"Me, too," he said. "Can we come in? I know it's late."

"If you're cool with me wearing my soft pants."

He laughed. "I saw teenagers wearing those at the airport. I don't think it'll offend my sensibilities."

She stepped aside, then closed the door behind them. "You want something to drink?"

"I'm good."

"What about your friend?"

He grinned. "She looks okay, too."

And she did, content sniffing and snuffling as they made their way back to the keeping room. Located off the kitchen, positioned to look out over the courtyard, the room was a cross between a garden room and family room.

Jeff had pronounced it Mira's space and let her decorate it any way she wished. Not surprisingly, she'd chosen bright, feminine fabrics and minimal, airy furniture. She sat on the end of the floral sofa, tucking her feet under her. Nola waited until Connor sat in the chair to decide where to rest herself. She chose the floor by Mira.

"Sorry," Mira said, reaching down to give the animal a pat. "Looks like she *is* a good judge of character."

"Nice." He mock-glowered at Nola. "Traitor."

Mira smiled. "Thanks for coming over."

"No problem. What's up?"

"You were right. About the way the police questioned you. They came to the studio and questioned me, Deni and Chris."

"About that Preacher guy?"

She nodded. "He's dead. He was murdered the same night he brought my cross back."

"That's why the detectives were so weird with me."

She clasped her hands together. "They're wondering if I had something to do with it, aren't they?"

"Or if I did. Yes, that's the way I read it."

"They even asked Deni and Chris where they were that night." She leaned down and stroked Nola, finding the feel of her soft fur comforting. "It's just unbelievable."

"Is it?"

She looked at him in surprise. "You can't be serious."

He leaned forward, elbows on knees, fingers laced. "Look at it the way they must be. This guy was killed within twenty-four hours of stealing your cross, but not before he returned it."

"Obviously, he did return it. I'm wearing it."

He went on as if she hadn't spoken. "Very odd. Even more problematic, there are no signs of a break-in at your home. And all the doors and windows are locked. Basically, all they have is your version of events. Preacher broke in, returned your cross and left without taking anything or bothering you."

It did sound lame, she thought. And far-fetched. But it was the truth. She told him so.

"I believe you, because I know you."

"What should I do?"

"Nothing. You haven't done anything wrong. They're fishing. It's what they're supposed to be doing. The morning they called you and asked for my name and number, they knew Preacher was dead but didn't say anything about it to you or me. Instead, they asked a lot of questions about the time. Where I went, if anyone saw me. Trying to trip one of us up."

"Trip us up?" She shook her head, smile tugging at her mouth. "You sound like you've done this before."

He grinned. "I told you the service made me paranoid."

They fell silent a moment; he broke it first. "That call just now, what was that all about?"

For a second she didn't even remember. In that moment she realized all her anxiety, all the frantic desperation she'd felt, was gone. Connor being here had obliterated it.

Could she tell him that? She wanted to, but at the same time she felt a little embarrassed, as if it revealed something too personal. Something she didn't even understand.

Even as she told herself she was being ridiculous, she shook her head. "I was overwhelmed and overreacting. Between the police and my father-in-law and everything, I . . . I just needed someone to talk to."

His expression shifted subtly. "I'm glad I could help." He glanced at his watch. "Before I take off, I brought you something. It's in the car. I'll be right back."

She started to stand, but he stopped her. "Stay put. I know the way."

Mira nodded and patted her leg. Nola stood and laid her head on Mira's lap. She stroked the dog's silky head and ears.

Several minutes passed, and she frowned. "What's taking him so long, girl? Maybe we should check on him?"

Nola wagged her tail and Mira stood. Moments later, at the front door, she peered out at the drive. Connor's car was gone.

From the keeping room came the chirp of her cell phone. Realization dawning, she hurried to answer.

"Where the hell are you?" she said. "This isn't funny."

"Nola's for you. I left a bowl, a bag of food and a leash in a box on the driveway."

"You did *what*?"

"I bought her for you. To replace Ginger."

Mira froze, startled by the angry heat that surged through her. "You had no right, Connor."

"We're old friends. Isn't that enough of a right?"

"No, it's not. I don't want a dog."

Nola whimpered and thumped her tail. Mira looked down to find the dog gazing earnestly up at her.

"Yes, you do. When I saw the way you were with her . . . for a moment there, I actually recognized you."

Hurt took her breath. "Nice, Connor. Perfect."

"I'm sorry." He lowered his voice. "You need her, Mira.

Someone broke into your house the other night. They were in your bedroom, they could have killed you."

"But I'm fine and he's dead. It's all over."

"Is it?"

"Why wouldn't it be?"

"Let's say the police are on to something. That's why they're asking all the questions. Something's not adding up."

"Like what? What could be wrong?"

"The time line maybe."

"The time line?"

"Yeah, maybe Preacher couldn't have been the one who broke in and left the cross." He paused. She heard the sounds of traffic. "Because he was already dead."

It took a moment for her to fully comprehend what he was suggesting. When she did, she went cold. A killer, standing beside her bed.

"My sweet star. How I've missed you."

She cleared her throat. "Are you purposely trying to scare the crap out of me?"

"Yes."

"So I'll take the dog?"

"So you'll be careful."

Nola whimpered again and Mira looked down at her.

"She's housebroken," he said.

"It's not that."

"You don't want her to go back to the pound, do you? You know what happens there."

"That's not fair."

"You loved Ginger. She was *your* dog, Mira. Not Jeff's."

Tears stung her eyes. "Yes, she was mine. And I lost her."

"Don't be afraid to love."

"I'm not, dammit! Get your ass back here, Connor Scott!"

"Not happening."

"I'll turn her out. Anything could happen to her."

"Yeah, right, that's going to happen."

He knew her too well. It infuriated her. "I'll see you tomorrow, Connor. You might think about reenlisting before then, because it won't be pretty."

Chapter Twenty-seven

Mira sat bolt upright in bed. Heart thundering, she flipped on the bedside lamp. A pool of light spilled over her. Nola, she realized. She had left the dog in the courtyard. She was barking.

Mira groaned and dragged her hands through her hair. Right, she *needed* a dog. Thanks, Connor. Like she'd been getting a full night's sleep without Little Miss Loudmouth.

She threw aside the covers and climbed out of bed. If she didn't shush Nola, cranky old Louise Latrobe would call the cops. Just what she needed: more NOPD attention.

The floor was cool beneath her bare feet. Hoping to stay at least a little groggy, she didn't bother with more lights. She padded out to the hallway and froze.

Jeff. The spicy soap and aftershave he'd used, the scent hung in the air.

She closed her eyes and breathed in the scent, memories flooding her. Jeff, stepping out of the shower, a billow of fragrant steam filling the bathroom. Cuddling in front of the television, nuzzling his neck, his scent filling her nose.

He was here, she realized. Home at last.

It'd all been a bad dream.

A distinct click, like a door being shut, startled her out of the moment. Reality hit her with the force of a wrecking ball.

Nola's barking.

The smell of aftershave. The door.

She wasn't alone.

With a cry, Mira ran for the kitchen and the door to the courtyard. Her steps faltered as she realized Nola had gone quiet. How long ago? Minutes? Because the danger had passed? Or because someone had shut her up?

No! She broke into a run. *No, no, no!*

"Nola!" she called. "Come!"

The dog responded to her cry. She heard her at the courtyard door, clawing.

Just as fear had played a litany of denials in her head, relief played one of thanks. She reached the door, fumbled with the lock, then yanked it open. The dog barreled in, nearly toppling her, obviously no worse for wear.

She wished she could say the same of herself.

Trembling, she sank to the floor and put her arms around the dog's neck. Whoever had been in the house was gone. She was unharmed. Nola was fine. Take a deep breath, she told herself. It was okay. Everything was okay.

She pressed her face into the dog's soft fur, comforted. Nola seemed to understand what she needed, and the normally boisterous animal sat immobile, just letting Mira hug her.

A prayer of thanksgiving played in her head. For Nola. Her high-pitched barking. For Connor bringing her the dog, tricking her into taking it.

Connor. As she thought of him, gratitude and affection speared through her. What if he hadn't insisted she needed a dog? Where might she be right now?

Someone had been in her house. Again.

She struggled to keep her terror in check, focusing instead on her gratitude. Her relief at being healthy and safe.

She hadn't felt that after Katrina. Instead she'd felt guilty.

Survivor's guilt, Dr. Jasper had told her. Normal under the circumstances. Many storm survivors were suffering from it. And she had more reasons than most.

She was glad to be alive.

The realization took her breath. She was thankful, with every fiber of her being, from the top of her head to the tips of her toes. She hadn't felt this way since before the storm. Mira laughed, reveling in the incredible heady feeling.

She had to share this with Connor. She had to thank him. Jumping to her feet, she retrieved her phone, located his number and dialed it. He answered immediately, sounding fully awake.

Without pausing to consider the oddness of that, she rushed on. "It's Mira."

"Mira? Are you okay?"

Her words came out in a rush. "Yes. No . . . I mean, maybe I shouldn't be, but I am."

"Now you've lost me." He yawned. "Did you just wake up or something?"

She had, Mira thought, and laughed. She knew she sounded like a total whack job, but she didn't care. "Thank you. For Nola. That's all I wanted to say."

She heard a rustling from his end of the phone, as if he was moving the bedclothes, sitting up. "I'm glad you two have bonded."

"That happens with a near-death experience."

"You're talking so crazy. Have you been drinking?"

"Nope. Just high on life."

He laughed. "You don't have any idea what time it is, do you?"

"None."

"Three in the morning."

That penetrated her euphoric bubble. "Oh, my gosh! Connor, I'm so sorry. I'll let you go."

"No," he said quickly. "I don't sleep much anyway. Why don't you tell me what brought on this middle-of-the-night, near-death, canine-bonding experience."

"Someone was in the house tonight. Nola's barking woke me—"

He cut her off. "Someone was in your house tonight?"

"Yes. But that's not—"

"Are you certain?"

"Yes. But that's not why I'm calling."

"It should be. I mean, shit, Mira . . . have you lost your frigging mind?"

Her bubble of euphoria deflated completely; fear began to fill it. "Oh, my God . . . someone was in my house again."

"I'm on my way over."

"You don't have to do that. I'm—"

"Yeah, I do. What was the name of that detective from before?"

"Malone," she said. "Detective Malone."

"Call him. I'll be there as soon as I can."

Chapter Twenty-eight

Fifteen years on the job, and Malone still hadn't adjusted to the middle-of-the-night calls. The blood and gore he could handle. The disregard for human life displayed by some, the sick behavior many accepted as normal. He had learned to let the distrust, discrimination and stupidity roll off his back. And he did it without drink or drugs.

But damn, he missed a good night's sleep.

Bayle pulled up behind him. She had wanted in, no matter the hour; he'd given her what she wanted. She climbed out of her vehicle and headed his way. From the look of her, she needed her sleep as well.

"What the hell?" she said when she reached him.

"Apparently, someone broke into her house. Again."

"Lucky us." At her scowl, he decided she had no sense of humor in the middle of the night.

As they approached the entrance, a dog began to bark. Gallier opened the door before they rang the bell. She held the dog, a big golden retriever, by the collar. "Detective Malone, thank you for coming."

"Ms. Gallier. You remember my partner, Detective Bayle?"

He saw her slight frown. He suspected Bayle had noted it as well.

"Of course. Come in."

"I see you took my advice and got a dog." Malone squatted and scratched behind her ears. "What's her name?"

"Nola. But I didn't actually take your advice. Connor—"

The other man emerged from the back of the house, carrying two mugs of coffee. The brew smelled wonderful, obviously a good-quality dark roast.

"Hello, Detectives," he said.

"Mr. Scott."

"Call me Connor." He handed Mira one of the mugs. "Can I get either of you a cup?"

They both refused, then turned back to Gallier. Bayle spoke first. "You were telling us about how you got Nola."

At her name, the animal trotted over to Bayle for some attention. She patted her head.

"Connor tricked me into taking her."

"Tricked?" Malone repeated. "Interesting choice of words. How does one do that?"

Scott answered for her. "Mira told me about that Preacher guy attacking her at her studio, then breaking in here. It just didn't seem smart or safe for her to live here alone. So I brought Nola over and persuaded her to keep her at least for a night." He smiled. "No tricks involved."

Malone glanced at Gallier. An emotion moved across her face, an expression of surprise or confusion, then was gone. Scott, he thought, was lying.

Bayle stepped in. "Good thing you did."

He took a sip of his coffee. "That's the way it turned out."

Malone assessed him for a moment, before turning back to Gallier. "Tell us exactly what happened."

"Nola's barking woke me up."

"What time was that?" Bayle asked.

"I'm not certain, I didn't look at the clock. About two thirty, I guess. I'd made up a bed for her in the courtyard."

"And where's your bedroom?"

She pointed down the hall. "I use the downstairs suite. It's more convenient."

"And she was loud enough to wake you?"

"Yes. She was going berserk." She rubbed her arms as if cold. "At first I thought she was just being a dog and I worried she would wake Mrs. Latrobe."

"Who?"

"My neighbor. On the right. She can be cantankerous. So I got out of bed to go fuss at Nola. But when I got to the hallway, I—"

She stopped and Malone frowned. "What, Ms. Gallier?"

"It's going to sound silly, but I smelled men's aftershave."

Scott frowned. "You didn't tell me that."

"I didn't?" She clasped her hands together. "I guess I forgot."

"And then?"

"I heard a door click shut. That's when I realized—"

She bit the last back, looking uncomfortable. Malone prodded her again. "What did you realize?"

She lifted her chin slightly. "That the smell wasn't my imagination."

Bayle cocked her head. "Why would you have thought that?"

Gallier glanced away, then back at them, expression almost defiant. "Because the scent I smelled was the one my husband wore."

Chapter Twenty-nine

Tuesday, August 16
4:05 A.M.

Mira shut the door behind the detectives. She held the knob a moment, aware of Connor standing behind her. Once again, they'd found nothing. No sign of a break-in. The windows and doors locked from the inside.

She looked at Connor. "It doesn't make any sense. I know what I heard. I smelled his aftershave. I didn't imagine it."

"I've got to go."

"Please don't." She caught his arm; it felt like rock beneath her hand. "Stay."

"I can't do this, Mira."

"What? I don't understand."

"Nothing." He freed himself from her grasp. "I need to go."

"You're angry," she said. "Why?"

"You don't want to know."

"Yes, I do." She held his gaze. "Please, don't go."

"I can't do this," he said again, gesturing to her, then himself. "You and me. I can't be your go-to guy."

His words hurt. She held her ground. "I didn't ask you to be."

"No? You called me, remember?"

She tilted up her chin. "To thank you for Nola. You brought me the damn dog, I didn't ask for that."

"What was I supposed to do?" He ran a hand over his close-cropped hair. "You tell me about some derelict attacking you, then breaking into your house, and you expect me to sit back and do nothing? I'm not that guy either."

"I know. I'm sorry. I didn't have anyone else to turn to." This time she caught his hand, laced her fingers with his. His hand was warm, solid. She didn't want to let go. "Please, don't be angry with me. Don't leave."

He looked at their joined hands, expression torn, then back up at her. "Jeff's aftershave, Mira? It's been almost six years. Is he still so real to you?"

"Yes." She searched his gaze, heart thundering. "He's not for you?"

"No. Jeff . . . he . . ." Connor swore and freed his hand. "I've got to go."

She stepped in front of the door. "He was your best friend."

His lips tightened. She sensed he was holding back, that the things he longed to say burned on his tongue. "Whatever you're thinking, say it, Connor. Just tell me!"

"Move away from the door."

She held her ground, furious. "Why'd you change the story about Nola?"

"What?"

"The police, you lied to them."

"It told them too much about us. About you. I don't trust them."

"You don't trust *them*? They're the police."

"And that doesn't mean squat."

"Wow, you have changed."

"War'll do that to you, sweetheart."

She cringed at the brutal edge in his voice. "Trust me," she said softly, reaching out to him. "Please."

"I want to trust you, I really do."

"That's not the same thing."

"I know. But it's all I've got." He gently moved her away from the door. "Goodbye, Mira."

He said it as if this was the last time they would see each other. She couldn't bear it. But she didn't know how to stop him.

He climbed into his car and backed out of her drive. And her life. Again.

Chapter Thirty

Malone sat at his desk, gazing at his computer screen. His eyes burned with fatigue, his stomach from too much coffee and too little food. A couple cubicles over, Bayle was doing the same—a little investigative work via the miracle of the Internet.

They'd agreed that something about Gallier's story and Scott's presence didn't add up. They had decided to divide and conquer: he would search out information about Scott, she about Gallier. He'd also wanted to do a little research into the origins and meaning of both *He will come again to judge the living and the dead* and *Judgment Day.*

The saying wasn't biblical but liturgical. Called the Apostles' Creed, it was used by nearly every Christian denomination. Both referred to a belief in a God who would come and collect the faithful and banish all others to hell, wherever and whatever that might be.

Many religions had some concept of a God who judged and a final judgment day, but only the Catholic and Lutheran denominations used those exact words in their creed.

So their perp was raised in the church, most probably

Roman Catholic, since the New Orleans area was heavily Catholic.

Malone made a mental note to discuss that with Bayle and turned his attention to Scott. Something about the guy just didn't sit right with him. It was too convenient that all this crap started at the same time he returned home from military service.

Military records were damn difficult to access, but it could be done with a subpoena. Whether the military released them was their call. Scott's premilitary record was nonexistent. No arrests, no convictions. If he'd had a juvenile record, it had disappeared. He'd made a few calls, done a little legwork. Apparently Scott had been a bit of a hellraiser, but nothing more than teenage rich kid crap.

No marriages, no children. Graduation with honors from Tulane University. Attended prep school in Virginia.

"Hey, partner."

Malone looked up at Bayle and smiled. "You find something that's going to make me stand up and dance?"

She smiled back. "I wish. Actually, I'm starving and hope you are, too."

"I am. And a break from this sounds really good right now."

"I know a place that serves out-of-this-world shrimp and grits."

"You had me at hungry." He stood and stretched. "Let's go."

She drove. The place was a hole-in-the-wall diner called Freddie and the Red-Headed Lady. Pure dive. Sketchy part of town. Heaven-on-earth, down-home cooking. She had the shrimp and grits, he Sista's soul food omelet with red bean gravy.

"Okay, how did you find this place?" he asked, mopping up the last of the gravy with a chunk of buttermilk biscuit. "I thought we Malones knew all the best local dives."

"My old boyfriend introduced me to it. He had a nose for places off the beaten track."

"The beaten track? More like off the gravel path." He glanced around. "Certainly not a place to see and be seen."

Something flashed in her eyes, then was gone. "Is that a problem for you?"

"Hell no. I appreciate the introduction, believe me." He leaned back in his chair as the waitress refilled their coffee cups.

"Can I get y'all anything else?" she asked.

"Not me," Bayle said and looked at him.

He shook his head. "Me either. It was great."

The woman hesitated a moment, gaze on Bayle. "I hope you don't mind me askin', but are you Detective Karin Bayle?"

"I am."

The waitress's eyes filled with tears. "During Katrina you saved my cousin's life. Brittany Ann Martin. She was trapped in her car."

"I remember." She did, he saw by the way her face softened. "How is she?"

"Really good. She just had a baby. A girl. I'm her godmother."

"Tell her I said hi and congratulations."

"I will." The waitress ripped their bill off her pad and stuffed it in her pocket. "This is on me."

"You don't have to do that—"

"Yeah, I do. Thank you, Detective."

"Wow," Malone said when the waitress was gone. "So that's what being famous is like."

"Stop. It's embarrassing."

She meant it, he realized, and did as she asked. "You find anything new about Gallier?"

"Not much. Born and raised in New Orleans. Went to public schools, attended the Center for Creative Arts, then Tulane's Newcomb College on a full scholarship."

"She didn't come from money, then?"

"Far from it. Parents are both dead. Dad when she was young. Mom before Katrina. One sib, a sister who lives in Knoxville."

"Run-ins with the law?"

"Other than the charges leveled on her after Katrina, nada."

It was hard for him to imagine such a small family, coming from one that extended like the plumes of an oil spill. "Anything else?"

"Her husband's death made her a rich woman." She picked up her coffee cup. "What about you? Turn up anything on Scott?"

"Damn little. Wealthy family, old-school New Orleans. A page in the Krewe of Rex. Years later, he was in the royal court. Went to work at the family financial services firm after university.

"I asked around, Scott did his share of hell-raising. Underage drinking, reckless driving, fighting, that sort of thing. I'll keep digging."

"They seemed pretty cozy tonight."

"That they did," he agreed. "No crime in that, though. What're you thinking?"

"About Gallier?" He nodded. "There's something going on there. Whether she's hiding something, lying or just plain crazy, something's not right with her."

"Just my opinion," he said, "but Scott's the one who sets off my alarm bells. His story's too convenient. He just happens to bring her a dog on the same night someone breaks into her house? Please."

He drummed his fingers on the table. "Twice now she calls us out. Both times we find all the doors and windows locked from the inside. Nothing's taken or disturbed and Gallier's unharmed. It's almost as if someone has a key and is sneaking in to play with her."

"But why?"

"To terrorize her. Exert control. Make her pay for some slight, real or imagined."

"Motivated by?"

"Love. Hate. Jealousy. Anger. Shame. All of the above. Her dead husband's aftershave sealed the deal for me."

She leaned back in her chair. "Explain."

"I put myself in her shoes. If I'd lost Stacy that way, and somebody wanted to screw with me, that'd do it. Big time."

Bayle pursed her lips. "Interesting. Who's your bet on?"

"How about the in-laws? They failed to get her through legal channels, so they go this route. Makes sense they might have a key to the house. Considering their social and economic stature, they'd hire it done."

"And murdering Preacher was part of it?"

"Hell, no. Preacher was offed by a badass who'd had enough of his sermons."

"What about the vandalized windows and Father Girod? Related to Gallier?"

"I'm thinking not. One of those weird coincidences I typically don't believe in."

"But you do now?" She folded her arms across her chest. "Why?"

"It just makes more sense to me."

"No." Bayle dropped her arms and leaned forward. "I'll tell you why. Because such a sweet, doe-eyed little thing couldn't possibly be at the heart of something so ugly."

"Whoa, hit the brakes. Give me a little credit."

"Sorry, but she's the kind of woman men do things for. Things they wouldn't normally do."

"Like commit murder?"

"Don't discount it."

"I'm not discounting anything at this point. Happy?"

"Works for me."

His cell phone buzzed. It was Percy. "Hey, bro. Got something good for me?"

"Define *good*."

Crap. "Okay, so who got whacked?"

"Anton Gallier."

"Any relation to—"

"Yup. Her father-in-law."

"Where?"

"French Quarter. Royal and St. Philip."

"Bayle and I are on our way."

Chapter Thirty-one

Gallier had been gunned down leaving his French Quarter apartment. Since he was married, Malone figured the man called it a corporate apartment, then generously allowed his company to pay for it. In the meantime, it served as his place to party.

He and Bayle ducked under the inner perimeter tape and signed the log. He moved his gaze over the scene. Like all French Quarter buildings, this one was old. Three stories with wraparound balconies. Gallier's apartment had been a third-floor corner unit.

A sweet place to be during Mardi Gras.

The coroner's photographer was doing his thing, the CSI team waiting patiently. The scene reminded Malone of one from the original *Godfather* movie: mob guy, dressed to kill, crumpled in the corner of the old-time elevator car. Blood and guts. Big mess.

Percy ambled over. Spencer introduced him to Bayle. "My new partner, Karin Bayle."

Percy grinned and held out his hand. "My condolences."

She took his hand, frowning. "Condolences? I don't—"

"At pulling the dead wood here."

"Little brother's under the misconception that he's funny." Malone punched him in the arm.

"Know what's really sad? Dude's wearing a two-thousand-dollar suit. Custom. Nice threads. Italian wool." He whistled low, under his breath. "No good to anyone now. That shit'll never come out."

A crime scene tech looked over her shoulder at them. "Even if it did, how you gonna repair a hole like that? There's no reweave to that."

"Damn shame," Percy agreed, then turned his attention back to Anton Gallier. "His girlfriend found him. He'd gotten up for a meeting and she'd slept in. Entire building is corporate apartments. Six apartments, two each floor. One elevator, two staircases, one for each side of the building.

"Shot twice," he went on. "Close range. Both times in the chest. First officer checked his ID. Wallet's in his jacket, plenty of green. Wearing a wedding ring and a Patek Philippe watch."

"Certainly wasn't a robbery," Bayle said.

"More like a mob-style execution," Spencer said, thinking again of the gangster movie. "If our perp knew Gallier was here, he waits until he hears the elevator. The door opens and *pop, pop,* he takes care of business. He walks away, not even a drop of blood on him."

"Let's find out if any of the other five units were being used last night. If so, maybe somebody saw something this morning. No place to hide here in the lobby, so if our scenario is correct, somebody could have seen him."

"Let's ask the folks at the grocery across the street as well. They open early."

"I'll get started on that," Percy offered.

Spencer nodded. "Girlfriend still here?"

"Oh, yeah. She's recuperating upstairs. I've got a uniform with her."

"Have you questioned her yet?"

"Nope. She's all yours."

Spencer collected her name and other pertinent information. He and Bayle took the stairs to the third floor.

The girlfriend sat on the couch, a bottle of artesian water clutched in her hands. She looked more bored than upset and lifted her gaze hopefully when they entered the room.

"Ms. Jessica Zurich, is that right?" Spencer asked.

"Jaz," she said, "like the music. My middle name's Ann."

"Gotcha," he said. "Very cute."

She was young. Mid- to late twenties, Malone guessed. Certainly beyond the age of consent, but considering her paramour had been in the neighborhood of his sixth decade, he found the thought of their relationship a little creepy. He supposed they'd had one big thing in common: Gallier's money.

"I'm Detective Spencer Malone and this is my partner, Detective Karin Bayle. We need to ask you some questions."

"That's cool. Is it going to take long, though? I've got a lunch appointment."

No real love there. She was already thinking about lunch.

"You're obviously very upset," Bayle said softly. "We'll make this as quick as possible."

If the young woman picked up on the sarcasm, she didn't show it.

"Thanks. I'd like to smoke. Do you mind?"

"Okay by me," Spencer said. Bayle nodded.

She dug a pack out of her tiny, ridiculously sparkly handbag. "Anton didn't allow it."

"I think he'd understand, considering the circumstances."

She giggled, the sound young and inappropriate. But what about this situation *wasn't* inappropriate? Malone thought.

She lit up, took a drag, then let out a stream of smoke. Something about the way she sucked in and blew out was decidedly sexual. It was almost like she was giving the damn thing a blow job.

Malone cleared his throat. "Tell me about last night and this morning."

"Anton and I spent the night here. We'd been out with friends."

"What did you do?"

She looked momentarily confused, like he was asking what the two of them had done in bed.

He clarified. "With your friends. Where did you go? Who were you with?"

"Some of his business associates. Their girlfriends. We spent most of the night at the Ritz dining room, but we also stopped in a couple clubs. Republic, Club 360."

"What time did you get back here?"

"Around one. Anton had a meeting in the morning. He let me sleep in."

"Considerate."

"He always was." Regret tinged her voice.

"You didn't hear anything? Nothing disturbed your sleep?"

"No. Anton said goodbye before he left and I slept like a baby until nine."

"Anybody else in any of the apartments last night?"

"No clue. I didn't see anyone."

"So you got up?"

"Had a cup of coffee and a piece of fruit, called my mother, then showered and dressed." She took a quick breath, as if preparing herself for something unpleasant. "I called the elevator and . . . there he was."

For the first time he heard real emotion in her voice.

"It must have been a shock."

"It was horrible. The most horrible thing I ever—" She squeezed her eyes shut. Malone suspected she was trying to force the image of Gallier out of her head.

"What did you do then?"

"I called the police."

"Did you touch him at all? Check his pulse? Anything?"

"Are you kidding?" She shuddered. "That was the last thing I'd do."

"How did the elevator get back to the ground floor?"

"I reached inside and pressed the button. I wanted it as far away from me as possible."

"Interesting. Why didn't you take the stairs and go for help?"

She looked at him blankly. It was obvious the thought hadn't crossed her mind. Either that, or she hadn't even realized there were stairs.

"Mr. Gallier was married, wasn't he?"

She nodded. "For like thirty-five years or something ridiculous like that." Her lips lifted. "He'd been married longer than I've been alive. I always thought that was kind of funny."

Malone cocked his head. There was something off about her. Her eyes. Her response. He wouldn't be surprised to learn that Jaz here had a little bump this morning. He'd bet a month's salary that sparkly little bag concealed something that'd get her sparkly little ass busted.

As if reading his thoughts, Bayle said, "When you got back here last night, you two use any drugs?"

Alarm raced into her eyes. "Why would you say that?"

"It's just a question. Whether he was using will turn up in the pathology report anyway."

She tossed her long blond hair over her shoulder. "I don't use drugs, Detective. Once in a while Anton would have a little something. You know, to aid his performance."

"And he did last night?"

"Yes. And we had sex." She lit another cigarette. "I enjoyed it."

Bayle rolled her eyes, but Malone was able to resist the temptation. "Did Gallier's wife know about you?" he asked.

"Me and the others. There've been lots of others. They had an agreement about it."

"An agreement?" Malone asked. He could feel the dislike of this woman emanating from Bayle. He figured the same was rolling off of him, too.

"Like the army." She smiled. "Don't ask, don't tell."

He could tell by her expression that she was disappointed by their lack of response to her cleverness. He decided she was completely narcissistic.

"You don't seem all that upset by this, Jaz."

"By what?"

"Your boyfriend's murder."

"I'm devastated." She brought a hand to her chest. "Absolutely."

"Devastated? Really?" Spencer cocked his head. "Were you in love with him?"

"No. But I was in love with us."

"Us?"

"Being together. Doing the things we did. We had fun, he bought me lots of nice things."

Like the gold watch and diamond earrings she wore, he thought. Very nice things, indeed.

"Did he have any enemies that you knew of?"

"He was a peach. Everyone loved Anton."

Malone found that very hard to believe. You didn't achieve what Anton Gallier had without pissing off a lot of folks.

"Although," she went on, "he said something about a fight with his daughter-in-law."

Malone glanced at Bayle, who responded with a slight nod.

"Do you know when the fight occurred?"

She pursed her lips. "A day or two ago at his club. I wasn't paying that much attention."

"What's the name of his club?"

"The Crescent City Club."

"Is there anything else you can recall him saying about it?"

She shook her head. "He called her white trash and a gold digger. He *really* didn't like her." She leaned forward. "He blamed her for his son's death."

"May I see your hands, Jaz?"

She held them out and Spencer inspected them, looking for gunpowder residue. They were clean.

"We're going to conduct a search of the premises. Also, may we have permission to search your things? If we can do that, you're free to go."

She immediately agreed. Her handbag and overnight bag were clean—no gun, anyway—and two minutes later she was exiting by way of the stairs.

After a cursory search of the apartment, leaving a more

thorough search to the CSI team, they headed downstairs. When they reached the main floor, the coroner's reps were carrying the body bag out of the elevator. The CSI guys took their place in the car. The doors slid shut.

Malone looked at Bayle. "After chatting with the unlikable Ms. Zurich, I've *got* to interview Gallier's wife."

"No joke." She made a face. "Just think, he was escaping from his wife to be with *that*."

The elevator door slid open behind them. "Detectives," the CSI tech called, "I think you'd better come take a look at this."

They did. On the inside of the door, the perp had written: *He cast out Seven Demons.*

Bayle looked at Malone. "What the hell does *that* mean?"

"I'll tell you what it means," he said, frowning. "We've got a damn big problem on our hands."

Chapter Thirty-two

Malone and Bayle stepped out of the elevator just as Percy entered the lobby. He took one look at their expressions and said, "What? Did someone else die while I was gone?"

"Take a look." Malone jerked his thumb toward the elevator. "Then we'll talk."

Percy stepped into the car; Spencer reached inside and pushed the button to close the door. A moment later, Spencer heard his brother swear. Not once but three times.

The door reopened, and Percy stepped off. "This pisses me off."

Spencer moved his gaze between his brother and Bayle. "I think it's safe to say at this point that we've got a serial on our hands." He ticked them off. "Sisters of Mercy, Preacher and now Gallier. All connected by a biblical reference."

"And Mira Gallier," Bayle added.

Percy scratched his head. " 'He cast out Seven Demons.' What the hell does that mean?"

"Specifically?" Spencer said. "Don't know. How about you, Bayle?"

She shook her head. "My mother fancied herself a Buddhist. The closest I got to Western religion was when my grandmother dragged me to her Baptist church. But it has to be biblical, right?"

"Right." Spencer frowned. "No doubt it refers to Christ's works, so we're talking New Testament."

"I could call Mom," Percy offered with a smirk. "Of course, then she'd know that we didn't know and she'd have our asses in mass like this." He snapped his fingers.

"That's so not happening, bro. Besides, that's what the Internet's for. How about the folks over at the grocery? Anybody see anything this morning?"

"A kid making a delivery. That's about it."

"Delivering what?"

"Food, they thought. That's what it looked like. Coffee tray, white bag."

"Makes sense," Spencer noted. "Anybody sees him in the lobby, he's got an instant explanation."

"The beauty of this kind of kill is how quick and clean it is," Bayle said.

Malone agreed. "This perp is highly organized."

"According to the cashier across the street, his hands were full." Percy frowned in thought. "So how'd he accomplish it all?"

"He wrote the message *before* killing Gallier," Bayle offered.

Percy nodded. "Gallier steps into the elevator, sees the message and assumes the building's been vandalized."

They returned to the elevator car and examined the writing. Unlike the message scrawled beside Preacher, this was definitely not written in blood.

"In my opinion, he would have had to put down the coffee tray to write this. The gun he could have fired with one hand," Bayle said.

"Looks like marker. Black, wide tip." Malone leaned close and sniffed. The slight ether scent lingered. "Permanent marker, not water based."

"Maybe he didn't take it with him?"

"And what about the coffee he was delivering? Once the deed was done, he would have wanted to cut out fast."

Malone headed outside, the other two on his heels. Sure enough, a trash receptacle was located right around the corner. He peered inside.

Coffee carrier, two cups and a white bag.

Bayle and Percy came up behind him. Percy whistled. "Pay dirt."

"Cups are definitely full." Malone nudged the take-out bag with his pen. "Something's in it."

"Maybe we're living right," Percy said, "and the asshole tossed the gun? That'd be sweet."

Implausible. But sweet. "I'm more interested in what's on the bag. It's five thousand degrees out here, no way he was wearing gloves. Should have prints, DNA from sweat. Maybe other trace."

"I'll alert the CSI guys," Bayle said, unclipping her phone.

"Cups and bag are generic, but we might be able to identify a business from the contents. What about the grocery's surveillance cameras?"

"I already checked them out," Percy said, "and they don't look promising. The one outside the entrance is pointed in the wrong direction."

"Let's check it anyway."

"Done."

"How about the lobby and elevator?" Bayle suggested. "Cameras are fairly standard these days."

"Let's check it out, but I'm not going to hold my breath."

A couple of the CSI techs tromped out of the building. Spencer gave them directions, then returned to his brother.

"Let's get some uniforms to canvass the neighborhood. See if anyone saw or heard anything. Apparently Gallier recently argued publicly with his daughter-in-law. Percy, I want you to go to the Crescent City Club and interview anyone who witnessed their fight. Bayle and I will deliver the news to Gallier's widow and see what she has to say. Whoever gets back first, set up an interview room. I'm hauling Mira Gallier in for questioning."

Chapter Thirty-three

Mira sat across from Dr. Jasper. The woman waited silently. Mira had called this morning and begged the therapist to fit her in. The woman had given up her lunch break in order to see her, but now Mira had no idea what to say.

She told her so and the woman's perfectly shaped eyebrows arched. "We could sit here and stare at one another for an hour, but that seems a tragic waste of a perfectly good lunch hour."

"It's just that so much has happened in the past week, I don't even know where to start."

"Interesting. Throw some of the events out and see what happens."

"I was attacked in my studio. The street corner preacher who did it was murdered the next night. My old friend Connor showed up after being missing since before Katrina. Someone broke into my house twice. I smelled Jeff's aftershave in the middle of the night. I had a fight with my ex– father-in-law. Felt genuinely happy for the first time since Jeff died. Oh, and I got a dog."

Dr. Jasper stared at her, her expression so classically

dumbfounded that Mira laughed. "I'm sorry, but your face . . . you look so shocked."

Dr. Jasper laughed, too. "When clients come in and tell me so much has happened, they're usually talking about their feelings. Not the makings for a made-for-TV movie. Which makes me think we should start with your feelings. You only directly referenced them once."

"I was happy?"

"Yes, that's the one." The therapist leaned back in her chair, looking comfortable as a cat. "Tell me about it."

Mira clasped her hands tightly in her lap. "I was glad to be alive. For the first time since the storm I was glad I didn't die with Jeff."

She paused, guilt and shame rising up in her. She fought them off. "It doesn't mean I'm glad Jeff's dead, does it? Isn't it okay to want to live?"

Without speaking, the therapist handed Mira the box of tissues she hadn't even realized she needed. She plucked one from the box and blew her nose. "It was the most wonderful feeling. I don't know if I can describe it."

"Try."

She searched for the right words. "It was like I'd been wearing this heavy, dark cloud. No," she corrected herself, "a shroud, that's what it was." Mira stopped, allowing the aptness of her own description to sink in. "Like I'd been dead," she murmured, "and at that moment had come back to life."

"Like Christ?"

"No." Mira looked at her and shook her head. "Like Lazarus."

The therapist nodded. "If I remember my Sunday-morning lessons correctly, Jesus brought Lazarus back to life."

"Yes. It was one of his miracles."

"So who brought *you* back to life?"

The question smacked her in the face. Connor? Nola? Her fear? The circumstances?

All of the above?

"I'm not sure. Maybe it was just time?"

"It *was* time, but time wasn't the catalyst. Tell me how it happened."

Too antsy to sit, Mira stood, crossed to the window, then turned back to the therapist.

Mira told her first about Preacher and her necklace, the words coming out in a rush. Then about reconnecting with Connor and his bringing her the dog for protection. "I was so pissed at him. I didn't want another dog. I wasn't about to fall in love with her. So I left her in the courtyard for the night.

"Her barking woke me up. When I went to see what was wrong, I smelled Jeff's aftershave."

"Are you certain?"

"Ralph Lauren's Polo Blue. He never wore anything else. For a moment, I was lost in memories and I almost imagined he was there, you know? Like I'd just awakened from a bad dream and it was . . . finally over."

"Then what?"

"I heard the sound of a door shutting and I knew . . . I wasn't alone. That someone had broken in, the way Preacher had."

Dr. Jasper made a note, then met her eyes. "Go on."

"I was terrified. I ran to get Nola. She was suddenly quiet and I was so afraid that I'd lost her, too."

Mira's voice cracked. "When I saw she was okay, something happened, like a switch flipping inside me. I was a deranged person. Laughing and crying, giddy and silly, even though just a moment before I'd been terrified."

Dr. Jasper laid aside her pen and pad and leaned toward her. "As a therapist, my job's not to draw conclusions for you, but to help you draw your own conclusions. If you were the therapist here, and I your client, how would you help me do that?"

"I don't understand."

"Everything you need is in the story. Let's pretend for the moment that none of that really happened. It was all a dream, or a creation of your subconscious. What are the important elements of the story?"

"Smelling Jeff's aftershave for sure. The way that made me feel."

"And then?"

"The sound of the door closing, snapping me back to reality. The realization that I wasn't alone."

"Go on."

"My fear of losing Nola. My joy to find her alive and unharmed."

Alive. Unharmed. Her overwhelming joy at being alive.

The therapist went on. "You say that nothing was taken, all the doors and windows were locked from the inside?"

"You're suggesting no one was there? That it was my subconscious creating it all?" Mira shook her head. "Nola was barking."

"Was she?"

"Yes! That's what woke me. It is, I . . ." Her voice trailed off, she crossed over to the sofa and sank back onto it. When had she noticed Nola wasn't barking anymore? The moment she climbed out of bed? When she reached the hall and smelled Jeff's aftershave? Or when she heard the door click shut?

"Did you know that of all our sensory memories, those associated with the sense of smell are the strongest? A smell can bring us back to a place or time, inspire us to relive the feelings associated with that time, better than anything else."

Mira shook her head and Dr. Jasper continued. "And what of the sound of a door closing? Other than the obvious, what could that mean?"

"An ending. A departure." She made a sound of frustration. "I see where you're going with this. But I know what I heard."

The therapist glanced at her notes. "In that moment, you said, you knew you weren't alone."

"That's right. Someone was in my house!"

"Those were your words, Mira. And they're powerful. Symbolically powerful."

Tears flooded her eyes and she shook her head in denial. She wasn't ready for this. "No," she said. "No."

Dr. Jasper reached across the table between them and

grasped her hands. "A door was open, in your mind. And there was Jeff. You relived him through your sensory memory." She tightened her fingers. "Then you shut the door. Because you knew you weren't alone. Not anymore."

Tears trickled down her cheeks. "I ran for Nola."

"And when you thought something had happened to her, you panicked. You were terrified." She squeezed, then released, Mira's hands. "You're choosing the present, Mira. You're letting someone—something—into your life and you want to live."

She was. It was so obvious.

"What did you do then?"

"I called Connor. I wanted to share my happiness with—" Mira bit the last back.

"I think that's significant, don't you?"

She did. But she wasn't ready to admit it. They finished out their hour in silence. When it was up, Dr. Jasper walked her to the door. There, she gave her a quick hug. Hands on her shoulders, she looked her in the eyes. "Be careful, Mira. It's good to feel again. It's important. But it's easy to be hurt."

Chapter Thirty-four

Anton Gallier had lived well. His home was of the same ilk as Scott's, only grander. Bayle parked on the street in front of the man's St. Charles Avenue mansion. Malone stepped out of the vehicle, his gaze settling on the home before him. In New Orleans, there were pieces of ground, the structures that sat upon them, so rarefied that only royalty could reside there. The Big Easy's own brand of royalty.

Anton Gallier's home was one of those. Neither newcomer nor Yankee would be allowed the honor of owning such a home. A smart guy could come to town, he could buy car dealerships and professional sports teams, could even become the mayor, but he could not possess this house or the pedigree that went along with it. Rumor had it that the actor Nicolas Cage had attempted to buy such a property and was shut out.

Malone didn't doubt other cities had similar unwritten rules, but he couldn't imagine it being as ingrained as it was here. In New Orleans, some things were simply not done. These gems were passed down within families and through marriage. Period. End of story.

Malone swept his gaze over the property. Spanning a half block on arguably one of the most beautiful avenues in the

United States, it represented the Old South. A privileged existence where one class did not mix with another, where the help was ever-present but unacknowledged, and real life, as experienced by everyone else, rarely came knocking.

It was coming to call today.

Malone and Bayle stopped at the iron gate. Gallier had a sophisticated video intercom. They pressed the call button.

"NOPD detectives here to see Mrs. Gallier." They held their shields up to the camera.

A moment later the iron gate swung open and they made their way through and up the tree-lined walk to the front door.

They were greeted by a uniformed houseman. The man held out an envelope. "Mrs. Gallier asked me to give you this and to thank you for your service."

"What's this?" Malone asked.

"Mr. and Mrs. Gallier's annual contribution to the benevolence fund."

Typical. Money was the answer to everything. He saw by Bayle's expression that she was thinking the same thing. "Go tell Mrs. Gallier we're not here for a donation. It's official business and a serious matter."

Something akin to glee lit the houseman's eyes, then was gone. "One moment."

As he walked away, Bayle said, "I get the feeling he looks for ways to fuck up her day."

"You got that, too?"

"Oh, yeah." She motioned around them. "Are you believing this? Makes my place look like a hand-me-down dollhouse for trolls."

He chuckled. "Tell me about it."

The butler reappeared and indicated that they should follow him. He escorted them to a room filled with Mardi Gras memorabilia. Not the cheap trinkets tossed from floats to the masses, but collectibles in glass display cases: crowns and scepters, jeweled masks, elaborate invitations and dance cards.

The New Orleans elite took Mardi Gras very seriously. To be named the King of Rex was a monumental achievement.

The young woman anointed his royal consort was also bestowed a huge honor—never mind that Rex was always some rich geezer, old enough to be her father. The parents of the lucky young woman spent tens of thousands of dollars on the honor. Parties were thrown, gowns purchased, votes ensured. None of it came cheap.

Apparently, Charlotte Gallier had been been Rex's consort in 1968. She had the photograph, crown and scepter to prove it.

"Ma'am, Detectives Malone and Bayle." She waved them in but didn't look up from what appeared to be thank-you notes she was writing.

"Mrs. Gallier," Malone began. "We—"

She held up a hand, stopping him. "One moment, please."

How like royalty, Malone thought, deciding to grant her the moments so he could use the time to study more of the room's interior. He was drawn to a grouping of photographs of the Krewe of Rex and its court going back at least a century.

He wandered over to a display of shadowboxes on the wall to his left. Cloisonné doubloons and real glass beads. From the time before made-in-China plastic beads and cheap aluminum doubloons. Amazing.

"Excuse me, Detective, what are you doing?"

"I've heard about these," he said, indicating the shadowboxes and their contents. "But I've never seen any."

"They're quite rare." She folded her hands in front of her. "How can I help you, Officers?"

"Detectives," he corrected. "I'm afraid we have some bad news."

She waited, though she barely looked interested. He wondered how she would react, if at all.

"Mrs. Gallier, your husband was murdered this morning. I'm very sorry."

She blinked three times; her lips trembled. "Oh my, that is bad news."

That was it. He glanced at Bayle. She was as blown away as he was.

"We're eager to find his killer. To that end, we need to ask you a few questions."

"Of course." She cleared her throat. "Can you tell me how he . . . how they did it."

"He was shot. In an elevator in the French Quarter."

"I see."

"Did you know he kept a second residence?"

"The apartment on Royal Street? Yes, I knew. It's the company's apartment."

Malone took a spiral notebook from his breast pocket. "When did you last see him, ma'am?"

"Yesterday morning when he left for work. He had business last night."

Monkey business.

Bayle stepped in. "Mrs. Gallier, are you aware your husband had a mistress?"

"Of course." She said it matter-of-factly. "We had no secrets from one another."

"And that was okay with you? You didn't care?"

"His dalliances meant nothing. I'm certain you can't understand, but he and I are partners. Much like you two are. We watched out for each other, always."

"You didn't worry that he'd leave you? Ask for a divorce?"

The way she looked at Bayle was condescending. "He would never have left me. Nor I him."

"Where were you this morning, Mrs. Gallier?"

"Here. I haven't left the house yet today. Now I'll have to."

"Is there anyone who could corroborate that?"

"Any number of the help."

"May we have permission to speak with them?"

"Certainly."

"Did he have any enemies?" Bayle asked.

The woman looked at her. "He was very rich, Detective. Very powerful. He had many enemies."

How different her response and Jaz's to the very same question, Malone thought. Interesting, too, her lack of embarrassment. Money equaled power. Power bred contempt.

And the earth revolved around the sun. Just the way it should.

"Let me rephrase that, Mrs. Gallier. Anybody want to kill him?"

She laughed, the sound brittle. "I imagine so, perhaps fantasizing about doing it. But to actually pull the trigger?"

She drummed her fingers on the desk. "My money would be on that little tart my son was married to. Just the other day, she threatened Anton. Barged into his club and did it in front of everyone. It was very ugly. Connor Scott was there as well. Everyone's talking about it."

And now they would be talking about this. "You called your daughter-in-law a tart. Was she cheating on your son?"

"Not that I know of."

"Is there a reason you and your husband disapproved of her?"

She made a dismissive gesture with her hands. "He married beneath himself, Detective. She had nothing and was nobody. A stained-glass artist? Dear God, please."

"Do you believe she killed your son?" Bayle asked.

"I wasn't as convinced as Anton; they did seem happy with each other. But now, with this . . . She got away with it once, so she did it again. Isn't that what these people do?"

"These people, ma'am?"

"Criminals. Murderers. First my son—" Her voice grew so thick she could hardly speak. "Now my husband. I'm alone now, Detectives. Completely alone."

Neither Malone nor Bayle had any more questions, and with her permission they questioned the staff. They learned she had been telling the truth—she hadn't left the house since the evening before.

As they buckled into her Taurus, Bayle said, "I don't think that woman has a heart."

"Either that or ice water runs in her veins."

Bayle eased into traffic. "Can you imagine that being your mother?"

"I can't. My mother's Italian, she's got plenty of fire. All that icy restraint, hell no." He laughed. "If she found out my dad was having an affair, that little woman would have killed him."

"Exactly. Thank you." She took a left to cross the neutral ground, stopping for a streetcar rumbling past. "Rich people, I swear."

He waited for her to say more, but she didn't. After a couple moments, he unclipped his cell phone. "I'll see where Percy's at and let him know we're on our way."

Chapter Thirty-five

Mira left the studio early, realizing after she had screwed up four consecutive breaks and sliced her finger open that it'd be safer for everyone if she went home. She couldn't stop thinking about the things Dr. Jasper had suggested. They played over in her head, stealing her ability to concentrate on anything else.

Was she closing the door on the past and on Jeff? Had the entire event been a creation of her subconscious: Nola barking, the sound of the door clicking shut, the smell of Jeff's aftershave?

It had all been so real.

"You're choosing the present, Mira. You're letting someone—or something—into your life and you want to live."

She turned onto her street, mind racing. She recalled Dr. Jasper's final warning about it being easy to be hurt. The words, something about the way she had said them, had sounded like a threat. They had certainly affected her like one, sending a shiver of apprehension up her spine.

Why would Dr. Jasper threaten her?

She wouldn't. Period. Another case of her runaway imagination.

She rounded the corner, Mrs. Latrobe's house coming into view. *Nola barking.* Of course. That's why she had gotten out of bed. She'd been afraid her cranky neighbor would be awakened.

Mira stopped in front of her neighbor's house and stepped out onto the sidewalk and into the blinding sunlight and suffocating heat.

She hardly noticed as she hurried up the walk to her neighbor's front door. She rang the bell. A moment later, the woman responded. Dressed in a crisp hourglass suit and pillbox hat, she was like a picture out of a 1950s *Life* magazine. Except for the baby blue slippers on her feet.

"Hi, Mrs. Latrobe," she said. "I'm Mira Gallier, your neighbor from next door."

"Just because I'm old doesn't mean I'm addled. I know who you are."

"Right." Mira cleared her throat. "I just wanted to apologize if my dog's barking woke you up."

"A dog?" The woman frowned. "I expect you'll keep the animal leashed."

"Of course, Mrs. Latrobe. And again, if she woke you up last night, I apologize."

"No, thank goodness." She narrowed her eyes. "But what has bothered me is the comings and goings over at your place all hours of the day and night."

"If you're talking about the police, I had an intruder—"

"And the men! It's not proper. I'm sure your poor husband is turning over in his grave."

Angry heat climbed Mira's cheeks. Several sharp retorts sprang to her lips, but she swallowed them as the image of the woman's hat, gloves, and house slippers filled her head. Nothing would be gained by pointing out that she was the one who should be ashamed for spying and jumping to nasty conclusions. Nor would she believe in Mira's innocence, even if she proclaimed it.

Mira took a step backward. "I'm glad you weren't awakened by Nola. Excuse me, Mrs. Latrobe. You have a good day." She turned and started back to her car.

"If it's one of those kind of dogs, I suggest you muzzle it," the woman called after her.

Mira held her tongue, though she wanted to defend Nola with every fiber of her being. Funny how the urge to defend her pet was stronger than the urge to defend herself.

She reached her Focus, climbed in and started the engine. In the short time the car had been off, the interior had become like an oven.

She set the air on high and sat with cool air blasting her face.

Mrs. Latrobe hadn't heard Nola.

But why? Because the dog hadn't been barking? Or because her neighbor simply hadn't heard?

Mira had a hard time believing her nosy neighbor would have slept through the jarring barkathon she had awakened to.

Jarring, she thought. Her choice of description fit Dr. Jasper's theory—to be jarred awake was sort of like getting a kick in the butt to get busy.

As she parked in her driveway, a car pulled in behind her. A police cruiser. A uniformed officer alighted from the driver's side and walked toward her.

She lowered her window. "Can I help you?" she asked.

"Mira Gallier?"

"Yes."

"Officer Gonzales, NOPD." He held up his shield.

After inspecting it, Mira lifted her gaze back to his. "How can I help you?" she asked again.

"You need to come with me, ma'am."

"Where?" She frowned. "Why?"

"To police headquarters. For questioning."

"Questioning," she repeated. "About what?"

"I don't know, ma'am."

She hesitated. "I should let my dog out. She's been cooped up since early this morning."

"I'm sorry, ma'am. I was ordered to bring you directly downtown."

Mira glanced at the house, then back at the officer. "I'll follow you in my car."

"I was told I had to bring you in myself."

A queasy feeling settled in the pit of her gut. He held the cruiser's back door open, then slammed it behind her. She breathed deeply, trying to calm herself.

Another first for her—riding in the back of a police car. At least she wasn't handcuffed.

By the time they reached Perdido Street and NOPD headquarters, she had worked herself into a bundle of raw nerves. If someone had come up behind her and shouted "Boo!" she probably would have had a heart attack.

Her escort radioed that they had arrived. A detective who looked remarkably like Spencer Malone greeted her.

"Ms. Gallier? Detective Percy Malone."

"I've talked to another Detective Malone. Your brother, I'm guessing."

He smiled. "Spencer. One of my brothers. I have four of them."

"Four? Oh, my."

"It gets better. Most of us are cops."

"I see the family resemblance."

He grinned. "But I got the looks and the height."

"And what did he get?"

"A wicked right hook."

She began to relax and smiled weakly. "Funny."

"Yeah, I got that, too." He motioned ahead. "Come this way and we'll get this over with as soon as possible."

"I don't have a car. The officer wouldn't let me drive."

"Standard procedure. Don't worry, we'll give you a lift home." He stopped and swung open a door marked with a *2*. The room was bare except for a table and three chairs.

"Home sweet home."

She swallowed hard. "Why am I here, Detective Malone?"

"For questioning."

"About what?"

"Let me get us all set up, then we can have a nice chat."

She hugged herself, the beginning of a headache at her temples. Why did she think this experience was going to be anything but nice?

"Have a seat." He crossed to the corner of the room, reached up and switched on a camera mounted in the corner. A tiny green light illuminated. "You married, Ms. Gallier?"

"Was. He died in Katrina."

"Oh, man. I'm sorry."

"How about you?"

"Still fishing. But Spencer's getting hitched. You have a big wedding?" He crossed to the opposite corner, did the same as before. Again, a green light illuminated.

She rubbed her temples. Something about this felt very wrong. "No, eloped. Vegas."

"I wish he'd gone that route. This thing's turning into a whole lot of trouble. I'm gonna have to wear a tuxedo and make a toast."

It sunk in what he was doing. "You're recording this?"

"For your protection and ours."

"I'm not under arrest, am I?"

"Not at all. Now why would you think that, Ms. Gallier?"

She cocked an eyebrow, unconvinced by his good-ole-boy routine. "Well, let's see. A police officer shows up at my door, insists I come here with him, won't even give me time to let my dog out to pee and now I'm sitting in a small, windowless room with two video cameras pointing at me."

"Did he cuff you or read you your rights?"

"No."

"There you go, not under arrest."

He shot her a knock-your-socks-off smile, but she wasn't distracted. "Why am I here, Detective?"

"For questioning. About a murder."

"A murder," she repeated. "Preacher's?"

"No, ma'am. Your father-in-law. Anton Gallier."

She stared at him, thunderstruck. When she could find her voice, she said, "You must be mistaken. I just saw him on Saturday."

"He was shot to death this morning."

"My God."

"I'm sorry for your loss."

A dozen different memories flew to her mind, none of them good. She met the detective's gaze. "There was no love lost between me and my father-in-law, Detective. But I think you already know that."

"Where were you this morning, Ms. Gallier?"

Cold, she rubbed her arms. "What time this morning?"

"Between six and ten."

"I got up about six o'clock, took my dog for a long walk, ate, dressed and called my therapist to beg her to fit me in today."

"And was she able to?"

"Yes. She gave up her lunch hour."

"Her name?"

"Dr. Adele Jasper."

"Why do you see her, Ms. Gallier?"

"None of your damn business."

"'He cast out Seven Demons.'"

"Excuse me?"

He repeated it, then asked, "Does that mean anything to you?"

Her expression altered slightly. "It's from the Bible. It refers to Christ's casting out of the Seven Demons that possessed Mary Magdalene."

"Wow, I'm impressed. You knew it just like that." He smiled. "You must have spent a whole lot of time in Sunday school."

"Actually, I spent the last year restoring the windows of Our Lady of Perpetual Sorrows Catholic Church. The centerpiece of those is the image of Mary Magdalene at the foot of the cross. With any historical restoration comes a massive amount of research."

"I don't understand. How would research make a difference in a restoration?"

"Because the art of stained glass is considered the work of craftsmen instead of artists, it's mostly anonymous. So I dig, find every reference I can to the church in question, the creation of its windows, unearth any photographs that exist of the window."

"And that led you to the Bible?"

"Yes. And no. I was really taken with her."

"Her? You mean Mary Magdalene?"

Mira nodded and went on. "And I wanted to know more. So I read everything I could find about her." She cocked her head. "Haven't you ever been fascinated by a historical figure?"

"Not that fascinated. Unless Michael Jordan counts." He smiled again, and again she wasn't buying. "These demons, what do you know about them?"

"Nothing. The Bible doesn't say."

"And none of the other books you read did, either?"

"No. We just know that they were causing her to sin. Why so interested, Detective?"

He ignored her question and went on. "I understand you recently had an argument with Anton Gallier."

They knew about the fight. With a sense of horror, she recalled her and Anton's exchange. She couldn't remember what she had said but knew it had been ugly. That it would incriminate her.

It would make her a suspect.

"I'd like to speak with my lawyer before I say any more."

"Of course." He smiled slightly. "If you feel that's necessary?"

The way he said the words made her feel guilty. Which was what he intended. He hoped to manipulate her with the emotion.

She wasn't falling for it. "It's my right." She returned his slight smile and repeated his words from earlier. "Set up for my protection and yours."

Chapter Thirty-six

"She's nobody's fool," Spencer said, taking his eyes from the video monitor to look at Bayle. "Didn't fall for our bullshit."

Lawyering up was the smartest thing she could have done, which is why they hated it. It's why they always played the if-you-really-think-it's-necessary card. Oldest trick in the book.

"She made the call," Percy said, stepping into the viewing room and shutting the door behind him. "Sorry I couldn't hold her off longer."

Malone turned to his brother to comment, but Bayle beat him to it. "I'm surprised she waited as long as she did. This isn't her first rodeo."

"She seemed genuinely shocked by news of his death," Percy said. "Though I've seen some award-winning performances over the years."

"Who else looks good?" Bayle asked.

"Who doesn't?" Spencer flipped through his notes. "By most accounts, the man was a complete bastard. Universally disliked, feared but respected."

"Respected?"

"For being such a bastard. Weird shit, huh? Even his wife was proud." Spencer poured himself a cup of coffee. He took a sip from the Styrofoam cup, made a face and set it on the table. "What about Connor Scott? Charlotte Gallier said he was at the club with Mira and witnessed their argument."

Percy flipped through the pages of his notepad. "More than witnessed. Anton Gallier got into it with him, too. According to witnesses, Scott looked pissed but pulled himself together and walked. The victim was challenging him to 'tell Mira the truth.' Something about why he joined up."

"Maybe he felt the need to shut the man up—permanently," Malone suggested. "It makes sense."

"Let's pick him up, bring him in."

A uniformed officer stuck his head in the door. "Gallier's lawyer's arrived. He's in with her now."

"You want me to continue?" Percy asked.

Spencer thought it would be for the best and Bayle concurred. Twenty minutes later, the recorder was on and transmitting. Malone recognized the lawyer. Lance Arnold. A solid player in the criminal defense community, known for being deliberate rather than flashy.

Percy began. "When was the last time you saw Anton Gallier?"

"Saturday. Midday."

"Can you describe that meeting?"

"Unpleasant. Very."

"Why?"

"Truthfully? Every interaction I had with him was unpleasant."

"Why's that?"

"He believed I killed his son." She laced her fingers together. "He'd made it his mission in life to ruin mine."

"In what way?"

"Ways," she corrected. "First he tried to have me charged with murder. When that wasn't successful, he attempted a civil suit. His latest was a post-Katrina documentary. He used his influence with the local PBS affiliate to broadcast barely veiled accusations against me."

"He owned the station, is that correct?"

"Yes." She rubbed her temple. "The reporter who'd done a segment on me gave me a heads-up. It was airing that night. She brought me a disc."

"So you watched it?"

"Yes."

"And you were angry. Furious, even."

The lawyer cut in. "You're putting words in her mouth, Detective. How about letting her tell you how she felt?"

"Sure." Percy held up his hands. "My mistake. Ms. Gallier, how did you feel after viewing the piece?"

"At first, overwhelmed. Hopeless."

Her emotions played easily on her face. Like an open book, Spencer thought, staring at the monitor. Emotionally, anyway.

She went on. "I felt like, what's the point of even trying to fight him? He was rich and powerful. But then I—"

She didn't finish the thought, but Percy didn't give her the out. "What, Ms. Gallier?"

She drew a deep breath. "Then I got mad. Really mad."

"Understandable." Percy nodded. "He'd been a thorn in your side for a long time."

"From the beginning."

Her lawyer cleared his throat in warning.

Percy pretended he didn't hear it and pressed on. "I'm sure you wanted nothing more than to get him out of your life once and for all."

"Detective," Arnold snapped, "I don't think—"

Gallier laid a hand on his arm, stopping him. "Yes, I would have loved not to ever have to deal with him again. But not like this. Not enough to want him dead."

"Really?" Percy glanced at his notes. "You threatened him."

"Not really." She glanced at her lawyer. "I don't feel like I did. I just told him I wouldn't let him drag me down anymore."

"No, Ms. Gallier. You did threaten him. I interviewed his lunch companions, they all confirmed it."

"What did I say?"

Percy looked at his notes again. "The victim said, 'What are you going to do, little girl? Kill me?' And you replied, 'Maybe I should. I doubt anyone would miss you.' That sounds like a threat to me."

"I was just mad. He laughed at me and I—"

The lawyer cut her off. "The heat of the moment, Detective. People say things like that all the time. Do you have anything else specific to ask her?"

"Tell me about your relationship with Connor Scott."

"Connor?" She looked confused at the change of direction. "We're old friends."

"He just reappeared in your life, is that right?"

"Yes." Malone noticed that she flexed her fingers. "He was serving in the military."

"A marine?" She nodded and he went on. "I understand he was with you at the Crescent City Club."

"No. He followed me there."

"Followed you. That seems a little weird."

"Not really. He was worried about me. He knows how Anton can be. Could be," she corrected.

"And how's that?"

"Mean," she said simply.

"Mean?" Percy repeated. "Lots of people are mean. Kids are mean. Still seems a little extreme to follow you. You're a grown woman."

"True." She shifted in her seat. "But Anton had a special gift for cruelty. And Connor knew how upset I was."

"Just how upset were you, Ms. Gallier?"

The lawyer stepped in. "I think we already established that. Let's move on."

"Was he afraid of what you might do? Is that why he followed you?"

"Detective!" Arnold said sharply. "Again, already established."

Spencer smiled as Percy continued without missing a beat. "I understand that Connor and Mr. Gallier got into it?"

"Anton was taunting him."

"About what?"

She shifted in her seat again, looking, Malone thought, decidedly uncomfortable. "I don't know."

"You were there, weren't you?"

"Yes. But Anton had been drinking and he didn't make a lot of sense. I don't know what he was talking about."

Malone glanced at Bayle. She had her gaze fixed on the monitor. He wondered if she too was thinking that Gallier was protecting Scott. But why?

He returned his attention to the interview in process. His brother was jogging her memory.

"According to witnesses, Ms. Gallier, your father-in-law challenged Scott to tell you 'the real reason he joined up.' Is that right?"

"I guess," she said.

"Yes, he said that? Or no, he did not?"

"Okay, yes. He did say that. A couple times, actually."

"And did Mr. Scott share the reason he joined the marines?"

"At that moment?"

"Then, before, or after? Has he shared it with you?"

She hesitated. "He told me it was a personal reason."

"And he shared what that personal reason was?"

She hesitated again and Malone knew the answer: he had not.

"Yes or no?"

"No, he did not."

"What's he hiding from you?"

"Nothing. It's not like that."

"Really? Old friends like the two of you are, and you don't know why he packed up and joined the military?"

She tilted up her chin. "Some things are intensely private, Detective. I get that. There's a difference between hiding something and just not wanting to share it."

"Is there?"

"Yes!" she cried and got to her feet. "And you know it! Stop playing with me."

"Maybe I'm not the one who's playing with you."

The lawyer caught her arm and eased her back to her seat. Spencer saw that Gallier was shaking. "I think we're done here," the attorney said.

"One last thing, if you don't mind. Mr. Gallier accused your friend Connor of being glad your husband was dead. Do you recall that?"

She nodded. "But it's not true. Jeff and Connor were best friends."

"Why do you think he said that?"

She lifted her gaze. Malone saw she was crying. "Because he was drunk. And bitter and angry and as mean as a snake. And because he couldn't let go of Jeff. He couldn't accept he was dead and move on."

"What about you, Ms. Gallier? Have you been able to move on?"

Chapter Thirty-seven

When the detectives released Mira from questioning, it took all her energy to stand, then put one foot in front of the other. She felt as if she had been hit by an SDT garbage truck. Hit and run smack over.

Garbage truck, she thought. That fit.

As if he sensed how close to collapsing she was, the lawyer kept a hand on her elbow. He steered her into the empty, waiting elevator car. He had been her stalwart champion through both Anton's attempt at a criminal charge and the civil suit that followed. She trusted him completely.

"How much trouble am I in?" she asked.

"They've got nothing but suspicions. You had a motive, a compelling one. Of course they're going to question you."

A compelling motive. A public argument and a threat. She was surprised they hadn't locked her up.

"I can't believe this is happening. It's such a nightmare."

He patted her shoulder. "Anton Gallier had lots of enemies. They'll find who did this."

But what if they didn't? she wondered. Would this continue to shadow her, the way her in-laws' claims had? Would she ever again have a slate unclouded by suspicion?

The elevator stuttered to a stop. The doors slid open and they stepped off. "We should talk some more," Lance said.

"I agree. But not now, okay?"

"The morning's fine. I don't think you're in any danger of being arrested. Rest well tonight, we'll talk then."

"Thanks, Lance. And now, I hate to ask, but could you give me a lift home?"

"Mira!"

She turned. Chris was hurrying across the lobby toward her. Her eyes flooded with tears of gratitude.

She ran toward him and threw herself in his arms. She clung to him and he held her tightly. "Thank you," she said. "Thank you for coming."

"Deni had her evening class. We wanted to make sure you were okay." He set her away from him so he could look her in the eyes. "Are you okay?"

"Define *okay*." When alarm raced into his eyes, she nodded. "I'm fine."

The lawyer came over. Mira introduced them. The men shook hands, then Lance turned to her. "You still need that lift home?"

She looked hopefully at Chris. As much as she appreciated Lance's expertise, he was her attorney, not her friend. And at this moment, being with a friend was what she needed.

"How about I drive you?" Chris said. "I'd like to, really."

A couple minutes later, Mira and Chris were climbing into his battered Ford pickup truck. After giving him directions, she sighed and rested her head against the seat back. The truck sputtered to life and she glanced in his direction. "How did you know I was here?"

"We heard about your father-in-law's murder on TV. Deni couldn't reach you on your cell or at home, so she figured the worst. To be certain, she called your lawyer's office. When his secretary told her he was at police headquarters, we knew for sure."

"My saviors." She closed her eyes a moment, then looked at him again. "Thanks for coming for me."

He met her gaze. "Of course I would, Mira."

Something in his eyes felt deeper than friendship. She looked quickly away. "Deni's a lucky girl."

"She doesn't always think so."

"Really? I haven't picked up on that. She seems happy."

He lifted a shoulder. "It's about my beliefs. See this ring? It's a promise ring. I vowed to wait until marriage."

She almost asked "For what?" then realized he meant remain celibate. She'd heard of the rings; they were in the news when the pop trio the Jonas Brothers started wearing them. But still, it ran so counter to popular thinking, she wasn't sure what to say.

"I've surprised you." She didn't deny it and he went on. "She thinks it means I don't want her. But I made a promise and I've lasted this long, I'm not going back on it now."

"I admire you sticking to your convictions. Not many people do."

He didn't reply and she closed her eyes again. She found the rumble and hum of the pickup melodic. And calming.

The way she found Chris. Calming. Centered. Grounded for a young man his age. She opened her eyes and asked him about it.

"You really want to know?"

"I wouldn't have asked if I didn't."

"It's not a pretty story. I saw a lot of bad stuff growing up. Death was a way of life. I learned that early."

"Where was that, Chris?"

"Edge of Gert Town, in Mid-City. Most of the guys I came up with got hooked up with gangs. And drugs. They're all dead now."

"I'm so sorry."

He shrugged again. "I could have gone that way."

"Why didn't you?"

"I grew up without a dad. Life was tough. My family depended on me."

"I'd bet there're a lot of gangbangers out there with the same story. Why're you different?"

"Don't know. Lucky? Blessed, maybe? It's one of the reasons for the promise ring."

It made sense, she thought. He'd saved his life by being different from the people around him.

He smiled at her. "What was your childhood like?"

"We didn't have much. It was just my mom, sister and I. We worked hard, depended on one another. I wouldn't change a thing about it."

"That's the way I feel," he said, sounding pleased. "Simple but beautiful. Katrina made me realize that even more. Made me aware of time and how precious—how important—every day is."

Her eyes filled with tears. His expression puckered with regret. "Geez, Mira, I'm sorry. I didn't mean—"

"It's okay. Katrina made me realize the same thing. Life is short." They fell silent once more. After a block, she said, "Frenchmen's up ahead. You'll take a left."

When he'd done as she directed, she added, "Mine's up on the right."

As his truck rattled to a stop, Mrs. Latrobe's side light snapped on.

"My neighbor's a little cranky. I sometimes think she wishes I'd died with Jeff."

As the words left her lips, she regretted them. "That sounded horrible. She's old and lonely, I should cut her some slack."

He climbed out of the truck. "Is that her?"

Mira looked over. Sure enough, there was Louise Latrobe at her window. Mira waved. The woman didn't return the greeting, just continued to stare.

Give her the benefit of the doubt, Mira. Maybe she can't see well enough to know you waved.

"I'll walk you to the door."

"That's not necessary, Chris. Really."

"Yes, it is. A gentleman makes sure a lady makes it safely inside."

She smiled. Another anachronism. He was one surprising young man.

When they reached her front door, Mira heard Nola on the

other side, snuffling and whining, anxious to see her. And, no doubt, to relieve herself.

Mira unlocked the door, then turned back to Chris. "Thank you so much. You don't know how much it meant to me that you were there."

She stood on tiptoes and kissed his cheek. "Tell Deni thanks, too. Tell her I love her and I'll be in as soon as I can in the morning."

"Sure." He started off, then stopped. "Mira?"

She looked back in question. He seemed uncertain what he had wanted to say. After a moment, he said simply, "Sleep well."

Chapter Thirty-eight

Malone sat across from Connor Scott. The man looked at once on alert and completely relaxed, no easy feat. Malone figured it was the military training.

"I suppose you're wondering why we called you in for questioning," he began.

"Not really." Scott moved his gaze between him and Bayle. "Anton Gallier was murdered and he and I had a skirmish three days ago. Seems reasonable you'd want to talk to me."

Smart guy. "Glad we're on the same page. How well did you know Anton Gallier?" he asked.

"Fairly well."

"How's that?"

"I was best friends with his son, Jeff. We went to prep school together, then university. I spent a lot of time at Jeff's house and he at mine."

"What was your opinion of Mr. Gallier?"

"He was smart. A skilled businessman. A political animal of the highest order."

"Meaning?"

"He knew how to get things done. Whose palm to grease to make things happen."

"So you liked him?"

Scott laughed, the sound humorless. "Hell, no. He was a prick. Jeff thought so, too. He hated his old man."

"That's pretty strong."

"It's true."

Malone let seconds of silence tick by, waiting for Scott to look away or shift uncomfortably in his seat, anything.

Scott didn't react at all.

"Where were you this morning between six and ten?"

"Running."

Malone arched his eyebrows. "The entire time?"

"No, from about six thirty to eight."

"Where did you run?"

"St. Charles streetcar line, from my house to Carrollton and back."

"Anybody see you?"

"I'm sure they did, Detective."

Malone struggled to keep his frustration at bay. "Anyone you know?"

"Not that I recognized."

"What did you do from eight to ten?"

"Returned home. Showered. Ate breakfast. Answered e-mail."

"Did you interact with anyone there?"

"The household staff."

Malone made a note, then looked back up at Scott. "Three days before Gallier's murder you two got into it at the Crescent City Club?"

"I guess you could call it that."

"What would you call it?"

Scott shrugged. "One of those things. It happens."

"And when 'one of those things' happens, does somebody end up dead?"

"One has nothing to do with the other. Obviously."

"Maybe not so obvious, Mr. Scott." Malone flipped through his notes, more for show than because he needed to refresh his memory. "Tell me, why were you at the Crescent City Club that day?"

Malone noticed the other man stiffen slightly. "To back Mira up."

"Why would she have needed backing up?"

"Why don't you ask her?"

"We already have. Now we want your version."

"I was at her studio when she learned Anton had manipulated the Katrina documentary to make her look bad. She was going to call him out on it."

"She was angry."

"Do you blame her?"

"That's a yes, then."

"Yes, she was angry. She said she wasn't going to let him beat her."

"Did you take that as a threat against Mr. Gallier?"

"Not at all." He shook his head, as if for emphasis. "I didn't want her to face him alone."

"Yet you arrived separately?"

"She refused my offer of help."

"You followed her anyway. Why?"

"I thought she needed me."

"You have a special relationship with Ms. Gallier, don't you?"

"We're friends. Old friends."

"And that's all?"

Malone noticed that for the first time, Scott shifted his gaze. "Yes."

"What was happening when you arrived?"

"Anton was threatening her. I told him to stop."

"Threatening? With bodily harm?"

Scott smiled grimly. "That wasn't Anton's way. His attack was more insidious."

"How would you describe it?"

"Emotional and psychological torture. He was very good at it."

"Then Gallier turned his attack on you, is that right?"

"He was drunk."

"That wasn't my question. He turned his attack on you."

"Yes."

Malone shuffled through his notes. "According to witnesses, Gallier accused you of 'being glad' Jeff was dead. What did he mean by that?"

"I'm sure I don't know."

"Bullshit. You know."

"Prove it."

"Is it true?"

"Is what true?"

"Are you glad your friend is dead?"

"No. It's not true."

"I think you're lying."

"Think whatever you like. It's your right."

Malone opened the file folder. He slid the top page across the table to Scott. "What is that in reference to?"

" 'He cast out Seven Demons'? No clue." He slid it back.

"Is it biblical?"

"Like I said, no clue."

"How about these?" He slid two more sheets across the table, reading them aloud as he did. " 'He will come again to judge the living and the dead' and 'Jugment Day'?"

Scott cocked an eyebrow. "What it refers to? I think it's pretty obvious."

"Humor me."

"It refers to the Judeo-Christian belief in heaven and hell and a God who decides who goes where." He glanced at the printed words. "And, just so you know, you spelled judgment wrong."

"Pardon?"

"Left out the *d*." Scott tapped the page.

Spencer looked at it and feigned surprise. "That I did. Thanks for pointing it out." He refocused on Scott's confrontation with Anton Gallier. "What was Gallier urging you to tell his daughter-in-law?"

"I have no idea."

"Why'd you join the marines?"

"I had my reasons."

"I'd like to know what they were."

"Too bad. It's none of your business and has nothing to do with Anton's death."

"I'm not so sure about that." Malone leaned slightly forward. "You're very secretive."

"Everybody has secrets."

"But not everyone would kill to keep a secret."

"But some would."

"Exactly. What would you do to keep your secrets safe?"

He held Malone's gaze evenly. "I didn't kill Anton Gallier, if that's what you're suggesting. Am I finished here, Detective? Or do I need to contact my lawyer?"

Spencer stood. "Thank you for your time, Mr. Scott." He walked him to the door and opened it. "Officer Armstrong will show you the way out."

A moment later, Bayle was at Spencer's side. "That's one cool customer."

Malone agreed. "And he knows how to spell."

"Which doesn't mean jack. The guy's smart. Could've deliberately used the misspelling as a way to throw us off."

"True, but he didn't seem that interested. If they'd been his, he would've shown a little more interest. Preened a little, something. He hardly even glanced at them."

Bayle agreed. "The only time he really came alive was when you asked about Mira Gallier."

"What do you think he's going to do now?"

"Run straight to his good friend—"

"Mira Gallier."

Chapter Thirty-nine

Unable to sit still, Mira paced. Jeff's father was gone. Murdered.

She had despised him. Many times, secretly, she had wished he would disappear. Be struck by lightning, a bus or a fatal heart attack. That's how angry she had been.

But now he was gone and it hurt. How could she feel grief over the death of a man who had been so cruel to her? Who had attempted to ruin her life and reputation?

Because he'd been Jeff's father. She didn't mourn the loss of Anton Gallier. No, she mourned the loss of yet another piece of her past with Jeff.

Time to let go, Mira.

She stopped and brought her hands to her eyes. She couldn't let go. She wasn't ready.

Her doorbell sounded and she ran to the door, Nola at her side, and peered through the sidelight. Connor. With a cry of relief she flung the door open and flew into his arms. "Did you hear? Anton's dead! He was murdered this morning."

He held her tightly. She felt that he trembled. "I heard," he said.

She tilted her head back to look at his face. "They think I

might have done it, Connor. They took me in and questioned me. I was there for hours."

"Maybe we should go inside?"

Mira realized he was right. Mrs. Latrobe was probably getting an eyeful right now. Spinning some sort of tall, sordid tale about what was going on.

She closed and locked the door behind them, then turned to find him gazing at her, his expression twisted with some strong emotion.

"What's wrong?"

"They questioned me, too. They suspect me as well. Maybe both of us."

"It's crazy!"

"Not really. Not from their perspective. We had a public confrontation with him. It looks bad."

"I know." She brought her hands to her face. "I wish I could take it back."

"Mira?"

At his tone, she dropped her hands and looked at him. "Yes?"

"That's not why I'm here tonight. There's something I have to tell you."

Suddenly, like a child, she wanted to press her hands over her ears. It was going to change everything. She didn't know why she was certain of it—maybe the timing, maybe the tone of his voice or the sadness in his eyes.

"All right," she said instead, softly. "Maybe we should sit down?"

"I think that'd be good. But not the kitchen."

She nodded and led him into the front parlor. She sat on the couch, he in the chair across from her.

He looked her in the eyes. "I need to tell you why I joined up. I want you to hear it from me."

"Okay." She laid her palms on her thighs. "I'm ready."

"I left because of you. Because I was in love with you."

She stared at him, her heart thundering, every fiber of her being recoiling from his words. She wasn't certain what she had expected him to say, but not that.

She shook her head. "We were friends."

"It was agony being around you all the time. He was my best friend. And I was in love with his wife."

He stood and crossed to the fireplace. "It was eating me alive. Being around you, wanting to touch you, keeping up the 'just friends' charade. I told myself a million times to just let it go. Stay away, find someone else . . . I couldn't make myself do it."

He turned and looked at her, taking in her shocked expression. "Come on, Mira. Think back. How could you not have suspected?"

She searched her memory. At first, all she recalled was the three of them together. Nothing to indicate he'd felt something different for her than she for him. Then a moment leaped to the front of her brain. Of catching him gazing at her, longing so palpable in his eyes she had been uncomfortable.

She had blown that off as nothing. Just as she had blown off other things. The way he would sometimes jerk away from her touch. The way he would glance away when she and Jeff kissed, or the times he had seemed angry with them for being so obviously in love. The New Year's Eve when he had kissed her and it had gone beyond the brush of one friend's mouth against another's.

Why hadn't she seen it then?

She hadn't wanted to. Because she hadn't wanted anything to change. She had been happy.

But he had been in pain.

She looked at him, heart breaking. "I'm sorry, I didn't know."

"You didn't want to. I respected that."

She stood and crossed to stand before him. "You could have told me. Sometimes, getting things out in the open changes them. Maybe you would have realized—"

"I wasn't in love with you?" He let out a bark of laughter. "I repeat, he was my best friend. And I was in love with his wife. What was I supposed to do? Tell you? Ask you to choose?"

She opened her mouth to tell him there would have been no choice. He held up a hand stopping her. "I know how that would have gone. And I wouldn't have done that to Jeff, anyway."

"But you didn't have to leave. We could have worked it out."

He swung away from her, rigid with anger. "How? Gone on the way we had been?"

"No. You two could have done things without me. The things you used to do before Jeff and I got together."

"You don't get it, Mira. I didn't want to spend time with him." His voice lowered. "Only with you."

She wrapped her arms around herself, wishing she could hug him but not daring to. It still felt wrong to her. What could she do but accept it?

"But to go away without a word? Forget my feelings. What about your folks? Jeff called them. They didn't know where you were."

"They knew, Mira. Of course they knew."

"They lied for you like that? My God." She thought back to the calls Jeff had made. The times he had begged Connor's folks to tell him where their son had gone.

Her eyes burned. "Jeff was devastated when you left. He called everyone, including your parents. Not once, but many times. When I think of all those calls, all those times—"

"Jeff knew."

For a moment she was sure she had misheard him. When she realized she hadn't, she caught her breath. "That's not true."

"I told him the day I left for basic."

"No." She shook her head. "He wouldn't have kept it from me. We didn't keep secrets from each other." She brought a hand to her cross, curled her fingers around it. "He wouldn't have lied to me. Not that way. Never."

"I told him why I was leaving. I thought he should know. I thought it was the honorable thing to do." He paused. "I left it up to him whether to tell you or not."

She began to tremble. "Why are you doing this?"

His expression hardened. "You wanted the truth."

"The truth," she whispered acidly, "yes. But not this. He would not have kept this from me. Would not have . . . pretended not to know where you'd gone. Or to be so hurt."

"Are you certain of that?"

"Stop it!"

"Maybe you didn't know him as well as you thought."

"Get out!" She marched across to the door and yanked it open, shaking with fury. "Leave me alone!"

"He wasn't perfect, Mira!" Connor grabbed her upper arms, forcing her to look at him. "He was just a man."

"He was your best friend! Why are you doing this?"

"Because I'm still in love with you, dammit!" He set her away from him, expression twisting with pain. "But not only are you still in love with him, you're more in love with him than before. You've made him into a saint. The perfect husband. But he wasn't. People have secrets. Even from their spouses. Jeff had them."

"I can't believe you're doing this. Trying to tear him down. Trying to take away all I have left of him."

"I'm not trying to destroy your memory of him. The last thing I want to do is hurt you. Why do you think I left?"

"Get out."

"I wanted you to hear the truth from me, not the police or anyone else."

Then she understood. "That's why you're here. The police questioned you. You had to tell me because you told them."

"I didn't tell them. But I know I'm going to have to and I didn't want you to hear it from them."

"That's what Anton meant," she realized. "When he said you were happy Jeff was dead. Because now you might have a chance with me?"

"I'm not glad he's dead. And I hate that his death has you clinging to a memory that's a lie."

"Get out, Connor." She jerked the front door open. "I don't want to see you or hear from you. We're no longer friends."

Chapter Forty

The moments ticked past, becoming minutes. Still Mira stood frozen, his words—and hers—ringing in her head: "*I was in love with you ... I'm still in love with you, dammit ... Jeff knew ... I told him the day I left ... Jeff had secrets ...*"

"*I don't want to see you or hear from you ... We're no longer friends.*"

She brought a hand to her mouth to hold back a cry of despair. She didn't want to lose him. Not again. She wanted him in her life.

She didn't know how they could stay friends. But she wanted to try.

She yanked the door open. The driveway was empty, the street dark. He was long gone.

Gone.

Mira sagged against the door frame, tears choking her. Maybe it was for the best. She could forgive him for saying those things about Jeff. But if he couldn't stop loving her and she couldn't love him back, how could they have any kind of relationship?

They couldn't, she acknowledged. It's why he had exited her life the first time.

From deep inside the house came the chirp of her cell phone. Connor, she thought. Calling to talk it through. Start over.

She ran for it. "Connor?" she said. "I'm so glad—"

"Hi, babe, it's me. Hold tight, I'm almost there."

The voice moved over her like thunder. She couldn't breathe. Couldn't think.

Jeff's voice.

The phone slipped from her fingers, hitting the floor with a sharp crack. The sound penetrated her shock, and with a sob, she scrambled for it, dropping to her knees, bringing it to her ear. "Jeff? Jeff, I'm here!"

Nothing.

She checked the display; it had gone dark.

No, no . . . it couldn't be broken. What would she do? She had to call him back. Hands shaking so badly it took three tries, she restarted the phone.

As it came to life, her landline rang. She leaped to her feet and ran to the kitchen, snatching it from its cradle and bringing it to her ear.

"Jeff!" she cried. "Don't hang up! Where are you?"

"Mira? It's Dr. Jasper. Are you all right?"

She careened back to earth. Not Jeff. Maybe never again.

"Are you all right?" the therapist asked once more, this time in a tone that demanded response. "Talk to me."

Her head went light. She grabbed the counter for support. "I think I'm going to pass out."

"Find a chair or sit on the floor." Mira sank to the floor. "Did you do that?"

"Yes."

"Deep breaths," the therapist said. "In and out. If you still feel dizzy, lie down or put your head between your knees."

Mira did as she suggested, lying back on the wooden floor, breathing in and out, mind racing. Did it really happen? she wondered. Did Jeff just call her? Or had she imagined it?

"Mira? Are you there?"

"I'm sorry, what?"

"Talk to me, Mira. What's happening?"

Concern resonated in the woman's voice. It penetrated Mira's shock. "I'm fine now. I just— Why are you calling me, Dr. Jasper?"

"I saw on the news. About Anton. Have you heard?"

"He's dead. Yes, I heard. The police questioned me about it."

"They questioned you? Why?"

"My confrontation with him on Saturday. Our history. I think I'm their number one suspect."

"Did they say that?"

"They didn't have to. I called my lawyer."

"But they didn't charge you?"

"No. I didn't kill him."

"Of course you didn't." She paused. "Why did you think I was Jeff calling?"

Mira started to tell her, then changed her mind. "I was asleep," she lied. "I was dreaming . . . Jeff was trying to reach me. It was so real." She paused. "Dr. Jasper? Can I ask you something?"

"Of course."

"How do we know Jeff is really dead?"

The long silence on the other end of the line spoke volumes. When the therapist finally spoke, her tone was soft but measured. "Mira, it's been almost six years."

"But we don't have proof."

"Do you still have hope he's alive?"

"I didn't. Not really. Until—"

Tonight. When I heard his voice.

She couldn't bring herself to say it. Not even to Dr. Jasper, with whom she had shared all her secrets, her highest highs and her darkest lows.

Why? Fear of looking insane? Or fear of the hope evaporating?

"How crazy would it be, Dr. Jasper? To believe he was alive?"

"You tell me, Mira."

"His body was never positively identified."

"True. But if he's alive, where has he been these past years?"

"I don't know." Mira hugged Nola, who had responded to the noise and was looking concerned. "Maybe he's had amnesia?" Even as she offered it, she knew how pathetic it sounded. The stuff of pulp fiction and movie-of-the-week plots. She pressed on anyway. "Isn't there a type of long-term amnesia?"

"Yes, severe retrograde amnesia. But it's extremely rare. And considering all the media coverage of Katrina, I feel certain someone would have contacted authorities about a man with injuries who didn't know his own name. Or he would have done so himself."

When Mira didn't respond, the therapist went on. "Besides, if he remembers now, why not call you? Why not knock on the door?"

"What if he did call me?"

"Are you telling me that Jeff called you?"

Mira stared at the clock mounted on the wall beside the sink. The minute hand ticked forward. Instead of answering, she said, "Without a one hundred percent positive ID, is it so wrong to have hope?"

"Not if it isn't interfering with your life. Not if you aren't putting a new relationship on hold because of it."

A new relationship. Connor.

"What else happened tonight, Mira?"

Connor told me he was in love with me. He told me that was why he joined the marines.

He also told me that Jeff knew. That Jeff had kept it a secret from me.

"Mira?"

"I'm not ready to talk about it."

"If you don't talk about it, I can't help you."

"Have I changed history? Have I idealized my marriage? Turned Jeff into a saint?"

"A certain amount of that is normal. And understandable. But too much, like anything, is unhealthy."

"Why? What would be so wrong in believing the absolute best?"

"Depends on what you're talking about. But just off the top of my head, what's wrong is it's a lie. It's difficult for real life to compete with a fairy tale. I can help you. But you have to tell me what's happened."

"I'm sorry, but I need to hold on to this for a while."

"Are you certain you don't want me to come over there? If you need me, I'll—"

"I'm okay. I'm not going to do anything drastic, including use."

"Then I want to see you in the morning. I'll come in early."

"It's not necessary."

"I insist. What's going on is huge, Mira. You can't handle this alone."

"Maybe I can. Maybe I should try."

"Trust me." Panic crept into the woman's voice. "We've worked together a long time. You've come such a long way. Promise me, you'll come in tomorrow morning. Eight o'clock."

"I promise I'll try."

Mira hung up before the therapist could object. She returned the phone to its base and dug her cell out of her pocket. She stared at it, heart thudding heavily.

The moment of truth. Just how crazy was she?

She accessed call history. And there it was.

Unknown caller. 11:03 P.M.

Chapter Forty-one

"Deni!" Mira called, pounding on her door. "It's me. I need to talk to you!" Her assistant lived in half of a shotgun double in Mid-City. Her house was dark, but her red VW Beetle sat in the drive.

She pounded again. "It's an emergency!"

The neighbor's porch light snapped on. Mira had met that neighbor: he was a butcher for Winn-Dixie with hands the size of meat hooks and the bulging biceps and chest that suggested he was no stranger to steroids.

Not the man you wanted to awake at midnight.

A light snapped on inside Deni's apartment. The door cracked and her friend peeked out. "Mira? My God, it is you. What the hell? It's after midnight."

"Let me in. Please. I need to talk to you." From the adjoining house came the sound of a dead bolt turning. "Quick before roid-rage Randy next door gets hold of me."

Deni swung the door wider and Mira slipped inside.

When she'd closed and relocked the door, Deni turned to her. "You're pale."

"I feel pale." She hugged herself. "Do you have anything to drink? Alcoholic."

"White wine or beer."

"Wine. Thanks."

Deni motioned the couch. "Sit down, I'll get you some."

Mira sank into the sofa. It was old and lumpy, in a good way. It swallowed her up, like her grandmother's lap used to. She laid her head against the sofa back. From the kitchen she heard the sound of hushed conversation.

Deni wasn't alone. She hadn't even considered that when she'd beelined over here at midnight. Geez.

Deni appeared with a tumbler of wine. Mira took it apologetically. "I can't believe I barged in like this."

"Don't worry about it. That's what friends are for."

"But with Chris here, it's so awkward. I just didn't think."

"Chris isn't here."

"But I heard you talking to someone."

"It was the cat." Deni smiled. "She's curious why I'm up."

As if cued, Mr. Suit trotted into the room. Deni had named him that because his gray and white markings made him look like he was wearing a gray flannel suit with a white shirt, socks and gloves.

The animal mewed and jumped onto Deni's lap. "What's happening, Mira? Chris told me what he knew, which wasn't much. Was it really awful? What did they ask you? It's unreal that they could think you'd have anything to do with Anton's murder, even if he was a horrible old son of a bitch."

"I think Jeff's alive."

Deni's mouth dropped. "Did you just say—"

Mira nodded. "Yeah, I did."

"You can't be serious."

"I am. He called me tonight."

Deni simply stared at her. Mira set the glass of wine on the coffee table and leaned toward her. "I haven't told anyone else. I didn't think they'd believe me." She searched her friend's expression. "Please believe me."

Deni blinked. "I'll try."

"He called me. On my cell. He told me to hold tight. He was almost home."

"How did you respond?"

"I dropped the phone. I was so shocked . . . I picked it up but the phone had shut off when I dropped it."

"Did you check your call—"

"History? Yes. Look." Mira accessed it and handed it over. "The call came in at eleven oh three."

"Unknown. That means the phone call was made from an unlisted number. Why would he do that?"

"Maybe he just didn't think about it."

Deni looked perplexed. "Wait. All those weird things that have happened to you lately . . . the two break-ins, awakening to the smell of his aftershave, do you think that was him?"

"I'm not sure what I think, but . . . maybe."

"Mira, honey, why would he play games with you? If he was alive and trying to contact you, why not just do it?"

"I don't know." Mira brought her hands to her face, then dropped them to her lap. "It doesn't make any sense. I'm so confused."

Deni stood and came around the couch to sit beside her. She took her hands. "What you should be is scared. Someone is screwing with your head. They've been in your house." She lowered her voice. "People are dead, Mira."

When she just stared blankly at Deni, her friend ticked them off. "Your father-in-law. That Preacher guy. Father Girod. I'm no cop, but you have a connection to all of them. Don't you find it all really freaky?"

The hair at the back of Mira's neck stood up. *Dear God, she did.* "No wonder the police questioned me that way. No wonder I'm a suspect."

Deni didn't respond, and after a moment, Mira met her friend's concerned gaze. "What if it is Jeff?"

"Seriously?" When Mira nodded, Deni said, "Then he's a sick son of a bitch who doesn't deserve your devotion."

"You sound like Connor. We argued tonight." She plucked at the blanket lying next to her on the couch. "He told me he up and left all those years ago because he was in love with me."

"I knew it! He's still in love with you, isn't he?"

"That's what he said."

Deni frowned. "And that's why you argued?"

"No." She rubbed the blanket's worn edge between her fingers. "He also said that Jeff lied to me. That Jeff knew all along where Connor had gone and why."

"Oh."

"How could he say that about Jeff? They were best friends."

"Maybe because it's true. How do you know it isn't?"

"Because I knew him. Did you?"

For a long moment, Deni simply stared at her, then backed down. "So it's not true."

"No, it's not." Mira shook her head. "Why would Jeff have kept that from me? Why the elaborate ruse of calling Connor's family, then sharing what they said?"

"Maybe there's more to it than you know?"

More to it than she knew? It made her dizzy to think there could be. "Or maybe Connor is lying?"

"Maybe." Deni yawned. "Look, it's late. Why don't you stay here tonight? We can talk more in the morning."

"I can't. Nola's at the house."

"She's probably sleeping. You can get up early and go home and let her out." She searched Mira's gaze. "I'm afraid for you."

"What if Jeff tries to call again?"

"You have your cell phone. And I'm here."

"What if he's . . . there? What if he's home?"

"He's not, hon. I'm sorry, but I have to say what I think. Look, if I'm wrong and he is there, he'll wait for you. You've waited almost six years for him, he can wait six hours for you."

Mira's eyes welled with tears. Exhaustion rolled over her and she shuddered. "Okay, I'll stay."

"Good girl. I'll get you a pillow and another blanket."

Mira awakened with a start. She rolled onto her side, but with difficulty—it felt as if she was being held in a bear hug. The dark was unfamiliar, as was the quiet. Where was she?

Deni's, she remembered. The big, mushy couch. The last thing she recalled was laying her head on the pillow.

Now it all came crashing back. Anton's murder and being questioned by the police. Connor's claim that he was in love with her, that he had been for years—and that Jeff had known and kept it from her.

"Hi, babe, it's me. Hold tight, I'm almost there."

She'd gone to sleep with her cell phone tucked under her pillow. She retrieved it and checked the time.

4:20 a.m.

No calls.

Careful to be as quiet as possible, she eased off the couch and went in search of the bathroom. Using her phone's display to illuminate the way, she tiptoed down the hall.

She froze as she heard her name. The sound of voices. A quiet conversation.

Mira frowned, confused. What was Deni doing up? And who was with her?

She recalled the night before, thinking she'd heard Deni talking to someone. Deni denying it. Mr. Suit, she'd said. She'd been talking to the cat.

Why would Deni lie to her? She couldn't believe she was even thinking such a thing. They had been friends for years. Mira relied on her, trusted her completely.

The bathroom lay to her left. Dead ahead was the closed door to Deni's bedroom.

Even as she scolded herself for being an ungrateful, faithless friend, Mira crept nearer to the bedroom. The voices became more distinct. More than a murmur now but still indistinguishable. A male voice. And a female's, Deni's.

Almost there, she thought she heard her name again. Then, distinctly, she heard Jeff's. Her heart began to thunder. She moved one step closer to put her ear to the door.

A floorboard creaked loudly. The voices stopped. She heard steps. Hand to her mouth to hold back her gasp, she darted to the bathroom, closing the door behind her.

She sank onto the commode, dropping her head to her

hands. What the hell was she doing? Spying on a friend? A friend who had opened her home to her in the middle of the night. If Deni had something to hide, would she have invited Mira to stay?

Get a grip, Mira. Pull yourself together.

A tap came on the bathroom door. "Mira," Deni called softly, "is everything all right?"

"Yes," she managed. "I'm sorry I woke you."

"It's okay." Deni yawned. "I'm going back to bed. See you in the morning."

"Thanks."

Mira relieved herself, washed her hands, then rinsed her face with cool water. She stepped back out into the hall, glancing toward Deni's bedroom. The door was partially open.

Heart in her throat, she crossed to it. "Deni?" she whispered. "You still awake?"

She answered that she was and Mira poked her head into the room.

In the glow of the alarm clock's luminescent dial, she saw that Deni was alone in bed. Also that she sported a major case of bed head and wore an oversize, ratty T-shirt. Hardly the appearance of a woman who had a male visitor.

"Sorry again. For waking you up."

"S'okay, Mira. I'm just glad you're okay."

"Can I ask you a question?"

"Sure."

"Was somebody else here a little while ago? A guy?"

Deni shook her head. "No. Why do you ask?"

"I thought . . . I thought I heard a guy talking."

Again, Deni shook her head. "I talk in my sleep sometimes. Maybe that was what you heard?"

She was lying, Mira thought. But why?

"Maybe so," she said, working to keep her tone light. "Night, Deni."

As she headed back to the couch, Mira wondered why Deni would lie to her. What could be so awful that she would try to hide it with a lie?

Chapter Forty-two

Mira sneaked out at first light. At least that's the way it felt as she scribbled a thank-you note to Deni, propped it up by the coffeemaker, then quietly let herself out. She didn't know why, but the last thing she wanted to do this morning was face Deni.

On the front porch, she quickly scanned the block, though uncertain what she was looking for. Other than a stray dog poking around a garbage can, the street was deserted.

She unlocked her car and climbed inside, checked the backseat the way her mother had taught her to, then started the engine and drew away from the curb.

It was so early that even the Starbucks drive-thru wasn't open, so she settled for coffee from a 24-hour convenience store. Mira sipped as she drove, keeping the confusing jumble of her thoughts at bay by singing along with the radio.

Mira turned on to her street. Mrs. Latrobe had left her porch light on. She wondered how late the woman had waited up for her to return. Maybe she had fallen asleep spyglass in hand.

Nola did, indeed, have to go. When Mira opened the

front door, the dog darted out and squatted in the yard for what seemed like an eternity.

"Poor baby," Mira murmured when Nola had finished her business and loped up to the porch wearing a huge grin. Mira scratched behind her ears. "Feel better now?"

Nola wagged her tail in response and trotted into the house. Mira started to follow, then stopped. What if Jeff was here, waiting for her? She had imagined seeing him again, their reunion—had played and replayed the joyful, romantic scenario—hundreds of times. Maybe thousands.

But now, strangely, her mind was blank except for Deni's comment from the night before: *"He's a sick son of a bitch who doesn't deserve your devotion."*

The truth of that settled uncomfortably over her. She stepped into the foyer. A hum filled her head. Her blood rushing, she realized. As if sensing her master's hesitation, Nola looked back at her, head cocked.

Mira shut the door, the click of the latch seeming to echo in the quiet. She took a step deeper into the house, then another, doing so until she stood at the bottom of the stairs. She lifted her gaze to the upper landing.

Was he here?

"Jeff?" she called, his name coming out a choked whisper. She cleared her throat and tried again. "Jeff! I'm home."

Silence answered. She called once more, even louder.

Still nothing.

Swallowing hard, she climbed the steps, hand skimming the rail, head growing light. She reached the second-floor landing and turned toward the master suite.

The door was closed.

Her steps faltered. She always left it open.

"People are dead . . . I'm no cop, but you have a connection to all of them . . . I'm afraid for you . . ."

Mira reached the door, grasped the knob and twisted. The door slowly swung open.

Empty. Nothing out of order. She let out a shaky breath, feeling like an idiot. A complete ass. Sunlight tumbled across the made bed, falling on something shiny on the floor. By Jeff's side of the bed.

She crossed to it, bent and picked it up. A dime. She turned it over in her fingers. Minted in 2005.

The year Katrina struck.

Mira shifted her gaze to the bed. The spread was mussed, as if someone had sprawled atop it. The pillow bore the imprint of a head.

A small squeak passed her lips. *He'd been here. He'd lain in the bed. Waiting for her.*

She snatched up the pillow, brought it to her face. It smelled like him, she thought, breathing deeply. His aftershave.

". . . a sick son of a bitch who doesn't deserve your devotion."

A chill washed over her. She dropped the pillow and backed toward the door.

From downstairs, she heard her name called. She jumped and whirled around. *Jeff! He really was alive!*

Her name came again. "Are you home? It's Connor!"

She brought a hand to her chest. Beneath it, her heart beat so hard and fast she feared it might burst from her chest.

Working to slow it, she exited the bedroom and crossed to the top of the stairs. "I'm here," she said.

He tipped his face up. "Hey."

"Hey. What are you doing here?"

"I couldn't leave it the way we did last night."

She shifted her gaze from his, to the open front door, then back. "Did you ring the bell?"

"The door was open."

"What do you mean? Unlocked?"

"No, standing open."

"But I shut it. I remember shutting it."

"It was open, Mira. I don't know what else to tell you. Maybe it didn't close all the way and the wind blew it open."

She'd heard it click shut. Besides, it wasn't windy. The treetops beyond the door were still.

Was she losing her mind?
Or was everyone else going mad?

"I think you should go."

He didn't move. "You can believe whatever you want to believe. If you want to build an altar to Jeff, who am I to say you shouldn't? I told you the truth last night, but I'll take it all back if you want me to. If I can't have your love, I'll take your friendship."

Mira gazed at him, the strangest sensation moving over her. A mixture of relief and . . . longing. To hold him. And be held by him.

Jeff was within her reach, closer than he had been in almost six years, and yet she stood here wondering what Connor's mouth would feel like against hers.

And it wasn't the first time. God help her, she had wondered the same thing way back, before Katrina and before Connor disappeared.

That New Year's Eve kiss. It had sent her running for Jeff. Not because it had happened, but because her physical reaction had been anything but platonic.

"Jeff's alive." She blurted the words out as a defense against her thoughts. And against the urge to run down the stairs and throw herself at Connor.

His expression tightened. "For God's sake, Mira! If you want me to leave so badly, I'll go."

"That's not it! You don't understand. Last night . . . he called me." His pitying expression said it all and she held out a hand, pleading. "He called me last night. It was his voice, Connor. It was!"

He shook his head. "I'm sorry. I am. I see now, I shouldn't have—"

She ran down the stairs to him. "I slept at Deni's last night. This morning, I went upstairs. His side of the bed, he had been lying on it. There was an indentation in his pillow. It smelled like him. I'll show you."

She grabbed his hand and brought him upstairs with her. "See?" She crossed to the bed and grabbed the pillow. "Smell it, you'll see." When he hesitated, she asked again, pleading.

He brought it to his face, breathed in, then handed it back. "It smells like fabric softener."

"No. And look." She unpocketed her phone, pulled up the call history and handed it to him. "There, at 11:03 P.M. He called."

He looked at the display. "Did he leave a message?"

"No, I answered."

"What did he say?"

"That he'd be here soon. You know how he'd sometimes call me babe? That's what he said. 'Hi, babe.'"

Connor didn't believe her. She saw it on his face. He turned to her, cupping her right cheek in his palm. The expression in his eyes made her want to cry.

She covered his hand with hers. His trembled slightly.

"Do you want him to be alive so badly, Mira?"

"It's not that," she whispered. "I promise you."

He moved his hand to the back of her head, tangling his fingers in her hair. "I can't compete with a ghost or a perfect memory. I'm just a man. Flesh and blood."

He bent and pressed his mouth against hers, kissing her roughly. She responded instinctively, hungrily, tipping her head to better connect with his mouth, pressing herself against him.

And then it was over. He released her and she stumbled backward, not because of force, but because it felt as if her life had crumbled beneath her. Again.

"Flesh and blood," he repeated. "If you decide that's what you want, you know where to find me."

"Wait!" she called after him. "I thought you said we could be friends."

He stopped and turned back. "We can," he said, his lips lifting. "But it's not my first choice. And I have a feeling it's not yours either."

Chapter Forty-three

Mira knew the route from her Frenchmen Street home to the studio like the back of her hand. She had traveled from one point to the other in as little as fifteen minutes; she had made the trip while so exhausted she had arrived without memory of actually driving it.

But today she found herself taking a new path. Turning onto auxiliary streets, meandering, even at one point getting herself turned around.

After Connor had left, she had stood for a long time staring at the closed door, thinking of his kiss and the way she had responded to it. Thinking of the things he had said.

"I can't compete with a ghost or a perfect memory . . . I'm just a man . . . Flesh and blood. If you decide that's what you want, you know where to find me . . ."

She'd headed for the shower in the hopes of clearing her head. In the hopes that the water would wash away the way he had made her feel. Alive. In a way she hadn't been in a long time. Like a sexual being.

And to wash off her sense of guilt. Like she had been cheating on her husband.

How could she cheat on a husband who was dead?

Maybe he wasn't?

A cat darted into the street and Mira slammed on the brakes. As the car skidded to a stop, she glanced to her right, to the row of neat Creole cottages that lined the street. One jumped out at her: painted a soft blue with white trim, with its slightly sagging porch shaded by a blossom-covered crape myrtle tree.

In the front window hung a stained-glass panel.

One of hers. A fleur-de-lis and sunflower. The one she had sold to Detective Malone and his fiancée, Stacy. Maybe Detective Malone could help her? If he believed her, who better to help her find Jeff?

Or whoever was screwing with her head.

From behind her came the blare of a horn. She glanced apologetically in the rearview mirror, lifted her hand in acknowledgment and pulled to the side of the road.

She glanced at the cottage again. What she was thinking was nuts. Wasn't it? But it was an option. And it seemed to her she didn't have too many of them.

Without giving herself time to reconsider, she cut the engine, climbed out and headed to his door.

Mira recognized the woman who opened it. Blond, striking features. Like a tall Angelina Jolie but with less mouth and more nose.

Mira smiled. "Stacy?"

The woman's expression grew guarded. She shifted her arm from the side to behind her back. "Can I help you?"

"I'm your neighbor from up and around the corner. Mira Gallier." She indicated the stained-glass panel. "You bought your stained-glass piece from me."

The other woman seemed to relax slightly. She smiled. "I remember. What can I do for you this morning?"

"I was looking for Spencer . . . Detective Malone."

"I'm sorry. He's not here."

"Oh." Mira took a step backward. "Okay. Sorry I bothered you."

"You didn't." She smiled again. "Can I give him a message?"

"Don't worry about it. It was stupid. I probably shouldn't have stopped anyway." Mira started down the stairs.

Stacy stopped her. "Wait. Are you in some sort of trouble?"

Mira looked back at her. "You could say that."

"Let me give you his numbers. He'll get back to you, I promise."

"It's okay. I have those. I was just driving by, saw the window and thought maybe he could help." She shook her head. "Never mind. Again, sorry I bothered you."

"You didn't." Stacy stepped out onto the porch. "Look, Mira, you seem really distraught. Maybe I can help you? I'm a cop, too."

"I'd forgotten. How come you're here and not at work?"

"I was shot. Six weeks ago. I've been recuperating."

"That was rude, wasn't it? I'm sorry, I'm not myself."

"No problem." She indicated the two chairs on the small front porch. "It's not too hot yet. Sit down. We'll talk."

Mira didn't hesitate. She didn't know why, but something about the other woman calmed her.

Stacy took the chair closer to the door. "It's been a long six weeks, Mira. Truth is, I'm about to go out of my flipping mind here. But with the doctor's final okay, I'm heading back to work the end of the month. Would you believe on Monday the twenty-ninth?"

The sixth anniversary of Katrina. "That doesn't give you the willies?"

Stacy laughed. "The willies?"

"Like it's bad luck or something?"

"It's just a day, like any other." They fell silent a moment. "Spencer mentioned you not too long ago."

"He did?"

"He said someone had broken into your studio, something like that."

"The flesh will be peeled from their bones, roasted and eaten by demons."

She shuddered, recalling it. "Preacher. So much has happened since, it seems like a million years ago already."

"He was murdered, wasn't he?"

"Yes. So was Father Girod and Anton Gallier. My father-in-law." She looked at Stacy. "I'm so confused. I don't know what to believe anymore. Or who to believe in."

"Tell me what's happening."

"That's what's so confusing. Besides the murders there's—" She looked down at her hands, realizing she had them clenched into tight fists. She relaxed them. "I wonder . . . My husband died in Katrina, but . . ."

She couldn't bring herself to say it. Stacy gently prodded. "But what, Mira? You can tell me."

"I wonder if he's alive."

"Why would you wonder that?"

"I think he's been in our home. I smelled his aftershave, saw the indentation of his head on his pillow and . . . he called me. Said he'd be home soon."

Stacy didn't comment and Mira went on. "I know I sound like a pathetic lunatic. It's so impossible but so . . . real. I don't know what to do." She looked Stacy in the eyes. "Do you think I'm losing my mind?"

"Can I tell you a story? Six years ago my sister Jane was being stalked by a psychopath. Someone from her past. He turned her life upside down. She nearly died."

"What happened? I mean, how did she—"

"Beat him?" Mira nodded and Stacy went on. "Let go of everything you *think* you know. Start over. A fresh slate. It's what good cops have to do."

"How so?"

"Look, sometimes cases are simple. They come together neatly, just the way you expect them to.

"But sometimes, what we know, without a doubt, is leading us in the absolute wrong direction. To get the job done, we have to clear the slate."

It made so much sense. Mira smiled weakly. "You're a good cop, aren't you?"

"I like to think so." She stood. "When's the last time you ate something?"

She honestly couldn't remember and said so.

"How about I get us both a muffin and a glass of iced tea?"

"That would be really nice." She pressed a hand to her suddenly rumbling stomach. "I'm starving."

Stacy smiled. "Great, I'll be right back."

When Stacy turned to walk into the house, Mira saw she had a handgun tucked into her waistband at the small of her back. Mira stared at the weapon, heart leaping to her throat.

What the hell was she doing? Was she out of her mind? Stacy was a cop and she was a suspect. Yet here she was, spilling her guts, acting like some sort of freaked-out psycho.

Stacy was probably calling Spencer at that very moment.

Mira leaped to her feet and hurried across the porch and down the stairs. She didn't look back until she was in her car, driving off. Stacy stood on the porch, staring after her, two glasses of tea in her hands.

Chapter Forty-four

Spencer moved his gaze around the table. Bayle sat beside him, his brother beside her. Percy's partner and the district commander were also in attendance, as well as Captain O'Shay, the head of Community Relations and the deputy chief.

On the walls and whiteboards were photographs of the three victims, along with the particulars of each homicide. Richards, the new Community Relations point man, was talking. "Okay, so nobody out there gives a shit about Preacher, he's not even on the media's radar—"

"Which is good," Deputy Chief Krohn said. "The superintendent and I want it kept that way. The last thing we want is the public fully aware that these three victims are linked."

"—but," Richards continued, "the other two have caused an uproar. First a popular parish priest and now Anton Gallier, a former King of Rex. The media is having a field day whipping the public into a frenzy."

Captain O'Shay shifted her gaze to Spencer. "What do you have so far?"

"Two strong suspects. Gallier's former daughter-in-law, Mira Gallier, and her friend Connor Scott."

Bayle stepped in. "Scott's a bit of a mystery. But Gallier has a connection to all three victims. She has a motive for two of them, and a strong motive for Anton Gallier."

"Which is?" Captain O'Shay asked.

"She hated his guts. He tried his damnedest to have her charged in the death of his son. When that failed, he brought a civil suit against her."

Malone took over. "Apparently, days before his murder he'd launched a new attack against her. She had a very public argument with him about it at the Crescent City Club."

"Scott was with her," Bayle continued. "The victim also challenged him. According to witnesses, Scott was visibly angry. The two could be in this together. I suspect they're romantically involved."

"What about the biblical messages?" Krohn asked. "Any help there?"

"Not much," Malone answered. "The first two are pretty universally Christian. Everyone we questioned knew them. But the third, from the Gallier scene, is more obscure."

Bayle jumped in. "Mira Gallier is the only one who knew it referred to Christ expunging Mary Magdalene's demons."

"The only one who *admitted* knowing," Malone corrected.

Captain O'Shay looked at Malone. "And what do you think? Are she and Scott together in this?"

"It's possible, though I like Scott for it. There's something with this guy that's just not right. For me, the coincidence that he comes home from the war and all this shit starts is a little hard to swallow. With her, I just don't see it. My sensors aren't going off."

"Not those sensors, anyway," Bayle muttered.

He looked at her, eyes narrowed. "What the hell's that supposed to mean?"

"It means it's hard for you to think the pretty, little widow did it."

"That's complete bullshit," he said, furious that she would suggest this, especially at a table with their superior officers. "Wherever you're coming from—"

Krohn cut him off. "You two work it out and do your jobs. What I want to know"—he tossed a couple copies of the day's *Times-Picayune* on the table—"is how'd the press get this?"

A headline from the front page screamed: JUDGMENT DAY KILLER?

A groan rippled over the group. Spencer held up his hands. "Not from anyone on my team. Right?" He moved his gaze between Percy and Bayle. Neither said a word. They didn't even blink.

Spencer turned back to the deputy chief. "Source could be EMTs, CSI, or even the suspects."

Krohn leaned forward. "The crimes are connected, no doubt. But do we have a serial killer on our hands?"

"Not in the traditional sense," Captain O'Shay said. "The acts of true serial killers are rituals, ones they repeat over and over. We're not seeing that here."

"True," Spencer agreed. "But what if, instead of a ritual, our perp is telling a story? What if all we have so far is the prologue?"

Krohn's face reddened. "Three victims, a prologue? Son of a bitch, Malone. Are you out of your fucking mind?"

"Explain," Captain O'Shay ordered.

"It's the biblical shtick. Judgment Day, casting out demons . . . Sure, it may be a smoke screen by a perfectly sane, methodical killer to throw us off. Or it may be a religious whack job who really believes he's the one sent to do the judging."

"By way of murder," Percy said. "His own little holy war."

"I don't like the sound of that." Deputy Chief Krohn looked directly at Captain O'Shay. "We don't want another victim. Is that understood?"

"Of course," she answered. "Absolutely, sir."

Spencer and Percy exchanged glances. The brass was always saying shit like that. As if the captain or any of the detectives under her command wanted *more* victims. Or the fun those victims brought with them—the superintendent crawling all over their asses.

She turned to Spencer and Bayle. "What about physical evidence? What do we have?"

Bayle jumped in first. "We retrieved a bullet from Gallier. A .45 caliber. Ran it through national ballistics network. Came up empty."

"Lifted some clean prints from the Gallier scene," Percy offered. "From the coffee cups and take-out bag. Didn't get a hit from the local database, running them through IAFIS now."

Bayle took over. "The prints gave us a rock-solid link between the Father Girod and Gallier homicides. Prints taken from the two scenes were a match."

Spencer nodded. "Additionally, we located three French Quarter restaurants that use the same combination of those cups, lids, tray and take-out bag. They also sell the same croissants and scones, acquired from the same supplier, Bakers Dozen.

"We've questioned the bakery's owner and are making the rounds of the three cafés with photos of Mira Gallier and Connor Scott."

Spencer's cell, holstered at his hip, vibrated. He glanced at the display, saw it was Stacy and excused himself from the table.

"Is everything all right?" he asked the moment he stepped outside the room.

"I'm fine. Mira Gallier was just here. Looking for you."

"What the hell?"

"She was behaving strangely. Keyed up and anxious. Said a few bizarre things including that she couldn't remember when she'd last eaten."

"And how did you learn that?"

"I invited her to breakfast."

"Son of a bitch, Stacy. She's a suspect in a murder investigation."

"Exactly why I invited her. Also why I kept my friend Mr. Glock with me the whole time."

Stacy was a cop. A good one. She knew all the right things

to do, but he'd be a liar if he didn't admit being shaken by the thought of a murder suspect showing up on his doorstep.

"She give you anything I can use?" he asked.

"She said she didn't know what to believe anymore. Or who to believe in. She also mentioned three victims, Father Girod, her father-in-law and Preacher."

"That's it?"

"Nope, there's one more thing. She thinks her dead husband's been paying her visits. She claims he called her last night."

"In other words, she's certifiable."

"Or close to it."

He let out a frustrated breath. "She's gone now?"

"Yes. Up and left when I went to get the tea and muffins."

After extracting her promise to call immediately if Gallier showed up again, he hung up and headed back to the table.

"Everything okay?" Captain O'Shay asked.

"That was Stacy. Mira Gallier was just at my home, looking for me."

No one spoke. The silence was heavy. They all worked law enforcement, some were married, some had kids. A perp learning where they lived, showing up and exacting revenge on the ones they loved was their worst nightmare.

Finally, Percy spoke. "That's screwed up, bro."

"Did Stacy feel threatened?" Captain O'Shay asked.

"No. In fact, she asked her to stay for breakfast." A ripple of laughter moved around the table. When it died, he added, "According to Stacy, Gallier was acting weird. Hyper. Said she didn't know who or what to believe. Mentioned all three vics. Thinks her dead husband's been paying her visits."

Another ripple of laughter circled the group. Captain O'Shay spoke up. "How did she find your residence?"

"Her glass studio is in the neighborhood. Stacy and I had been in before, bought a piece of her art for our front window. Gallier and I made that connection when I questioned her after her encounter with Preacher."

The captain nodded, expression thoughtful. "When we brought Gallier in, did you interview her?"

"No, Percy did. I interviewed Scott."

"Good. She thinks of you as a neighbor, a friend. That's why she just 'stopped by.' You need to maintain that trust. Let Percy or Bayle be the bad cops. You're there to 'help' her. If there's a chance she'll confide in anybody, it'll be you."

"Got it," he said. "What do you want our next step to be?"

"Pay her a visit. Just you, Malone. Real friendly. Tell her you hate it, but your captain is making you bring her downtown for questioning. Tell her, if it makes her feel more comfortable, you could request to be the one who interviews her. My guess is, if she knows anything, she'll either give it up for you or go a long way toward it."

"And me, Captain?" Bayle asked.

"I want you and Percy in the viewing room."

The meeting wrapped. As they dispersed, Spencer touched Bayle's arm. "Can I talk to you for a minute?"

"Sure." She stepped back into the conference room. "What's up?"

"That's what I want to know."

"I don't follow."

"That crack. About Gallier."

"What are you talking about?"

"Come on, Bayle. You questioned my judgment by suggesting I was influenced by Gallier's looks. I haven't done anything to make you think that."

She opened her mouth as if to argue, then shut it. "You're right," she said stiffly. "I was out of line."

It wasn't good enough. Not this time. "So what's your problem, Bayle? Is it with me? Men in general? Or do you have some issue with Gallier?"

She looked away, then back at him. "I don't have a problem with you. Or anybody else. Just doing my job."

"Bullshit."

She didn't respond and he shook his head. "Partnership is about honesty. And trust. I've got to trust you've got my back, no matter what. And after the stunt you pulled in there, I'm feeling a little shaky about that."

"Does having your back mean keeping my mouth shut while you mess up? 'Cause I'm not built that way."

He leaned toward her, tamping down his anger. "That's not what you did in there, and you know it."

"You're right." She sighed. "I've seen a lot of that sort of thing on the job, but I shouldn't have lumped you in with those types. It won't happen again."

Bayle moved past him, into the hall. As she walked away, Malone wondered what it would take to get Tony Sciame to reconsider retirement.

Chapter Forty-five

Mira let herself into the studio. The bell over the door jangled. Deni's Beetle and Chris's truck were both in the lot, so she called out a greeting.

Her assistant appeared at the workroom door, face flushed. "Where have you been? I've been worried sick!"

Mira stashed her purse behind the counter and headed for the workroom. "I'm fine."

"You show up last night, talking crazy—"

"I wasn't talking crazy."

"Yes, you were. You tell me Jeff's alive, that he called you—"

"He did. It was his voice. I promise you, Deni."

"Then this morning, I wake up and you're gone!"

"I left a note."

"You didn't show up for your appointment with Dr. Jasper."

"Dr. Jasper?"

"You had an eight o'clock appointment with her. She called, looking for you."

Shit. She'd forgotten. "I'll call her."

"And," Deni continued, following her into the workroom,

"you were supposed to call Lance this morning." At her blank stare, she said, "Lance Arnold. Your attorney."

"Crap. I forgot that, too. I'll take care of it."

Mira crossed to the Magdalene window and stopped before it. Deni followed. "I tried to call you. A bunch of times. You never picked up."

"I left my phone at the house."

Deni shook her head in disbelief. "People are being murdered, your dead husband may or may not be paying you visits, you're a suspect in a homicide and you just leave your phone at home?"

When she didn't comment, Deni went on, clearly exasperated. "We still have to set the date for the installation. Sister Sarah Elisabeth called; she wants to know when we're coming."

"Not yet. I'm not ready."

"The window's complete. Mira, you can't put it off forever."

"I'm not ready," she said again, looking over her shoulder at Deni. "I need to be at my best. With everything going on . . . my head's not straight. I'll make a mistake. I won't chance that."

Mira glanced away, then back at her friend. "I've got to ask you a question, Deni, and I hope you're not mad. I know you weren't alone last night. When I went to the bathroom, I heard you talking to someone. I heard a male voice. Why'd you lie to me?"

"I didn't." She shook her head, eyes wide. "Maybe you heard the TV?"

"It wasn't the TV. I heard my name. And Jeff's."

"Mira, honey, I don't know what you're talking about."

Mira knew what she had heard.

What could Deni be hiding? What could matter so much?

She crossed to her friend and caught her hands, holding them tightly. "You can tell me anything. We're friends. And I count on you. To help me run this place, but more important, for your friendship."

The words came out thickly; she cleared her throat. "I really need you right now. I don't think I can do this without you, whatever *this* is."

Her friend's eyes filled with tears and she hugged her. "Thank you. There is something I need to tell you, something I've been wanting to tell—"

"Hey, you two," Chris said, coming in the side door. "What's going on? It looks like a lovefest in here."

"Mutual appreciation society," Deni said, releasing Mira.

"I forgot my cooler. Mind if I grab a water out of the fridge?"

"Get all you want," Mira said. "I really appreciate you coming down to the police station for me last night. I owe you."

"That's what friends do for each other." He started for the kitchen. "Anybody else need anything?"

"Coffee?" Mira said.

"I'll make some," Deni offered, falling in step with Chris.

Mira watched them go. What had Deni been about to tell her? The truth? That she had lied about having company? Or something else entirely? Chris's arrival had shattered the moment.

Deni hadn't wanted Chris to hear.

But why? They had been romantically involved for a while now, what secret would she have from him?

Mira shifted her attention to the Magdalene panel. Detective Malone had asked her if she knew what the phrase "He cast out Seven Demons" referred to. Why, she wondered, had he wanted to know that?

He'd been questioning her about Anton's murder. So, obviously, it must have had something to do with it. But what?

Mira focused on the panel, tilting her head as she studied the saint's grief-stricken expression. Strangely, she didn't feel the connection with the saint that she had before. As if someone—or something—had broken it.

Her friends returned and Deni handed her the coffee. Mira curled her hands around the mug. "Do either of you know Magdalene's story?"

"I do," Chris said. "She was a prostitute and Jesus saved her. Something like that, anyway."

"He did save her, by casting out demons. Seven of them." She met Chris's eyes. "But she wasn't a prostitute. It doesn't say that anywhere in the Bible. The early church made it up."

Mira sipped the coffee, mind tripping forward. "Detective Malone asked me about the casting out of Seven Demons. He asked if I knew what it meant."

"Why?"

"He didn't say." Mira searched her memory, then shook her head. "But don't you think it's odd that he asked that and here she is in my studio? Think about it. The three murders are connected to me and so is Mary Magdalene."

"Maybe I should call Dr. Jasper," Deni said, going for her phone.

Chris caught her arm, stopping her. "She's okay. Let her talk."

"He's right," Mira said. "I am okay. I'm just processing. Trying to work a few things out, that's all. Maybe make a point."

Although Deni didn't look happy about it, she nodded and Mira went on. "For centuries, people believed the lie about Magdalene. Just because someone said it was so." She paused. "More likely she was Mary, the sister of Martha and Lazarus."

"The Mary who dried Jesus' feet with her hair?" Chris offered.

"Yes. She was absolutely devoted to him. Some speculate they were married."

"Like in that book, *The Da Vinci Code*."

"Right. But way before Dan Brown, people made the case they were married. Take Jesus' first recorded miracle, the wedding at Cana. It makes sense the wedding in the story was actually Jesus'. Why else would his mother have come to him about providing wine for the guests? Providing food and drink would have fallen on the party's host. In this case the host was the groom."

"And he did," said Chris. "He turned water into wine."

"Exactly." Mira glanced at her two friends again. "If I were possessed by demons and someone came along and set me free of them, I'd certainly be devoted to him. Wouldn't you?"

"Yes," Deni agreed. "I suppose I would."

"Demons in my head," she said under her breath, more to herself than them. "Is that the same as being nuts? In Jesus' time, was a mental illness, like schizophrenia, considered demonic possession? Or is the reverse true?"

"The reverse?"

"Is what we call mental illness today really demonic possession?"

"You're scaring me now," Deni said.

She was scaring herself, Mira acknowledged. But she pressed on anyway. "And just imagine, Magdalene had to watch her beloved die. That's the story of this window."

"I still don't understand," Deni murmured.

"You can't always believe what people say . . . They told me Jeff was dead and now it may not be true. Jeff told me he didn't know where Connor had gone and now I learn that might have been a lie. We believe all sorts of things, just because people tell us it's so."

Chris came off his stool, crossed to her and drew her to her feet. "You've been through so much, Mira." He hugged her. "I'm so sorry. I know how much it sucks."

Tears choked her and she rested her head on his chest. "I just don't know what's real anymore."

"You can believe in me," he said simply. "I'm real. You can believe in Deni. We're your friends. We love you and won't let anything happen to you."

The bell above the shop's door jingled. "I'll see who it is," Deni said, heading that way. Moments later, she appeared in the doorway. Her expression showed that she had bad news.

As the thought registered, Mira saw who the bad news was: Detective Spencer Malone.

Chapter Forty-six

If looks could kill, Mira's assistant would be wanted for murder, Malone thought. Ditto for the carpenter. Gallier, on the other hand, just looked as if she had been put through the wringer.

He nodded toward the stained-glass panel she stood in front of. "What saint is she?" he asked, though he suspected he knew.

"Mary Magdalene."

The window she had told Percy she'd done all the research for. He crossed to stand beside her. "It's incredible."

"Yes, it is." She turned to fully face him. "I talked to your fiancée this morning."

"She told me."

"She was a lot of help. I like her."

"I'll tell her you said so. I've got a bit of bad news." She stiffened, as if preparing herself. "My captain needs me to bring you back downtown for further questioning. I'm really sorry about that."

"Can't you just talk to me here?"

"I wish. But this is a homicide investigation and we have to cover all our bases. Standard procedure."

It was a good thing none of that was a lie, because as she silently studied his expression, he sensed she was trying to decide if he was being straight with her. To that end, he added, "I can ask permission to be the one who interviews you, if that would make you feel more comfortable?"

"It would, thanks. Will it take long?"

"Shouldn't." He smiled. "Scout's honor."

"Were you a Scout?"

"No, I was a hellion."

She laughed, though it sounded forced. "I should call my lawyer."

"Go right ahead."

Mira did, only to learn that he was in court. She left a detailed message, then looked at Deni. "I'll be back as soon as I can. If Lance calls, fill him in."

"I could come with you?" she said. "Or Chris could?"

"Somebody's got to keep things running here. I'll be fine."

The assistant wanted to argue, Spencer saw. The boyfriend looked ready for a fight. Mira reassured them both, and several moments later, Spencer held the door open for her as she stepped out onto the front porch. He joined her. "Do you know where we're going?"

"If it's the same place I was yesterday, headquarters on Perdido Street."

"Good, then I'll follow you," he said, knowing she would see his letting her drive herself as a sign of trust on his part. Which was exactly what he wanted her to think. The truth was, he didn't believe she was a flight risk and even if she did try, she couldn't outrun him.

Buckled into the Camaro, he used his voice-activated dialing to call Stacy. "What are you doing?" he asked when she answered.

"Going out of my effing mind. You?"

"Heading back to HQ to question Gallier. How would you like a bit of undercover work?"

Stacy laughed. "Are you kidding?"

"That's what I thought. I want you to tail Gallier when

she leaves HQ. She's driving a blue Ford Focus. When she parks it, I'll let you know where."

"What am I looking for?"

"Where she goes, who she speaks to. And look, I'm not certain we don't have this thing all wrong and Gallier herself is in danger. In which case—"

"I watch my own ass as well as hers."

"Yes." The phone beeped, indicating another call coming in. "Got to go. Keep me posted."

He clicked through. "Malone here."

"Hey, bro. Where ya at?"

Percy. "Poydras near the Dome. Any luck with the café employees?"

"None. One of the women from Café Express thought Scott looked familiar but couldn't place him at the restaurant Monday morning. Have you seen Bayle?"

"She's not with you?"

"Nope. I thought maybe there'd been a game change."

Spencer frowned. "Not that I'm aware of." The light turned green. Mira eased through, Spencer followed. "Be there in ten minutes. If we can't find her then, release the hounds."

His brother laughed and hung up.

Exactly ten minutes later he and Mira Gallier arrived on the third floor of NOPD HQ. He kept the conversation flowing and light. He didn't want her revealing anything before they had an audience and a tape running. He supposed he should feel at least a pinch of guilt at his tactics, but didn't.

He was investigating three homicides. If she was guilty, she didn't deserve one iota of his guilt. If she wasn't, that would be proved out as well.

"Yo, Malone. Bayle was looking for you."

He turned toward his fellow detectives. "Hey, Waldon. Johnson. Tell her I heard she was MIA and I'm heading in for an interview."

"Did you say Walton and Johnson?" Gallier asked as they walked away. "Like the Radio Gawds?"

"Waldon, with a *d*. But yeah, it's kind of their claim to fame." He leaned his head closer to hers. "Only not funny.

Distinctly unfunny, actually. But they don't get that, which *is* funny. Pretty crazy, huh?"

They reached the interview room and headed inside.

He went to switch on the camera. "You want to wait for your lawyer? It's no problem."

She took a seat. "That's okay. Let's go ahead and get started."

"If at any point you change your mind, just let me know." He sat across from her. "Why were you at my home today?"

"I thought maybe you could help me."

"With what?"

"Some bizarre things had happened. I was confused."

"When I spoke to Stacy, she said you told her you didn't know what to believe. Or who to trust. Is that accurate?"

"Yes."

"Does your confusion have anything to do with Connor Scott?"

She looked surprised. "Why do you ask?"

He smiled. "Answer my question first. Okay?"

She nodded, though she looked uncomfortable. He repeated the question. "Did your confusion have anything to do with Connor Scott?"

"A little, yes."

"Could you explain?"

"He said some things—" She shook her head. "It doesn't have anything to do with this."

"Let me be the judge of that. What kind of things?"

"About my husband. They're really personal."

"Maybe I can help?" When she didn't respond, he added, "That's why you stopped by my house this morning. For my help. Right?"

She nodded, then met his eyes. "We were friends, the three of us. But—"

"He was in love with you?"

Color flooded her cheeks. Not embarrassment, he thought, but discomfort at having been so easily read. "That's what he said."

"You don't believe him?"

"I do. I didn't expect . . . I never . . ." She looked at her hands, folded on the table in front of her. "He told me that's why he joined up."

"Okay. So far, not too confusing."

"He said Jeff knew all along."

"Knew what, Ms. Gallier?"

"Where Connor had gone. And why. But Jeff always claimed he didn't."

"Which, if true, would mean he lied to you?" He paused. "Is honesty important to you?"

"Of course."

He changed direction. "Do you trust him?"

"Connor?" She hesitated. "I did. Until . . ."

"This."

"Yes."

"He's very secretive."

She shook her head. "No."

"Really? He doesn't keep secrets from you?"

"He doesn't. Not anymore, anyway."

"Honesty is important, Ms. Gallier. And I'm going to make a promise to you right now. I won't lie to you. And I'm telling you, I don't trust him. And I don't think you should, either."

She pressed her lips together, her conflicted feelings easy to read.

"Why are you protecting him?"

"I'm not."

He looked her straight in the eyes. "He's a mystery. And I find it odd, very odd, that all these things didn't start happening to you until he came back into your life. Don't you?"

She didn't reply and he continued. "You don't think it strange that all these things—these bizarre things, as you called them—began since he returned to New Orleans?"

Spencer didn't wait for an answer. "August ninth: Sisters of Mercy Church is vandalized and Father Girod is murdered. A 'judgment' message is graffitied on the windows you restored. August twelfth: a street evangelist comes into your studio and attacks you, spouting frightening things about the end of the world. He snatches your cross and runs. August thirteenth: your cross is mysteriously returned. Preacher is murdered. August sixteenth: Anton Gallier is shot to death. Interestingly, that occurs after he challenged Connor Scott to tell you the truth."

Mira was shaking. Spencer waited a moment, then pressed on. "Ms. Gallier?" She looked helplessly up at him. "When did Connor come to see you for the first time?"

She thought for a moment. "The same day that Preacher took my cross."

"The twelfth," he said. "And do you know the date he returned to New Orleans?"

"He said he'd been home a few days. Something like that."

"Would you be surprised to hear that Connor Scott returned to New Orleans on the morning of the seventh?"

"The seventh," she repeated.

"Two days before the first incident. That's pretty weird, don't you think?"

He saw that she did. "Could it be a coincidence, that all these things have occurred since Mr. Scott returned from Afghanistan? Could it also be a coincidence that, in addition, they all lead back to you?"

When she didn't answer, he asked again, "Could it be, Ms. Gallier?"

She jumped to her feet. "I don't know! Yes, maybe it could be! Or—"

"Or what?"

"Or maybe it isn't. I don't know what's happening! Why don't you believe me?"

"I want to, Mira," he said. "I really do. Please, sit down."

She did and he continued. "Let's talk about the things that have been happening to you personally." She nodded. "You believe someone broke into your home twice now."

"Someone did."

"Yes, but your house was locked up tight and we found no sign of a forced entry. How do you explain that?"

"I can't."

"After Katrina, did you change your locks?"

She frowned. "Why would I have?"

"I take it that's a no?" She confirmed and he continued. "What about your alarm code, did you change it?"

"No, I didn't. I didn't see any reason to."

"Did Connor Scott, as one of Jeff's oldest and most trusted friends, have access to both?"

As if completely nonplussed by his question, she just stared at him.

"Ms. Gallier," he pressed, "did he?"

She met his gaze defiantly. "Yes."

"And your dog, Nola, she was a gift from Mr. Scott, is that correct?"

Uncertainty flickered in her eyes. "You know she was."

"Nola seemed pretty fond of him. Bet she wouldn't even bark at him if he showed up unannounced."

"I know what you're doing and it's bullshit!"

Malone ignored her and pushed on. "He would know what aftershave your husband wore—"

"Stop it!"

"What else would he know and be able to use to unhinge you?"

She got to her feet, face white, shaking with anger. "Are we finished here, or do I need to wait for my lawyer?"

"I tell you what, let me clear you leaving with my captain." He stood. "I'll be right back."

Spencer joined his colleagues in the viewing room. No one spoke or even looked his way. They sat gazing at the video monitor, watching Gallier's every move.

She was pacing. Clasping and unclasping her hands. Talking to herself. Every so often she would stop and hug herself or drag her hands through her hair.

Suddenly, she stopped and went still. Her expression shifted from confused desperation to understanding.

"Jackpot," Percy said.

"She's got something," Bayle agreed, obviously excited. "Let's go find out what."

"Uh-uh," Spencer said. "I say we release her. See where she goes. What she does. I've already got someone in place."

"Tail her." Percy nodded. "Perfect. I'm with my bro here, Bayle."

Bayle looked frustrated. "But she knows something!"

"She's not going anywhere. Besides, if we don't release her now, she'll wait for Arnold and the moment's lost."

"Agreed," Bayle said, though she didn't look happy about it. "With a caveat. Give her a last chance to share her aha moment."

Malone agreed and reentered the interview room. She was sitting, hands folded in her lap. She looked hopefully his way.

"Free to go." He smiled. "Thanks so much for doing this, Mira. I really appreciate it."

She scooped up her handbag. He could tell she was eager to leave. He didn't blame her, but it seemed to him that her desperation had been replaced with determination.

"Is there anything else you want to share before you—"

She shook her head. "No."

"You're certain? Even the smallest realization can lead to something big."

"I agree," she said. "And I'll let you know if I have a small realization."

Which meant, maybe, that she'd had a big one.

"Are you okay to drive?" he asked. "I could give you a lift? Have an officer bring your car?"

She shook her head again and together they walked to the elevator. He pushed the call button.

"I'll escort you down," he said as the car arrived.

She didn't respond and they didn't speak again until they reached her Ford. He saw Stacy, waiting in her silver Camry, several rows down.

"I'm here for you," he said as Mira opened the car door and slid inside. He bent to meet her eyes. "If you need anything, just call. You can trust me."

She held his gaze a moment, then nodded. "Thank you."

She backed out of the parking spot. Spencer started for the building's entrance, careful not to glance Stacy's way. Even so, he was aware of the exact moment she fell in line with Gallier.

He had complete confidence in Stacy's abilities and trusted her to anticipate trouble and respond appropriately.

Trouble. Truth was, he wasn't positive they were coming at this from the right angle. They'd focused their attention on her and Scott as being the guilty parties. But what if they had this all wrong? What if she was the perpetrator's focus? What if they were, indeed, dealing with a lunatic who believed himself final judge over all?

What part might Mira Gallier play in that scenario?

Not liking the answer to that, Malone went back to the squad room. Bayle was waiting for him.

"You did it," she said, grinning. "She trusts you." She delivered a friendly punch to his upper arm, seeming almost gleeful. "Good job, partner."

"I'm not so sure about that."

"Why not?" She fell into step with him. "This is practically a no-brainer."

"A no-brainer," he repeated. "Are you for real? Have you even considered the fact that instead of the perp, she's the intended victim?"

"No. Hell no, in fact." She shook her head. "The one who looks guilty usually is. It's a fact of police work, Malone. And you know it. We see it played out that way every day, year after year."

It was true. But still, his gut instinct was leading him in another direction. He told her so.

She shrugged. "Maybe you're right. But I don't think so."

"And you're never wrong?"

She grinned. "Of course not. You?"

"Never." He returned her grin. "May the best man win."

He started off. She called after him. "You're so full of crap, Malone."

He looked over his shoulder at her. "Clearly, I'm not the only one. Catch you later, loser."

Chapter Forty-seven

Mira knew what she had to do. Stacy Killian had told her that morning. A clean slate. Question everything. Start with what she *knew* was true. Lay it all out with the possibility it wasn't.

And look for what?

For someone who would want to hurt her. A liar. A betrayer.

Mira glanced at the dash clock and noted the time. Deni's morning class would have just let out. She grabbed her cell and dialed her assistant.

"Where are you?" Deni answered. "Are you okay?"

"I'm on my way home. I'm fine."

"You're not coming in?"

"No. I need some time to think. To try to sort things out."

"I could help you. Mira, I . . . I don't think you should be alone. I'm afraid for you."

"I've got to do this by myself. I'll be fine." She paused. "But thanks, Deni. I'm really glad you're my friend."

But maybe she wasn't.

Mira shook her head against the thought. Why would Deni try to hurt her?

"What happened at the police station?"

"They asked me a lot of questions. Mostly about Connor."

"Connor?" she repeated. "Do they think he's the one who killed all those people?"

"They didn't come right out and say that, but that's the way it seemed."

"What are you going to do?"

"Clean the slate."

"I don't understand. What does that mean?"

She didn't answer. "I've got to go. I'll check in later."

"Wait! Have you called Dr. Jasper?"

"Not yet. Did she call again?"

"No, but . . . I thought I saw her drive by the studio."

"Dr. Jasper? Really?"

"I was taking some glass out to the bin. At first I thought she was going to turn in to our drive, because she was going so slowly. But then she just rolled on by."

"Are you certain?"

"Almost a hundred percent. Doesn't she drive that beautiful silver-blue Jag?"

"She does."

"This is going to sound really nuts, but"—she let out a long breath—"Dr. Jasper wasn't alone in the car. There was a man with her."

Mira waited, wondering what would come next. Wondering if, after everything that had happened so far, she could be surprised.

"Mira," Deni went on, "he looked like Jeff."

Like Jeff? A man with Dr. Jasper— The blare of horns and scream of brakes jolted her attention back to the road. She dropped the phone. A red light, she'd realized, heart leaping to her throat. She had run right through it. She could have killed herself or someone else.

She made it through the intersection and to the side of the road, then stopped the car. She rested her head on the steering wheel, breathing deeply. The feeling passed and she remembered Deni. She recovered the phone from the car floor.

"Deni?" she managed. "Are you still there?"

She was. "What happened?"

"I . . . I ran a light and nearly caused an accident."

"It's my fault, I shouldn't have said anything. Maybe it was my imagination. I mean, the man probably just looked similar and after what you told me last night . . . Besides, I was up by the building and she was rolling by . . ."

Her assistant's words trailed off and Mira drew her eyebrows together. Why would Dr. Jasper have driven by the studio? And who could have been with her? Not Jeff. Of course not.

Question everything. And everyone.

"I shouldn't have upset you. She's probably worried about you and drove by to see if your car was in the lot. And the guy could have been anyone. There are a lot of tall, dark-haired—"

"Don't worry about it," Mira said, forcing calm into her voice. "I'll call her as soon as I get home."

Mira eased carefully back into traffic. Even as she fixed her attention fully on the road, her thoughts began to wander. Why would Dr. Jasper have driven by that way? Why not just call again?

The man with her had looked like Jeff.

Mira thought back to the previous evening. Dr. Jasper's call had come in moments after Jeff's. So close, in fact, she had thought it had been Jeff calling back.

A weird coincidence? Or carefully timed?

The thought took her breath. Dr. Jasper—better than anyone—knew her innermost thoughts, her hopes and fears. She knew intimate details of her and Jeff's life together. But she hadn't known Jeff. She would have mentioned if she had. Wouldn't she?

She shook her head. Ridiculous. Why would Dr. Jasper want to terrorize her? What could she possibly gain from it?

Mira tightened her fingers on the steering wheel, forcing herself to focus. She'd found Dr. Jasper through a recommendation. Not her regular physician. A friend or acquaintance. Who? Someone who had known Jeff, she remembered.

She turned on to her street. Mrs. Latrobe's porch light

was still on. She glanced that way, frowning slightly at how uncharacteristic it was.

Mrs. Latrobe. Ask her, of course.

Mira slammed on her brakes, jerking to a stop in front of the woman's home. She stared at the porch light. Louise Latrobe's reason for living was spying on her neighbors. And she seemed to have a special interest in Mira. What had she said the other day? *Men coming and going, all hours.*

Louise Latrobe would have seen everything. Who had been breaking in and how. She would be able to describe them.

And Louise had known Jeff. If it had been him—back from the dead—she would have recognized him.

Mira pulled to the side of the road, hopped out of her car and hurried to Louise Latrobe's wide front porch. She rang the bell, waiting, thoughts racing as she searched for what she would say. Subtlety, she thought. She would start in a neighborly fashion: she was there to advise her she'd left her porch light burning. She would ease into who the woman might have seen "coming and going at all hours." Mira couldn't believe she hadn't thought of this before.

She rang the bell again, then knocked forcefully.

"Mrs. Latrobe? Louise? It's Mira Gallier."

Still the woman didn't answer. Mrs. Latrobe rarely left her home. Her Friday-afternoon shampoo and set at the beauty salon and the occasional doctor's appointment. She even had her groceries delivered.

Could she have fallen ill? Or had an accident? Could she be in the hospital? It would explain the light burning in the daytime. And it wouldn't be so surprising, considering her age.

Mira peered through the leaded-glass sidelight. A lamp was on in the front parlor as well. Of what she could see, nothing looked out of place.

"Mrs. Latrobe," she called again, pounding this time, urgency tugging at her. "It's Mira Gallier. Please, I need to talk to you!"

When there was still no answer, Mira darted down the

steps and circled around back. She knocked on that door as well, with the same outcome. Feeling like a thief, she tried the door.

Locked.

She made her way back around front. It was as hot as hell and unbearably muggy. Welcome to New Orleans in August. Sweat beaded her upper lip and rolled down her back. Her cotton shirt clung to her sticky skin.

The woman wasn't home, Mira told herself even as she climbed the steps. She could try back later, question her then. That's what a logical, completely sane person would do.

At this moment, Mira felt anything but logical. Or sane.

Somebody was tormenting her. It might or might not be tied to three murders—ones the police believed she had something to do with.

And Louise Latrobe very well might know—or be able to identify—the person responsible.

Mira glanced quickly over her shoulder, then reached for the doorknob.

It turned. The door clicked open.

Mira's heart sank. She hadn't expected that. She'd tried out of desperation, out of an unwillingness to give up.

Mrs. Latrobe trusted no one. Just as she wouldn't leave lights burning all day, she wouldn't leave her front door unlocked.

This was bad. Something was wrong.

In life, moments presented themselves where a critical choice had to be made. Go forward? Or back away? Both held risks. And either way could be second-guessed for a lifetime.

Now was one of those moments.

"Louise," she called softly, stepping into the foyer, "it's Mira Gallier. I'm checking to make sure you're all right."

The house was quiet save for the tick of the massive grandfather clock standing sentinel against the opposite wall. The interior was warm with a subtle, underlying sour smell.

Like food that had gone bad or garbage that hadn't been covered. Mira wrinkled her nose in distaste. She headed for the parlor where she had seen the light burning. It was the parlor on the side of the house that bordered hers. A large wingback chair faced the window, its broad back toward the entry. On the small table beside it sat a pair of binoculars.

"Louise?" she called again. Nothing appeared out of order. She swept her gaze lower, to the floor. It landed on a small, pale hand peeking out from in front of the chair.

Mira caught her breath. "Mrs. Latrobe," she whispered. "Please say something."

But she didn't. And never would again. Louise Latrobe lay faceup on the floor in front of the chair, face twisted into a terrible death mask.

On her forehead, in the same orange color that tinted the woman's lips, was the number 4.

Mira stood in frozen horror. She wanted to run but couldn't move. She heard herself scream, yet no sound escaped her.

The grandfather clock struck the hour. The sound jolted her from her terrified state. She turned and ran, one scream after another ripping past her lips.

She'd left the front door open. Mira darted through it, onto the porch—and smack into Stacy Killian.

Chapter Forty-eight

Wednesday, August 17
1:03 P.M.

"Help!" Mira cried. "It's my neighbor. I think she's . . . she's dead!"

Stacy grasped her upper arms. "Slow down, Mira. Look at me. That's right. Focus. Take a deep breath."

Mira did as Stacy ordered, holding her gaze, breathing deeply. At first, her legs shook so badly she feared she would fall if Stacy let her go. But gradually, as the seconds ticked past, they grew steadier, her head less light.

"Good," Stacy said, dropping her hands. "Tell me what happened."

"Mrs. Latrobe . . . Louise . . . I came over to talk to her. She didn't answer . . . I went in and . . . there she was."

"Where?"

She shuddered, remembering. "On the floor. In the parlor."

"Did you touch her?"

She shook her head.

"Did you touch anything else?"

"No."

"Good. Now I have to go inside, just for a minute, then I'll be right back. I need you to stay here. Can you do that?"

Mira nodded, though her teeth began to chatter.

Stacy disappeared into the house. Mira squeezed her eyes shut against the image that popped into her head: of the woman's horrible expression and that vile orange 4 on her forehead.

Poor Mrs. Latrobe. Who could have done this?

Stacy reappeared. She was on her cell phone. "I'm at the scene. Yes, she's with me. You got it. Love you, too."

Detective Malone.

It suddenly occurred to Mira how much trouble she was in. How this must look. "Oh, my God."

Stacy pocketed her phone. "What's wrong?"

"I didn't do this."

"No one said you did."

"But Detective Malone . . . he's been questioning me about those other murders . . . now—" She brought her hands to her face. "What's happening to me?"

Stacy came to stand directly in front of her. "Spencer's on his way. He's on your side and so am I. Tell us everything and we can help you."

She dropped her hands. "Do you really think you can?"

"I do, Mira. I promise." Stacy took a small spiral notebook and pen from her back pocket. "What was your relationship with Mrs. Latrobe?"

"We're neighbors."

"Were you friendly?"

"Not especially. But we never had words. Not really."

"Not really? What does that mean?"

Mira hugged herself. "She was a busybody. Spent most of her time spying on her neighbors. Especially me. Sometimes she would make a comment. Or complain."

At the sound of a car door slamming, Mira glanced at the street. Detective Malone, she saw, hurrying up the walk. A moment later came the sound of sirens. An ambulance and two police cruisers.

"Okay, Mira, look at me," Stacy said. "Let them do their job, you talk to me. Like we're just two girlfriends, out for lunch."

She nodded, wishing they were. "Strange things have been happening to me. I thought Mrs. Latrobe could help. Because of her spying."

"I'm not quite following that. Could you explain?"

"Yesterday I stopped here to see if Louise had heard Nola's barking. And to apologize if she had. In case it woke her up." Mira twisted her fingers together. "She said she hadn't heard Nola but made this comment about men coming and going from my place. At all hours. I thought she meant the police and—"

"The times you've called Spencer?"

"Detective Malone, yes. And Connor had been by, visiting. So I didn't ask her to explain. She was kind of prickly."

"I understand," Stacy said. "When I talked to you this morning, you said you were starting to think your husband might be alive. Why's that, Mira?"

Detective Malone came up beside them but didn't say anything. Mira glanced at him, then back at Stacy. "He called me. Last night. It was his voice. He said he was going to be home soon."

"Did he say anything else?"

"No. I . . . I dropped the phone and the call got killed."

"What did you do then?"

"I didn't know what to do. He didn't call back and I was sort of . . . freaking out. So I went to a friend's. I slept there."

Stacy cocked an eyebrow. "You didn't wait at your house for him, just in case?"

"It doesn't make sense, does it?" Mira brought a hand to her forehead. "My therapist called—"

"What's his name?"

"Her. Dr. Adele Jasper. She called right after Jeff did. But on my landline."

"Did you tell her what happened?"

"No, not exactly."

"Why not?"

Mira looked away, feeling like a complete fool. "I just . . . couldn't. I knew what she'd think."

"And what's that?"

"That I was cracking up." Mira pressed her lips together, using the moment to try to compose herself. "I needed to talk to somebody. Somebody who I thought would believe me. So I went to Deni's. She convinced me to stay the night. I had my cell phone. And if it had really been Jeff, wouldn't he call me again?"

"That makes good sense," Stacy said. "Why didn't you call him back?"

"I couldn't. It was an unlisted number. My cell wouldn't dial it back."

"So this morning, what happened before you stopped and talked to me?"

"I came home really early. Because of Nola and because . . . I wondered if he would be there."

"But he wasn't."

She shook her head. "But it looked like he had been. His pillow, there was an indentation . . . like his head had been on it. And it . . . smelled like him."

She looked down at her clasped hands, then back up at the two detectives. "That's why I came over here. That and the porch light. I remembered what Louise had said, about men at my place." Connor's image filled her head. The memory of his mouth against hers, the way it had made her feel. She wasn't about to share that with them. "She knew Jeff; if he was alive she would have recognized him. And I figured she could describe who she had seen and when."

"Good thinking. And the porch light?"

"It was on during the day. Louise never did that. Once she lectured Jeff and me about how much electricity we used."

Mira saw Stacy's lips twitch slightly. "So why did you let yourself into her house?"

"I shouldn't have. I knocked and called out. Front and back, then just checked the knob. The door was open so I went in." Her voice shook. "I wish I hadn't. She looked . . . it was so horrible. I don't think I'll ever be able to get it out of my head."

"It'll get better, Mira, I promise." Stacy squeezed her hands. "When's the last time you saw your neighbor alive?"

"Let me think, so much has happened." She brought her fingers to her temples. "I talked to her Tuesday afternoon, that's when she made that comment about people coming and going."

"And that was the last time?"

"Yes. No, wait. That night. About nine o'clock, when I got back home. After being questioned by you guys."

"You're certain it was her?"

She thought a moment, then nodded. "Positive. Her porch light snapped on, then she appeared at her side window. I waved, though she didn't wave back."

"Thank you." Stacy jerked her thumb toward Spencer. "He and I need to talk. Stay put, okay? I'll be back."

As the two started off, the improbability of the situation occurred to Mira. "Stacy?"

The woman looked over her shoulder at her. "Yes?"

"Where did you . . . I mean, how did you happen to be here, just now when I needed you?"

She smiled. "I wondered when you'd ask. Spencer tasked me with keeping an eye on you. It worked out pretty well for both of us, didn't it?"

Mira drew her eyebrows together. "I don't understand what you mean."

"Kept me from another day of daytime TV and gave you someone to back up your version of events."

Stacy had been following her. Malone had set that up. It was why he had let her go.

She had been so easily duped by his manufactured concern. But as Stacy had pointed out, it seemed to have worked in her favor.

Where would she be right now without Stacy as a witness?

Mira shuddered and turned toward the house's big front window. A reflection in the glass caught her eyes. A Jaguar. Silver-blue. Easing past.

Dr. Jasper. The street was choked with police and emergency vehicles, providing only a single lane for moving traffic. She didn't see the Jag, but that didn't mean it wasn't there, halted beside the crime-scene van or ambulance.

She jogged down the steps and traversed the lawn to the street. She looked up, then down. No silver-blue Jag. If it had been there, it was gone now.

Chapter Forty-nine

Through the doorway, Malone caught sight of Bayle striding toward the house. She looked pissed. She signed in then jogged up the porch steps.

A moment later she stood before him, all but breathing fire. She nodded at Stacy, then turned to him. "A word, Malone. In private."

They found a quiet corner and Bayle rounded on him. "How did you get here so much faster than I did?"

"I made all the lights?"

"More like Stacy called you first. And then you called me when you were en route?"

"Pretty much."

His honesty seemed to momentarily throw her. "What's Stacy doing here, anyway?"

"I told you I put a tail on Gallier. You never asked who."

"Son of a bitch, Malone." She lowered her voice. "What kind of game are you playing?"

"No game. You got a problem with Stacy now?"

She flushed. "Don't make me the bad guy here. I've got no problem with Stacy. My problem's with you."

"Welcome to the frickin' club. Look, it made sense. We

didn't have to pull anybody off another detail, she's a damn good cop—one, by the way, who knows Gallier. Plus, I trust her completely."

"To put your interests first."

He narrowed his eyes. "This isn't about me, Bayle. And it's not about you. It's about catching a killer. And the interests I'm putting first are the department's. Can you say the same?"

She couldn't. He saw it in her eyes. She tried to mask it, but whatever her agenda, it ran too deep to hide completely. What the hell was going on with her?

"What do we have?" she asked, voice tight.

Spencer motioned the front parlor. "Take a look for yourself.

"Her name was Louise Latrobe," he said a moment later, as they joined Stacy beside the vic. "According to her driver's license—yes, she still had a valid Louisiana license—she was eighty-nine. She was a widow and lived alone."

Malone allowed himself to see the victim through Bayle's eyes, as if for the first time. Latrobe lay on the floor between a large window and a wingback chair. She'd been a petite woman, bony in the way some elderly became, neither fat nor muscle to anchor the skin. Her body was twisted slightly, as if she had tried to stop her fall. One hand rested on her chest, the other at her side. Her face had settled into one of those grotesque expressions that made crime-scene humor necessary.

But still, the most startling thing was the orange 4 on her forehead.

"What the hell does that mean?" Bayle asked.

The coroner's investigator was finishing his examination. He looked up at Bayle. "Indeed, Detective."

"What are you thinking, Ray?"

"No signs of a struggle. No visible marks on her body. Other than the numeral four, of course. Nails look clean. We're not going to get a lot from her."

"How'd he kill her?"

"I'm not certain he did."

"Excuse me?" Malone said.

"This may be a case of cardiac arrest."

"Cardiac arrest," Bayle repeated. "How do you figure?"

"We see this with heart attack victims, hand at her chest, clutching. Not warding off an attacker."

"So before she had her sudden, excruciating heart attack," Bayle said, sounding annoyed, "she got her god-awful orange lipstick and marked her forehead with the four?"

"Hardly." The man made a face as he shook his head. "I'm not saying the killer wasn't here, I'm just saying I don't think he touched her."

"So what happened?"

"The son of a bitch scared her to death."

The room went momentarily quiet. Then Spencer asked, "Where's the lipstick?" When none of them responded, he directed the question to the CSI team. "Anybody collect a tube of lipstick?" They hadn't.

He turned back to Stacy and Bayle. "The binoculars corroborate Gallier's story."

"Which was?" Bayle snapped. "I missed it."

Stacy quickly filled her in, finishing with, "Apparently, Latrobe was the neighborhood busybody."

"Are you buying Gallier's story? Seems to me, a spying neighbor's a damn good motive for murder."

"Oh, I think it's a motive, all right. Only I don't think it's Gallier's."

"I'll play devil's advocate here," Bayle said. "I like Gallier for this. It makes four deaths, all connected to her. We've got a snooping neighbor who keeps tabs on her comings and goings. Gallier knew it was only a matter of time before we questioned her."

"I get that," Stacy said. "Big problem, though. I was tailing her. Her story dovetails perfectly with what I witnessed."

"Really?" Bayle cocked an eyebrow. "Where were you when she stopped her car?"

"End of the block."

"And from that distance you could see her expression and tell that none of this was planned or rehearsed?"

Stacy narrowed her eyes. "Of course not. But as she described, she turned onto Frenchmen, then a couple car lengths in, slammed on the brakes. She sat several moments stopped in the middle of the street, then pulled over and parked.

"Next thing I know, she's racing across the lawn, heading to Latrobe's. I watched her knock, peek through windows, go around back, then come back around the front. She was the picture of determination. And _then_, agit_ation_."

"Agitation? Interesting."

"When she entered the house illegally, I went after her. She was completely terrified."

"That convinces me," Bayle said sarcastically. "I've never run across a perp who deserved an Academy Award for acting."

Stacy didn't tolerate sarcasm well. Malone stepped in quickly. "Let's assume this is the work of the same perp. Accompanying the other three vics was a message. The first, 'He will come again to judge the living and the dead.' The second, simply, 'Judgment Day.' And the third, 'He cast out Seven Demons.' Here, all we have is the number four. What's he"—he looked pointedly at Bayle—"or _she_ telling us?"

"I've got it," Stacy said. "The countdown has begun."

"The countdown? To Judgment Day?"

"No. The Seven Demons. Father Girod was number one, Preacher was two, Anton Gallier was three, Latrobe is four. Three more to go."

Chapter Fifty

When Detective Malone had finally given Mira the okay to return home, Stacy insisted on escorting her. Although Mira had assured the woman it was unnecessary, she was oddly comforted. While being questioned by Detective Bayle she'd gotten the feeling that if Stacy hadn't been there to back up her version of events, she'd be in handcuffs instead of walking free.

"Do you have someone you can call?" Stacy asked as they made their way down the walkway to the street.

It had rained while she'd been waiting on Louise's porch. A typical August afternoon shower, it had left the air soupy. "I'll be fine."

"That's not what I asked."

No, it wasn't. But she hated to lie to the woman. The one person she wanted to call, she didn't think she should.

Connor.

A lump formed in her throat. Did she want to call him because of their past relationship? Because he made her feel safe? Or because he said he loved her—and right now she really needed that?

"Mira, do you?"

"Yes, of course."

"Who?"

"My assistant Deni or my friend Connor. I haven't decided which."

"You don't have any family?"

The question crushed her. She fought to keep it from showing. "No, but they're like my family."

They reached the street. The ambulance, coroner's wagon and a couple cruisers had cleared out. The crime-scene van remained, as well as a number of personal police vehicles.

"Which car is yours?" Mira asked.

Stacy pointed to a silver Camry parked across from her house. "Why?"

"I want to know who to look for if trouble comes knocking."

Stacy smiled. "Let's hope it won't. Besides, I have a feeling that once my captain hears about this, I'll be back to watching daytime TV."

"I feel your pain."

Their eyes met and they both laughed. It struck Mira as bizarre that she could laugh now, but at the same time she was grateful for it.

They reached Mira's drive. Stacy held out her card. "I know you have Spencer's number, but here's mine as well."

Mira took it. "Thank you."

"Think of me as a cop *and* a friend. I mean it, okay?"

Nola was waiting at the front door for her. Mira unlocked the door, let her out to do her business, then called her into the house. The dog barreled inside and down the hall to the kitchen. Mira followed slowly, listening to the quiet, assuring herself she was alone.

Would she ever feel completely safe here again? she wondered. Acknowledging that only time would tell, she headed to the kitchen, fed Nola, then sat.

Take the next step. Figure this thing out. Mira took a pen and notepad from beside the phone. *Deni,* she wrote. *Chris. Connor.*

Dr. Jasper. Her silver-blue Jag.

She reached for her cell and dialed the therapist. The woman answered right away.

"Mira, where are you?"

Instead of answering the question, she posed one of her own. "Have you been looking for me, Dr. Jasper?"

"Yes. You and I had an appointment this morning. I came in early to meet you, but you didn't show."

"Do you still drive the Jag sedan? Silver-blue color?"

"Silver Cloud. Yes, but—"

"I just saw you drive by my house. Deni saw you drive by the studio."

"I'm at the office, Mira. I have been since our scheduled appointment this morning."

Could Deni have been mistaken? Could she have as well?
Or was Dr. Jasper lying?

"Deni thought she saw Jeff with you."

"Excuse me, did you say Jeff?"

"Yes. Was he with you?"

"Of course not. He's dead."

"He called me last night."

"What did you say?" She sounded stunned.

"Jeff called. Said he'd be here soon."

For a long moment the therapist was silent. When she spoke, her tone was measured, her voice low and soothing. As if she were trying to talk sense to a crazy person.

A crazy person. Her.

"Mira, I wish it had been me driving by. I wish Jeff had called or that he'd been in the car with me. But I've been here all day and Jeff is dead. He's dead," she said again. "I'm so sorry."

Mira held tightly to the phone, wishing she knew what the hell she was doing.

"You saw what you wanted to see," the therapist continued. "Last night, you heard the voice you wanted to hear."

"I was trying to remember, Dr. Jasper. Who recommended you to me?"

Again a moment of silence. "I don't remember. That was years ago."

"It was someone from the memorial service. Someone connected to Jeff. Or his family."

Then she remembered. It hit her like a thunderbolt.

Not a friend of hers or Jeff's. Charlotte's friend. Another former Queen of Rex.

Mira pictured her. One of those perfectly preserved matrons, never a hair out of place or nail chipped.

Like Dr. Jasper.

"The mind has power beyond anything we can really imagine," Dr. Jasper was saying. "I had a patient who 'believed' her body into pregnancy. Morning sickness, sore breasts, a swelling belly . . . She wanted to be pregnant so badly she 'made' it happen. Was there a real, live fetus growing inside her womb? Of course not. But her mind had convinced her body there was."

"Why are you so desperately trying to convince me all this is in my head?"

"Mira, this *is* all in your head. And I'd hardly call my actions 'desperate.' I've always had your best interests at heart. You were doing so well. We were on the precipice of stopping therapy. Now . . . your psychological state is more fragile than when we began our work."

"Whose side are you on, Dr. Jasper?"

"How can you ask me that? Yours, of course."

"Why didn't you tell me you were friends with the Galliers or that you knew Jeff?"

"I'm not friends with the Galliers and I didn't know Jeff. Charlotte and I have served on a few committees together. But that's all."

"You should have let me know that up front, considering what they've put me through."

"I would have," she said firmly, "had I thought it anything that would interfere with my ability to counsel you."

"I trusted you."

"You still can. I promise you."

"I've got to go."

"Did you hear anything I said? I'm frightened for you. You're in a very dangerous place."

"I heard everything you said. And I'm thinking I might be in danger from you."

"Mira," she coaxed, "you know that's not true. It's false and it's destructive. Someone planted that seed. Ask yourself why."

"I'm hanging up now. Goodbye, Dr. Jasper."

"No, wait! The police were here. Asking me questions about you."

"What kind of questions?"

"About your treatment and state of mind. Your feelings for your father-in-law."

Mira went cold. "What did you tell them?"

"That what we discuss is privileged. But they also asked a lot of questions about Connor Scott. Your relationship with him. Whether I had met him. If you talked about him much. I'm worried about it. They know something. I don't think you should trust him."

Mira's hackles rose. "You're warning me about Connor? You don't even know him."

"I know this all started after he returned to New Orleans. I know you're emotionally vulnerable right now. I know that when Connor reappeared in your life, so did these . . . manifestations of Jeff."

"Are you the one, Dr. Jasper?"

"The one?"

"Who's been terrorizing me? Who somehow re-created his voice? What about his aftershave? Did I mention the one he preferred? Or did Charlotte Gallier tell you?"

"My God, Mira! Please stop this. Come in. We'll talk. I have your best interests—"

"Goodbye, Dr. Jasper."

She hung up. Almost immediately, her cell rang. The therapist calling back. Mira silenced the call. Moments later a text message binged through.

I do have your best interests at heart. You can trust me.

And then, in another text: *Be careful, Mira. Please.*

Mira stared at the two text messages, torn. What if she was

wrong? What if the therapist was the one person she *could* trust?

She sank onto a bar stool. They'd worked together just over four years. She had helped Mira through some harrowing times. If the therapist hadn't had her best interests at heart, would she have helped her so much?

How could she be certain?

Call Charlotte and ask her.

Her ex–mother-in-law wouldn't take her call. She didn't doubt that for a second. She had people who screened her calls: a butler, housekeeper or social secretary. To make it through the screening process, the woman had to want to speak to the caller. Or want something from him or her.

That was it. Dr. Jasper would call Charlotte.

Mira still had the Galliers' home number in her contacts list. She dialed *67 to mask her number and called it. The butler answered. "Dr. Adele Jasper," Mira said, "calling for Charlotte Gallier."

A moment later, Charlotte came on the line. "Adele, darling, how lovely of you to call."

That told Mira everything she needed to know. She ended the call and stuffed her phone into the back pocket of her capri pants. Dr. Jasper had kept the truth from her. She and Jeff's mother were more than just "board member" acquaintances.

Was Dr. Jasper the one who had been terrorizing her?

But why now? After almost four years?

The man in the car looked an awful lot like Jeff. The smell of his aftershave. His voice on the phone.

Mira began to pace. It didn't make sense, did it? No, she thought, answering her own question. None of it did.

She stopped pacing and lifted her face to the ceiling. What should she do now? Who could she turn to?

Connor.

She wanted to trust him. She wanted it so badly. Why not just let go and allow herself to? He'd said he was in love with her. He made her feel safe. He'd brought her Nola, for Pete's sake.

But he'd also called Jeff a liar. All this craziness had begun after he'd come back into her life. The police suspected him of being a killer.

A killer. Father Girod. Preacher. Anton. Poor Mrs. Latrobe. Mira shuddered as the image of the woman filled her head. That horrible grimace. The orange 4 on her forehead. As if she had been just a number, one in a line of many.

One in a line of many.

Mira caught her breath. Is that what the number had meant? Was there to be a five and a six? Was there a number waiting for her?

Fear shot through her. She sank into the sofa. Suddenly, knowing who she could trust became urgent. This wasn't simply about someone playing a sick game with her.

People were dying.

She hadn't really connected the two before. She hadn't thought the murders had anything to do with her. Not really.

But they did. Dear God.

A betrayal by Connor would crush her.

She needed him in her life, but she had to know if she could trust him. She couldn't discover the answer to that question sitting here.

Mira grabbed her purse, keys and Nola, then hurried to her car.

Chapter Fifty-one

Captain O'Shay moved her gaze from Malone to Stacy to Bayle and back again. Her expression let them know she was not a happy camper. "We have four victims already," she said, "and you're telling me to expect three more?"

"Maybe," Malone offered. "If our theory is correct."

"Explain."

"The perp left us a message at the Gallier scene—"

"He cast out Seven Demons."

"Yes. Today we have another victim. This one with the number four on her forehead."

"And you believe it means . . ."

"That Latrobe was 'demon' number four. Gallier was number three."

"It's a countdown," Stacy said. "Seven demons, four down, three to go."

Captain O'Shay drummed her fingers on the desktop. "Which would make Father Girod and Preacher numbers one and two. You're certain it's the same perp? Different MO."

Spencer shook his head. "Not really, Captain. Each murder's been different. What's remained the same is the UNSUB's method of communicating with us and—"

Bayle jumped in. "The connection to Mira Gallier."

"Why these victims?" Captain O'Shay asked. "If your theory's correct, what's our guy's motivation? Clearly, Gallier's a key piece of the puzzle. It's a question of how she fits in."

"Someone's killing these people for her?" Stacy offered. "Anton Gallier was an enemy and the busybody neighbor was an annoyance."

Malone agreed. "Connor Scott, maybe. It all started when he came back into her life. And he's in love with her."

Captain O'Shay frowned. "So who's next? Who's number five?"

"We find out who else Gallier has issues with?" Stacy said.

"Seems to me we might all be on that list." Malone grinned. "We better watch our backs."

"Not funny," Stacy said. "I'm not even officially recovered from my last run-in with a perp."

"Maybe no one else is on the list?"

Malone looked disbelievingly at Bayle. "How do you figure?"

"Anton Gallier was the intended target. The busybody neighbor saw something. Everything else has been a smokescreen to cover her father-in-law's murder."

"I was tailing her," Stacy offered. "Her story checks out."

"An elaborate ruse."

"Ridiculously elaborate," she said. "Come on, Karin. She didn't know she was being tailed."

"Think about it," Bayle insisted, "Mira Gallier and Scott create the scenario together, then they act it out. Real time."

Stacy shook her head. "I see where you're coming from, but it just doesn't feel right to me. I've got to go with Spencer on this one."

"Of course you do."

"What's that supposed to mean?"

"You know damn well. He's your fiancé. You're not going against him. At least not until you've got that ring on your finger."

"Detective," Captain O'Shay said sharply, "that's enough!"

"Is it? I don't think so. What's she doing here, anyway? Not only is she *not* working this case, she's on leave."

Bayle turned back to Captain O'Shay. "Of course, considering the circumstances, bringing that to your attention probably won't do any good."

"What circumstances are those, Detective?"

"It's all in the family, right?"

Malone winced. Challenging Captain O'Shay's ethics was a dangerous move.

"You'd better back down, Detective. Right now. If you're going to accuse me of favoritism, you better be ready to back it up."

Bayle flushed. "Requesting a word in private, Captain."

"I think that might be a good idea. Detectives, give us a minute."

Malone and Stacy filed out of the office, closing the door behind them. He looked at Stacy. "What's Bayle's deal? You worked with her briefly, she always like this?"

"That's not the Karin Bayle I worked with. The Karin I know is a level-headed, good cop."

"Her breakdown, what was that all about?"

"Not sure. We weren't working together then."

"Who was?"

She thought a moment. "Donna St. Cloud. She's DIU, First District."

"You know her?"

"Not well, but well enough to ask a couple questions."

The captain's door opened; Bayle stepped out. "She wants you both inside."

Captain O'Shay stood in front of her desk, arms folded across her chest. "Take a seat." They did and she pinned Malone with her gaze. "Bayle's made a serious accusation against you."

"It's bullshit."

"Conflict of interest. Dereliction of duties. Impaired judgment."

Stacy snorted in disgust and Captain O'Shay turned that steely gaze on her. "You have something to add, Detective Killian?"

"Yeah, Captain, I do. It's *absolute* bullshit."

"Let's see. Malone, you manipulated an investigation by insinuating Detective Killian, not only your fiancée but an officer out on medical leave, into it. According to Bayle, you did it so you could shut her out. Case in point, you learned of the Latrobe homicide first and notified your partner last. She arrived to the scene after you had questioned the witness."

"That's Bayle's interpretation, Captain. Yes, I asked Stacy to tail Gallier. A decision that had nothing to do with my relationship with her and everything to do with her relationship with Gallier. Do I trust Stacy not to screw up? A lot more than some minimal-experience uniform you might have agreed to assign to her."

"That's right, Malone, *I* would have assigned. I'm in charge here. I call the shots, not you."

"Yes, Captain."

"Your reckless arrogance has put me in an extremely awkward position."

"I apologize, Captain."

"And you," she said, turning her gaze back to Stacy. "You think you're ready to come back, Detective? Fine. You bring me an okay from your physician and I'll welcome you with open arms. Until then, you're on medical leave. Is that clear?"

"Crystal, Captain."

Malone stood. "I respectfully request you take Bayle off the case. She has her own agenda and, frankly, I don't trust she has my back."

"Funny, she said the same thing about you."

"What's your decision, Captain?"

"Put your ass back in that chair, Detective." She motioned to Stacy. "Thank you, Detective Killian. That will be all. Send Detective Bayle back in."

A moment later, Bayle had rejoined them. Malone noticed that she wouldn't look at him.

"You two will put this petty, inappropriate bullshit aside

and work together. We have four victims and I expect you to get your collective acts together. If you don't, I'll pull both your asses off this case and park them at desks."

Bayle jumped to her feet. "Captain, with all due respect—"

"Can it, Detective. My focus is making sure we don't have another victim. I suggest you get Scott back in here for questioning. If you haven't already, create a time line. I want to know the last time someone saw Latrobe alive and what Scott was doing every minute after. And work together, dammit!"

"But, Captain—"

"That'll be all. Keep me posted."

Chapter Fifty-two

Scott came with an attorney this time. Malone recognized him from the newspaper. Phillip Knight was a celebrity law-yer. One of the best criminal defense attorneys in the city, he was as smart as he was slippery. Scott wasn't taking any chances. Of course, rich people rarely did.

They took seats in the interview room. Malone studied Scott and had to give the guy props—he looked completely relaxed.

Malone introduced himself to the lawyer, then turned to Scott. "Thank you for coming in, Mr. Scott. Have you ever heard the name Louise Latrobe?"

Scott shook his head. "No."

"You're certain?"

"Yes."

"You and Mira Gallier are good friends, correct?" He agreed and Malone went on. "And when Jeff Gallier was alive, you spent a good bit of time in their home?"

Again, he agreed.

"In all that time, did you meet any of their neighbors?"

Scott appeared to think a moment, then shook his head. "No."

"Did Jeff or Mira talk about any of their neighbors? Socialize with them?"

"Not that I remember."

"They never mentioned a neighbor who was difficult? Nosy?"

His expression altered slightly. "Wait, there was something . . . a neighbor who spied on them. The old lady who lived to their right."

Malone made a note of Scott's sudden recollection. "Would it surprise you to learn her name was Louise Latrobe?"

"I wouldn't feel any particular way about it." He folded his hands on the table. "Since I didn't know her."

"How about if I told you she was dead? That she had been murdered?"

That got a reaction. From both Scott and his attorney.

The lawyer leaned forward. "That has nothing to do with my client. He's already told you he didn't know her."

"Where have you been the past twenty-four hours, Mr. Scott?"

"Around."

"Could you be more specific?"

"Could you?"

"From the time you left here last night until now."

"Are you serious?" asked Knight, indignant. "Surely you don't expect my client to give you a minute-by-minute account?"

"But I do, Mr. Knight. With an emphasis on the highlights."

Knight pressed. "If you have a victim—"

"We do."

"—you have an approximate time of death. I don't appreciate you wasting our time."

"Sometimes TOD doesn't tell the whole tale. She was last seen alive around this time yesterday."

The attorney started to argue, but Scott stopped him. "Yesterday I left questioning here and went to Mira Gallier's."

"Why?"

"Because we're friends. And because I needed her to know the truth."

"About what?"

"My feelings for her."

"Which are?"

"None of your business."

Malone decided to let that go. "How long were you there?"

"Not long. Maybe thirty minutes. At the outside."

"Then where'd you go?"

"Home."

"You still at your parents'?"

"I was. It was my last night there."

"What time was that?"

"Eleven, eleven thirty."

"Can anyone corroborate that?"

"Nope. My parents are in the mountains of North Carolina. They go every August. And the staff had left for the day."

"How about security video? I noticed the property was wired."

He looked surprised but unconcerned. "It is. You can check the alarm code record as well. My code is unique to me."

Malone made a note. "Then what?"

"Had a beer. Or two. And went to bed."

"This morning, what time did you wake up?"

"Early. Five or just before."

"Wow, that's early for a guy who's not working."

"Since the war, I don't sleep like I used to."

"Sorry to hear that." Scott shrugged. Malone continued. "Up around five, what then?"

"Grabbed a coffee. Left before the staff arrived."

"Left for where?"

He hesitated, looking uncomfortable for the first time. "Mira Gallier's."

Interesting. By his own admission, Scott had been in the vicinity of the crime scene twice in twenty-four hours. The attorney didn't look pleased.

"What time was that?" Malone asked.

"I got there around six."

"Seems a little early for a social call."

"She was up."

"What was the reason for the early visit?"

He shifted slightly in his seat. "Personal."

"A woman is dead. And you, Mr. Scott, just happened to be steps away from where the murder occurred, not once but twice within a matter of hours."

The lawyer leaned over and whispered something in Scott's ear. Scott nodded, then met Malone's eyes once more. "We'd left it in a bad place the night before. I wanted to make it right."

"You fought?"

"Had a disagreement."

"About?"

"Her husband. I tried to tell her he hadn't been a saint. My mistake."

"Not a saint," Malone repeated. "What does that mean?"

"That's between me and Mira."

Again, he let that pass. For now. "How long were you at her home?"

"Twenty minutes tops."

"You left there and did what?"

"Started moving into my new place."

"Renting?"

"No. My maternal grandmother died recently. It was her house, she left it to me. I spent the day doing that."

"See anyone?"

"The guys I hired to move me."

Malone asked the name of the company, then jotted down his answer.

The lawyer spoke up. "Is that all, Detective?"

Malone flipped through his spiral, pretending to consider the question, then shut it. "For now."

They all stood. "By the way," Malone said, "Mira Gallier found the body."

Scott stiffened. "Excuse me?"

"She found the body. She was pretty shook up."

The information threw him, although Malone could see he tried to hide it. He could almost feel sorry for the guy—if he didn't suspect him of being a murdering son of a bitch.

"You don't find it odd, Mr. Scott, that these murders have all occurred since you returned to New Orleans? Or the fact they all connect to your friend Mira?"

"I haven't thought about it."

"Really? I find that hard to believe."

"Why should I? I had nothing to do with them. It's an odd coincidence, that's all."

"I don't believe in coincidences."

"That's your problem then, isn't it?"

"Mira Gallier's thought about it. She's thought about it a lot." Malone paused a moment to let that sink in. "And she finds it odd, too."

Scott flinched. Malone pressed on, deciding to take a stab at him. "I understand you have both a key to Mira Gallier's home and knowledge of the alarm code."

"Pardon me?"

"You were Mira and Jeff Gallier's best friend. They trusted you with a key and alarm code."

Scott was scrambling to right himself. "That was years ago. What could that have to do with now?"

"What indeed?" He looked down at his imaginary notes. "I see you're in love with your *friend* Mira Gallier."

Scott blanched. "Mira told you that?"

Bull's-eye. "Love is one of the most powerful motivators there is. Love, hate, greed: the holy trinity of murder."

Knight stepped in. "That's enough, Detective. Connor, we're leaving."

"I'll walk you to the elevator," said Malone.

They stepped into the hall. Bayle appeared at the door of the viewing room. Scott saw her and stopped. They stared at each other, and in those seconds Malone couldn't see Scott's expression, but Bayle looked like a deer caught in headlights.

Then the expression was gone, replaced by cool indifference.

Malone frowned, recalling the first time he and Bayle had questioned Scott. He'd sensed a strong, unpleasant emotion between them. He had asked Bayle about it. What had she said?

That she had met him before. Through a guy she'd been dating. The relationship had ended badly.

It didn't add up. Could Bayle be so distraught over a relationship that some guy she had been introduced to once stirred that kind of emotion? In both of them?

Maybe it wasn't some other guy she'd been in a relationship with. Maybe it was Scott. It could explain why she was so set on Gallier's guilt.

It would also mean her work on this case was anything but objective.

After dropping Scott and his attorney at the elevator, Malone walked back to the viewing room, thoughts racing. He couldn't bring his suspicions to the captain. Not now, after she had ordered the two of them to put their differences aside and work together. He needed more than a suspicion to take to Captain O'Shay.

Bayle and Percy were waiting. "What did you think?" he asked.

His brother spoke up first. "My guess is, he'll go straight to her. If they're in this together, we've poked a serious hole in his trust."

"Bayle?"

"Brilliant, insinuating she shared the same personal information he'd withheld."

"Did you notice, he never asked where the body was found or how she died?" Malone didn't take his gaze from Bayle. "I like that he admitted being in the vicinity of the scene. That helps."

"In my opinion," she said, "that supports his version of events."

Malone inclined his head. "Maybe. When I told him Mira had discovered the body, he looked as if I'd punched him in the gut. He didn't expect that."

"Or like it," Percy added. "He's definitely got it bad for her. You must've hit it earlier, Bayle. The father-in-law was the intended target. He did it for the woman he loves."

Something vulnerable crossed Bayle's face, then vanished. She cleared her throat. "Where do we go from here?"

"Let's stay on the pathologist. Also, I want the security video and code records from the Scott residence."

"I got that," Percy said. "I'll check in as soon as I have something."

His brother left them alone. Malone turned to his partner. "You're quiet, Bayle."

"Am I?"

"No thoughts?"

"I'd like to go over the interview again, then I'll contact the moving company."

As she started off, he stopped her. "What happened earlier, can we put it behind us?"

"I don't know, can we?"

"I'd like to try." He held out a hand. "Partners?"

She hesitated, then took it. "Partners."

Chapter Fifty-three

Connor hadn't been home. Mira had waited outside his parents' home for a few minutes before getting cold feet and driving off. She had tried his cell phone but had hung up without leaving a message. She had no idea what she would say to him. She couldn't ask him to prove she could trust him. What would that even take?

And where did she go now?

Not home. Not yet. She couldn't stand the thought of being in the house. Alone with her thoughts and the memory of what had happened just across the lawn.

So she drove, with no particular destination in mind, Nola riding shotgun, nose pressed to the cracked window. The mindlessness of it calmed her. Focusing on the road and the simple chore of driving helped to chase away the horrific image of Mrs. Latrobe. And to keep her own terror at bay.

Did the killer have a number waiting for her?

Mira found herself in front of her old studio. She hadn't been by in a long time, since just a couple months after the storm. She parked across the street, lowered the window and stared, remembering it as it had been on her first visit after the water retreated.

Like a futuristic scene after nuclear war. Everything painted the gray of dried, cracked mud. The trees covered in it. Bushes and lawns. The dilapidated structures that had once been homes and businesses. And no sound. Not of birds singing or children playing.

No life.

Slowly but surely the area was being built back up. The devastation had been so complete that the dotting of homes seemed to her a monumental act of courage. And faith.

While she sat and stared, a woman emerged from the house, carrying a bag of trash. She saw Mira and looked curiously at her, then went around to the side of the building, dumped the garbage and made her way back around front.

As the woman reached the porch, she stopped and looked back at Mira in question.

She didn't belong here anymore. This wasn't her life.

Dump the garbage, Mira.

It was time to let go. Time to move on.

The truth of that burst through her, leveling the protective walls she'd erected, shattering the layers of grief, regret and guilt that held her in their grip.

The garbage. Take it out.

Let it go.

She wanted to live again—life with all its complicated, messy pieces. Chores. Work. Friends. Relationships.

Love.

She *could* love again. She could be loved.

Connor.

Take a chance, Mira. Live again.

The thought startled her. The garbage: everything holding her back, good memories and bad ones. The past. Jeff. It was time to let go. Time to move on.

Now she drove with purpose. Uptown toward the Riverbend, taking Carrollton to Oak Street. She eased into the parking lot beside her current studio.

She gazed at the structure, satisfaction washing over her. This felt right. She belonged here now, it was home.

Mira climbed out. "Come, Nola," she said, snapping the leash to the dog's collar.

They made their way around front. Just as it should have been, the studio was locked up tight. Mira let herself in, then disabled the alarm. It was Nola's first visit to the studio and although she was excited by the new smells, she seemed to understand it wasn't the place to romp.

Mira slid open the pocket doors and headed into the work-room. The Magdalene window was waiting for her. The saint gazing out at the world, forever brokenhearted.

How like the saint she had been. Grief unchanging. Separated from the world—and from life—by a grim wall of her own making.

Had been. No more.

She laughed, feeling young and free. And new. Amid the blood and the death, she had come back to life.

Suddenly, Nola growled. That sound was followed by another. *Tap, tap, tap.*

Mira froze. Nola growled again.

Tap, tap, tap . . .

She looked at Nola. Her attention seemed to be trained on the rear door and windows. Something moved outside. A scream rose in her throat.

Then she saw what it was. Or rather, who it was.

Chris. He'd been tapping on the window.

She hurried over and opened the door. He stumbled in, a huge gash in his arm.

"My God, Chris, what happened!"

"I was working. I slipped."

"Working? Do you know what time it is?"

"I have work lights. I thought I'd work late, since it's cooler. I got sloppy."

"Because you're tired! Come on, let me get a look at it."

She led him to the kitchen. In her line of work, she dealt with a lot of cuts. She was well versed in how to tend them and when they needed professional attention.

She cleaned the wound, being as gentle as she could. She knew it hurt.

As if on cue, he winced. "That stings."

"I'll bet. Sorry." She examined the cut. "Not as deep as I thought it would be."

"That's good."

"Your call, Chris. I think you're okay without stitches, but if you—"

"No stitches. Just a bandage."

"You got it." She collected what she needed. "No more night work, okay? Besides, you scared me to death. And you're lucky Nola didn't eat you."

He grinned sheepishly. "I guess I am. No more night work. What are you doing here tonight?"

"I'm not really sure. I just am." She cut off strips of tape.

At his silence, she glanced up at him. "I'm not trying to be vague. I really don't know for certain. Could be I wanted to see Maggie." She motioned the window. "She helps me focus sometimes."

"Or?"

"I didn't want to be home."

"How come?"

She applied antibiotic cream to the square of gauze, then carefully fitted it over the wound. "My neighbor was murdered. I found her."

"Good God, Mira. That's awful." He touched her hand. "Are you all right?"

"I am now." She thought about sharing her newfound freedom with him, then decided not to. "There you go," she said, finishing taping the bandage. "Keep it clean and dry."

He smiled. "Yes, Dr. Gallier."

She returned the smile. "You go on. I've got this."

He hesitated, watching her pack up the first-aid kit. She glanced at him. "I'm fine. You don't have to stay. I know you're tired."

"But I could, if you need me to."

She smiled slightly. "That's really sweet, but I'm good."

"What are you going to do?"

"Spend a little time with Mags, then head home. I've got to go sometime, right?"

"I suppose."

She carried the kit back to the pantry. He hadn't moved. "You can go. Really."

He didn't look comfortable with it, but he nodded. "See you in the morning?"

"See you then."

He started off; she stopped him. "Chris?" He looked back at her. "Tuesday night, when I was over at Deni's, were you there?"

"Tuesday night?" He shook his head. "I didn't even know you were at Deni's."

"I spent the night. I thought she told you."

"Nope. Why did you think I was there?"

"In the middle of the night, I thought I heard you talking. Probably just the TV."

"Probably. She sometimes leaves it on all night."

"Are you guys okay?"

He hesitated a moment. "Yeah, we're good."

She frowned. "You don't sound convinced."

"It's just that sometimes . . . never mind."

"No, tell me."

"Sometimes, it's like I don't know her at all. It's like she's . . . a whole different person."

The comment chilled her. Maybe because it mirrored what she had learned about Dr. Jasper. And what she was feeling about everyone in her life.

He was looking at her strangely and she wondered what he was reading in her expression. She cleared her throat. "Women can be moody. Maybe it's just that."

"Maybe." He paused. "Look, it's getting late and I don't feel comfortable leaving you here alone. Especially with the . . . all the crazy stuff that's been happening."

"I've got Nola."

"Still, please let me walk you to your car. If you're not ready to go, I'll wait in the kitchen or something."

Mira looked back at the Magdalene window, realizing that everything she had wanted to glean by sitting here, she already had.

"You're right, Chris. It is late and I would appreciate you walking me out."

Chapter Fifty-four

Connor was waiting for her when she got home, sitting on her front step. He stood when she climbed out of the car.

Nola bounded over to him. He bent and scratched behind her ears and thumped her side. "Hey, girl. You doing good?"

The dog went spastic with pleasure, running circles around him, then rolling onto her back. Connor laughed at her antics and rubbed her belly.

Mira headed their way, using the moments to collect herself. He had left the ball in her court. She had taken it but now wasn't sure what to do with it.

When she reached him, he straightened; their eyes met. His tormented expression broke her heart. "Connor? What's wrong?"

"I heard about your neighbor. I'm so sorry."

He took her in his arms and held her. She clung to him, thoughts reeling. Could she trust him? She wanted to so desperately.

If this was wrong, it wouldn't feel so right. If he was a killer, she would know.

Wouldn't she?

"The police questioned me again," he said. "Detective

Malone said you thought that I . . . Mira, I've had nothing to do with any of these murders. I couldn't. Please tell me you believe me." He rested his forehead against hers. "I need you to believe in me."

She did, instinctively. With her heart. With her body's response to his. With every part but that small corner of her brain where Detective Malone's comments about keys, alarm codes and odd coincidences nagged at her.

Mira shut those doubts out. She wanted to believe him. On some elemental level, she *needed* to.

"I believe you," she said softly. "Maybe I shouldn't. Maybe I should run. But right now, I don't want to be anywhere but with you."

He cupped her face in his palms. "Thank God. The police, they made it seem like you—"

She brought her fingers to his lips. "I don't want to talk about that, not now. Not about Detective Malone or the murders. Not about anything that's been happening. I just want to be with you."

She caught his hand and led him into the house. In the foyer, alone, door closed and locked behind them, she stood on tiptoe and brushed her lips against his. When he didn't stop her, she deepened the kiss, pressing herself against him, winding her arms around his neck.

For the longest second of her life, he stood as still and unresponsive as a wall. Then he shuddered, his hands dropping to her backside, cupping her, deepening the kiss even more.

Without breaking the kiss, he lifted her. She wrapped her legs around his waist as he carried her to the bedroom.

Her bedroom. Not the one she and Jeff had shared. The one she had never shared with anyone. A first. Special.

They tumbled onto the bed. Mira took the lead. Impatiently tugging at clothing, greedily tasting and taking. Each time he tried to slow her pace, she defied him.

There would be time for leisurely lovemaking, but that time was not now. Now was for heat. And greed. And animal gratification.

It had been six years since she had been with a man. And impossibly, it felt like she had been waiting for this one, for Connor, forever.

He thrust into her; she cried out in pleasure, bucking up against him. Just like that. No coaxing or cajoling. No advance and retreat. He joined her, crying out her name.

Afterward, they lay together, a tangle of arms, legs and damp bedding. Beneath her palm, his heart pounded, its wild beat matching her own. She turned her face to his chest, breathing in his scent. So different from Jeff's. Earthier. Not as sweet, more . . . masculine. But not offensive. Heady. Exciting.

He cleared his throat. "Mira?"

She lifted onto her elbow to meet his eyes. "Hmm?"

"What the hell was that? Not that I don't like—" He grinned. "I do. But damn, girl."

She laughed, pleased. "It's been a long time."

"Forever, actually."

She searched his gaze, a lump forming in her throat. She bent and kissed him. "What do you want to do now?"

He'd waited "forever" for the first time. And only ten minutes for the second—though he made her wait in other ways, dragging out her pleasure and his own.

Long after they'd both succumbed, Mira lay in his arms, drifting and relaxed. And happy. Sweetly, deliciously, ridiculously happy.

She ran her hand along his back, stopping on a jagged ridge below his shoulder blade. She smoothed her fingers over it, following the ridge down his side and around, nearly to his abdomen.

At her exploration, he grew still. Over the years she had seen him shirtless many times; this was new. "What is this?"

"A souvenir from my fun-filled days and nights in Afghanistan."

"What happened?"

He rolled onto his back and gazed up at the ceiling. She propped herself up on an elbow, so she could see his face. "If you aren't ready to talk about it, I understand."

"On foot patrol in Helmand Province, an IED went off in the middle of my squad." He cut his gaze to hers, expression harsh. "It's war. Men die. I'm not worried about a little scar."

She held his gaze. "I can't imagine what it must have been like."

"You're right, you couldn't even come close. You think Katrina was bad. At least you knew which direction she was coming from. And who the enemy was. Over there, the enemy mixes with the civilians. How're we supposed to—"

He bit back what he was about to say and started again. "We're walking down this damn dirt road, I see a young guy and his grandpa in the field ahead. Jones spots the buried IED—"

"A roadside bomb?"

"Yeah. An improvised explosive device. So he sees it, turns to tell us and *boom.* He's not there anymore. Someone had to pull the detonator to make it explode. Was it grandpa? The kid? Someone in the trees? I don't know.

"The smoke clears, Jones and I are in a ditch. I hear Orazio call in a chopper for us."

"What happened to Jones?"

"He died."

Mira caught his hand, laced their fingers. "I'm sorry."

"Yeah, well, it happens."

Her eyes burned with unshed tears. She blinked, fighting to keep them from falling. They were both battle scarred. And they were both survivors. "I'm glad you're here."

"Me, too." He cleared his throat. "I was lucky."

Lucky, she thought. Her, too. She hadn't realized just how lucky until this moment. For the first time in forever the future seemed bright. Something she looked forward to.

Her stomach growled loudly, and he laughed. He looked at her, grinning. "Hungry?"

"Starving, obviously. You?"

"Oh, yeah."

He climbed out of bed, then helped her to her feet. They re-dressed and headed for the kitchen. She sent Connor to the wine closet to pick out a bottle while she poked through the refrigerator.

"Red or white?" he called.

"Are you kidding?"

"That's what I thought." He exited the closet carrying a red. "Does a 2007 Sonoma Coast Pinot Noir sound okay?"

"Sounds perfect. I'm thinking omelets."

"If there's cheese involved, I'm with you."

Nola, who could hear a refrigerator door open from a mile away, had padded into the kitchen. Mira filled her bowl.

Mira and Connor worked together, choosing and chopping ingredients, sipping wine. Discussing nothing more serious than favorite meals. She cleared the bar, then set two places.

The eggs came out perfectly, delicately turned, light and fluffy yet crisp at the edges. Mira ate ravenously, finishing before him, all but licking her plate clean.

He smiled at her, amused. "I guess we should have made more."

"I would have eaten it." She carried her plate to the sink, then went back for his. He was studying the notepad she'd had earlier, the list she'd started.

"What's this?" he asked, glancing up at her.

"Nothing."

He frowned. "Not nothing. My name's on it. Deni's. Chris and Dr. Jasper."

"This morning a detective suggested that to find the truth, I needed to take everything I knew to be true and put it back on the table. Question it. Start over."

"What detective? Malone? Or Bayle?" The venom in his voice startled her.

"No. Detective Killian."

"My name's on this list."

"Right. I made a list of all the people in my life who I trusted."

"But worried you couldn't."

"It wasn't like that."

"Then what was it like? You told me you believed in me. That you trusted me. So why's my name on this list?"

"Because I was trying to do what the detective suggested."

He shook his head. "There's trust and there's not, Mira. It's like faith. You believe or you don't."

"Earlier, you asked me to make a decision. Right then and there. And I did. I went with my gut."

"Your gut. What does that mean?"

"You know what it means. It means you push away your doubts and go with—"

"Great." He tossed the pad angrily onto the bar. "Isn't that what men get accused of all the time? Of following the brain between their legs?"

"It's not like that."

"Really?"

"I was following my heart, idiot!"

"Ask me if you can trust me."

She tipped up her chin. "Can I trust you?"

"With your life."

A whisper of doubt flickered through her. It must have registered on her face because he swore. "I can't believe this! Son of a bitch!"

She took a step toward him, hand out. "You're not being fair."

"I'm not being fair? Mira, I'm in love with you. I've laid my heart bare for you. If that's not trust, I don't know what is."

"Six years ago you didn't trust me enough to tell me the truth. Instead, you ran away."

"That was different. You were married to my best friend."

"But *we* were supposed to be friends! You told him. Why not me? What would have been so difficult? How can you love someone when you don't trust her enough to be honest?"

"I was protecting you."

"Right," she said sarcastically. "You were protecting yourself."

"You want honesty?"

"Total."

They stood nearly nose to nose, gazes locked. His hands were clenched into fists. Mira leaned toward him, silently daring him.

"That list of names you scribbled. Why isn't Jeff's name on it?"

"You're being ridiculous."

"His name should be on the list, too. He was cheating."

She must have heard wrong. He couldn't have said what she thought he had.

"Jeff was having affairs."

She caught her breath and took a step back, feeling as if he had physically struck her. "You're lying."

"I couldn't be a part of it. I told him so."

She shook her head. "I don't believe you."

"Think back, Mira. How many nights did you wonder why he was late? How many times did you call me or the Crescent City Club looking for him?"

Not many at first, she remembered. Then, toward the end, a lot. He always had a logical explanation. "He was out with you," she said. "Or business associates. Sometimes Anton and his cronies."

"No. He was out with other women."

"I don't want to hear this," she whispered. "Please stop."

"You need to hear it." He caught her hands and brought them to his heart. "In the past six years you've built Jeff into a saint and your marriage into this idyllic paradise."

He lowered his voice. "I couldn't tell you. But I couldn't sit back and watch. I couldn't be party to it."

She dropped her head to his chest, too drained even to cry. To-the-bone exhausted.

Ironic, but the one thing she had believed in, one hundred percent, had been a lie.

"I should have told you before. I wanted to. I started to a hundred times back then and since I've been home. But each time, I couldn't do it."

She lifted her face to his. "I think you should go."

"Mira—"

"It's not you. I just . . . I need to be alone for a while. I've got to process this."

"That detective, what she told you to do, I think she was right." He searched her expression, his determined. "Everything's on the table now."

"What are you saying?"

"I think the murders and everything that's been going on have something to do with Jeff. I'm going to try to find out what."

Chapter Fifty-five

Despair clawed at him. Doubt picked at him, like the constant drip, drip of a faucet in the night. What if he had been wrong? What if he had misinterpreted his Father? What if this wasn't his time? If she wasn't meant to be his?

The thought knocked the wind out of him. He sank to his knees, where he belonged. Pleading for mercy and forgiveness.

He closed his eyes. His head filled with the image of the latest felled demon. Her eyes wide and terrified. She had known who he was. And what he was capable of. His power had grown so strong, his presence alone had killed her.

So why couldn't Mary see him? He could root out evil ones, fell them with not more than his gaze, and yet his beloved didn't recognize him.

Worse, she turned to others. Like a prostitute. Like a cheap whore.

His guttural cry shattered the silence. He raised his hands heavenward. "Why does she still not see? I've followed Your instructions, been a good and faithful servant. This one thing is all I ask!"

When his Father didn't respond, he lashed out. "You never

liked her! I know that. But to turn away from me now?" He
fisted his fingers, angry—yet deeply ashamed of the emotion and where it wanted to lead him. "If only you could see
her as I do!"

The anger left him and he collapsed. "Tell me what to
do," he whispered. "Help me."

Why do you despair? You are the Chosen One.

The voice in his head. His Father. He started to cry. "Forgive me, Father, for my anger and my doubt. I'm unclean.
Mary doesn't recognize me because of my sin."

*The pull of the earthly world is strong. It's not Mary who
turns away from you. It's the Evil One who pulls her away.
Your mission is not yet complete.*

He grew still, heart racing. "Haven't I brought judgment
on four who meant to harm her? Demons set on keeping me
and Mary apart? Didn't I announce, through the Holy Scripture, what I had done for her? Why won't she open her eyes!"

*There are Seven Demons, my Son. Why would this time
be any different than in Bethany? She is still in their grasp.*

"Yes," he said, nodding, "I must expel them all."

*Until then, she'll be in the grip of the Evil One. Only you
can save her.*

Only he could save her. It was as it should be. Trembling,
he lifted his face to heaven. "Thank you, Father. I owe you
everything and I am your servant."

Chapter Fifty-six

Malone wished the caffeine would kick in. He'd worked most of the night, heading home to catch a few hours of sleep and a shower, only to return with the sun. He felt like crap. He bet he looked even worse—warmed-over crap, maybe.

He leaned against the war room table and swept his gaze over the whiteboard. A large map of the metro area with pushpins marking the location each victim was found. Time line with corresponding victim photos, notes on evidence, time and cause of death.

What was he missing? Malone swore and dragged a hand through his hair. Four victims. Four different means of death. Victims unrelated except for a line of Scripture and a connection to Mira Gallier.

For about the hundredth time since Scott's questioning the night before, he started at the beginning. Father Girod: death by blunt-force trauma. Weapon recovered, usable prints. No witnesses. Preacher: throat slit with a piece of broken glass. No usable prints. No witnesses. Anton Gallier: death by gunshot wounds to the chest. Weapon unrecovered. Prints recovered from coffee cups and take-out bag. Match prints from Sisters of Mercy homicide. Louise Latrobe: means of death unresolved. Still awaiting lab results on lipstick used to write 4 on victim's forehead.

"Hey, partner."

He looked over his shoulder at Bayle. She looked haggard. "Hey."

"Been here long?"

"A few hours. Looking for answers."

"Find any?"

"I wish."

"Coffeed-out yet?" She held up a cup from the local PJ's. "If not, I've brought a peace offering."

He eyed it with mock suspicion. "How do I know it's not poisoned?"

She smiled and crossed to him. "I guess you'll just have to trust me."

He took the cup and sipped.

She met and held his gaze. "And I'll trust you, Malone."

He nodded and they both turned to the wall and its display. Bayle spoke first. "I've been thinking. What if the break-ins and such that've happened to Mira Gallier have nothing to do with this?"

He looked at her in surprise. "That's a pretty big turn-around from yesterday."

"I know she's involved somehow, but I'm much less certain she had anything to do with the murders."

He drew his eyebrows together and studied her a moment, confused. "I don't get it. What changed for you?"

She met his eyes. "Stacy. Her statement of what she saw."

"You seemed pretty adamant yesterday."

"I've been called stubborn once or twice."

Malone didn't fully trust her turnaround. Not that it didn't happen in the investigative process when new evidence emerged. It did. Often. But this shift represented a monumental change in attitude.

"And the bizarre things happening to her?" he asked.

"The manifestations of a troubled woman. Or staged by her for attention. Again, because she's unbalanced."

"Entirely possible. We have nothing solid to show any of it actually occurred."

"Exactly." Bayle made a sweeping motion, taking in the display board. "The perp is trying to communicate directly with us through his messages. Obviously, they're extremely important to him."

Malone nodded. "It's something he wants us to know."

"Badly enough to take the chance of exposing himself. Leaving those messages at the scene is a risk. They take time and planning."

Malone went to stand in front of the photographs of the graffitied windows. " 'He will come again to judge the living and the dead.' Our first message. What's our UNSUB's thought process here? Why does he want us to know this?"

"Because he believes it."

"A religious fanatic?"

She cocked her head. "Maybe."

"Even if Father Girod hadn't been murdered, it's too deliberate to have been a simple act of vandalism."

"Who is the 'He' in that message?"

"The son of God. Jesus Christ."

"Our perp thinks it's the end of the world? He's reminding us what comes next."

"Judgment Day," Malone said.

"Which just happened to be our next 'message.' "

Malone gazed at the photographs, pieces clicking into place. "He's not reminding us what's coming next. He's telling us what has come."

"I don't get it."

He looked at Bayle, excited. "He is the one who's come to judge the living and the dead."

"Our guy has a Christ complex?"

"Yeah. Think about it. Judgment Day's our next message. He's telling us it's happening. That it's begun."

She pursed her lips in thought. "Then why 'He cast out Seven Demons'? Why not a continuation of what he'd begun with Preacher?"

"I don't know." Malone moved his gaze over the wall and whiteboard, looking for the answer. "If I'm remembering my New Testament lessons, while on earth Jesus performed a number of miracles. They included casting out demons."

"Right," she agreed. "And seven is a significant number in the Bible: seven seals, seven deadly sins, the seventh day He rested."

"Although only once does it refer to Seven Demons."

"In reference to Mary Magdalene."

"Maybe we're being too literal. We're assuming our whack-job perp knows that. We're assuming he really knows the Bible." Malone started to pace. "I skipped as many catechism classes as I slept through, but I'd heard about the casting out of demons. I didn't know it had anything to do with Mary Magdalene. He may not have, either."

She nodded. "Okay, let's put ourselves in our perp's head. He thinks he's the reincarnated Christ, come to judge the 'living and the dead.' He's getting rid of demons. The bad guys."

"It works," he agreed. "I only have one problem with it."

"Mira Gallier?"

"Close. The fact she's been restoring a Mary Magdalene window. Maybe she's not the connection? Maybe the window is?"

It was one of those aha moments that elevated police work from a follow-the-trail-of-bread-crumbs kind of drudgery to a creative endeavor. Some of his ahas turned out to be dead ends or bullshit, but it still made the game exciting. He rubbed his hands together, going with it. "Let's go back to the beginning, the initial scene at Sisters of Mercy. Why that church?"

"Because he's comfortable there. He's spent time there."

"Exactly. Because it's *his* church. Did we ever get a list of Sisters of Mercy parishioners?"

"Not a complete one. We focused on anyone who might've had a beef with the church or school."

"Let's get it."

"It's going to be big."

"But we have a small suspect list."

"How do you figure?" she asked, frowning.

"All the murders have a connection to Mira Gallier. Let's see if somebody on that list does as well."

"I've got this. What about you?"

"Think I'll follow up on the Mary Magdalene angle. Find out where the window came from and how it came to be in Gallier's workshop."

"Sounds good." She started off. "I'll keep you posted."

His cell rang. He saw it was Stacy. "Hey, babe. What's up?"

"I have that information you were looking for. I spoke with Donna St. Cloud. She and Bayle were partners for several years, from 2003 to 2006, when Bayle moved over to ISD. She said Bayle had been having an affair with some guy. It was a big deal, she was totally gone over him."

"What happened?"

"It didn't end well. Bayle comes in one day distraught. Says the affair is over. That he left her."

"What was his name?"

"Bayle would never tell her. But St. Cloud did know he was somebody important. He had big bucks and was Uptown society."

Connor Scott. Malone felt the realization like a kick to the gut.

"St. Cloud did some digging, thought maybe she could connect the dots and figure out who he was. But by then it was after Katrina, things were really screwed up. Including Bayle. St. Cloud said she was moody and her work became inconsistent. Said she was relieved when Bayle got the promotion to ISD and that she wasn't surprised when she heard about her meltdown."

"The promotion makes sense. Bayle made a name for herself early in her career. And her performance during Katrina was nothing short of heroic."

Malone recalled the stories of acts of courage that bordered on death defying, ones that reflected little concern for Bayle's own safety. In retrospect, it made sense. She'd been in a personal crisis and didn't care if she lived or died.

"Nobody noticed how close to snapping she was," he said.

"I'm not surprised. It was the end of the world. Total, freaking Armageddon."

"How come it takes so long after Katrina for her to publicly fall apart?"

"I'm sure her therapist could tell us, but I can only guess. There were a lot of distractions after the storm. She was a hero. She became NOPD's Katrina poster girl. She was interviewed on TV and for magazines, honored by civic organizations."

"And there's the distraction of the cleanup."

"She melts down when it quiets down."

Malone nodded. "Exactly. And I get all that. It's her story and not my concern. What is my concern is whether the man she was in love with was Connor Scott. If so, her involvement in this investigation compromises it."

For a moment, Stacy was silent. "You told me Bayle had an attitude about Gallier. That she accused you of falling for her poor-little-victim routine."

"Yeah, something like that."

"If Scott's the one, those comments make sense."

"Because Scott's in love with Gallier," Malone said. "And has been for years. Bayle would hate her guts."

"What are you going to do?" Stacy asked.

"I wish I knew."

"A word of advice, my love. You're in tricky territory, proceed with caution."

Chapter Fifty-seven

Thursday, August 18
9:20 A.M.

Malone took Stacy's advice. He decided to pursue the information on the Magdalene window and set his questions about Bayle on the mental back burner. It was an effective technique he used often. It gave his subconscious a chance to work on one issue while he acted on another.

A call to Gallier Glassworks had provided him the information he'd needed. Gallier wasn't in yet, but her assistant had been happy to fill him in. The Magdalene window had come from Our Lady of Perpetual Sorrows Church in Chalmette, the largest city in St. Bernard Parish. The church, along with its magnificent windows, had been destroyed by Katrina. A nun named Sister Sarah Elisabeth had championed the cause of resurrecting both the church and its windows. She had found Gallier Glassworks and turned the windows over to Mira for restoration.

He contacted the sister and she agreed to meet with him. He was on his way now.

Malone called Bayle from the road. "Update," he said when she answered. "I'm heading to Chalmette to meet with a Sister Sarah Elisabeth. She's the one who brought the Magdalene window to Gallier."

"Progressing on my end as well," she said. "Father Mc-Linn from Sisters of Mercy agreed to get us the information on parishioners."

"How long until we have it?"

"It'll take the rest of today, maybe even tomorrow, to get the information together. Current parishioners are easy, it's the lapsed and nonactives that'll take time. They lost a lot of their information in the storm and have had to piece it back together and reenter data."

"Gotcha. How many years did you ask them to go back?"

"Ten. I thought that'd give us a reasonable data cushion."

"Good call." At times like these, he wondered if he wasn't totally off base regarding Bayle's motivations. She seemed impartial and on point; they seemed to be on the same page every step of the way.

Maybe he should just ask her? Get it out there and out of the way?

Not now. Not over the phone. He had to be able to see her expression when she responded, needed to evaluate her body language. "When will you be back to HQ?"

"Before you."

"See you then."

He ended the call and drove in silence. He couldn't remember the last time he'd been to St. Bernard Parish. "Da Parish," as it was called, comprised the southeastern border of the now infamous Lower Ninth Ward and held the distinction of being one hundred percent uninhabitable after Katrina.

He still had a hard time comprehending the destruction. The numbers blew him away—the once thriving community was now only a third the size of its pre-storm population. A hopeful sign was that homes were in the process of being rebuilt. The smokestacks of the Murphy Oil Refinery towered in the distance.

A sign announced the turn for Our Lady of Perpetual Sorrows. A tragically ironic name, considering what had transpired. He wondered if they had considered changing it, then rejected the thought. The people of St. Bernard Parish wouldn't stand for it. To them, it was a matter of pride and community. This was their home, for better or worse, and they wanted it to stay the way it had always been.

The church itself was smaller than he had expected. It was still unfinished, judging by the activity going on around it. The sign out front listed the times for mass.

He went on a search for the church office. He found it and identified himself to the woman at the desk.

She smiled and stood. "You're here to see Sister Sarah Elisabeth. She told me to expect you. Follow me."

She led him down a short hall to a kitchen area. The smell of baking bread hung in the air as several women worked.

"Sister," she said, "the detective's here."

The woman who greeted him was small in stature, with a wizened face and huge protruding eyes. Like a female Yoda.

"Sister," he said, "thanks for seeing me."

"Of course I would, silly boy."

Her voice was a surprise. Young and lively, it matched the expression in her eyes. He laughed. "It's been a long time since anyone called me a boy."

"Come, let me show you where our beautiful lady will reside."

"Your beautiful lady?"

"The Magdalene window. Come."

Malone walked with her. She commented on this and that as they walked, detailing present updates and past damage. He heard the love in her voice, but surprisingly not pain, regret or even fatigue.

He commented on this. She shook her head. "God has a plan for everything. Who am I to question that?"

She swung open one of the sanctuary's double doors. Inside, she made a sweeping gesture, taking in the wall of boarded-up windows. "Soon, this room will be filled with colored light."

Her hand caught his attention, small and gnarled. Rheumatoid arthritis. He'd seen the devastation the disease had wrought many times before.

She saw his gaze and smiled. "We all have our crosses to

bear. It's how we carry them that reveals our character. And our faith."

"I didn't mean to stare. My grandmother suffered with the disease. I know how difficult it can be."

"'I can do all things through Christ who strengthens me,'" she quoted. "Philippians 4:13. And what I cannot do, He provides an angel to do it for me."

He cleared his throat. "And the Magdalene window, did God provide an angel for that?"

"You know He did. Mira Gallier." She crossed to an aisle of pews, genuflected and crossed herself, then slipped into the pew and sat. He followed her.

"What you don't know, Detective, is how He brought us together. It was a miracle."

Malone found her devotion charming. Humoring her, he told her to go on.

"I can see you don't believe in miracles, Detective."

"It's that obvious?"

"I'll tell you my story, then you decide." She didn't wait for him to comment, simply went on. "As I'm sure you know, Katrina took all this away. Not just our church, but our people. Our community.

"Our building broken, our beautiful windows destroyed. There was nothing left. We were inundated with the water. And oil from the Murphy spill."

Adding insult to injury, Malone remembered. One of the oil company's storage tanks had come loose and spilled a million-plus gallons. Anything within two miles of the facility had been affected.

"Time passed. Our parishioners were gone. Even Father Clementine had been forced to go.

"So here our beautiful lady lay in pieces, moldering, fouled by oil. A year passed. Then two. I prayed every day, Detective. I prayed for a miracle. A way to save our church and restore our windows. One day, as I prayed outside the church, a sudden gust of wind blew a page from the *Times-Picayune* against my ankles. I bent and retrieved it and there she was. My angel."

"Mira Gallier?"

"Yes." She crossed herself, then went on. "An article about her restoration of the city's stained-glass windows. And I knew she was the one God had sent to me."

"That's quite a story."

"Not a story." She smiled serenely. "A miracle."

He wished he could believe that way. He wished he could accept the idea of an ultimate power for good and in miracles. He told her so.

She reached out and covered one of his hands with her deformed one. "There's only one thing that separates a believer from a nonbeliever."

"And what's that, Sister?"

"You already know," she said softly. "Faith."

He wanted to tell her it wasn't that easy. That it was hard to have unshakable faith in good in the face of unrelenting evil, day in and day out.

Instead, he asked, "Sister, was anyone else a part of getting the Magdalene window into Mira Gallier's hands?"

She shook her head. "Just me and the Almighty."

"Did anyone else show a special interest in it?"

"No. I'm sorry."

"How about transportation of the pieces?"

"She arranged all of it."

"I'm going to read you some names. If you know any of these people, or if they have any connection to your window, let me know."

The names were people close to Mira, the victims and anyone else associated with the case.

He began with Scott, then moved on to Deni Watts.

"I know her," she said. "She's the one who took window measurements. I talked to her on the phone just last week."

"What about?"

"The windows. When we should expect to have them installed."

"Did she give you a date?"

She shook her head. "She said Mira wanted to wait until after hurricane season."

He went on, naming Chris Johns, Dr. Adele Jasper and Anton Gallier.

"I'm sorry, I don't know any of them."

"Ever heard of a street evangelist called Preacher?"

When she replied again in the negative, he passed Latrobe by her, then, surprising himself, Karin Bayle.

"What was that last name?" she asked.

"Karin Bayle."

"It sounds sort of familiar, but . . . no. I'm so sorry."

"Are you certain?"

"I think so."

He handed her the list and one of his cards. "Keep these. If something jogs your memory, call me."

Chapter Fifty-eight

Back at HQ, Malone made his way up to ISD. The department was like a ghost town—everybody was either out on call or out to lunch. Not Bayle, however. He found her at her desk.

"Hey, partner," he said. "The list from Sisters of Mercy show up yet?"

"Nope. But it's early."

"Just wishful thinking." He perched on the edge of her desk. "What do you have there?"

She angled it so he could read it. "Coroner's report on Latrobe. She died of natural causes. Cardiac arrest."

"No shit?"

"No shit. Hollister called it at the scene. Autopsy showed this wasn't her first heart attack."

"So our guy did, literally, scare her to death."

"Or he found her conveniently dead, marked her forehead and left."

"Maybe." He thumbed through the report. "No marks on her body or other signs of trauma. No defensive wounds; nails were clean."

"Which adds up to a big fat nothing for us to work with."

"Lab get anything on the lipstick?"

Bayle slid over another report. "Estée Lauder. Coral Sunrise. Actually, it's a discontinued color. Techs found three more tubes upstairs. All three brand-new, never been used."

Malone frowned. "How does that happen?"

"Easy. She learns from her usual salesgirl that her color is being discontinued. So she buys up whatever's left. We girls do that all the time."

"No shit," he said again. "I wonder if Stacy does that?"

"Ask her. My bet's on yes." Bayle leaned back in her chair. "How'd it go in Chalmette?"

"Interesting." He held her gaze. "Have you been out to Our Lady of Perpetual Sorrows or met Sister Sarah Elisabeth?"

She didn't even blink. "Never. Why?"

"She's a hoot, that's all. It's worth the trip just to meet her."

"Did you get anything we could use?"

"Nada."

"Could she be our killer?"

Malone had to laugh, as a picture of the Yoda-like nun wielding a gun or a deadly shard of glass entered his mind.

Bayle looked irritated. "Maybe you should explain why that's funny?"

"Sorry. You sort of had to be there. She would have needed to ask Preacher to get on his knees to be able to reach his throat to slit it. Plus, she's about a thousand years old."

Bayle frowned slightly. "I've got a question, Malone. Donna St. Cloud called a little bit ago. She said Stacy was asking some questions about me. My history. My breakdown. You know anything about that?"

He hadn't expected this, especially after the things St. Cloud had said. But he didn't let it throw him. "You know I do."

"What the hell, Malone? What's that all about?"

"I had some questions."

"You could have asked me."

"Really? I'll ask now. Why'd you break down?"

"Post-traumatic stress disorder stemming from Katrina."

"Nothing to do with some guy? A rich, Uptown guy?"

Her steady gaze faltered a bit. "What does that have to do with anything? And why would it be any of your damn business if it had?"

"If it influenced your performance on this case, you bet it'd be my business."

"It's not. That's bullshit."

"Did you have an affair with Connor Scott? Is he the guy who broke your heart? The first time I saw you together, is that what I picked up on?"

"This is outrageous!" She stood and started past him.

He caught her arm. "Is that why you haven't been able to move past Mira Gallier as lead suspect? Because he was in love with her then and he's still in love with her?"

"Let go of my arm."

"Answer me."

"No! Okay? I did not have an affair with Scott. He is just who I said, a coworker of the guy who did break my heart. You're right, you got me, the breakup sent me into a tailspin, then Katrina sent me over the edge."

"What was his name?"

"None of your damn business."

"His name?"

"James," she said, yanking her arm free. "Sterling. Look him up. I'm sure he'd love to talk to you. Excuse me, I'm going to lunch."

She stalked past him, then stopped and looked back. "Nice trust, Malone. Appreciate it. As soon as we're finished with this case, I'll ask for a change."

Chapter Fifty-nine

Malone admitted it. He'd screwed up. Handled the whole thing with Bayle wrong. Going behind her back that way. It unraveled the very fabric of what a partnership was supposed to be.

Honesty and trust. The unshakable belief that even if everybody else out there turned their back on you without a second thought, your partner would still be there.

Actually, Bayle had taken it damn well. If their roles had been reversed, he'd have been furious. Wait for the investigation to conclude before severing the relationship? Hell, no. He would have demanded she be removed from the case and another partner assigned. Immediately.

Time to eat some humble pie, Malone. He owed her an apology.

She hadn't returned from lunch, he learned. Back at his desk, he dialed her cell. He hadn't really expected her to pick up for him, so he wasn't surprised when the device clicked over to voice mail.

"Okay," he said, "I'm a jackass, I admit it. I'm sorry. Call me back." Oddly enough, his desk phone jangled just as he ended the cell call. "Malone."

"Detective Spencer Malone?" a woman asked.

"Yes. Can I help you?"

"My name's Dr. Adele Jasper. I'm Mira Gallier's therapist. I wonder if we could meet?"

He grabbed his notebook and a pen. "What's this in reference to?"

"I think you know."

"It would help if you could give me something specific."

"Never mind, this was a mistake."

"When?" he said quickly. "I could meet you now."

"No, I have a two thirty appointment. A new client. Let's say three forty-five?"

He agreed, and she gave him her address.

Chapter Sixty

Malone pulled up at the Uptown address. Located just off the Avenue, on Soniat Street. It was a lovely, tree-shaded property, not over-the-top but solid. Dr. Adele Jasper practiced out of the carriage house behind the home.

Percy was waiting for him, Bayle was not. He muttered an oath. He'd called her again, left the time and address. He'd been certain she'd be here. Bayle might be hopping mad at him, but she'd made it clear she wasn't giving up on this investigation.

He glanced at his watch. He was early. She could still be en route.

Malone met his brother. "Where's your partner?" Percy asked.

"Maybe on her way. I'm not sure."

Percy cocked an eyebrow. "What's up?"

"We had a disagreement. I questioned her integrity and went behind her back. She's pretty pissed off."

Percy knew him well enough not to comment. "Should we wait?"

Malone glanced at his watch again, then shook his head. "She's smart. She'll catch up."

They followed the path around to the carriage house's entrance. They entered a waiting room, a buzzer sounding as they did. Jasper had outfitted it with elegant but comfortable furnishings in a muted, soothing color scheme. Several chairs, a coffee table with a fan of trendy magazines, a small writing desk with a chair and a phone.

A sign hung on the closed door at the back of the room: DO NOT DISTURB. IN SESSION.

"No receptionist," Percy said. "An open door. Risky, considering crime in the area."

Malone moved his gaze over the room. He indicated the camera mounted in the corner and trained on the door. "Not that risky. Bet there's one in front, too."

Malone wandered over to the magazines. *Southern Living, Metropolitan Home, Vogue.* Pretty obvious the demographics of Jasper's clients. Not a *Field & Stream* or *Sports Illustrated* in sight.

He glanced at the time and frowned. Three fifty. "She said her appointment was coming in at two thirty."

"So?"

"Aren't these sessions usually an hour?"

"They are on TV. Maybe her client was late?"

Malone slid his gaze toward the closed door, then the camera. "Something's not right. She knows we're here. If her session was going to run this long over—"

"She'd let us know."

They crossed to the door, drawing their weapons. Malone knocked. "Dr. Jasper? Detective Malone."

She didn't reply. He tried the door while Percy covered him. It opened. The interior boasted large windows, cypress wood floors and high ceilings.

It would have been a lovely environment to work in.

Would have been. Past tense. Just like Adele Jasper.

Chapter Sixty-one

Jasper had put up a fight. Malone swept his gaze over the scene. Furniture toppled, knickknacks broken, a smear of blood across the wall, a framed Crescent City Classic poster, glass shattered. Jasper lay sprawled in front of the desk, hands frozen claws, face bloodied.

On her forehead, a bold, black number 5.

News that there had been another victim had brought out the brass and CSI had arrived in record time. Ray Hollister and his photographer were on the scene. The only one who hadn't shown was Bayle.

Where the hell was she?

Captain O'Shay asked him the same thing a moment later. She didn't like his answer. "You're telling me your partner is MIA?"

"Something like that."

"You'd better be a little more specific, Detective. I've lost my sense of humor."

"She's not answering her cell. I've called three times."

"When'd you last have contact with her?"

"Noonish. We had a difference of opinion."

"Explain."

"I questioned her integrity concerning this case. She was pretty pissed off."

"I take it that was the abbreviated version." It wasn't a question and she went on. "And your last message to her?"

"After we discovered Jasper."

"Dammit, Malone! Your partner's been out of contact for four hours, and I'm just hearing about it now?"

"Until now, I figured she was licking her wounds."

Captain O'Shay was furious. He'd seen her this mad on only a handful of occasions. "I'll be waiting for the nonabbreviated version of events, Detective. Until then, do your fucking job!"

"Glad it was you and not me," Percy muttered.

"No joke."

The photographers had gotten their shots and Ray Hollister was examining the body. He looked grumpy. "Good afternoon, Detectives," he said, not looking up. "Trouble seems to follow you two."

"Tell us something we don't know, please."

"And here I thought you Malones knew it all." Hollister inspected Jasper's hands. "We've hit the jackpot, boys. It looks like she got a couple good whacks in, there's blood and tissue under the nails."

"That'll help us eliminate suspects," Malone said. "How'd she die?"

"Don't know yet." Using a scalpel, Hollister probed the laceration on her right cheek. "Glass fragments embedded in her skin."

Malone shifted his gaze to the Classic poster, then to Percy. "Did our perp smash her face into it, or did it break her fall?"

"Either way," Hollister said, "it might have done the trick."

"Killed her?" Percy asked.

"Immobilized her long enough for the UNSUB to get his hands around her throat." He indicated her neck. "Bruising. Hyoid bone broken, petechiae in eyes and lips."

"He strangled her?" Malone shook his head. "What? Just to keep things interesting?"

"How long's she been dead?" Percy asked.

"Not long. She's pretty fresh. A couple hours max."

Malone checked his watch. "I talked to her at two o'clock. We arrived around three forty. Deed was done, perp was gone." He looked at Percy. "She said she had a new client. At two thirty."

"Wonder if he, or she, showed?"

"And if that's our perp."

"What about the video-monitoring system?" Percy asked.

One of the techs answered. "Just a live feed. No recording set up."

Malone nodded. "Let's check her appointment book, get a name. New appointments usually fill out paperwork as well."

They left Hollister to do his thing. Jasper's desk was in a private office at the very back of the carriage house. The door had a key lock, though they found it open.

The appointment book lay open on the desk. Today's page had been ripped out.

"Perfect." Malone flipped forward and back in the planner. "Look at this. Two thirty is her last appointment time on Tuesdays and Thursdays." He tapped the Thursday before, then turned to the one before that. "She takes a five o'clock Pilates class at Simply Fit."

Percy narrowed his eyes. "If he's our perp, he knows these appointments last an hour. He also knows this is a solo practice. No receptionist."

"He'll have her all to himself for an entire hour. More than enough time to kill her and get out."

"But she sees it coming. And now we have a real crime scene."

Malone frowned in thought. "I wonder if our perp realizes the game just changed? If so, he's going to move quickly."

Percy agreed. "Take chances he wouldn't have before. He'll be completely focused on finishing his 'work' before he's caught."

They looked at each other. Malone didn't doubt his brother was thinking the same thing he was.

"He cast out Seven Demons." Five down, two to go.

"Son of a bitch," Percy muttered. "We've got to get this bastard."

Jasper's desk phone rang. Malone looked at it, then back up at his brother. "What did you say?"

"That we needed to get this bastard."

Malone smiled. "I think we might be one step closer."

He pointed to a message pad beside the phone. There, written big as life, was Connor Scott's name.

Chapter Sixty-two

Thursday, August 18
5:20 P.M.

He stood naked in front of the bathroom mirror, his image distorted by fog on the glass. He wiped the fog away, but still the distortion remained. Who was that man? he wondered. The one with blood on his hands? The blood of the lambs.

This wasn't the way it was supposed to be. This wasn't what *he* was supposed to be.

He backed away from the damning reflection. The wall stopped his progress and he sank to the damp tile floor, drawing his knees to his chest. His heart raced and his head hurt. Something was wrong, had gone terribly wrong.

He lowered his gaze to his arms, the deep gouges that had again begun seeping blood. She'd fought him, digging her nails into his arms, flailing and kicking. She had cried and pleaded, had invoked his Father's holy name.

He didn't understand. The others had been extinguished so easily.

A shudder rippled over him. He squeezed his eyes tight shut, wanting to block out the memory.

Another came forward. A violent memory. He'd been eight years old. His mother and grandmother at the top of the stairs, yelling at each other. His mother had ahold of one of his arms, his grandmother the other.

"You're delusional," his mother shouted. *"And you're going to make him crazy, like you are! He's my son and I'm taking him away from you!"*

Their suitcases waited by the door. His grandmother released his arm. At his mother's direction, he ran down to wait by them.

"It wasn't a virgin birth, Mother! I had sex; he didn't love me and he left. My baby's just a regular little boy. You have to accept that."

His grandmother's howl of rage filled his head. He saw his mother pitch forward and tumble down the stairs, her head hitting the foyer floor with a sickening crack.

You're going to make him crazy, like you are . . . crazy . . . crazy . . . crazy.

"I can't bear it!" he screamed, pressing his hands over his ears. "Father, where are you? Make it stop, please!"

But he didn't make it stop. The memory continued to unfurl. His grandmother making him help her drag the body out to the backyard, then dig the hole deeper and deeper.

"Push," she ordered. *"Harder!"*

His mother's body landing in the hole with a *thump.*

"Stop!" he screamed.

And then his Father was upon him. *Your grandmother did what she had to do. Your mother didn't believe. Not in your mission or in your divinity.*

"I loved her."

She meant to take you away.

She had. His grandmother couldn't allow that and had stopped her the only way she knew how. He looked heavenward. "Today, where were you while she fought me? The others went so quickly, but this one—"

Do you not think the Evil One is strong? That he will fight with all his wiles and might? Do not fool yourself, Son. He is very powerful, indeed.

"But she called on your name, for protection and intervention. As if it was I who was the Evil One."

The tricks of the serpent. Finish your mission. Expel the last of the demons. Once Mary is cleansed and by your side, you'll be at peace.

Peace, he thought. Yes, how he longed for it. And now, it was so close. Two more demons, that's all that were left.

Chapter Sixty-three

Thursday, August 18
5:55 P.M.

Mira opened her eyes. It took her a moment to realize where she was: her garden room, on the couch. She struggled to sit up, her limbs heavy and her head fuzzy.

What time was it? She shook her head, hoping to clear the cobwebs. She felt like she had been sleeping off a bender. But she hadn't imbibed, not even a glass of wine.

Connor. The things he'd told her.

She had faced the moment totally sober.

That was huge. Monumental. But she had no desire to celebrate.

Jeff had been cheating on her.

After Connor had left, she'd sat here. Reliving her marriage and trying to reconcile it with what Connor had told her. And with the fact that the marriage she had believed to be a real-life fairy tale had been a sham.

She hadn't known. She hadn't simply "chosen" not to see, or looked the other way out of cowardice or unwillingness to let go of her fairy tale.

Yes, she recalled occasionally wondering where Jeff was, or why he was so late getting home. But she had never seriously considered he was with another woman. Or been suspicious enough to ask him if he was cheating.

Yet he had been. Not one affair. Multiple ones.

If she could trust that Connor had been telling her the truth.

She did. A week ago, she wouldn't have. She would have fought the suggestion to the death.

Not anymore. She felt like such a fool. A starry-eyed, idiot ingenue. For her blindness then. And for spending the past six years mourning the "perfect" love she had lost.

Who else had known? His family? Probably. No wonder they didn't respect her. No wonder they believed she'd killed him. Mira imagined their thoughts: she found out Jeff was cheating, or he confessed and asked for a divorce; in a fit of jealousy and rage, she killed him.

What if one of the women had become more than an affair? What if Jeff had meant to leave her?

Mira closed her eyes, conflicting emotions of anger and pain ricocheting through her. She had given Jeff everything, put herself, heart and soul, into their marriage. And what had he done? Given her a piece of his life. A little slice to nibble on when he wasn't out sharing the rest with someone else.

Where did she go from here? Mira wondered. She couldn't confront him. Couldn't scream, yell or even flail her fists against his chest. She couldn't even divorce the bastard.

She would do the only thing she could—move on with her life. What she should have done long before this.

Connor. If he would forgive her doubts and give her another chance. Give *them* another chance, she thought.

Her cell phone sounded from the kitchen. Mira climbed off the couch and hurried to find it, hoping it was Connor.

It wasn't, she realized, as she snatched it up off the counter and answered.

Deni greeted her. "Hey, Mira. Just checking in with you. Are you okay?"

"Up and breathing. What time is it?"

"Just after six."

"At night?" Mira looked over her shoulder at the clock on

the microwave. It was, indeed, after six. "My God, I slept all day. I can't believe it. I'm sorry you were worried."

"It's all right. I'm just glad you're fine."

"Anything happen today that I should know about?"

"Chris said you were in last night. And that you bandaged his arm."

"I did. How is he? It was a pretty nasty cut."

"You know guys, the less fussing the better. He went right back to work, sawing and hammering like nothing happened until it started bleeding again."

"Did he go home?"

"I sent him to the Redi-Med for stitches. He didn't want to do that either."

Mira changed the subject. "Did Dr. Jasper call or come by today?"

"No. But Lance Arnold called again."

Mira made a mental note to call the attorney. "Thanks. I'll definitely be in first thing tomorrow."

"Mira, wait. There's something I have to tell you." She cleared her throat. "The other night when you were over, I lied to you about being alone. I wasn't."

Mira had known it, though she had tried to convince herself otherwise. She didn't know what to say, so she said nothing.

Deni pressed on. "Please don't be mad at me. I just, I lied because . . . it wasn't Chris who was with me. I was embarrassed and it was really awkward."

Not Chris? Mira frowned. "Last night when I asked, he said you guys were fine."

Deni's silence spoke volumes.

She thought of Jeff, of what Connor had told her and how much it hurt. "Running around that way is wrong. You're better than that, Deni."

"I know," she said, her voice taking on a whiny edge, "and I really like Chris. He's a great guy and I could see us having a future together. But—"

"But what?"

"He's a little weird."

"How so?"

"For one, he wears that purity ring—"

"He told me about that."

"For another, he never wants to go out or party. I like to have fun. That's how I met Bill. Chris was too tired to go out, so I went without him and one thing led to another."

Mira wondered if that's the way it started with Jeff's paramours. Chance and boredom? Lack of satisfaction with her? Or some deficiency in him?

"Chris is a good guy, Deni. But if it's not going to work, it's not. You need to be honest with him."

"He says he knows you."

"Who knows me?"

"Bill. Through Jeff. They were friends."

Chill bumps crawled up Mira's arms. "Who is this guy?"

"He's a bartender. We met at Daiquiris."

Had Jeff ever mentioned a friend who tended bar? She didn't think so. But it didn't mean it wasn't true. Jeff had had lots of friends. And, apparently, a whole other life she hadn't known about.

"Have you talked to him about me?"

"Just a little." Her tone turned defensive. "With everything going on . . . I mean, how do I not talk about it?"

"And the other night, when I came to you, you told him everything? About Jeff, that I thought he was alive?"

"I didn't know I wasn't supposed to."

"You insisted you were alone."

"What was I supposed to do? He was there, I had to tell him something!"

A stranger who said he knew her and Jeff. A stranger who had secretly insinuated himself into her life through Deni. One who knew everything about her—where she was and what she was doing and feeling.

Again, through association with Deni.

Could he be the one? "When did you meet him?"

"I don't know, a few weeks ago."

"It's important, Deni. When?"

She was silent a moment. "The same day that Preacher person attacked you."

He was the one. He had to be.

"What's his full name?"

"Why does that matter—"

"It does, dammit! What's his full name?"

She hesitated. "Bill Smith."

She might as well have said John Doe. She told Deni so.

"What's that supposed to mean?"

"That's an awfully pat name, don't you think? How can you be sure that's his real name?"

"Because he told me it was! Geez, Mira, why are you acting like this?"

"Because four people are dead! Did you know that it's four now?" Her stunned silence told Mira that she hadn't. "My neighbor. And I found her. It was awful. Horrible. The killer wrote a number four on her forehead!"

"Bill isn't a killer. He's really nice. You need to trust me." It sounded like Deni was crying. "He said he liked you. That he met you and—"

"Last night you were afraid for me. Remember? And now you're blindly trusting someone you don't even know."

"I know him! That's what I'm trying to tell you, but you won't listen!"

"Don't you get it? What if this guy wants to put a number on *my* forehead!"

"Oh, my God! Why would you think that?"

"Because the only thing the victims have in common is me!"

"He opens doors for me and doesn't curse. And he's religious. In fact, last Wednesday night he didn't come over because he promised his grandmother he'd take her to mass."

"*He will come again to judge the living and the dead.*"

Fear gripped her. "Where are you?"

"Home. Why?"

"Stay there. Promise me. And don't answer the door or call anybody—"

"Bill's going to call any minute. We're going out tonight."

"No! Please, Deni, this is life and death."

"You're losing it, Mira. Are you sure you're not using?"

"Please," Mira begged, "don't talk to this guy, don't let him into your place until I call you back. Promise."

"No. I'm sorry I lied to you. And I'm sorry all this is going on, but it doesn't have anything to do with me or Bill. You need to chill. I've got to go."

"Deni, don't—"

Her assistant hung up.

Mira immediately dialed her back. Deni didn't pick up and Mira didn't leave a message. Instead, she dug out Malone's number and dialed it.

"Malone here."

"Detective, thank God!" The words came out half sob. "I think I know who the killer is."

"Whoa, slow down, Ms. Gallier. What are you saying?"

"The killer. I think it's a guy who Deni's been seeing in secret. He told her he knows me, that he knew Jeff . . . she's told him everything . . . I'm afraid for her."

"Tell me everything," he said flatly. "Don't leave anything out."

"Deni called me," she said as calmly as she could. "She confessed that the night I stayed with her, there was a man there. His name was Bill Smith."

"Bill Smith," he repeated. "Do you know him?"

"No, though he claims he knows me. That he knew Jeff." Her voice rose slightly, though she tried to control it. "Turns out he came into her life the same day Preacher attacked me. She's been keeping him posted on everything that's been going on!"

"Calm down, it's going to be okay. Has he threatened her?"

"No. She thinks I'm overreacting. But it's just too weird, with everything going on . . . If I'm right and he's the killer and she tells him I'm suspicious of him, he'll kill her. Won't he?"

"Let's not go there right now. Bill Smith, you said. Do you know anything else about him?"

"He's a bartender."

"Where?"

"Deni said they met at Daiquiris, but I don't know which one or even if he was working when they met."

"I'll check it out. Where are you?"

"Home."

"Your dog's with you?"

"Of course, what . . . If you're trying to make me feel less freaked out, it's not working."

"Look, I need you to stay put. I'm going to send a cruiser by to keep you company."

"A cruiser?" For a moment, she was confused. Then she understood. And went cold with fear. "Something's happened. What?"

"There's been another murder."

"Who?" she managed, the sound small and strangled.

"Dr. Adele Jasper. I'm sorry, Mira."

Chapter Sixty-four

Dr. Jasper was dead. Mira struggled to wrap her mind around that fact. She had been murdered, though Mira didn't know how. She wondered if the killer had placed a number 5 on her forehead.

She had accused Dr. Jasper of being the one who was terrorizing her and now she was dead. Regret settled like a fist in the pit of her stomach. And guilt, gnawing at her, whispering that if Louise Latrobe and Adele Jasper hadn't known her they would still be alive. The same guilty voice that had taunted her over Jeff's death.

Should she call everyone she knew, warn them they were in danger? Connor and Chris, the rest of her neighbors, Sam from the Corner Bar?

But now, this moment, it was Deni she had to warn.

The image of Louise Latrobe filled her head, face a ghastly death mask, the 4 painted on her forehead like an obscene exclamation point. She squeezed her eyes shut against it. She couldn't let that happen to Deni. She wouldn't.

She had made the right decision, coming here. Ignoring Detective Malone's order to sit tight and wait. Deni could be in trouble. Bill Smith could be a killer. And if Deni told him about their phone call and that Mira thought he was a murderer, he could kill Deni to protect his identity.

She had put her friend in danger.

Mira looked at Deni's double, at her red VW Beetle parked in the driveway. Without giving herself another moment to wimp out, she climbed out of her car. As she hurried to her friend's door, she considered the things she would say, how she would convince her. She would beg her to hold off seeing Bill Smith until the police questioned him.

Mira reached the small covered porch and stopped short. Deni's front door was open.

Just an inch or two. Just enough to send a shiver of fear racing through her.

Mira told herself to return to her car, call Malone again. Or 911. Then wait until help arrived. But what if she was the help? What if Deni needed her now, not ten minutes from now?

Heart thundering, as if her every instinct was resisting her will, she nudged the door open with just the tips of her fingers. Poking her head inside, she called out. "Deni? It's Mira."

No answer.

She had been in this same predicament yesterday. Standing on Mrs. Latrobe's front porch, easing her door open, calling out hopefully.

She felt like she might throw up. An endless chant of *Please, God, not again* played in her head.

She pressed a hand to her stomach. She couldn't bear finding her friend in the same condition she had found Louise. She couldn't.

Wait for the police, Mira. Do not do this.

Even as she told herself she wasn't a hero, she stepped gingerly into the apartment. "Deni," she whispered, "are you all right?"

Absolute silence greeted her. She moved her gaze over the room—nothing looked out of place. At least for Deni, or in a way that aroused her suspicion. Newspapers, magazines and sketches littered most surfaces. Empty soft drink cans and water bottles, throw pillows on the floor, shoes scattered about. At least a dozen pairs. Tacked on an easel in the corner was a beautiful charcoal drawing of an angel, art materials covering the table beside it.

Creative clutter, Mira thought. Much the way Deni worked at the studio.

However, she wasn't totally reassured by the absence of overturned furniture or signs of a struggle. There hadn't been any of that at Mrs. Latrobe's the day before, either.

Mouth dry, light-headed with fear, Mira tiptoed forward. She reached the kitchen and peeked inside.

She let out a shuddering breath. *Nothing. Thank God.*

"Who the hell are you?"

Mira whirled around. The man standing just inside the doorway was huge, and judging by his expression, he wanted to tear her apart.

She took a step backward, a scream ripping past her lips and bouncing off the walls of the tiny kitchen.

The big guy went white. He threw up his hands. "It's okay. I didn't mean to scare you, please don't do that again."

Mira glanced wildly around her, looking for something she might be able to use as a weapon. The closest she came was the teakettle sitting on the range top. Even filled with water she didn't think it'd be much good against Gigantor. "Who are you?" she managed. "Bill?"

"No, I'm Randy. Deni's neighbor."

Roid-rage Randy. Of course. If she hadn't been so freaked out already, she would have recognized him.

"Wait," he said, "we've met before. You're Deni's boss."

"Her friend, too. Mira Gallier. What are you doing over here, Randy?"

"I saw you creep in and decided to come see what was going on." He frowned. "What is going on? Where's Deni?"

"I was hoping she was here."

He scratched his head. "She was a little bit ago. I heard her arguing with somebody."

"With who?"

He shrugged. "I don't know. It was pretty intense, though."

"What was it about?"

"I couldn't really make it out. Heard a lot of f this and f that. He called her a liar."

"He? It was definitely a man she was arguing with?"

Randy paused. "Actually, I'm not sure. I just assumed. She's been dating a couple different dudes."

"Is one of them named Bill Smith?"

"I don't know. She didn't introduce me or anything, I just saw 'em around."

"What'd they look like?"

"One has blondish-reddish hair. Kinda long and shaggy. Scruffy looking."

"Scruffy, what does that mean?"

"You know, the way young people dress. Baggy cargo shorts, T-shirts, flip-flops."

That sounded like Chris. "What about the other guy?"

"Real sharp looking. Short hair. Older."

"How old?"

"I just got a couple of glimpses of him. Maybe in his thirties?"

"Did you notice what type of vehicle he drove?" she asked hopefully.

"Sorry."

Sudden tears flooded her eyes. What was she supposed to do now?

"Hey, are you okay?"

"Not really. I'm afraid she's in trouble. I'm afraid"—she struggled not to cry—"that this guy, the short-haired one, might have hurt her."

He looked alarmed. "Have you checked the rest of her place?"

She shook her head. "I guess I should, huh?"

"I'll look with you, if you want?"

She did and together they checked the rest of the house. No Deni. No sign of a fight or struggle. Judging by the pile of clothes and the damp towel hanging over the shower rod, she'd showered and changed clothes.

"This is starting to feel a little weird," he said, averting his eyes from the discarded clothing. "I don't think she'd be comfortable with us being in here like this. Especially me."

Mira nodded but didn't move. "Where could she be?"

"Probably went out. She's almost never home at night."

"Then why was the door open?"

He thought a moment. "She left in a hurry and didn't close it tight?"

"And didn't lock it?"

"If it's like mine, it's one of those that you lock from the inside, before you go out. All you have to do then is slam the door."

She didn't respond and they returned to the kitchen.

"Look," he said, "she left her cell phone."

He picked it up off the kitchen counter and held it out.

Mira stared at it, a funny tingly sensation moving over her. More than any other person she knew, Deni was attached to her phone. She used it for e-mail, social networking and games. She checked the weather on it and used it to keep up with the news. If somebody asked her a question about anything she didn't know off the top of her head, she went to her phone.

Mira had never known her to be without it.

Randy must have seen the upset on her face. "She probably just forgot it."

Mira didn't believe that, even though she really wanted to. She glanced a last time around the kitchen. An empty Lean Cuisine frozen meal box sat on the counter by the microwave. She crossed to the appliance and popped open the door. Inside sat an untouched, cooked meal.

She bit back a squeak of dismay and shut the microwave. Who cooked a meal, then just left it to sit? Wouldn't she have at least covered it with foil and stuck it in the fridge?

Randy went on. "My guess is, she's out with one of those dudes. Too bad you can't just call and ask."

Call and ask. Of course.

"Can I have the phone?"

"Sure." He handed it to her.

She tucked the device into her pants pocket. "How long ago did you overhear that argument?"

He tipped his face to the ceiling for a moment. "*Jeopardy!* was on. I'd say about forty minutes. Maybe an hour."

Forty to sixty minutes ago. Shortly after she'd talked to Deni. She didn't know what that meant or if it was even important, but she liked having the information, just in case.

"I think you're right, Randy. This feels weird, we should get out of here."

Outside, she thanked him for his help, then hurried to her car. After starting it and setting the A/C to arctic blast, she dug Deni's phone out of her pocket.

She quickly accessed the call history: Deni's call to her, and hers back, then a call to a number she didn't recognize, one from Chris, then two calls from the first number.

Using her own phone, she called Chris. He answered right away. "Hi, Mira. What's up?"

"Just wondering if Deni's with you?"

"Deni? Nope. Haven't talked to her in an hour or so."

"When was that?"

"I don't know, I could check my phone if you want. I called to see if she wanted to go out for a pizza, but she said she wasn't in the mood."

More like she had another date.

"Is everything all right?" he asked.

"I have some bad news. Dr. Jasper is dead. She was murdered." She heard his sharply drawn breath. "And now," she went on, "I'm worried about—"

She couldn't tell him about Bill Smith, not like this. Not over the phone. "Where are you?" she asked instead.

"New York Pizza. Picking up. My taste buds were all set for it, you know how that is."

"I do." Her thoughts tumbled forward. Maybe Chris could help her? Maybe he knew where Deni hung out? Or maybe he knew more about Deni's secret life than she thought he did?

But she could only find out face-to-face with him.

"What size pizza did you get?"

"A large. Vegetarian. Why?"

"How 'bout we share? We could meet at the studio?"

He liked the idea. They agreed to head there immediately and hung up. But Mira wasn't done. This time she made a call from Deni's phone, dialing back that last call Deni had placed.

It rang several times before an automated message announced: *I'm sorry, but the subscriber you have dialed has a voice mail box that has not been set up.*

She tossed the phone on the seat beside her. She would try Mr. Bill Smith later.

Chapter Sixty-five

Mira pulled into the studio's parking area, taking the space next to the only other vehicle in the lot—Chris's truck. She hurried around to the studio entrance.

She had expected him to be waiting on the porch for her, but that wasn't the case. She crossed to the door—and found it locked. A locked door, imagine that?

She stepped inside. And smelled pizza. Her stomach responded with a growl. "Chris?" she called out. "I'm here."

The pocket doors to the workroom stood half open. Light tumbled through, illuminating the darkened retail area.

"Chris?" she said again and started that way.

He appeared in the doorway, his expression strange. Distraught. She stopped. "What is it?" Her words came out a whisper.

He slid the doors shut behind him. The light bled out the cracks and crevices around the old doors. "Don't go in there."

"Oh, my God." She brought a hand to her mouth. It was shaking. "Is it . . . Deni?"

"Deni?" He looked confused. "It's the Magdalene window. It's gone."

For a moment, Mira wondered if she had stopped breathing. If she might never breathe again. "What do you mean, gone? Moved?"

He shook his head. "It's not here. I searched the studio. None of the other panels are missing."

"Maybe Deni packed it for transport?"

"I don't think so. I mean, why would she pack it without an install date?"

She started toward him. "Let me see."

He hesitated, then stepped aside. Mira took a moment to prepare herself, then resolutely slid the doors open.

Nothing could have prepared her for the empty place where the Magdalene window had been.

"You're trembling," Chris said softly. "Are you all right?"

"Who would take it? What could they possibly want with her—"

And then she knew: *"He cast out Seven Demons." Mary Magdalene.*

"Oh, my God. I know who has it."

"You do? Who—"

"The Judgment Day killer."

"Mira, there's something I have to tell you." At his serious tone, she stopped and looked at him. "It's about Deni. Something the neighbor said she saw."

Mira waited, heart thudding heavily.

"When I knew for certain that the window was gone, I went across the street, to ask the neighbors if they saw anyone. Carol, directly across from us, said she saw Deni here earlier tonight. She was with a guy. They carried something big and loaded it into a van. It was crated. About the size of a large window."

She struggled to make sense of what he was telling her. "Was Carol certain it was Deni?"

"Positive."

"What time was that?"

Chris looked sick. "Around seven, she said."

Mira thought back. What time had Deni called? Around

six o'clock, she remembered. She'd checked the time, been surprised she had slept all day.

"Did she recognize the man?" she asked.

"No, but . . . she said he looked like military."

"Military?" She stared at him. "He was in uniform?"

"No, just . . . He had a buzz cut. And light hair."

"No," she said, shaking her head for emphasis. "I know what you're implying, but it wasn't him."

"Then who was she with? I'm afraid for her. She wouldn't hurt you or anyone else. And she wouldn't take the Magdalene window unless she was being forced to. Connor tricked her somehow, got her to let him into the studio and—"

"His name's Bill Smith." Mira caught his hands. "Deni was seeing someone else. That's who she's with. I'm sorry. I only just found out."

For a moment, he simply stared at her, then he shook his head. "That can't be right. We see each other every day and almost every night. Everything's been good."

"I'm sorry," she said again, squeezing his fingers.

"How long—" He cleared his throat. "How long's it been going on?"

"A few weeks. Since the day Preacher attacked me."

He struggled to come to grips with the information. "That was the same day your friend Connor showed up."

It was. She hadn't put that together. "But Deni told me the guy's name is Bill Smith. That he's a bartender she met while out partying . . ."

But Deni had also told her, not once but three times, that there had been no one at her house the night she'd slept over.

She'd lied before. So why not tonight, too?

Mira pressed her fingers to her forehead. Connor and Deni? In this together? Coconspirators? Killers? It didn't make sense.

She dropped her hands and met Chris's gaze evenly. "It wasn't Connor. I have to believe that. And if Deni really was here and helped steal the Magdalene window, she was being forced to."

"Okay," he said, "I'm with you, then. What do we do now?"

"Good question. Problem is, I'm not exactly sure."

"Call the cops?" he offered. "That Detective Malone. He'll know what to do."

"Yes," she said. "But before we do, let's look at it all again, see if we can figure out why the killer would take the Magdalene window."

Headlights cut across the front of the building. They both turned in that direction.

"Mira," he whispered, "I don't want to scare you, but if this guy's killing people around you, maybe this isn't the smartest place for us to be?"

From outside came the slam of a car door.

It was too late to turn off the lights. Too late to make certain she had relocked the front door. Fear took her breath.

Chris grabbed her hand and pulled her toward the tall racks in the corner. Between the two racks and the wall was a slim space, just big enough for them to hide.

She slid in first, all the way to the wall. He behind her. Completely in shadow, they stood pressed together. He found her hand and laced their fingers together.

Moments later came a rapping on the front door, then the definite sound of the lock being tested. Mira pressed her lips together to hold back a cry. Chris squeezed her fingers tightly.

In the next moments, the person was at the workroom emergency exit, trying it. Then a beam of light darted crazily over the floors, walls and ceiling. Mira went light-headed with fear. She breathed as deeply and silently as she could, working to concentrate on her breath and the reassuring sound of Chris's wildly beating heart.

For a long time after whoever had been trying to get in had given up, Mira and Chris didn't move. Finally, Chris released her hand, then whispered, "Stay put. I'll make sure he's gone."

She nodded. "Be careful."

He slipped silently out. She counted in her head, imagining where he was with each number. At ninety-eight, he reappeared at the opening of their hiding place.

"All clear," he said and reached a hand out for her. She took it and shimmied out.

"Did you check the parking lot?"

"I did. Your car and my truck, that's it. But I think we should get out of here."

She did, too. "But go where?"

"I have a place," he said. "Deni doesn't even know about it. We'll be safe there."

Chapter Sixty-six

Malone sat at his desk. Things had gone from bad to worse. He'd sent a cruiser to Gallier's—neither she nor her vehicle had been there. He'd sent another by her studio, but hadn't heard back yet. He'd tried calling her but she hadn't picked up. In addition, Scott had slipped through their fingers. Malone feared the man had figured out they were on to him and gone into hiding. Scott was no uneducated, low-IQ street criminal. If he was their UNSUB, he'd have to know that taking out Dr. Jasper that way had screwed any hope of his getting away with it. The Jasper scene was a virtual mother lode of physical evidence: phone records, DNA, trace, even his name, written in the victim's handwriting.

Knowing that, he'd either be on the run or focusing on completing what he'd begun—which would include two more folks, one of them most probably Mira Gallier.

And Bayle was still MIA.

Percy appeared at his cubicle. "Captain's ready for us."

Malone nodded and stood. His brother looked as frustrated as he felt. How the hell had this case suddenly spun so far out of their control?

Captain O'Shay waved them into her office. "Any word

from Bayle?" she asked. When Malone indicated no, she swore. "What the hell happened between you two? The long version, Detective."

"Nothing that I would have thought—" He cleared his throat. "I knew that she'd been in a relationship that ended badly. Badly enough that it precipitated her meltdown. I asked if the man she'd been involved with was Connor Scott and suggested she wasn't as objective about this case as she should be."

"Connor Scott? How the hell did you draw that conclusion?"

"The intense dislike I'd observed between them from the first time we questioned him. Her unexplainable bias against Mira Gallier. Her former partner told Stacy the guy she'd been involved with was Uptown old money. It sounds like a stretch now, but at the time it felt right."

"How did Bayle respond?"

"She told me I was full of shit and, basically, a piece of it as well. I decided she was right, called and apologized via cell phone message. She never called me back."

"And now, no Scott either."

"No, Captain."

She moved her gaze between them, then settled on Malone. "Any chance Bayle and Scott could be in this together?"

He thought a moment. "Not in my opinion. It was animosity I picked up between them. Not heat."

"Bayle's in trouble," she said. "She would have come to me with her grievances, asked for a change. No way the detective I know would shirk her duties by running off."

"Unless I was right."

"Or," Percy offered, "she had another breakdown?"

"There's more, Captain," Malone said. "We have a new lead." At her expression, he quickly filled her in on Bill Smith.

When he'd finished, she narrowed her eyes and pursed her lips. "What do you think?"

"Gallier could have stumbled onto something. It makes sense. By hooking up with someone close to Gallier, the perp would have been able to stay connected to the investigation and be continually apprised of her movements and frame of mind. In addition, through Deni Watts they might have had access to the keys and alarm codes to Gallier's home and studio."

Percy jumped in. "What we don't have is his name at the scene of the last crime. Though," he added, "this Smith would have known Connor Scott was a prime suspect and used his name instead of his own when he made an appointment with Jasper."

"I told Gallier to sit tight and that I was sending a unit over to keep an eye on her. She chose to run off instead."

Captain O'Shay frowned. "Any idea where she might have run to?"

"My best guess is Deni Watts's to try to warn her about this Bill Smith. If not there, I'm not certain. I'd say Scott's or her studio."

"Let's start with Watts's place. Get a cruiser over there. Next, I want to know who this Bill Smith is, where he works, if he has a record. Then I want him in here for questioning. Find out where Watts hangs out and who she hangs with. If she has family, question them. Wasn't there another boyfriend—"

"Chris Johns," Malone said. "Carpenter, handyman. Also works for Gallier."

"Let's talk to him. If Watts dumped him, he'll know something and be happy to help. And look, bring Jackson and Phillips on board. With a generic name like Bill Smith, you're bound to have a lot to sift through."

They nodded, stood and filed out, heading toward Malone's office. "This thing's eating at me," he said. "What am I missing?"

"Same thing I am, obviously."

Malone realized they'd stopped in front of Bayle's cubicle. He glanced in at her desk, something plucking at his memory.

"You okay, bro?"

Then he remembered. Catching Bayle crying. Her trying to hide it, stuffing something into her desk drawer.

He stepped into the cubicle and crossed to her desk, going behind it.

"What're you doing?"

"Something I may regret." He slid open the top drawer and started rifling through the contents. Nothing. Forms, a notebook, a Crescent City Connection toll receipt and a couple energy bars.

"Okay, now you're starting to scare me. Uncool, bro."

He didn't reply, though he knew his brother was right. Instead, he slid open the bottom drawer. Nothing again.

Malone straightened, looking sheepishly at his brother. "I feel like an idiot. Let's get out of here before somebody—"

He stopped, his gaze going to a slash of bright orange peeking out from under a file folder. A hideous shade he would recognize anywhere: Coral Sunrise.

What he was looking for had been right in front of his eyes.

Percy followed his gaze. "Holy shit," he said.

"You have gloves?" Malone asked. He did and handed them over. After fitting them on, Malone carefully extracted the paper.

On the unlined sheet, printed in all caps, were two words: *I KNOW.*

Following the words, drawn with the garish orange lipstick, was a smiley face.

Chapter Sixty-seven

Malone sat outside Bayle's small Bayou St. John home, a neighborhood defined by the bayou that ran along its western edge. He flexed his fingers, eager for the warrant to arrive so they could begin.

They had compared the smiley face symbol from the Sisters of Mercy scene to the one found on Bayle's desk. They were nearly identical, a circle with the smile and eyes inside, a distinctive swoop at the top of the circle. It had been a piece of information they had deliberately kept from the press, just in case it turned out to be important. Now it looked as if it had. Unfortunately, it linked Bayle to the crimes.

Malone searched his memory. Who had seen the graffitied windows? Law enforcement who had worked the scene. Paramedics and CSI. A few members of the Sisters of Mercy staff. Mira Gallier and whoever helped her clean the windows. Deni Watts? Chris Johns?

And the killer.

He frowned. Where did Bayle fit in all this? Had she created the note, then never delivered it? Or had she been the recipient? And what did the note's originator "know"?

A cruiser pulled up behind him. Another vehicle behind

that, probably a tech to unlock the house. Despite what Hollywood liked to portray, they kicked in doors only when faced with no other option. Two uniforms stepped out of the cruiser, one of them with search warrant in hand.

The officer handed it to him, and Malone scanned it to make certain it listed everything and in a way that would least restrict their search: photos, journal, letters, e-mails, .45 caliber gun, lipstick in Coral Sunrise, sales receipts, Sharpie, broad tip in black. The list went on.

Malone nodded. "Let's do this."

They fell into step together, making their way up the brick walk to the front door. Within moments, the tech had it open. The uniformed officers shone their flashlights into the dark space, then stepped aside so Malone could enter.

He flipped on the foyer light. None of them spoke. It felt wrong. A violation. Bayle was one of their own, a decorated officer, a Katrina hero, a friend. And they were readying to poke through her life as if she were a stranger to them.

She was, Malone told himself. The woman they were investigating was not who she had portrayed herself to be. Not completely. This woman had, at best, withheld information pertinent to an investigation, and at worst, was a murderer.

"Where would you like us to start, Detective?" the officer who'd handed him the warrant asked.

"You take in here," he said, indicating the living room. "Follow up with the kitchen. I'll start with her bedroom. You've reviewed the list of what we're looking for?"

He had, and they split up. Malone made his way into her bedroom, fitting on gloves as he did. He reached the room and switched on the overhead.

He swept his gaze over the interior. For a tough cookie like Bayle, it was surprisingly feminine. Soft colors, a ruffled bedspread. Bed pillows with beading and decorative tassels.

He crossed to the cluttered nightstand. A single framed photograph sat on its top. He picked it up. Bayle with a guy. Malone gazed at the photo, a simple three-by-five. It looked as if it had been taken at a bar, the lighting was bad and the resolution poor. The man with her wasn't Connor Scott, but he did look familiar. Handsome, short hair, a winning smile.

Malone frowned in thought. Where did he know him from?

He studied it a moment more, then shifted his attention to the other items on the nightstand: moisturizer, cell phone charger, a bottle of Tylenol PM, a paperback novel.

Percy arrived. He greeted the other officers, then entered the room. Malone looked over his shoulder. "Take a look at the guy in this photo, see if you recognize him."

Percy picked up the photo, then whistled. "Holy shit, I do know this guy."

Malone met his brother's surprised gaze. "Yeah? Who is it?"

"Jeff Gallier."

Chapter Sixty-eight

Mira had convinced Chris to swing by her house to collect Nola and grab a change of clothes and some other personal items. He'd been spooked and eager to get somewhere safe, but she'd insisted. After all, she didn't know how long it would be before she returned home.

It had taken longer than she'd expected. She'd had to feed and walk Nola, then gather her things together. Now she realized she had forgotten her cell phone somewhere in the house.

Chris waited on the porch, playing lookout. Nola stood beside him, tail wagging. Mira brought him her duffel. "Anybody suspicious drive by?"

"Nada. All quiet."

"That's a relief. I need one more minute, I left my cell phone inside." As if cued, it began to ring. "Be right back—"

He caught her hand. "Don't answer it. Let's just go. I've got a feeling we're running out of time."

She shook off his hand. "Don't be silly, it'll only take a minute. Besides, it may be Detective Malone with news."

It was the detective, she learned moments later when she answered.

"Ms. Gallier, are you all right?"

"Fine," she said, catching her breath. "I had to run for the phone, that's all."

"Where are you?"

"I'm at home."

"There have been some developments in the case. I'm going to send a cruiser to pick you up. Wait for it this time."

Her heart leaped to her throat. "Is this about Deni? Is she all right?"

"Your assistant? As far as I know she's fine. This is good news. We're closing in on the killer."

"Thank God! Was it that Bill Smith Deni was dating?"

"I can't say much more than I already have, but I can tell you that it was not Bill Smith or anyone else Deni was dating."

"Are you certain, Detective? When I went to her house, she wasn't there. But she'd left her cell phone and her neighbor heard an argument before I got there."

"I'm positive. Look, I bet she and her boyfriend had a fight, then made up. She forgot her phone when they went out."

"What about the Magdalene window? Someone's stolen it."

"Excuse me?"

"It's gone. Chris discovered it. He questioned the neighbor across the street from the studio. She told him she saw Deni and a guy putting what appeared to be a wrapped window into a van around seven tonight."

"We'll look into it, but if she did take the window, it was unrelated to the murders."

"How do you know? Maybe he killed her? Maybe—"

"Mira," he said, cutting her off, "I've got to go. The cruiser is on its way, it's urgent you stay put. The names are Officers James and Fosse. Don't go with anyone else, not even Detective Bayle. Do you understand? I'll be able to tell you more soon."

He ended the call and she frowned, realizing she should feel relieved but was confused instead. Something about this felt really wrong. And why that final comment about Detective Bayle?

"Who were you talking to?" Chris asked from behind her.

"Detective Malone. He arranged for a couple officers to pick me up and take me to a safe location. Apparently, they've identified the killer."

"We have a safe place to go, you and I."

He sounded strange. Hurt, maybe. She tucked her phone into her pocket and turned around. "I'm not leaving you, Chris. I'm bringing you with . . ."

Her words trailed off. He was bleeding—blood stained the arm of his shirt and dripped from the cuff. "Oh, my God, you're hurt!" She turned and grabbed a dishcloth. "What happened—"

Before she could finish the words, she was pressed face-first against the refrigerator, arms twisted behind her back. He was wrapping something tightly around her wrists.

It took that moment for her rational mind to come to grips with what was happening and begin to struggle. When she thrashed against his grip, he caught the back of her head, his hand like a vise. She gasped in pain.

"Stop it, Mary! I don't want to hurt you."

"Let me go, Chris . . . This is crazy . . . Please."

Where was Nola? she wondered. Why hadn't she come to her aid? Then she heard her, barking and clawing at the courtyard door.

"You're possessed by demons. I'll finish this and we'll be together."

She screamed then, the sounds ripping from her throat, one after another. Nola went nuts, barking and growling, throwing herself against the door.

Her only warning of what was coming next was the sudden jerk of the hand at the back of her head; in the next moment stars exploded in her head as her face smashed into the refrigerator.

Her knees gave. She crumpled to the floor, doubling over at the excruciating pain.

"It's almost over, Mary. It's going to be fine. We'll be together forever." He dug her phone from her pocket, dropped it, then stomped it with the heel of his work boot.

Her brain told her to try to run. She fought her way to a crawl, praying the police were close, that someone had heard her scream or Nola's frantic barking.

He stepped on her lower back, anchoring her in place. "None of that, my dear. We don't have time."

She heard something tearing and a moment later knew what—a dishcloth, the same one she had grabbed to help him. He fitted it over her mouth, tying it tightly behind her head. She tasted blood and started to cry.

At her tears, his face puckered with regret. For a moment, she thought he might free her, then his expression hardened.

"Demons," he muttered, using another strip to secure her ankles. "I'll free you from them, I promise."

He scooped her up and carried her out to his truck. So the killer wouldn't know they were there, they had deliberately extinguished the porch and driveway lights. Hysteria bubbled up inside her. But the killer had known all along. Waiting for just the right moment.

Mira heard sirens in the distance. But she saw his truck, just steps away, passenger door open and waiting, engine running.

The police weren't going to make it in time.

In a last, desperate attempt to escape, she rocked and twisted against his grasp. He tightened his arms, squeezing until she couldn't breathe and feared her ribs were going to break.

He tossed her into the truck and slammed the door. A moment later, he was behind the wheel, tearing out of the driveway. No one to see them, she realized. Her closest neighbor was gone, murdered by the same monster who had her now.

Chapter Sixty-nine

Thursday, August 18
10:00 P.M.

Malone couldn't believe what he'd just heard. He pressed his cell tighter to his ear. "What do you mean, Gallier's not there?"

"Her vehicle's here, her dog's barking its fool head off, but all the lights are off and she's not answering the door."

"Did you identify yourselves?"

"Yes, Detective. Even used my big-boy voice. What do you want us to do now?"

Even though the woman had run off when he ordered her to stay put before, this felt different. And in light of the circumstances, terribly wrong. "Hold on a moment."

He snapped his fingers to get Percy's attention. "Call Gallier's cell. She's not answering her door."

Percy did and a moment later shook his head. "Went straight to voice mail."

Why would she have turned her phone off?

She wouldn't have. Not now.

Heart thundering, Malone returned to the holding officer. "Do an exterior search of the premises, look for anything that seems out of order. Let me know what you find."

The officer called back almost before Malone had gotten his cell reholstered.

"Detective, we found what looks like blood on the front steps and front door casing. You want us to go in?"

"Hell, yes. Sending backup and on my way now."

By the time Malone and Percy got to the scene, there were three cruisers in place and Fosse and James had searched the house.

"Gallier's not here," Officer Fosse said, "and it looks as if she was taken by force."

Malone followed the officer to the kitchen. Blood on the floor and front of the refrigerator. A bloody, ripped towel and what had been an iPhone. Mira Gallier's, he'd bet.

He wanted to bellow with frustration but kept himself in check. What the hell did they do now?

"Crime-scene techs are on their way," Percy said. "Officers have already begun a canvass of the neighborhood. If anyone saw or heard anything, we'll know."

Malone's cell went off; he saw it was headquarters. Not just headquarters, he learned—Captain O'Shay.

"Where are you?" she asked.

"At Mira Gallier's. And it's not good news. She's not here and there are signs of a violent altercation."

"They've located Detective Bayle."

"Where is she?"

"Downtown. The InterContinental hotel."

"Percy and I are on our way. With your permission, I want to be the first to interview her."

"Sorry, Spencer, but that's not going to be possible."

He stopped, hearing the edge in his aunt's voice. He asked, though he suspected he wouldn't like the answer, "Why the hell not?"

"She's dead. It looks as if she killed herself."

Chapter Seventy

Malone and Percy crossed the InterContinental's stunning lobby, aware of the anxious gazes of employees. The manager hurried over with another man who Malone surmised was hotel security.

"Detectives," the manager said, tone hushed. "Thank you for coming so quickly. We hope to get this taken care of quietly, before the guests become aware there's a problem."

"We understand," Malone said.

"This is my head of security, Hector Tabor. He will accompany you to the twelfth floor and room 1212. Hotel policy demands a member of our staff remain with law enforcement at all times."

Malone nodded and Tabor showed them to the elevator.

On the ride up, Malone worked to center himself and his thoughts. He needed to focus on this scene, unemotionally, not on the past or his relationship with Bayle.

Come to it clean, Malone. Do it.

The elevator doors opened with a soft *whoosh*. Room 1212 lay dead ahead on the right. He didn't need to count down or check room numbers. The NOPD officer standing sentinel outside the door told him everything he needed to know.

He let his breath out in a resigned sigh. Percy, standing beside him, made a similar sound. The officer looked their way, nodded in recognition. Joey Petron. Nice guy. Solid cop.

There'd be no jokes at this scene. No smiling or banter. Just a heavy silence.

"We the first?" Malone asked.

"You are. CSI's on the way. Contacted the Coroner's Office. Her superior officer's been notified."

Malone didn't bother telling him that "her superior officer" was also his own. He signed them both in. "Anything else we should know?"

He shook his head. "Damn shame. I feel real bad about this."

Welcome to the club.

Malone and Percy entered the room, Tabor following. Bayle had rented a suite. They made their way through the elegantly appointed living room and into the bedroom. She'd shot herself with her service weapon. One bullet to her right temple.

He stopped at the end of the bed, struggling to catch his breath, fighting not to be sick, though it had been years since that had happened. In a strange way he felt grateful for the nausea—he still had enough humanity to feel ill at the sight of a colleague in this state.

He wondered if Percy felt the same. A quick glance his way suggested he did.

Percy spoke first. "Downstairs, they said she'd checked in around one thirty this afternoon. Took the suite for one night."

"Had she left the room since?"

"They didn't know but offered the elevator surveillance tapes."

Malone glanced at the service cart parked by the bed. She'd ordered champagne and chocolate-dipped strawberries. Only one glass, he noted. He pointed that out to Percy, who nodded and took out his notebook. "I'll double-check that with room service."

"Do we know what time she ordered room service?"

"Three o'clock," Tabor offered. "She accepted delivery twenty-five minutes later."

Malone glanced Tabor's way. Although he stood in the bedroom doorway, his gaze was fixed on a point on the wall opposite the bed. Two things hit Malone at once: Bayle had made the decision to do this shortly after their argument, and there was no way she'd killed Jasper or nabbed Gallier.

Malone moved his gaze back to her. She had showered. Her hair was still wrapped in a towel, turban style. The turban had slipped as her head had jerked with the force of impact, then fell back against the velvet headboard. She wore one of the hotel's fluffy white robes. Both it and the towel were soaked with blood and dotted with brain matter. The headboard was in a similar condition.

Her hand was still on the gun. Malone moved closer to get a better look. "Gun powder residue," he said. "No doubt she pulled the trigger."

On the dresser, in a neat pile, she had stacked her shield, key ring, ID badge and wallet. Beside that, a small leather-bound book.

"No note here," Percy said. "I'll take a look around."

Malone fitted on gloves and crossed to the dresser. A journal, he saw, and picked it up.

The entries dated from February 2004 to November 2006. Bayle and Jeff Gallier had met at the Columns Hotel bar. At first she hadn't known he was married; she'd been so smitten by the time he'd told her that she'd bought his tired tale about his marriage being over.

As he read, Malone learned Bayle had wrestled with being "the other woman," had broken up with Gallier a number of times, but he'd always wooed her back.

Malone supposed he should feel good that he'd been suspicious of her, that he'd questioned her motives. He didn't. He was embarrassed for her. Angry with Jeff Gallier for being such an asshole, the kind of guy who gave them all a bad name. And furious with Bayle for allowing herself to be manipulated that way.

He read on, two things becoming obvious as he did: Bayle had been obsessively in love with Jeff Gallier and to an equal degree she'd hated his wife.

He flipped forward, to her writings in the weeks after Katrina. They were short, sporadic entries. At first they conveyed her concern for her lover's welfare and her frantic attempts to contact him, following with the knowledge that he was "missing," presumed dead.

Through her words, he learned that Bayle believed Jeff had confessed his affair to Mira, then in a jealous rage, she had killed him—and used the storm's chaos to hide it.

Malone turned to the next entry and stopped, surprised. Bayle had gone to Anton Gallier with her suspicions. She had provided the inspiration for the man's campaign against his daughter-in-law.

But that last entry was not her last. "I found the note, Percy. It's right here in her journal."

"Mary Mother of God."

Aunt Patti. He glanced over his shoulder at her. She looked stricken.

"You shouldn't have come," he said.

She met his eyes, the expression in hers steely. "Step back, Detective. I was her commanding officer, of course I had to come."

Malone acknowledged his mistake. "Of course, Captain. I was out of line."

"You found the note?"

He nodded and held out the journal, open to the last entry. "Just now. Haven't even read it yet."

She crossed to him, and the three of them read it together.

> *To whoever finds this first—my money's on
> Malone, but if it's not, get it to him, please.
> You are one astute son of a bitch, you know that?*

*You saw through my shit right away—I respect you
for that. Don't think for a minute you had anything to
do with this, it was all me. The jig was up, you know?
I was over it. The grief and anger. The hatred. The
games—life, I guess. I'd just had fucking enough of it.*

*I was just screwing with Gallier's mind. The
aftershave, the phone call—a brilliant use of a saved
voice message, if I do say so myself. I wanted to
punish her. I wanted to drive her crazy. The way I
was being driven crazy. I wanted her to miss him, the
way I was missing him. In the end, looks like she
moved on and I never did. Even though she was still
living in his house . . . I used to imagine sometimes
that I . . . we used to meet there and I . . . You know
what? Fuck this.*

Ciao, partner

They simultaneously finished reading and lifted their
heads. None of them spoke. Malone supposed it was because
Bayle had just said it all. And because it was such a waste. A
great cop. A hero. It just didn't make any sense.

CSI arrived. The techs entered without their usual banter.
As they came in, the three of them filed out. Once clear of
the bedroom, Captain O'Shay broke their silence. "Shake it
off, Detectives. We've got a perp out there who's already
killed five people and, we presume, intends to kill two more.
What's our next step?"

Before Malone could respond, his cell phone went off.

"Detective? This is Sister Sarah Elisabeth, from Our
Lady of Perpetual Sorrows."

"Sister?" he said in surprise, glancing at his watch. "Is
everything all right?"

"It's late, I know, but I was in prayer and the Lord spoke
to me."

"I'm sorry, Sister, what?"

"You said I should call if I recognized someone from that
list you left me. God had to give me a nudge, but I realize I
do know one of these people."

He was aware of Captain O'Shay and Percy waiting. Of the danger Mira Gallier was in, that others' lives might depend on him.

"I hate to hurry you, Sister, but time's not on my side here. Who—"

"Christopher," she answered. "Chris Johns. It didn't ring a bell, because Christopher's the only name I knew him by." She laughed. "He was such a sweet, helpful young man I always called him Saint Christopher. He installed all the pews in the sanctuary."

Chris Johns.

In that moment, Malone believed in miracles. "I've got to go, Sister, but thank you. You've helped more than you can imagine."

Chapter Seventy-one

Friday, August 19
1:40 A.M.

The first thing Mira became aware of was a stabbing pain. Behind her eyes. At the back of her head. She moaned and tried to roll onto her side. Her body refused to cooperate, her limbs were leaden, her hands and feet numb.

Not leaden, she remembered. Bound. Tightly. Her wrists behind her back; her ankles. At least he had removed the gag.

Absolute, unadulterated terror rocketed through her. Panic with it. She fought against her bindings, pain shooting through her head, shoulders and back as she did.

After a couple minutes she stopped, out of breath, tears streaming down her cheeks. This couldn't be happening. But it was. Chris was the Judgment Day killer. He'd brought her here, wherever that was. A sob passed her lips.

Get a grip, Mira. Breathe. Freaking out isn't going to help.

She squeezed her eyes shut. She had to get out of this. There had to be a way.

Keeping the panic at bay, she moved her gaze over the room. Totally black, save for traces of moonlight peeking in around window coverings.

She certainly wasn't home, or anyplace else she recognized. The air was stale. Old and dusty and rancid. It made her throat and nose burn.

"You're awake."

"Chris?" She turned her head in the direction the voice had come from. More blackness. "I can't see you."

"I'll come closer."

She heard his footsteps. Soft-soled shoes, not the work boots from earlier. He was almost on top of her when he came into view. The face she knew but suddenly didn't recognize. It was the strangest feeling, surreal and frightening.

Who was this person?

"Please untie me."

"I can't," he said, voice thick with emotion. "I'm sorry."

She wanted to sob and scream. She held both back. "It hurts, Chris. My hands and feet are numb. Please untie me. I won't run, I promise."

"He told me not to trust you. Because of the demons."

"Who told you that?" she asked. "It's not true. It's not! Please believe me."

He lifted his gaze to the ceiling. "Father, what should I do?" He paused, as if listening. "But she promises she won't run."

Again the pause, then his face puckered with regret. "I'm sorry," he said again. "It's too soon."

"What do you mean?" She struggled to free her arms. "Untie me, Chris. Please."

He looked distressed. "Don't make this harder than it has to be, Mary. I can't."

"Why are you calling me that?"

"It'll all be over soon. Then we'll be together."

Do not fall apart. Figure out what he wants and give it to him.

"My wrists and ankles really hurt," she whispered. "You can trust me. I trust you."

He studied her, expression hopeful. She realized that he wanted to believe her. That he longed to trust her. It was something.

"Please," she pleaded, batting her eyes at him.

"Who are you?" he asked.

The question threw her. "You know who I am. You know me."

"I do," he said softly, squatting beside her. He reached out and traced his fingers over her cheek. "But I need you to tell me."

Her every nerve ending recoiled at his touch, but she managed to keep it from showing. "I'm your friend, Mira Gallier."

His expression tightened, he snatched his hand away and stood. "You need your sleep."

"No—" Her voice broke on a sob. "Please, Chris."

"It's not your fault. It's the Evil One. Until his demons are expelled, you can't see who you really are."

With that, he turned and left her alone in the dark.

Chapter Seventy-two

Friday, August 19
6:05 A.M.

Murky daylight peered around the edges of the blackout paper. Flashes of lightning intensified the light, giving Mira glimpses of the far corners of the room that was her prison. And, maybe, the place she would spend the last minutes of her life.

Mira squeezed her eyes shut against the thought. She couldn't go there. If she did, she might not be able to muster the strength she'd need to get out of this.

An incredibly bright flash lit up the room. Two windows, Mira saw. Old, with heavy casings. The kind of molding found in homes all over the city. She lifted her gaze to the high ceiling. A large medallion in the center.

In a state of disrepair. Cracks in the plaster. Water marks. Patches of mold.

Was that what she smelled? Moisture? Moldy plaster?

After Chris left, she hadn't slept except for minutes when she'd drifted off against her will. She'd spent those long, dark hours fighting back terror by working on the predicament she was in.

She had to convince Chris to let her go. To do that she had to make him believe he could trust her.

How?

Mira had come to the conclusion that pleading wasn't going to work. Nor was approaching him from a sane perspective. She had to meet him where he lived, the place inside his head where all this made perfect sense.

Remember, Mira. Figure it out.

He'd called her Mary. He'd felt bad for not being able to believe her. He'd wanted to let her go. But couldn't because his father told him so. His Heavenly Father, judging by the way he had lifted his gaze heavenward.

He believed he was Christ. Returned to judge the living and the dead. That's why he'd graffitied the Creed on the Sisters of Mercy windows. It's why he had left the words *Judgment Day* by Preacher's body.

And that she was Mary Magdalene. His devoted servant and true love. That's why he called her Mary.

At the thought, stomach bile rose in her throat. He was trying to expel the demons from *her.* What had he said?

That it was the demons who were keeping her from seeing who she really was. That he had to expel them all.

The demons, she realized. Dear God. People in her life. Her father-in-law. Her neighbor. Her shrink.

Deni. Connor. Panic surged inside her. Despair. What if he had already killed them? What if that's what he was doing right now? Who rounded out the seven?

Unless he told her, there was no way to know. It could be anyone.

No, Mira. Focus on getting the hell out of here.

Give him what he wants. It would work. It had to.

Maybe. She pressed her lips together, fear and uncertainty growing inside her. She couldn't make a mistake. She might not have a second chance.

She heard him at the door. The dead bolt sliding back, the crack of the door opening.

Showtime, Mira. Don't blow it.

She closed her eyes, pretending to be asleep. She heard him crossing the room, setting something on the floor beside the bed.

Food, she realized as the smell of bacon and eggs tickled her nose. "Mary," he called softly. "It's me. Are you awake?"

She opened her eyes. The sight of him turned her stomach. She forced a welcoming smile.

"I brought you some breakfast."

"You're so good to me."

"Because I love you. I know who you really are."

"I know who I am now, too. And I know who you are." She paused. "My sweet savior."

He acted like he hadn't heard her. "Are you hungry, Mira?"

"Not Mira. Mary. And yes, I'm starving."

He helped her sit up. When he touched her, she felt him tremble.

"What time is it?"

"Almost six thirty."

They would have realized she was in trouble. The cruiser Detective Malone had sent for her. Surely, they would have gone into her house, seen the blood in the kitchen and her smashed phone on the floor.

"Untie my hands so I can eat. I won't run."

"I'm sorry, Mary. I can't do that."

"But I'm so hungry."

"I'll feed you."

She allowed him to do so, though it took an extreme effort not to gag with every bite.

When she'd finished, he patted her mouth with the napkin, then bent and kissed her. She longed to recoil, to scream her disgust. Instead, she closed her eyes and thought of Connor.

When he drew away, she looked up at him with what she hoped he would think was adoration. "Ask me who I am," she whispered. "I know now."

"Who are you?"

"Your devoted follower," she said, starting out vaguely, hoping to gauge his reaction. If she was wrong—and she could be—she would have blown her chance at freedom. "The woman who owes you her life. I love you," she said, forcing the words past her lips.

He looked unconvinced. Tears filled her eyes. "Don't you recognize me? I'm Mary. Your Magdalene. I washed your feet with my hair and anointed you with perfume. I watched you die, suffering every moment with you, feeling as if my heart was being ripped from my chest."

The words felt blasphemous leaving her lips. A part of her hated herself for them. Tears rolled down her cheeks. "But here you are. Flesh and blood, returned to me."

"Mary," he managed, voice trembling, "I've waited such a long time for you. So very long." He laid his head in her lap. "I've been so alone."

"No longer, my love. I'm here. You're not alone anymore."

He wept into her lap. Like a child, the sound heartbreaking.

She couldn't allow herself to worry about him. She would do whatever necessary to escape. Even if it meant killing him.

Mira murmured soft sounds of comfort, her mind racing, working on what she should do next. She didn't want to push him too hard, yet feared doing too little as well. Should she ask to be untied? Tell him she longed to hold him? Comfort him properly?

He lifted his head and tipped his face up to hers. At the expression in his eyes, fear shuddered through her.

"I have a surprise for you," he said.

The fear caught her in a stranglehold. She tried to speak but found she couldn't.

"There's someone I want you to meet."

She wanted to say no. To plead she wasn't ready. Every fiber in her being screamed she didn't want to do this.

"Who?" she choked out. "Who do you want me to meet?"

He didn't answer. He drew her to her feet. She couldn't feel them and started to topple over. He caught her, then lifted her into his arms and carried her as if she were a lamb to be laid upon an altar.

A sacrificial lamb. His lamb.

She started to cry. She didn't want to die. After all the days, months and years she had spent not just wishing she was dead, but making it happen, watching it happen—here she was now praying for another chance at life.

"Don't cry, sweet Mary," he said. "It'll be over soon. And no one will ever tear us apart again."

Chapter Seventy-three

Mira stood in the center of a small, old-fashioned bathroom. Chris had left her to "prepare," though he'd refused to say exactly what for. He'd unbound her wrists and ankles, leaving everything she might need: toothbrush and toothpaste, towel, washcloth, soap, toilet paper and comb. And a simple linen shift and cotton panties to change into.

Thirty minutes, he'd told her, then left her alone, locking the door behind him.

Thirty minutes until what?

She moved her gaze over the room for what felt like the hundredth time. Pedestal sink. Claw-footed tub. A single, small window with rippled glass, painted shut.

No way to escape.

She was still alive. And that was everything. It gave her hope; she still had a chance.

Aware of time passing, she relieved herself, stripped and, feeling frighteningly vulnerable, gave herself a quick sponge bath. She dried herself, then slipped into the shift and panties. She longed to defy him and put her own clothes back on, but she didn't want to do anything that might set him off.

The most important thing for her to do was to stay in

character. The more he trusted her, the further he would lower his guard.

Submissive. The picture of blind devotion. *She could do this.*

After brushing her teeth and combing her hair, Mira closed the lid to the commode and sank onto it. How many minutes had passed? It seemed like more than thirty already. Considerably more.

What if he didn't return? What would she do then?

Mira shook her head, as if trying to physically chase the thought away. A form of psychological torture, she thought. A way to keep her uncertain and guessing. Another way to control her.

She started to stand, then went still. The sound of a woman weeping. Low, hopeless.

Where was it coming from? The wall behind the commode?

She stood and wedging herself behind it, laid her ear to the wall. Sure enough, the weeping came from the other side. Tentatively, Mira tapped three times.

The weeping stopped, followed by *tap, tap, tap.*

"Hello," she called as softly as she thought she could and still be heard.

Tap, tap, tap.

Who was it? Another captive? Another Mary Magdalene? She pressed closer. "Do you need help?"

Tap, tap, tap.

She heard Chris at the door, inserting the key in the lock. "Shh, he's coming."

She sank onto the commode, just as the door opened. He stepped through, frowning. "What were you doing?"

"Waiting for you."

"I heard you talking."

"Praying. Giving thanks."

His expression cleared. "You look beautiful, Mary."

"Thank you, Rabbi."

In Jesus' time, *Rabbi* was a term of respect reserved for religious teachers. In the New Testament, the apostles often referred to Jesus in this way. She took a chance that he would know this and be further convinced of her sincerity.

The way his face lit up told her the gambit had paid off.

He held up a brown paper bag. "I brought you something."

He sounded so pleased with himself. She glanced at the bag, then back at him. Anything could be in that bag. A gun or knife. Something to mark her forehead. Rope to rebind her hands and wrists. Tears sprang to her eyes. She blinked against them.

"She was wrong about you."

"Who was?"

"Grandmother." He crossed to her. Reaching out, he trailed his fingers over the curve of her cheek, then dropped his hand. "Look in the bag, Mary."

She hesitated and he said it again, holding out the bag. She took it, eased it open and peeked inside. Hair. A head.

With a squeal of fear, she dropped the bag.

"What's wrong?" He retrieved it, reached inside and pulled out the contents.

A wig, she saw. Coppery red hair, wavy and long.

"You never should have cut your hair."

"No," she agreed automatically.

"Why did you?"

"I don't know."

"The demons," he said simply.

"The demons," she repeated, not knowing how else to respond.

He fitted the wig on her, smoothing his hands over the long strands, then standing back to look at her. As he did, his expression altered, his breathing grew quicker, more shallow.

He was becoming aroused.

She reached up to yank off the wig; he caught her hand, stopping her.

"Why do I have to wear it?" she asked. "You know who I am."

"But she won't."

"Who?"

"My grandmother. Come."

He held out his hand. Mira took it. His was warm and damp. Hers, she knew, was like ice. He led her out into the hallway. The staircase was so close. She could break free and run. If she could make it to the foyer and out the front door, she could scream for help. Someone would hear her.

But she had only one chance. Wait for the right moment, Mira told herself. It would come.

As if reading her mind, he tightened his fingers. "It's going to be all right, Mary. Don't be scared."

He stopped before another door. A second stairway, from back in the days of servants' quarters.

He urged her up, following so close she felt his sticky breath on the back of her neck. With each step the air grew hotter, thicker, more fecund. What was up here?

Two doors. He stopped at the one on the right, rapped his knuckles lightly on it. "Grandmother, it's me." He eased open the door. "I've brought Mary to you."

Without waiting for a reply, he led her into the room. Gray light filtered through the moldy draperies. Mira hung back, half hiding behind him.

"Look at us, Grandmother." The figure on the bed didn't move. He paused, head cocked slightly as if listening to a response, then said, "Give her a chance, you'll see."

Who was he talking to? Mira peeked around him. It was just them and the figure on the bed.

"Don't be that way!" he cried. "She's not a whore!" He grabbed Mira's arm and dragged her out from behind him, then forward. "My Mary's back. See her! She's back!"

Mira got a clear view of the bed. A scream filled her lungs even as she looked again, not believing what she was seeing. A corpse. Like something out of a movie or a house of horrors. Mostly skeletal with patches of what looked like decomposing flesh, muscle or sinew.

Was this a joke? It wasn't, Mira knew. She closed her eyes to block out the grisly image.

Chris dragged her toward the bed, even though she fought and clawed at him. He seemed not to notice, as if he was in a sort of trance.

"Grandmother," he pleaded, "you believed in me when no one else would. You told me of my virgin birth . . . you showed me my true purpose and believed in me when no one else would."

He looked at Mira, gaze strangely blank. "My mother was Mary, but she didn't believe. God had to strike her down."

"What are you saying?" she managed, realizing just how close she was to losing it.

"Grandmother told me everything. She was the one who taught me that the voice in my head was my Father's. That it was good. That I should listen."

"I don't want to be here," she said. "Please."

"Kneel beside the bed, take her hand."

"No." Mira shook her head. "I can't. Please don't make me."

He started to coax, then turned sharply toward the bed. "It doesn't prove anything!" he shouted. "Put yourself in her shoes!"

Mira jerked free of his grasp and ran for the door. He caught her before she even had it open, his arms circling her waist, dragging her backward.

"Mary, there's no reason to run. I'm here, I won't let her hurt you."

Panic overwhelmed her. Any plans of manipulating him evaporated. "She's dead, Chris! Why can't you see that?"

"No, sweetheart, she's old and very ill. But that's a part of life. You can't escape it."

"No! She's dead! You need help."

"You're talking crazy. Come, kneel beside her." His grip on her became steely. Mira fought him, begging, pleading. Despite her best effort, they reached the side of the bed. He forced her to her knees, practically sitting on her to keep her down.

She was sobbing now. "I can't do this. Please don't make me—"

He grabbed her wrist, his fingers digging into her flesh like talons. "Take her hand, Mary. Kiss it. Show her the respect she deserves."

"No!" Marshaling all her strength, she pushed him and scrambled to her feet. He fell sideways, against the bed, half onto the body. The corpse's head popped free and dropped onto the floor.

He screamed, face twisted with fury. "Look what you've done! She'll never forgive you now. Never!"

"I'm sorry." She backed away. "I didn't mean it."

In horrified fascination, she watched him carefully scoop up the decomposing skull and place it back on the pillow, arranging the wisps of hair just so, murmuring words of apology and adoration as he did.

When he'd finished, he looked at her. Only then did she realize her stupidity—she could have used those few moments to run.

"It's not your fault, Mary. It's mine."

She took a step backward as he took one forward. "I just wanted it to be true so badly, I rushed it. It's not your fault," he said again.

He eased a length of nylon rope from his jacket pocket. "The demons still have you. I have to finish expelling them."

"He cast out Seven Demons."

She shook her head. "No. There are no demons. You're sick, Chris. You need help—"

"There are only two left. The ones with the strongest hold on you."

"Chris, you have to listen to me. I'm Mira Gallier, your boss and friend. Not Mary Magdalene." She took another step backward, then another. "You're Chris Johns, and you need help. I'll make sure you get it, I'll—"

She whirled and grabbed the door handle. He lunged, smashing her into the door, knocking the air out of her.

"I didn't want to hurt you, Mary. I hope you know that." He flung her to the floor; her chin hit with a loud crack. Pain and stars exploded in her head, brilliant like fireworks, then dimmed to an empty black sky.

Chapter Seventy-four

Friday, August 19
8:40 A.M.

Mira came to with a throbbing headache. Her jaw hurt unbearably and she tasted blood in her mouth. Moaning, she tried to roll onto her back but found she couldn't. She cracked open her eyes.

"Mira, thank God . . . It's me, Deni."

Deni? Mira blinked, her vision clearing. Her friend kneeled beside her. She was crying.

"Where am I?"

"It's Chris, Mira. He's the one . . . not Bill—" Her voice broke on a sob. "He came to my house . . . he grabbed me and—" She started to cry. "He believes you're Mary Magdalene."

It all came crashing back. The corpse in the other room. Chris's curiously blank gaze. His throwing her to the ground, pain exploding in her head. "And that he's Jesus Christ." *Returned to judge the living and the dead.*

"Yes," Deni whispered. "And he has the Magdalene window. He told me."

Of course, Mira realized. He'd fabricated that whole story about a neighbor seeing Deni and a man taking it, to throw suspicion on Deni and Connor. And she had fallen for it, like an idiot.

Deni's eyes filled with tears, as if reading her expression. "I thought he was a good guy. It's my fault we're here."

"No. I believed it, too." Mira assessed their situation. Her hands were bound, but not her feet. With assistance from Deni, maybe she could sit. "Help me up."

"My hands are tied."

"Use your legs and feet."

"I don't want to hurt you."

"Look at me, could I be in more pain?"

Deni looked sheepish. "Okay, I'll try. Tell me what to do."

Mira directed Deni to try to wedge her feet under her hips and then, when she counted to three, try to help her over. After several tries, Mira was on her back. Using the same technique, Deni helped propel her to a sitting position.

Physically, it hurt almost more than she could bear, but emotionally she felt a hundred percent better. "I wonder what he wants with the window?"

"He's so whacked, Mira. It could be anything."

"We're getting out of here." Mira moved her gaze over the room. *Not even a boarded-up window.* "Somehow."

"Maybe Detective Malone will come for us?"

"Maybe, but we can't depend on it. I don't think we have much time."

Deni's eyes welled with tears, her lower lip began to quiver. "Then there's no way."

"Don't give up, you hear me? We're getting out of here." The bravado in her voice was almost laughable, considering their odds. "What has he told you?"

"He thinks I'm some sort of evil spirit. That I'm possessing you." She pressed her lips together for a moment, then went on. "He killed all those other people."

"Yes."

"And he plans to kill me. And Connor. In front of you."

Mira's stomach lurched to her throat, but she managed to hold it together. "Is that everything? Did he tell you when he was going to do it or—"

They heard him at the door. Mira looked at Deni. Her friend had turned deathly pale.

Chris stepped into the room, closing the door behind him. He carried a toolbox and set it on the floor by the door. "Mary," he said, "I'm so glad you're awake."

Her mouth went dry. She couldn't take her eyes from the box. "No thanks to you."

He ignored that and opened the box. He retrieved a pair of leather work gloves. He slipped them on, smiling benignly.

"What are you doing?"

He didn't answer. Instead, he drew another item from the box and crossed to stand before her.

Then she understood why he needed the gloves.

"Do you recognize this?" He held out a long, jagged piece of stained glass.

But not just any piece, she saw. One from the Magdalene window, the upper part of the saint's face, a strip that included the eyes.

She had worked for days restoring those eyes, trying to recapture the grief and longing emanating from them. Mira held back a cry of disbelief and despair—she wouldn't give the son of a bitch the satisfaction.

She looked him straight in the eyes. "You know I do."

"The window had an unnatural hold on you. I released you from its power." He smiled, obviously pleased with himself. "Now, I have a surprise for you."

"Another one?" she shot back, realizing she had nothing, no ideas. Nada. Just sarcasm. And bone-deep terror. "You're just full of surprises, aren't you?"

"That's the demons talking."

"No, Chris. It's me. There are no demons."

"Yes. There are two more." He glanced toward Deni. "Her and Connor."

She wanted to scream and curse at him, to kick or even spit in his face in an attempt to reach a sane part of him—if he had one. But even if she did, it wouldn't work. Anything that didn't play into his delusions reinforced them.

Mira worked at the rope binding her wrists. "Why Sisters of Mercy? Because I restored the windows?"

He looked at her strangely. "Because they depicted the life of Christ, of course. My first life. And because that's where it all began. My mother's church, where I was conceived, then baptized. Father Girod was the priest who performed the ceremony."

"And yet you killed him?"

"I'd come to realize that he, too, was a demon. If he wasn't, he would have recognized and welcomed me."

Deni began to weep. Mira longed to comfort her but kept her focus on Chris. "And Preacher?"

"I found him and got your cross back." Chris shook his head. "Preacher was a false prophet. And the second demon." He squatted down, cocking his head as he studied her. "I imagined you'd thank me."

For killing a man? For breaking into her house?

She couldn't bring herself to do it. "How did you get into my house?"

"Stole your key while you were in the studio working. Ran over to the hardware store and had a copy made. It took less than thirty minutes."

Her wrists burned, rubbed raw as she tried to free them from the rope. It could be her imagination, but it felt as if the ropes were loosening. "And the alarm code?"

"Got it from Deni."

"I'm sorry, Mira," Deni whispered.

"Don't call her that!" Chris said, whirling to face Deni. "Her name's Mary."

"Let her go," Mira said gently. "Please, Chris."

"I can't do that, Mary. I'm sorry. You'll thank me later."

"No, I won't. I'll hate you forever."

"Now for your surprise."

He left the room, returning moments later, dragging something heavy. Not something, she saw. Someone.

"Connor!" she cried. He was unmoving, the side of his head bloodied, face bruised and swollen. Blood seeped from his side. "What have you done to him?"

Chris didn't answer. Instead, he lifted his gaze heavenward. "You are the Father, I am the Son, everything I do is in Your name. May Your will be done in this and always."

"That's a lie!" she cried, scooting toward Connor. "This is *not* God's will. If you were truly the Christ, you wouldn't do this. His was a voice of love and peace. Not destruction. The voice in your head is a liar!"

Chris seemed to freeze. A spark of hope ignited in her. Maybe she could reach him through the very story he claimed to know so well. "*That's* the demon, Chris. Not Deni. Not Connor."

Chris turned to her, still holding the shard of glass. His hands shook. "You're wrong, you'll see. These eyes . . . Father promised me . . . I'll save you—"

"The voice in your head is the demon!" She was close enough to touch Connor, if only she could free her hands. Mira worked at the ropes so furiously her hands became slick with blood. "Remember the serpent in the garden, how he tricked Eve? And what of the devil's temptation in the desert? The Evil One uses God's good words . . . The voice is the devil, lying to you!"

He blinked, mumbled something and took a step backward. She saw what looked like confusion cross his features. "Are you certain, Father? But the eyes, she was meant—"

The piece of glass slipped from his fingers. He looked at Mira. "He tells me to do it quickly instead. To get the gun, the one I used to kill the third demon."

Her father-in-law. "No, Chris, listen to me! The voice is—"

"No." He hurried to the toolbox, began rifling through it.

"Yes," she pleaded. "If you were Christ, you would turn the other cheek. Do you remember, when the soldiers came to arrest you, and Peter used his sword against them? What did you say?"

He looked up. She saw he trembled. " 'Those who draw the sword will die by the sword.' "

"Yes. You know what that means. You know what you're doing is not the work of God."

His expression twisted as if with sharp pain. He doubled over, then fell to his knees and lifted his face heavenward. "The demons . . . they overwhelm me, Father, it hurts . . . Help me!"

Connor moaned, coming to. Mira gazed at him a moment, then turned back to Chris. "I'm telling the truth. You know it, Chris. You know it's true!"

He pressed his hands to his ears. "Help me, Father! Tell me what . . . the gun . . . yes . . . end it quickly."

Connor moaned again. His eyes opened and he looked at her. If she had ever doubted that he loved her, the expression in his eyes dispelled those doubts forever.

Chris got to his feet, clutching the weapon's grip, his expression strangely blank, gaze unfocused. "Look at me, Chris!" she screamed as loudly as she could, fighting for his attention. "You're being deceived. All these killings are wrong, they're a sin. They're—"

"No!" he cried. But not in response to her, she realized. To the voice in his head. "It *is* Mary! My Magdalene. You sent her to be by my side. You said it was she. What?" He shook his head. "God Almighty can't be fooled. He's all-knowing, all-powerful!"

Mira doubled her efforts with the rope. Blood streamed down her hands, the pain in her wrists excruciating.

"The Chosen One . . . I believed—" He turned toward Connor. "Liar and demon—"

"No!" she cried. "Don't hurt him, please! I love him."

Chris acted as if he hadn't heard her. Instead, he was lost in the conversation only he could hear.

"Mother . . . was right . . . all a lie—" His body convulsed. Tears rolled down his cheeks.

Her one hand came free, then the other. Too late, she saw.

Chris raised the gun, turned it on himself. And fired.

Chapter Seventy-five

Shouts filled the air. Detective Malone, Mira realized. Other officers. She crawled over to Connor. "Are you okay?"

"Are you kidding?" he managed, voice raspy. "I'm perfect." At her confusion he smiled, though the curving of his lips was half grimace. "You said you loved me."

"I do love you." She started to cry. "I thought he was going to kill you."

"You got through to him, Mira. It's over."

She looked at where Chris lay, blood pooling around him, then wished she hadn't—it would be an image she would carry with her forever. She turned quickly back to Connor, drinking in his battered face.

"Hey, you two." Spencer squatted beside them. He freed Connor's wrists, then ankles. He eyed Connor. "Looks like he got more than a few licks in."

"Bastard surprised me. Came to my door in the middle of the night, with this bullshit story about the Magdalene window being stolen and Mira freaking out."

He coughed; the sound was wet. "Told me she was . . . hysterical and wouldn't talk to anyone but me. I believed it . . . wanted to be her knight in shining armor." He laughed, then winced. "Some knight. The damsel in distress saved . . . us . . . all."

"Your side," Mira said, alarmed. "You're bleeding."

"It's no . . . big deal. After he clubbed me, he stuck me with a piece of glass."

"That's a lot of blood," Spencer said. "Medic," he called, "over here."

Mira moved to make room for the paramedic and watched him examine what looked like a scary, vicious wound.

"Sorry we're late," Spencer said, drawing her gaze from Connor. "We learned Chris was our guy around midnight, but it took until now to locate this house. It belongs to his grandmother, who has a different last name. Located it through the Sisters of Mercy records." He grinned. "My idea, by the way."

"Detective Malone?" an officer called from the doorway. "You've got to see this. This dude was off-the-charts crazy."

He stood. "Don't even think about moving until the paramedic gives you a thumbs-up. And we'll need a full statement as soon as you're up to it."

Knowing they must have found Grandma, Mira shuddered, then turned back to Connor.

The medic had cleaned and dressed the wound. "This will do until we get you to the hospital," he said, then turned to her. "Let's take a look at those wrists."

She hadn't even thought of them since she freed herself from the rope. She looked at them now and went lightheaded at the sight.

Connor sat up and drew her back against his chest. She leaned into him and closed her eyes while the paramedic tended to her hands, then her head.

"It's okay," Connor whispered. "It's over."

It was, she realized. All of it. Not just the tending to her new, physical wounds, but all of it, past and present. She rested her cheek against his chest, reassured by the steady beat of his heart. They were alive and safe.

And they were together. She lifted her face to his. "I love you, Connor Scott. Thank you for waiting for me."

Epilogue

"I now pronounce you husband and wife. You may kiss the bride."

Spencer bent and kissed Stacy. Not a chaste peck or brief meeting, a long, deep kiss that testified to both passion and commitment.

Mira curled her fingers around Connor's. He looked at her, happiness shining from his eyes. She knew he saw the same emotion shining from hers.

They turned back to the newly married couple. Mira thought of Chris and the final pieces of the puzzle, uncovered by the police investigation.

Chris's mother had been murdered, her remains found buried in the backyard, the remnants of a suitcase with her. According to old-timers from Sisters of Mercy, the last time Mary Johns had been seen alive was at the school, the day she'd picked up Chris and informed them that they were moving to Texas.

Those same parishioners remembered Chris's grandmother as extremely odd, refusing to believe her only child had gotten pregnant out of wedlock and claiming that Chris's had been an Immaculate Conception. When others refused to believe her, she'd left the church.

No wonder Chris had turned out the way he had, Mira thought. Knowing what his grandmother had done, then fed a daily diet of madness.

The forensic anthropologist determined that the grandmother had been dead for quite some time and had classified her death as a homicide as well—the woman's hyoid bone had been crushed, the probable manner of death strangulation.

What had happened? Mira wondered. Had Chris just snapped one day and killed her? Then, unable to deal with that reality, brought her back to "life"?

Back to life, she thought. To the world of the living. Leaving behind the demons of the past, letting go.

Mira supposed she should find it strange that she was recalling such events now, at the marriage of two people who had become her friends. But she didn't. If not for those events, she wouldn't be here. Not physically. And not emotionally. She could have ended up like Karin Bayle, so unable to let go of the past that she had thrown her future away.

Her future. Connor. She curled her fingers tighter around his, happier, more at peace than she'd ever thought she would be again.

The newlyweds started down the aisle, heading toward the open church doors and the beautiful day—and future—beyond.

Holding tightly to Connor's hand, Mira followed them.

"GET READY TO STAY UP ALL NIGHT."*

Experience these page-turning thrillers from
New York Times bestselling author
ERICA SPINDLER

BLOOD VINES
Her family tried to bury the past.
Now she'll risk her life to dig it up…

"PULSE-POUNDING."
—*Lisa Gardner

BREAKNECK
To catch the killer known as "Breakneck,"
one woman puts her own neck on the line…

"SPINE-TINGLING."
—*Star Magazine*

Available from St. Martin's Paperbacks